# Ozarium

# Ozarium

## Book Two of the Transitional Delusions Series

# Brick Marlin

SEVENTH STAR PRESS

Cover art: Enggar Adirasa
Cover art in this book copyright © 2016 Enggar Adirasa & Seventh Star
Press, LLC.

Editor: Scott Sandridge

Published by Seventh Star Press, LLC.

ISBN Number: 978-1-941706-45-9

Seventh Star Press
www.seventhstarpress.com
info@seventhstarpress.com

Publisher's Note:
*Ozarium* is a work of fiction. All names, characters, and places are the
product of the author's imagination, used in fictitious manner. Any
resemblances to actual persons, places, locales, events, etc. are purely
coincidental.

Printed in the United States of America

First Edition

# Acknowledgements

Much like most of my work these days this book was challenging. There is so much going on in this new world I've invented at times my brain has a hard time keeping up. Lori Marlin has been my biggest inspiration and supporter of this odd craft called writing. Without her at my side, I would be lost in a Sector, a bizarre dimension eating too many packages of Explosive Pop Rock candies and drinking sodas. At any rate, not only to I thank my lovely wife, my good friend and publisher Stephen Zimmer, my editor Scott Sandridge, my illustrator Enggar Ajar A, my longtime friends I've known since high school too many years to count, Chuck Lewis, Tim Lewis, Dennis Toby, Scott Francis, as well as Kathy Copas, and authors whom have inspired me such as Gary Braunbeck, Lucy Snyder and Michael Libling

# Dedication

*This one is dedicated to my readers.*

Transitional Delusions – a dark change from one state or condition to another; appearance is often…deceptive.

*Welcome my son, welcome to the machine*
*Where have you been? It's all right we know where you've been*

– Pink Floyd, Welcome To The Machine

The world had become a nebulous dread.

Martha whispered a prayer as she stumbled down the street, the Browning tucked under her good arm, her head and left arm radiating waves of pain from the monster's attack. Tears slipped down her cheeks. Somehow luck had sided with her when the severed desk leg impaled the beast. Her home town had decreed a sinister death by the hands of evil.

Bodies lay strewn in pieces in the streets, leaking abstract designs of human blood.

Her stomach churned. She wanted to puke.

There would be no more laughing, no more crying, no more giggles you'd hear from children who played outside in the summer evening, catching fireflies in glass jars or waving sparklers during the Fourth of July.

Had Wendy and Shro died? Could there be no one left to survive this apocalyptic blood bath with children being possessed, hacking away, murdering all the adults?

No clue.

Had she been bit? Damn, can't remember…

Chuckle. Wouldn't that be just great? Attacked by a five foot rat, chewed on, and not only gain rabies alongside the pain she already had. Ha! What a joke! That would be the least of her worries! She'd probably die long before being able to stand up to the evil. Her intentions would be shattered. Shredded. Martha wanted to confront this evil creature responsible for destroying her town, though …could she actually do something like that?

By herself?

Martha, what the hell are you trying to prove? You're too old to do this. You actually think you, Misfortunate Martha, could do such a thing? Isn't that what the kids used to call you a long time ago, when you went to school?

*Misfortunate Martha! Misfortunate Martha! Misfortunate Martha!* the kids would chant, swelling like a blood-sucking tick. The name stuck because of you always being accident-prone. Losing control of your bike and crashing it into a tree, turning your foot counter-clockwise until feeling a pop under your skin. Or when you showcased your talent, your legs pin-wheeled, mimicking a cartoon character, slipping in Richie Simmons' pile of vomit back in tenth grade.

For whatever reason she thought about this, she did not know. Nor did she understand why she had more memories flowing around inside her brain. Lots of good ones; some bad, as it is in the circle of life.

A large wave of pain severed the transmission. Nausea coiled inside her stomach. Too bad she couldn't saw her head and arm off and replaced it with new.

She leaned against a building as the pain subsided.

The park twenty-feet from her had been built a few years prior, shoving away anything but nice. A severed head could be discovered with every spin of the carousel.

Martha stumbled further. She needed to find a car. Vehicles were overturned, some not, some washed with human remains and blazing, billowing smoke, odorizing the air with copper.

The smell reflected memories of when her father slaughtered pigs and chickens on the farm.

Martha's legs wobbled, the pain becoming worse, wracking her husk. Her vision winked blurs. Again she leaned against a building until the waves subsided.

Two blocks' later an abandoned car with keys still in the ignition and its driver's side door hung ajar. Not quite her style of vehicle, a little blue sports car which looked as if it could damn near do zero to sixty in two clucks of a chicken's beak (something her daddy used to say) but it would have to do. No dead driver, no blood.

Bonus.

Martha slid inside the driver's seat before the pain gut-punched her. She doubled-over, letting lose the Browning in the passenger seat. Pain, being a sinister virtue, churned her stomach. Bile clawed its way into her throat.

She spewed red vomit onto the pavement.

Very red and very bright.

Jesus…am I…bleeding from the inside? she wondered.

Squinting, tears streaming down her bony cheeks, the pain in her head decided to sidle next to the hurt in her stomach, blurring her vision again. A helmet of pain slammed down on her scalp, increasing its war with her body. When she thought she couldn't take anymore, the switch flicked off.

Martha sucked in a breath, blew it out. She wiped her mouth with the back of her hand. Closing her eyes, a few seconds slid by.

Or hours.

Voices …

Her eyes opened.

Craning her neck, she looked behind her, seeing nothing but a desolate, decaying town she once called her home.

A light breeze snuck in and ruffled her grey hair.

She wiped a hand across her face, sucked in another breath, let it out, turned the key. The car's engine fired up. Putting it in gear she sped down the street. Similar-looking houses whipped by as if propelled on a moving canvas. Staving off an interest of glancing at them, she knew they had become skeletons, empty of life.

*\*\**

Jeff sure as hell did not deserve this. His own son had hacked him up while he had been asleep and his soul, a bright blue orb, had not left the flesh yet.

*Wasn't that what people said when you died? Your soul would leave your body and go to Heaven? So much for what people thought…*

Jeff's soul moved around inside the remains of his husk, surfing his bloodstream, bounced off the soft mass which used to be his beating heart and would have visited his own brain if little Robby hadn't used the electric knife to severe off his head.

Jeff did not dare exit the stump and leave his flesh. Not a chance.

*Where would he go?*

*Would he be trapped in his house forever, haunting an empty place where his wife Trish and Robby had so many great memories until yesterday? At least Trish had passed on a few years ago from cancer, the end of the world sparing her from its horror.*

Jeff patiently waited to be collected by – he hoped – God.

And, as he waited, outside grew darker.

\*\*\*

Jeannie's body lay slashed into ribbons in her tub. Her one hundred and fifty pound body had slipped under the water, undergoing a bloated transition. Her soul peeked out through her dead eyes at the world through a watery landscape.

Every so often a bubble would emerge in the cooled, red bathwater.

Jeannie still wondered why the alarm system had not went off when the two kids broke into her home and used butcher knives to kill her. She had come home, shut off all the lights in the house, lit some candles, slid into the tub, and intended to relax. Not die.

She also wondered why she wasn't in Heaven.

\*\*\*

Joseph had figured out how to animate the dead.

His own dead body to be exact.

After wondering for a good amount of time why he hadn't left his flesh and should already be standing in front of the Pearly White Gates, he grew bored, being an active gent in his mortal life: runner, hiker, biker and swimmer. Soon he discovered he could shift back and forth beneath his cadaver.

He used to love staying in shape. He ate healthy five days out the week, leaving the two remaining to have as his "binging days". Staying active made him feel great and energetic all the times. Plus, there was always a chick in his life – interchangeable ones at that. If he ever grew tired of one, there seemed to always be another who wanted to hang out with him.

It was way cool!

While he bounced around inside, his dead body lying spread eagle on the floor of his basement where he had his head caved in by that evil kid using a single hundred pound dumbbell

– Damn but they were strong! –

he sped through his husk, able to sift between the skin and the thigh muscle, slide beside his calf muscle, and clamber back up next to his waist and burrow into his intestines, carefully crawling into the interior of his stomach, reaching the inside of his mouth, feeling as if he was spelunking in an unknown cavern.

It was way cool!

However, for Joseph, he grew tired of things easily if there was no challenge to it, and this action grew old quick. Loneliness sidled next to this bright blue orb. Joseph began to think how un-cool this all was.

Was he ever going to see that great dude in the sky?

\*\*\*

In Martha's wake leaving Hampshire, four large transparent spheres emerged out of the clouds, each coming from the west, each harboring a single hooded figure inside. Each figure used specialized gloves worn on their hands to evolve and move the spheres. To distinguish them apart, the spheres were tinted with different colors: white, red, black and pale.

The Metempsychosis Quartet, once titled The Reckoning, are a quartet of demons who reside in the west part of Hell. In unison the figures used their gloves to blast beams into every existing human corpse, draining each soul. Rising high in the air as if someone had released thousands of balloons at once, hundreds of bright blue orbs oozed into the spheres.

The spheres vanished.

The clouds darkened, rumbled with thunder. Long fingers of lightening speared the ground, busting up pavement, splitting trees apart, setting a few afire.

Spearing out of the sky a funnel cloud touched the ground, chewing into the soil, until breaking apart into long fingers of tornados, driving spikes into the dead, severing flesh from bone. The wind snatched them and, with a drive to procure a malicious automation, propelled skeletons to grab hold of one another's boney hand, dancing in a circle.

A dance of the dead.

Video screens materialized inside the circle, pixels linked together to form bizarre pictures, such as a clown assassin, a graveyard where ghosts lurk on a nightly basis, and a sky filled with air traffic over a large colony of homes and tall buildings, even the addition of a river filled with the dead.

The tilt of their skulls, an uptick of their mandibles, hollow eyes stared up into the sky as they each let lose a shriek. A second slipped by as each skeleton blew apart, turning to dust, snatching away the screens.

In the blink of an eye there is a Shift, swallowing the old, regurgitating the new, layering the planet with a blend of mortal flesh and blood and machine, a genesis of a very bizarre world entitled Westersphere.

\*\*\*

Martha does not feel the Shift; does not feel the morph of the world in the air. Halfway to Woodbury she drives past a truck pulled off to the side of the road. WESTERSPHERE'S ~~BAILEY'S~~ FINEST CHEW IN THE TERRITORY! NOW IN WINTERGREEN AND WATERMELON FLAVORS! stenciled the side of the trailer along with the expanse of a grinning cartoon face of a guy wearing a straw hat. Giving a "thumbs-up", while the rest of his body did not fit into the picture, his huge eyes, rosy cheeks, and missing teeth approved this message.

The passenger side door of the truck hung ajar. Martha paid no attention to peek a look inside as she passed by, much less written on the trailer. If she had, she would have remembered a man named Tray who used to own the truck and would have noticed a silhouette sitting in the driver's seat wearing a cowboy hat. Back leaned against the driver's side door, long legs stretched out, boots rested on the dashboard.

If she had seen this shape, she would have seen it tip its hat to her, a gesture of saying howdy there, young lady.

If she had seen this, this story might have had to be adjusted.

At any rate, the road curved and the woodlands sat flush on her left and right. Once Martha drove over the hill a large sign sat on the shoulder, WELCOME TO WOODBURY! FAMOUS FOR THE APPLE FESTIVAL! A huge red apple was on the sign with two eyes and a wide smile, its plump body swollen with pride, as a cartoon worm burrowed out of where the apple's nose should have been. The worm cheesed with a rack of white teeth.

A few miles later Martha drove through Woodbury, noticing the similarity of Hampshire: desolate, dead bodies strewn in the streets. Patches of dried blood, some clumped up like small dirt piles added to the scenery. Passing by one house, an ensanguined path had long but crusted on the sidewalk leading from the front door, ending with a woman's lithe body hung from a tree limb. Stripped naked, a smiley face had been carved into her stomach. The smiley's mouth wide open, allowed her intestines to vacate her flesh and lie in a small pile on the ground below her feet.

Martha wondered if this could be where the horror started. Or could it have possibly started in the next town over? Could it have started as far as in another state? Martha hadn't a clue. She hadn't heard anything on the news about any odd occurrences before she went to bed, a night or so ago, right after reading a few passages out of her Bible, then awakened a couple of hours later to find Penny in her house. She sure hadn't expected it. She sure didn't expect the horror which came with Penny's visit. Penny was once a sweet child before the evil kidnapped her, changing her into that creature.

Martha missed the real Penny, the sweet little girl who loved eating freshly baked cookies, right out of the oven. Who didn't? Warm with a gooey chocolaty center. Martha always made sure to add extra chocolate chips whenever she made them for Penny. A must! Martha would place about six cookies on a plate, pour two tall glasses of milk, and retire to the living room with Penny who sat there playing with her dolls. Both would drink their milk and eat their cookies. If Penny's parents had known Martha allowed the girl to eat four cookies, they would be pissed. So that became Martha's and Penny's little secret, not speaking of it.

Martha captured and held onto those nice thoughts, as well as a few others for a little longer as she drove around the square until the terrible pain invaded yet again with razor sharp claws, snuffing away the memories her brain wished to spat. Wincing, she kept one eye open; one eye shut. She slowed the car, allowing it to come to a stop, bumping off a curb. There was no way she could drive like this.

It was too intense.

A large wave of pain crashed into her frame, nearly making her faint. Lasting longer this time, Martha waited until it decided to subside, withdraw away from her flesh.

Through the car's windshield sat a wooden gazebo where Woodbury always had bands set up to play during the summer months. Even a farmer's market had been set up where she loved to come pick out apples, tomatoes, green, red peppers and cucumbers. This was a place where she remembered a man half her age flirting with her about fifteen years prior. Not that she minded it, she felt flattered; made her feel a tad young even, didn't really know why, but, maybe there was some youth in her heart or –

The sound of another vehicle interrupted her thoughts, rolling up behind her, its breaks squeaking to a stop. The long black car replicated a sixties model Lincoln Continental with suicide doors. Two tall men in dark business suits stepped out of the car. One was holding some kind of an electronic tablet.

"Mrs. ...Martha Wells?"

Martha blinked. Who were these men? Their faces were sc... pale.

"Mrs. Wells, right?"

They hardly had an expression, too. "Y-Yeah. That's me. Wh-Who are you two?"

He tapped his finger on the tablet and swiped. "According to the Recog, you are in need of assistance. We are here to help you, Mrs. Wells. Please, come with us."

The other man opened Lincoln's door to the backseat.

"Help me? Help me...how? What is a Reco–"

"We are here to improve your life, Mrs. Wells. You are hurt. Allow us to accompany you to a place where they will attend to your wounds and bruises."

Frown. "You mean take me to a hospital?"

Nearly five seconds slipped by before the man who spoke blinked twice, as if processing this question before replying: "Yes. That is correct."

Why the short pause? Something didn't feel right. Who the hell were these guys? Where'd they come from? They darn near looked like government agents!

"Please, let us help you, Mrs. Wells."

And if they were from the government maybe they could get to the bottom of why this horror occurred. Did they already have an explanation of what had happened in Hampshire? How about here in Woodbury? Were they here to study this place and attempt to locate the monster responsible for all these deaths? Too many questions to be asked in this painful state she lived in. She hurt. Period. The waves of pain worsened by the minute. She really had no choice and knew she should go with them, hoping to God they could help her. If she intended on tracking down the evil, she needed to be patched up before she did so. Maybe there were a group of survivors somewhere who would help her in the fight against the monster. She sure as hell wasn't as young as she used to be, and even though her will to face the monster that snatched away her town and caused the murder of everyone was strong, she could not do it herself.

Pulling herself out of the car, she stepped toward the Lincoln and stopped. She forgot her gun. She needed the gun. It used to be her late husband's.

The man told her he'd grab it for her. "Please, allow us to help you into the backseat," he added.

Martha took two more steps before the ground reached up to meet her, one hard smack of her face, knocking her unconscious. Sometime later she remembered waking up, feeling as if the vehicle was no longer on the ground because the clouds seemed awful close.

She heard one of the men say: "Central, do you read? We are

in route back to Slader Corp. We have the subject in our custody.

\*\*\*

Static flutters across a television feed called a televid. An image tweaks, flutters, flips, showing the commercial of a man in a business suit and tie walking down a long staircase in an old house.

*"Do you know me?" Smile.*

*"Not so long ago I saved Ozarium by extinguishing Overcast, a time where people fought to survive in a post-apocalyptic world after the Shift — no thanks to the defunct leadership of Charles Krate who did nothing for the people. Overcast was a time where creatures from the previous world lurked, causing terror. Thank the gods I could develop a team to rid the world of those sinister beasts! Once they were disposed of, I helped create more jobs in the colony for the people. Those who were homeless, hiding in the streets, were given a roof over their heads and food in their stomachs and offered new jobs to support themselves.*

*The man walks down a hallway and opens a door, revealing a near-duplicate form of the Oval Office. Aside from the tall windows behind the desk, aside from the two flags sitting at opposite ends of a long desk, one harboring the design of an arachnid, the other with crossed scythes, odd pictures hang on the walls. One is of a man wearing the face of a clown, sitting in a dilapidated recliner in the midst of eating something from a small can and gazing up at the ceiling in his house; one is the view of a boy sound asleep in his room, the moon shining through the window, a figure sitting in a chair close by, its eyes glowing red, while there is an emanation of a low hum; and another picture shows a dark silhouette strolling down the street playing a flute while small hairy creatures lumber behind.*

*The man sits down on the edge of the desk.*

*"Do you know me?"*

*"I changed the game of the Lottery. It is all for the better good people of the colony, I assure you this. When we pick your name at*

*random, and you win, the demi takes security measures to make sure no harm comes to your skin." Pause. "Until due time."*

*"Do you know me?*

*"I am your leader. The one who you voted in office. Oh, and I am also responsible for inventing Bodykredd."*

*Grin.*

*After a close-up of a light green and yellow microchip is viewed and the words* MAXIMUS SLADER *etch themselves across it as a man's voice finalizes the commercial by saying:*

*"Bodykredd. Keep it under the skin of your palm, reload with cred when YOU need it!"*

*This has been an approved message from the Slader Corporation*™

\*\*\*

The Jake Velmer Checklist:

　　1. Samantha and the two extra mouths to feed are long gone, sent off in the bouncer.

　　2. Dog is fed.

　　3. Robot maid is shut down,

　　4. World Wrestling Federation X is on the vid. The Hammer rocks!

　　5. Beer is on ice.

　　6. Unlimited supply of Beanie Weenies Cajun Sardine Style.

　　7. The riding lawnmower has been modified to specs and is fueled up, ready to mow!

\*\*\*

I miss my Daddy. He decided to stay behind today and keep himself holed-up in our modified, double-wide trailer and go down with a fight.

During the three month period before daddy was scheduled to be picked up by the demi officials and put to death, he paid those nice guys from the Subterranean for lessons to be a sniper. He said he wanted to be just like his hero from that old movie in the archives, *First Blood.* He said that John Rambo dude had it together. He was real squiggly and could kick some major ass! Daddy loved how that dude had all kinds of weapons and stuff and knew how to build things. Daddy had begun comparing himself to John Rambo, grinning from ear to ear, after building the tree house for me and Tobi using titanium panels once used for the old rocket ship that delivered people back and forth from outer space.

I used to ask daddy where he got the panels, but he always changed the subject for some reason.

Then he'd knock me upside the head.

Daddy sure liked to do that to mommy, too. Told her she was dumb and stupid and since the day had come for her to be on her own she'd better shape up and learn how to cook because her food sucked.

I didn't think it did. I loved Mommy's cooking.

Daddy didn't want to hear about how bad her green bean gummy-worm casserole tasted while he floated around in the ghostly world of the Stygian Wake. Daddy warned he would leave it and come back and haunt her ugly ass as a ghost.

I believed he would.

Probably knock me upside my head while he was at it.

Daddy helped us inside the bouncer where me and mommy and baby Tobi were headed into the river of corpses to see if we can find a way out of Ozarium. Money from the lotto winnings were used to buy the expensive Ramjam device, jamming the waves of demi radar. A thing called an Oxy-Giin allowed an ample supply of oxygen to fill the cab to have the robot driver steer us underwater.

Mommy had gasped after Daddy told her about this last thing. She told him she had always been afraid of water. Didn't he remember why?

Daddy told her no and to get over it. Grow the hell up. Before we blasted off Mommy explained to him "It was when my daddy – grandpa – throwed me into the lake, Jake, telling me I need to learn how to swim, or sink like a sack filled with rocks and puppies."

"Oh." Daddy frowned.

"Luckily, there had been a boy who had seen this and come rescued me." Wink. "That was you, darling."

"Really?"

"Yup." She took a long drag off her cigarette, blew out shapes of miniature yard gnomes in various dance poses which floated into the air. (I always thought the gnomes were neat, even when they would take turns stabbing each other with knives) "You took off your shoes and shirt and dove head-first into that water in your jeans."

"I did?"

"Yup!"

Mommy continued the tale, telling Daddy that grandpa had knocked Daddy upside his darn head and told him to get the hell outta there. He was trying to show his daughter how to swim. Course, this didn't keep Daddy from sneaking over after dark and seeing Mommy. Nuh-uh! It was love at first sight, she said! She would always love Daddy, even if her demi checks never paid enough for the makeup to hide her bruises.

At least the demi cheese wasn't synthetic like its canned meat surprise! Blah!

Now as we flew through the water, corpses bouncing off the bouncer, tacking on a hundred miles behind us, huddled together, we watched the televid. Wherever you sit, you can see the TV screen without turning your head. Kinda cool, huh?

Mommy held baby Tobi on her knee as he sucked his dirt-caked thumb while we watched the Channel 6 news broadcasting live in the front lawn of our mobile home we'd never be allowed to return to:

*** 

"Howdy folks! Welcome to the *Whadda Ya Gotta Say, Ray?* news report. I'm Ray Manisquaski, and I'm here in Pikes Peak Park where Jake Velmer, our latest lotto winner, has tucked himself away inside his modified mobile home," the young reporter with short dark hair said with a grin stretched across his face. "We have another winner, yet again, who has decided to fight with force, not wanting to die as scheduled after the three month period stated under lotto winning laws. It is such a shame that people do this to themselves! We not only have the demi on site, we have one of the top demi agents, Mangdan Styles, here to talk to us as we wait out this stand-off."

A hovering automaton vid-camera panned backward, enclosing the demi dressed in a black suit, red tie and dark shades standing beside the reporter.

"Agent Styles, can you tell us why lotto winners sometimes choose this path? It is rare for winners to do what they're told to do and die without any trouble. Am I right?"

"Yes. For some reason winners decide to go against protocol. There's still a few who follow protocol, mind you, making our jobs easier. However, like Mr. Velmer, he has become a special case. There really is no rhyme or reason for it."

"How so?"

"Mr. Velmer has been trained to be a sniper in the Subterraneans. This will be a tricky situation. I do not want to lose any of my agents."

"The Subterraneans is where the rebellion is, correct?"

"Yes. The Subterraneans is their hideout. We have yet to locate it. What the rebellion is doing is against the law, and we are going to make sure it will never happen again."

"Have you not found the ones responsible for setting fire to one of the labs in Slader Corp?"

"No, but we may have a lead or two. The rebellion caused the fire and if found will be prosecuted."

"I am sure they will be. Will you not have to use Chainsaw Freckles for what is going on today?"

"We hope not. This situation should be taken care of fairly quick. This man has decided his own fate."

"Is it not true Chainsaw Freckles has the soul of a serial killer who used to prey on children in its processors?"

"We cannot comment on that, Ray. It's confidential."

"Okay. As far as the lottery, it just seems easier to spend your winnings the last three months of your life and go quietly without remorse or flag down a msu, or mobile suicide unit, when your time is up, I think."

"I could not agree with you more, Ray. We wish everyone would think like you and use msu's, but they don't, making it very difficult, like Mr. Velmer."

"Thank you, agent Styles! I often wonder how nice it would be to win all that money! How many times do you think situations like Mr. Velmer's ha—"

Gunfire sputtered out of a window from the mobile home.

"Get back!" Styles shoved the reporter. "Get behind the halftrack NOW!"

The vid-cam swerved around the van and followed Manisquaski, capturing a glimpse of a team of dark-clothed demi agents wearing black helmets, carrying shields, moving toward the mobile home as one unit like congealed, black blood.

As soon as the reporter took cover the vid-cam snuck a peek around the van, being not only the reporter's eyes, but the viewing area's as well, catching the action, as a bullet found its way around a shield, blowing off the demi's leg just below the knee. Another bullet blew off a demi's foot. If not for the ability to do a quick maneuver, a program built into the vid-cam's system, a third bullet would have taken it out.

"Medic!" a demi agent hollered. Two paramedics appeared. Bullets bounced off their shields as they covered the wounded agents, dragging them out of the picture.

"YOU ALL BEST STAY BACK, DARNIT!! I'LL SHOOT SOMEONE ELSE, YOU HEAR??" Velmer's voice warned through a speaker attached to the roof of the home.

As the vid-cam continued to roll, Manisquaski shouted orders at his men, and their shields blossomed like a flower covering their legs and feet, just as gunfire crackled once again out of a window from the mobile home.

Bullets *tink-tink -tink-tinked!* off their shields.

The demi continued to shove forward.

Styles stepped into the picture with another agent holding a shield wide enough to protect them. Through a bullhorn Styles shouted: "Give up, Velmer! You know as well as I do actions like these never result in your good faith for the colony!"

"THE HELL WITH THE OZARIUM! GET THE HELL OFF MY PROPERTY, DEMI SCUM!!" A red flash of a particle beam scraped ten demi off the lawn, leaving a juicy smear of crimson.

"PULL BACK!" Styles shouted.

Rapid gunfire followed seconds later, spraying demi shields, forcing the demi back, widening a view of a garage with a Mack truck grill hanging over a door that slid open. Velmer shot out on a modified twentieth-century Deer riding mower with an authentic, pre-Shift .50 caliber M2 machine gun bolted to its rear. He wore a hands-free wireless microphone on his head:

"YA NEVER GONNA TAKE ME ALIVE DEMI-SCUM! MY GREAT-GREAT-GREAT-GREAT- GRANDPAPPY TOLD THAT TO THE VIETNAMESE! HE STABBED AND SHOT

TEN OF THEM RIGHT BETWEEN THE EYES WHEN THEY TRIED TO KILL HIM AND HIS UNIT! I'M HERE TO HOLD UP THE TRADITION! AYUCK-AYUCK-AYUCK!"

Velmer chugged a beer, burped, swerved a bit when he threw the can to the side, and fired the .50 cal.

Bullets punched a hole in a demi halftrack.

"Stop that nonsense, Velmer! Turn that gun and mower off right now!" Styles demanded.

Velmer flipped him the bird, chugged another beer, burped again (a couple of beanie weenie chunks soaked in beer came with it and had to turn his head to spit them on the ground), spun the mower around in a one-eighty, shredding a hedge cut in the shape of an ostrich dancing a jig, and fired the .50 cal again, punching a fist-sized hole in another halftrack, shattering the skull of the driver inside.

"Stop that, Velmer! Give yourself up! This is your last chance!" Styles voice demanded, echoing out of the bullhorn.

Velmer said something very offensive in a drunken slur I will refrain from adding into this tale because it involved telling Styles to stick his private part into the mother who gave birth to him.

So, at any rate, Styles ordered the demi soldiers to pull back. "Okay, then. Have it your way, Velmer!" He lowered the bullhorn and told a soldier who stood next to him: "Bring in Freckles!"

With a whir and a clank a tall clown entered in front of the vid-cam, with a chainsaw slung over its shoulder, a hand scythe hanging from his wide belt harboring the designs of cyclopean skulls and wearing a grinning face of a holographic Halloween mask, sutured eyes, a sutured mouth…

**Commercial Break:**

*"Howdy, friends! My name's Tyler Ray Jim Bob Elrod III. You all know me as the smiling bouncer and replica car salesman. You all should remember this goofy commercial:*

*Someone dressed in Chainsaw Freckles garb towered over a five foot five and six inch Tyler Ray Jim Bob Elrod III. "Would ya look?" He made a wide sweep with his arm. "This is my opponent's sales lot, Gertrude B Tuffasnails', filled with WAY TOO MANY HIGH PRICED REPLICAS! This cannot be! Look behind me!" He points a thumb over his shoulder. "A Chevy Nova replica, WAY TOO MUCH CRED! Over there sits a Cadillac replica, you could buy millions of Bork burgers with THAT much cred! Over there sits a bouncer with all the dressings: amphibious, stocked with an Oxy Giin and a Ramjam device, auto pilot capable, not one but a pair of thermonuclear powered Wankel-McMeyer turbine engines – extra turbo – twin harmonic human marrow vaporizers, and many other great features.*

*The hells is Gertrude doing? Selling equipment for a war? Sheesh!*

*"And look at her prize possession, a Plymouth Barricuda replica! No way is anyone in their right mind living in Ozarium gonna purchase this beast for that sticker price! Gertrude must be on that awful drug goose or sumthin'!*

*"I think we need to make a stand, right Chainsaw?"*

*The Chainsaw Freckles' impostor nodded.*

*"What shall we do to show the viewing area Ozarium doesn't take that kind of crap?"*

*Freckles' grumbled.*

*"Thought so, big guy!" the vid cam zooms in. Tyler Ray Jim Bob Elrod III's face floods the screen.*

*He winks.*

*The vid flips, showing a close-up as the chainsaw roars to life and the blade connects to the metal, grinding the Plymouth into two halves.*

*"Now," Tyler Ray Jim Bob Elrod III, the commercial returning*

to the present, "I'm here to discuss sumthin' purrty darn serious with you. Darn near as serious as these bib overalls I'm wearin' with the holographic pigs pushing their wheel burrows across this large gut ah mine."

He looped stubby fingers under the shoulder straps, then used one paw to pat his gut.

"And I didn't get this from bein' a health nut." Wink. "I worked hard at widening this here load!" Tyler Ray Jim Bob Elrod's overweight body shook and shimmied while he went through a series of guffaws and hardy harr-harrs and a cough and hack. "Working hard eight hours a day sitting around in your undies and watching the Hammer put a smack down on an opponent while having to wait for a demi check to be electronically deposited into your Bodykredd is tiresome enuff without havin' to deal with pests, right? And, if you're like me, and don't live in one uh those uppity, snot-nosed sterilized communities, you need one of those pest control devices called Martha the Rat Exterminator X. Yes, folks, you need to rid those rats from the village! Those nasty creatures are dangerous! Sure as heck don't need 'em in your double-wide where your family sleeps. All my kids, the ten from the four marriages I've had, are safe n' sound in their home with a Martha. My ex's will stake claim to that!

"Here's what a Martha looks like, take a gander at this fine specimen right…here!" The vid-cam pans over to a grey-headed servo unit about four foot tall dressed in a blouse and slacks, its synthetic fleshed face filled with rage, a lower lip curled and protruding, holding a Browning Auto-5 shotgun.

"With God as her co-pilot, watch this baby in action!"

The picture flips to a scene where a family is being terrorized by rats scurrying all over the floors of their double-wide home. Surrounded by a pile of empty beer cans, a lightning bolt for their logo, the husband is freaking out in his drunken state of mind, reclined back in front of a televid in his stained white sleeveless t-shirt, playing tug-a-war with a rat that is desperately trying to steal his bag of extra-extra seasoned barbeque potato chips. "Gimme back my chips, rat! Let go of 'um!"

The rat bares its teeth and squeals at the man.

In the kitchen the man's wife is standing on a chair, attempting to make dinner on the stove with enough grease sizzling in the pan that could actually be used to create a miniature indoor grease rink for rats if one would want to venture in that direction while rats scurry back and forth on the faded linoleum floor.

Scooping up a greasy mess of demi canned meat surprise, artificial onion and potato-flavored, a few pieces of the food ooze like spit onto the floor and is instantly gobbled up by a rat.

It licks its lips and rubs its tummy and burps.

Five of the six children are being chased by the rats, while the sixth one, a toddler with a healthy pocket of feces still in her diaper is slowly being surrounded by rats baring their teeth. The baby seems to think it is funny and is giggling.

Suddenly, the front door bursts open, severing the hinges, and there stands Martha the Rat Exterminator X.

After the husband lets lose a long, throaty burp, wipes his chin from a discharge of beer caused by a pestering reflux he just cannot control with eating ten flavored antacids a day, losing the tug-a-war with the rat, he opens his mouth and says in a terribly acted out dialogue: "Bout time you got 'ere, Martha! We're in need of your assis... assis...assistah...assistan...Crap! Can't remember my words!

"Burrrrrp!

"Help... Yeah...that's it...help...Help us please!" He throws his hands up, dropping a perfectly good beer, splashing the liquid contents on the floor. "Aw, damn!"

"With God as my co-pilot, I swear vengeance!" the unit speaks through some unseen speaker without moving its lips, throwing her fist in the air. Bottom lip curled, rage in her lenses for pupils, Martha cocks the shotgun, targets a rat, and splatters not only it, but three more furry bodies from the spray of the buckshot, chewing a hole into a wall next to a bookcase which has not seen one book on its shelve since it was built.

Rats begin scattering, taking notice to this horror impaled into them.

The shotgun goes off again, smearing rat blood and guts over the toddler who is still giggling. Another blast and pieces of fur and a dismembered rat head lands smack dab inside the sizzling pan on the stove.

The wife scoops up the head. "Yuck!" She flips it over her shoulder and continues working on the family's dinner, unperturbed by the rat fragments.

Three more rats are blown apart, the bodies splatter against the televid. A windshield wiper appears, wiping away the goo.

More rats are assassinated and once the job is finalized Martha stands there in the living room, nodding her metal head, approving her destruction which includes the elimination of the rats, smoldering holes in the walls, and a bullet-chewed up couch that should have been discarded five years ago. The rest of the double-wide is in ruins but the folks are as happy and content as if a redneck Santa Claus just gave them an empty Mountain Dew two-liter plastic bottle to use as the leaking reservoir in their Camaro replica Bouncer.

"Whew! Glad you...uh...uh...um...Crap, what the hell are those words? Oh...I know...I know...It's: Glad you helped us out, Martha!" the husband fails miserably, acting out his part with his drunken dialogue, unsteady on his feet he rises from the recliner and falls face-first with a wet smack into a congealing pile of rat blood and fur.

The kids all gather around Martha. The unit picks up the toddler and places the girl on her metal shoulder. A mixture of baby peas, baby applesauce, baby carrots and baby sweet potatoes feces ooze out of a crevice of the diaper, leaking down the back of the metal rat assassin.

"This house is clean," Martha says, throwing her fist in the air for the second time.

"Dinner's ready!!" the woman strolls out of the kitchen, holding a large bowl of the greasy substance. "Who's hungry?"

*Her family raise their hands.*

*Her husband attempts to rise back up, slips on the pile of rat goo, hits his head on the corner of the coffee table and passes out.*

*Martha catches his body with one arm.*

*Switching back to Tyler Ray Jim Bob Elrod the third: "So, what are ya waitin' for, folks? Put that twelfth beer down and get off that couch and get your butt down here to Tyler Ray Jim Bob Elrod's Rodent Quarantine And Kill and buy you a Martha. She'll be mighty fine to ya and take good care of your problems! And, don't worry about that family's double-wide, we are one hundred percent insured and we are sure Slader Corp will offer its assistance for your loss!*

*"See ya next time, folks!"*


*This message is still pending approval from the Slader Corporation ™ but under section five dash three – a thirty day probation – it is allowed for viewing.*


*** 


"Did you watch the news last night, dude?"

"Yep. Un-freaking believable, Walts!"

Saturday morning. Walts and his friend Jonas laid on their backs on a hill, their hands tucked behind their heads, watching clouds drift slowly by at the blue sky. The white stream of a jet left a chalk mark on the sky's canvas.

"I wonder why the demi never fires back at the winners, like shooting them in the foot or something?" Walts asked.

"Remember that one rule, Walts?" Jonas explained. "It states that the winner is not to be hurt in any way shape or form before being put to death. It's against the law."

"They really broke the law last night! See when they had to send Chainsaw Freckles in? Did you see *that*?"

"Yep. They had to. Velmer was a maniac!"

"Chainsaw Freckles is squiggly, man! I'd love to meet him for myself!"

"Dude, the only way you're gonna meet him is if you win the lottery and not die like you're supposed to. Would be rad to meet the robot, though."

"Never gonna happen. Kids are exempt. We aren't allowed to play the lottery."

"Sure about that? I'm not. Don't count your cloned chicken eggs before they're hatched."

"Ain't gonna happen, Jonas!"

"I believe it could. Times are changing, like last night, dude. Look at that guy Velmer; he actually went out and paid for lessons to become a sniper."

"That's a first; haven't heard of other lotto winners doing that." Walts pondered. "Guess you may be right, Jonas. This world we live in *is* bizarre."

"Huh. You're telling *me!*"

"Say, why do people like Velmer try to fight the demi? They know they are never gonna win!"

"Well," Jonas scratched his nose, "maybe they figure since they're gonna die, why not go out with a bang? "

"I would never do that. I wouldn't do what Velmer did. That's nuts! Now his family is dead, too! The news showed their Bouncer being blown out of the river by a long range missile!"

"I saw it! I agree it is nuts, but part of me wonders: wouldn't it be really cool to go out with a bang like Velmer?"

"You crazy, Jonas? Been sniffing cinnamon astro glue or something? I wouldn't touch that in a squiggle moment! They'd rather see you stop one of the mobile suicide units and commit suicide on your own rather than try and fight to stay alive! And what happens when you get to the afterlife, they're now calling the Great Beyond? There may actually be Great Beyond laws that would work against you."

"Laws?"

"Yep. There might be something in the rules stating for you to bypass the Stygian Wake and heavens and sent straight to the hells; all because of not going quietly with the demi so they can kill you off!"

"You believe that?"

"Yep! And I'll tell you another thing, Grandpa says it's total weirdo in the Wake. Ghosts don't like the rules much. Residual ghosts replay their death over and over. Sounds creepy to me!"

"Yeah, me too! Don't think I want to watch someone hang themselves repeatedly."

"Or shoot themselves in the head."

"Or cut their throats."

"Right! Grandpa is under oath not to say much to mortals. But he has mentioned ghosts could go anywhere they want. Haunt anyplace they desire. It's not like that anymore."

"Huh. I bet whoever's in charge on the other side doesn't give a nuclear re-act how you die; whether you go out with a bang, or not. I wonder who makes the rules?"

"Dunno. Could be someone who worked as a demi agent in their previous life. Maybe they were recruited after they showed up. S'posedly there's a guy called the Shepherd who lives in Purgatory and places your soul in a glass jar if you don't obey him."

"Do *what*? You sure *you* haven't been sniffing cinnamon astro glue, Walts? Ain't never heard of a dude called the Shepherd. Did your grandpa tell you that brain-dribble?"

"Nope. Colin did."

"Colin?"

"Yeah. He's a raven. One of those kids who are always dressed in black."

Jonas chuckled. "I know who Colin is. He's cool. I don't know why he's a raven. They are one messed up group! They give me weirdo vibes!"

"Same here. Skulls and crossbones on their shirts, white makeup on their face making them look dead. I wouldn't say that around Colin, though. He's groove, real cool."

"They look like they're trying to be a vampire or something!"

"True! But look: Colin told me there was some kids teasing one of the ravens awhile back, calling him an idiot for wearing black all the time. Even said his mom slept in a coffin and drank blood. The situation didn't end well."

"What happened?"

"The way Colin told it was the raven punched one of the kids, and the kids all ganged up and kicked the raven's butt. It was three against one! The raven ran off crying to the master Raven, and he sent a few of others after those kids. The ravens brought 'em back and hung them up by their ankles in an old abandoned warehouse. They threated to hook 'em all up to Swipe and wipe out their memories."

"Dude, Swipe is like, *really* expensive! How could they get a hold of something like that?"

"Dunno."

"You believe this?"

"Sure. Guess so."

"I'm not sold on that, dude. Swipe is high-dollar material! It's supposedly only used by the demi. Colin is a beatnik, don't ya think, Walts? His elevator doesn't go to the top."

Walts shrugged his shoulders, which was more like a twitch since his hands were still tucked under his head. "Seemed like the truth at the time. I think the entire raven click is beatnik – but to each its own."

Jonas chuckled. "I agree…Hey, did ya hear about the lottery winner who bought that mini-sub with a cloaking device last year and took her kids with her, hoping to hide underwater? What the heck was *she* thinking?"

"The demi has some pretty wild toys used to locate people

who disobey the lottery laws."

Jonas scratched his nose again. "No doubt. Slader Corp can afford to pay their people to develop things like that."

"True. Like your father."

Jonas grinned. "He has developed cool stuff."

"He developed traffic lights for SkyDrive."

"Yup. Pretty rad."

Walts' stomach gurgled. "Man, I'm hungry! Wanna go to that new burger place?"

"Long as it's not beef-flavored synthetic, I'm in!"

"Groovatronic!" Walts paused, scrunched his face up. "The hells with synthetic stuff! I don't know how people eat it!"

"The schizos do."

"Yuk! They probably *choose* to be homeless."

"Maybe. I sure wouldn't."

"Me neither! If I was a schizo and the demi offered a roof over my head and food in my tummy and a job, I'd get off the street."

"I wouldn't do that."

"Huh? Why not?"

"Why do I want to work? I'm a kid!"

Walts chuckled.

"Seriously, though, I'd take the roof over my head and the food."

"Yeah. Me too. We might get good stuff like cheesy pops and barbeque chips and hot dogs and peanut butter sandwiches."

"As long as it's not synthetic, Walts."

"Right. There is that."

"Wouldn't want to talk to myself, either. They pegged the name for those schizos right!"

"I agree, man. Weird-oh!" Walts' brain switched gears. "I'm not sure if I have enough Bodykredd or not for a burger, dude!"

"Didn't your parents wire you your weekly cred for doing your chores?"

"Yeah…um…think I might've spent it all what was left in the cred's memory on arcade games at Time Riff." Walts ran his thumb over the middle of his palm where the microchip was under his skin. He always thought it was so weird to have the chip, placed there when he was born. He feared sometimes that it would eventually break apart and get lost in his body. Not only would he not be able to spend money, he'd have to go get another implant. He had heard they were *painful!*

Jonas sat up on his elbows. "You need to learn how to save your money, dude. Don't drain the chip's mem."

"I know. Need to learn how to manage it. I suppose the only good thing is I only receive half the cred. Dad wires the rest in a savings account for me."

"Cool. But I think I'm done going to the Time Riff."

"Do *what?* Thought you like that place!"

"I do. But you need to come over and see what my parents bought me." Grin.

"It can't be better than playing games at the time Riff!"

"It is, Walts. You'd be surprised."

Walts frowned. "Time Riff is like a pre-Shift enema, stepping back in time!"

Jonas screwed his face up. "A…*what?*"

"Enema."

"Dude. That's sick!"

Walts laughed. "They even have old posters on the walls like Farrah Fawcett. She's a fox!"

"You know, I really don't know anything about her."

"Say *what?*"

"I really don't, other than what you've told me."

"Farah. Fawcett. The most beautiful girl in the world, and you don't know much about her?" I told you to look her history up on the internet."

"Just never got around to it."

"Wow. She was the one who was married to Lee Majors; the one who played the "Six-Million Dollar Man" a really, really, really long time ago."

Jonas blinked. "Walts, you lost me. I'm not up on that vintage, pre-Shift stuff you have. You know more about it than I do, and we're the same age. You're a total spacer, man! You *sure* you're not a little old man living in a child's body?"

Walts chuckled. "Nope! "The Six-Million Dollar Man" was an old sci-fi show where an astronaut crashed-landed his space craft and the scientists replaced his legs, his right arm, and his right eye, making him super-human. He worked for a place much like Slader Corp that fought crime."

"Way squiggly! Sounds like my kinda material!"

"You'd like it! You're gonna have to go with me to the old movie vid house down on fourth and watch some flicks. I've never been there, and I bet it's groovatronic to the max! Free popcorn and Coke, too!"

"Synthetic?"

Walts snorted. "You kiddin'? Hells no!"

"Sounds real squiggly, Walts, but, um, I think I'll stay home and watch movies on Quasi-Cinematix."

"Wait. You have a Quasi-C?"

"Yep."

"That's what your parents bought you?"

"Yep. Got my own stash to eat and drink at home while watching flicks."

"Way groovy! But, dude, one day let's go down and check the old vid house and watch those movies on the big screen. I've heard its cool!"

"Mmmph. Not sure, Walts."

"Why not? Give me a good enough reason!"

"Too many schizos go there. Ever been around one? I have, once. Those people stink."

Walt pondered. "Can't remember being around any homeless folks. I didn't think they smelled funny. What do they smell like?"

"Like the smell after someone lights a match and blows it out. What's the word for it…?"

"Sulfurous."

Jonas blinked. "Wow. How'd you figure that one out?"

"Heard it the other day in English class. Mr. Handles always introduces a strange word for the day."

"Cool. Those schizos really smell sulfurous."

Walts screwed his face up in disgust. "Nasty!"

"Yep."

"They should make use of the Sterilizer Booths located on different corners downtown."

"I agree! I think someone else should to."

"Who?"

"You."

"What?"

"You smell, man!"

"Shut-up!

Jonas chuckled.

"I really don't smell…do I?" Walts lifted his arms and sniffed his arm pits.

"Like a bed of roses, Walts!"

"You are *not* funny!"

Jonas laughed.

"Dude, that's mean!" Walts continued sniffing himself. "I don't stink! You're lyin'!"

"Am I?" Grin.

Walts sniffed again. "Yep. You're messing with me! I wouldn't ever say that to you, man!"

"That's cause I don't stink."

Walts leaned over, couldn't smell a thing drifting from Jonas but said: "Ha! You smell too!"

"Nope. That's you, man."

Aggravation flicked Walts ears, making them red. "Man! I need to get home and change!" He jumped up, stomped around on the ground, pacing this way and that. "Geeeez!"

Jonas laughed.

"You're really serious, aren't you?"

"Yep." Jonas shook his head, instead of a nod.

Walts frowned.

"Gotchya! I'm only messing with you!"

"Now that isn't funny!"

"Shoulda saw the look on your face!" Jonas said. "A 35mm Turbo Camera moment!"

Walts wanted to get angry, though couldn't. He started laughing, too. Jonas liked messing with him, getting him riled-up sometimes. And there were times Walts could get under Jonas' skin, too.

"Looked like you were really getting mad at me!"

"I was!"

"Shoulda known I wouldn't do that to you! We're good friends!"

"Yeah…I know…"

"Seriously, though: you need to come over and play Quasi-C. You'll love it!"

"Dude, I don't want to sit there with a neon green fish bowl on my head looking zombiefied. Gives me the creeps thinking about being inside a virtual reality-driven world."

"Man, it's radically twisted! You just don't *know* what you're missin'! That helmet you call a neon green fish bowl is the turn of the century for movies and games! It'll place you *inside* the game fighting monsters! Heck with using a joystick and buttons! Quasi-C is where it's at! You become your own type of character!"

"Own type? I'm my own type while playing a game at the Riff."

"Not like this you're not. Instead of playing behind the eyes of a character who already has its own personality the computer chooses for you, you are your own person."

"Huh. That's weirdo. Sounds cool. Not sure if I can see myself *inside* a game. May freak me out! Besides, Cinematix is expensive. I can't afford it on my cred."

"I told you you can come over and play it at my house. If you decide to purchase one, ask your parents."

"Yeah, *riiight*! They ain't gonna buy it for me. You know they tell me if I want something I gotta save up for it. It sucks!"

"That's not bad logic, Walts."

"Still sucks. Wish my parents were rich like yours, dude."

"No you don't, Walts. It's not all fun and games at my house. You already know that."

Walts did.

"Dad is always working.  Never really get to hang out with him. Barely get to see Mom. She's always down at Shop n Save A Bundle or at church playing Bingo or Bunko or jacked into Nimbus on the Gridd where sermons are spoke by a virtual preacher."

This wasn't the first time Jonas had expressed this. Walts felt sorry for him. Jonas' parents were hardly around, and it seemed as if Jonas always had the run of the house. They had a new machine called Food Processor XR Turbo which spat out any kind of food you wished to program into it: hamburgers, pizza, French fries, vanilla ice cream with pieces of dark chocolate. An expensive machine to purchase.

"Come on, you know Slader Corp pays your father well," Walts tried to enlighten the subject. "Right?"

"Well. Yeah. They do pay dad a lot."

"He's got some great cred, Jonas! It's a good thing this day and age. Years ago, when Overcast hit, it screwed up stuff. Nowadays jobs are everywhere, thanks to the colony's leader, Maximus Slader."

"Guess you're right." Jonas smiled. "My dad does make good

cred as a scientist. Still, I wished I seen him and mom more. Glad you aren't like other kids, all jealous and stuff, calling me a rich kid who gets his way all the time."

"I just know you don't act all high and mighty like Wilson."

Jonas' laughter fizzled out. "I can't stand that kid! He's a lot of trouble!"

"Maybe we could sick the ravens on him. They'd beat the sarcastic out of him."

Jonas chuckled and pointed his finger at Walts. "Good one! Wilson would cry and boo-hoo and run home to his mommy!"

"Yep!"

Jonas laughed. "Hey, let's blow this defunct Popsicle stand and get some food, Walts. My treat!"

"Squiggly! See? That's why I don't tease you about being rich. You keep buying me food!"

"Yeah, yeah, yeah, you're gonna start buying your own food with that attitude!"

"Riiiight!" Walts chuckled. "Think you owe me an extra burger for messing with me a while ago."

"Not happenin'! Now you're messing with *me*!" Jonas laughed.

The two boys got up and walked down the hill into town and headed to Bork Burgers, Inc. A flying saucer stuck out of its roof like a bone torn through flesh. A line of lights winked green, blue, yellow and red around its exterior. The establishment's title scrolled along the edge of the saucer.

Inside the restaurant, a robot took their order and instructed Jonas to swipe his left palm over the scanner sitting on the counter. Data transfer informed the bot if a customer's Bodykredd had enough in its mem to purchase something.

It took a couple of minutes for Jonas to decide what kind of burger he wanted, an Astro-Beam, dressed, no pickles; or a Radiated Jupiter Jalapeno with extra jalapenos. Choosing two of the same of the latter – Walts agreeing to eat a spicy burger too– Jonas added two waffle fries and two drinks. Not only did the fries come in small shapes of Chainsaw Freckle faces, the cups depicted designs of the demented robot clown in action, using his chainsaw to rip through walls.

The boys took a seat and ate.

A few hours later they were off to go swimming at the public pool. After they went through the sterilization showers they jumped in.

The only bad thing ending their afternoon together had been Wilson showing up, a Jupiter waste, splashing Jonas by doing a meteor ball (similar to a cannon ball) next to him in the water. He teased Jonas, boasting his being richer, more important.

Jonas ignored him. If he hadn't, he would have knocked out Wilson's front teeth.

He and Walts finally parted ways, each heading home for the evening.

***

*"Good evening ladies, gentlemen and children of Ozarium, I do hope you are doing well, as I, Maximus Slader, am. We are nearing the first days of summer. The flowers and trees are blooming nicely, showing so many wonderful colors. I bet you, my good people, are probably planning your required by Slader Corp law holographic vacation for your family. Remember to choose your vacation promptly by the due date.*

*"As you know," he cleared his throat, adjusted his tie, "the Lottery is upon us once again. It is that time again. The tickets will be sent out this week, via snail mail, and should arrive in your mailbox soon. I am sure all of you, ladies and gentlemen, are wondering: 'Who will be the next winner? Will it be me? Will I win all that cash to credit my BodyKredd?'*

*"Now, if you are one of the lucky ones who are chosen anonymously,*

*one of the lucky ones to win all that money — congratulations to you! I hope you have a grand time with your winnings! Spend it anyway you would like to!*

*"Just remember to follow the rules stated at www.lottowinnings@ demi.com and be aware you only have a limited time to spend your cred. Your time could be up in one week; or it could be as long as three months. That is the nature of the lotto. That is the fun about it, making the winner spend as much cred as possible before the demi shows up at his/her door, ready to escort them to the Neutralization Center.*

*"Take heed, the rules change from time to time; however, it always states to never — ever — leave one penny of it with your family or friends. Make sure you do not do this. The demi will be watching. I assure you."* Smile. *"If you are the next winner, and when the demi does arrive at your house to collect you, please, go quietly. Don't resist them whatever you do; it only causes problems.*

*"I cannot press this enough, ladies and gentlemen!*

*"Stand tall. Hold your head up high, ladies and gentlemen. Know that in your heart you are doing your good deed for Ozarium! You are the next person helping to keep the population down, keeping it to a minimal count! You will be the next poster child for your great deed! As the next lotto winner you will be remembered as you go down in history to help the colony strive! And, to add, you may have a monument made of yourself here in front of Slader Corp. This will depend on your actions when the demi comes to collect."*

*He cleared his throat.*

*"As an example what I am relating to, I must touch base on the most recent case of Velmer. We all know what his tragic history is about, correct? I would hope that you, good people of the colony, do. Mr. Velmer decided to use his lottery winnings to not only buy weapons from the rebellion, hidden in secrecy in a place entitled the Subterraneans, but to become a sniper and fight to the death against the demi.*

*"That is going against the rules of the lotto. This action must never be repeated.*

"This rebellion is a horrible bunch of individuals who think the lotto is a bad thing. They think the way I rule the colony is terrible. They think they can brain wash individuals — not only the people who win the lotto — to follow their path. I detest this group. I would not waste another second if I could catch each and every one of them to send them to the Neutralization Center for their crimes, such as destroying one of my labs a short time ago. "

He blinked.

"Ladies and gentlemen, you know I pulled Ozarium out of Overcast and rectified the world right. I created more jobs for the people and stopped the banks from foreclosing on their homes. Business is booming. People are happy. People have the freedom to do as they wish. All I ask in return for my great deed is to keep the population from spreading out of hand. There are only so many jobs in the colony for employment. There are only so many homes to own in the colony. There are only so many apartments to be rented. And, there are only a small handful of the people who we call the schizos who choose to be homeless. Those people have that right to live on the streets. Sterilization Booths are nearly on every corner of the street and every Friday the demi gives out free food to these people. They have never been a threat.

"Now, have I done wrong, ladies and gentlemen? Do you good people think I've done something wrong?

"I think not.

"To add, the case of Jake Velmer, it was a dark day in history to file away. Not only was he executed by our best assassin, Chainsaw Freckles — a famous one to nearly everyone in the colony — Velmer's family, who thought they were safe, watching from their televid hundreds of miles away in their Bouncer holding onto a quarter of a million cred, were blown out of the air by a long range missile."

He paused, allowing the statement to saturate the fear.

"Ladies and gentlemen, I will leave you with this: Do the right thing. Play responsibly. Spend your money however you wish, just stay within the lotto laws. Don't leave it with your family. Don't leave it *with your friends. Spend, spend, spend!*

"*Think long and hard, remember who has pulled you out of the dark days of the fallen economy, pegged as Overcast many years ago. Understand that our population must be leveled to a minimum in the colony. People are living longer these days. Too many baby-makers, repros, are breaking the law by having babies, not filling out the necessary forms online to be approved before they decide to have off-spring. Those of you in this category know who you are. Take heed and stop having intercourse unless you were approved to reproduce!*

"*Remember, there will be only one winner for him or her to spend their money within the period allowed before their travel, crossing over into the Great Beyond. He or she will have the best casket paid for by me and the best headstone carved out of granite with a pure gold face where the loved one's name will be engraved.*

*Smile.*

"*There can only be one winner, and that may very…well…be… you!*" *He took the time to give heavy emphasis on each of the last six words and gave the viewing audience a wider smile.* "*Good night ladies, gentlemen and children. Thank you so much for tuning in!*"

\*\*\*

Sarah's cell phone battery was as dead as the cockroach and its babies she smashed on the stove.

Frustrated, she pitched her smartphone in the corner and grabbed a duffle bag, stuffed a few clothes in it, turned off the televid, shutting off the last of Maximus Slader's speech and bolted out the apartment door. Two of the twelve lights in the hallway were out. One flickered; one had been shattered. Pieces of glass crunched under Sarah's boots as she slipped down the stairs and into the night.

Kentil was supposed to pick her up out front of the apartment building at eight sharp. It was two minutes past.

*Where the hell was he? Did he not realize the consequences?*

Benny kicked her.

"Shhhh! It'll be okay, Benny," she soothed her unborn baby, rubbing her stomach. "Daddy is on the way."

The moon glowed. A wind shivered the leaves in the trees. Sarah had always heard people arguing in their homes, TV shows blaring out of open windows, or the guy above listening to heavy metal groups from decades past.

But not tonight.

Really quiet; almost as silent as a tomb.

Sarah stood alone outside, waiting on Kentil.

"Where *was* he?" she spoke aloud.

Her plans were for the both of them to leave town and find somewhere to hide. She had been receiving abortion notices concerning her upcoming birth, thanks to her quack doc, a One Stop Shop Medic, for turning her into the demi. She had never registered to have a baby and was not about to get an abortion. Out of the question. The demi could stuff that idea up their ass! She was going to keep this baby and that was final, whether against their stupid laws or not.

Who the hell did Maximus Slader think he was? So *what* if he was in charge of the colony? So *what* if he enlightened the dark days of the economy and helped the nation? What was up with this lotto business? Did he think it was an excuse to take an innocent person's life? Who the hells did he think he was: a god?

Thinking about people forced to play the lotto frightened her. If chosen, you were instructed by Maximus Slader and the demi to die. Period. You would die by being sent to the Neutralization Center, a place ran by a central processing unit, the heart of this death machine which chooses your destiny of how you will die.

Sarah shuddered, thinking about this. Maximus Slader was no god, he was the reaper!

Headlights sliced the dark, pulling her to its attention.

Sarah shouldered her duffle, took a step, stopped. The replica swung to the left, rolling around one of the other apartment buildings.

"Shit."

Minutes slithered by. Sarah wanted to leave so bad she could taste it. She had reached Kentil by cell right before it went cadaver and the battery died. Leaving work, he said he'd be there as soon as he could. He told her he loved her. When she replied, her words were severed before finishing "Love you, too!"

She couldn't figure out why it happened. Her cell had had a good battery charge. She had charged it up an hour beforehand. She even removed the battery, waited ten minutes, and stuck it back in, hoping it would reboot.

Nothing happened, giving her a dark screen.

Sarah looked at her watch. Half an hour gone by since she spoke to Kentil. Something wasn't right. He should have been here by now.

She licked her lips, sighed. Okay. She'd have to foot it into town and hope to gods she noticed Kentil pass by in his replica before she made it there. Walking that far did not amuse her. Her body already tired, her feet were swollen and hurt. Her hormones were attacking her neurotransmitters, making her patience nil.

Gods she wished she could sever *that* line of transmission! She hated the mood swings!

She huffed.

Twenty feet away from the front door of her apartment building she felt as if someone trailed in her wake.

She looked over her shoulder.

Nobody.

Sarah knew of the schizos who roamed the streets at night. She knew she did not want to be an inch – much less fifty feet away – from them. Said to be dangerous, schizos only came out once curfew commenced. They were called schizos for a reason, too.

Supposedly they were homeless people who were mentally unstable. No telling why the demi could not control them. A mystery to Sarah. The demi ran the colony under Maximus Slader. They were the law. They had the guns. So, what gives? Sarah had a gut-feeling the demi had something to do with the schizos existence, but she did not know how or why. Everyone was ordered to stay inside and keep their doors locked at curfew. Something she cared not to think about anymore. She and Kentil were hacking it up and spitting it behind them. They needed to get out of town and get out ASAP. That was the plan. They wanted to see if there was something beyond the Ozarium, perhaps another colony where freedom for her, Benny and Kentil lie. Restricted signs were posted at that old house sitting by the river and along the road which had been blocked a decade or so, long before her birth. The bridge connecting to the other part of the road had collapsed, never fixed because of the floating dead from the Neutralization Center making it their watery graveyard. Disturbing the current of the river would be blasphemy, like stepping on someone's grave.

Tonight she and Kentil were expecting to find out if they could actually escape this terrible place.

A bouncer hovered past as she strolled along the sidewalk. Another followed, music blaring out of the windows. Hardly any street lights burnt a glow in the darkness, something they always did. She wondered if Slader Corp was trying to save energy or what.

*Probably another stupid idea Mr. Slader came up with.*

Sarah hurried up one street, took a left and followed another, still on the lookout for Kentil, She hoped he would spot her, maybe in the bouncer's headlights, before she saw him. Otherwise, he'd miss her and go home to an empty apartment, wondering where she had gone.

She began to second-guess herself.

She prayed this wasn't a mistake, heading down to his place of work. Should she have stayed behind? What if they couldn't find each other? What would she do *then*? What if Kentil had crashed his replica and had been carted off to the hospital? Gods, she'd be in a pickle if that happened! She'd go to his work, find out the horror, have to travel – on foot, no less – off to the hospital and make sure he was okay. Knowing her luck the demi would be there standing by, ready to force her into an operating room where they'd do the abortion using a One-Stop-Shop-method. Quick. Painless. Benny would be pulled from her body, the umbilical cord cut, severing the life-feed to her little boy who she would never see laugh, cry, take his first step or ride his bike. What if –

Behind her, something buzzed, as if bees had been forced inside a glass jar, tiny holes punctured on the lid to reveal the sound of their displeasure.

She snatched a glance over her shoulder.

Nothing there. Darkness and an odd odor, as if something burned.

The buzzing quit.

*What the heck could that be? Was she hearing things?*

Sarah pressed on, turned a corner, saw the neon sign above titled Matt's Café and slipped inside.

The bell on the door jingled.

The small café' where Kentil worked, nearly shaved of customers, left the stubble of a man and woman sitting in a booth across from each other, chatting, holding hands. One man wore a business suit and a hat sat at the counter, the tip of his shoe touching the floor, the other snug against the foot rest on the stool. The café's owner worked behind the counter, wiping it with a rag.

"Sarah, hey, what's up?"

"Hey, Matt."

"What brings you down here tonight?"

"I'm looking for Kentil."

"He left a while ago. Ran an errand for me. Been gone, say," he looked at the clock on the wall in the shape of a grinning clown's face, "fifteen minutes or so."

"Really? Huh. I talked to him on the phone a little while ago, and he said he was on the way home. Wonder why he didn't tell me he was running an errand for you?"

"Dunno." Matt shrugged his shoulders. "Probably 'cause it was a short trip. Figured it wouldn't take him long. He should be back soon. Take a seat if you want. Cup ah jolt?"

"Um…sure." She slid into a booth.

Matt grabbed the pot of jolt off the burner and a cup. He noticed her duffle bag. "You two off somewhere this late at night?"

"Just out. Kentil and me planned on cruisin' a bit before bed." Sarah smiled.

"With a duffle bag?"

"We…we want to be prepared in case we have to make the hospital run."

Matt glanced down at Sarah's stomach. "Good thinkin'. Keep in mind curfew is only an hour away, you know. There won't be much time for you two kids to cruise – unless you have to hurry to the hospital." Smile.

"I know. I wanted to get out of the house for a few. Going stir crazy! Feel like a hermit, cooped up all day." Benny kicked again, she placed a hand over her belly.

The guy on the stool slightly turned his head, in her direction.

"Ah, I see. How much longer you got?"

"About a week."

"Bet you and Kentil are excited, huh?"

"Yep."

"Me and the wife wanted kids real bad, you know." Matt placed a white cup in front of Sarah, poured the black liquid. Sarah could have sworn she heard a buzz.

*What the heck was that?* "Really? You two wanted kids?"

"Yup. The demi didn't approve us." He frowned. "You would have thought the demi would have explained why they refused us to try and conceive a child. No reason why. Guess that's the way it goes, eh? I know my Marylyn didn't think it was fair. Hurt her feelings real bad. She thought they should have approved us regardless. Marylyn was livid, Sarah. She vocalized her disproval by sending them a nasty email." He returned behind the counter and gave it a wipe with a rag. He topped off the guy on the bar stool's cup with jolt.

The guy nodded, thanking Matt.

Again, buzzing, and Sarah wished she knew where it came from.

"Anyways, we got a not-so-friendly visit from the demi afterward," Matt continued. "They had a long talk with us, making sure we weren't going to take any violent action against them. If Marylyn had said yes that day, I wouldn't have been standing here talking to you. I assure you *that!* The guys in black were pretty serious, Sarah. Scared the shit out of me and Marylyn." He chuckled. "Scared us enough that we refrained from having sex for a long while – which I know sounds too personal, sorry – to make sure she didn't get pregnant. Man, if she had..."

He left his sentence open for Sarah to visualize the consequences which could have transpired. Consequences she and Kentil could very well face if caught.

"So...how'd you and Kentil get permission?"

"We....um..." She had a lump in her throat, the worry of the demi catching up to her and Kentil scrolling across her brain. "We applied online, like you're supposed to do, and were approved pretty quickly."

"That's really great, Sarah! You two are very lucky you were able to reproduce. Wished it went that smooth for me and my Marylyn." He smiled. Sarah read his expression, imagining he still thought how nice it would be to have a kid. "You know, they say you have a better chance if someone dies of old age, has a fatal accident, giving themselves over to a mobile suicide unit or winning the Lotto, allowing couples a chance to have a kid."

Sarah nodded. "I've heard that before."

"If people didn't die, they'd forbid a repro to happen. Sure, there's a lot of couples in line who have the paperwork in hand, ready to start a family, probably wishing more people would die so they could have more than one child. Hells, some might root for it! Sick folks, right? Odd world we live in, Sarah, here in the colony. I thank the gods every day for me and Marylyn's health and good fortune – which really isn't much, but, hey, it's a living; me working here at the café, her working at the laundry. I was really young when the Overcast happened. Slader really pulled us out of that dark hole and I commend him for that."

"Um…so do I," she lied.

She glanced over her shoulder at the door, hoping to see Kentil step through, caught the guy on the bar stool with his head turned, eavesdropping. "Where'd you send Kentil off to do, anyway?"

"Needed for him to go to the bank and deposit the earnings for the day. He should be back real soon…More jolt?"

"No. I'm fine, thanks."

"Excuse me a minute. Gotta wash some dishes before I close up the place."

"Sure."

Matt returned behind the counter. Time began to crawl by. The couple sitting in the booth got up and left. The guy on the barstool nursed his drink, faced forward. Sarah glanced at the door, hoping to see Kentil come strolling in.

No sign of him.

"I'll be right back, Matt. Gonna step outside for sec."

"Sure thing," he replied, his back turned to her while doing the dishes.

Another buzz.

Sarah didn't hear that one as she stepped outside to look for Kentil. She hoped to get a glimpse of the headlights of his bouncer coming toward her.

A creepiness crawled down her spine. Something unsettling and definitely not right. She stepped another foot closer to the curb. Kentil should have probably been back by now. Funny, he never mentioned about running the earnings to the bank on the cellphone. Unless he intended on adding it to the conversation right after telling her he loved her. In which case, her phone went mort, cutting off his words.

She went back inside, stopped.

The lights were on, but nobody home.

Vacant. No sign of Matt doing dishes. No sign of the eavesdropping guy sitting on the bar stool. The rag Matt had been using sat bunched up like a small, tightly wrapped sarcophagus.

"Matt? You in the back?" Sarah walked to the restroom doors. "Matt?" She rapped on the door marked **MEN.** "You in there? You okay?"

No response.

Had she missed seeing the guy who sat on the barstool leave? Had he come outside when she had been out there?

The right eye on the grinning clown face above winked, informing her the top of the hour. Curfew a half an hour away.

Sarah looked outside. She ran a hand through her dark hair. What the heck was going on? Kentil should have been back, they should have been long gone by now.

The toilet flushed in one of the bathrooms.

"Matt? You in there?"

No response.

"Matt! Don't scare me! I'm pregnant, and you know that ain't good for my nerves and my baby!"

A black Lincoln Continental replica with suicide doors pulled up to the curb outside, its brakes squeaked to a stop. Two demi agents got out and stepped inside the café'.

Sarah took a step backward.

"Ms. Sarah Lans?" one asked, reading his Recog. His face an expressionless mask of pale flesh.

"Y-Yes."

"You are in violation of the Repro law. You are ordered to come with us."

"Huh? You have the wrong girl!"

"Ms. Lans, I have the file on this tablet where your request was denied. Your picture is on here. The doctor you have been seeing has been taken into custody and is charged as an accessory for your crimes. Come with us, Ms. Lans."

"I'm not going anywhere with you people!"

"Do not make us use force, Ms. Lans," the agent holding the Recog said. "It will not be wise."

"This kind of treatment isn't right! You people should not have a right to say who lives and who dies! That's just sick!"

"The laws are in place for a reason. It keeps the population leveled, Ms. Lans. If not, there would be an overflow of humans in the colony. People would live longer, enduring disease, illness; more homeless people would roam the streets; riots would spark; more corpses would be in need of burial. The cemeteries are nearly at their max right now, Ms. Lans. We do not want to start dumping the good people or the lotto winners who have died for the colony in the river, unless we absolutely have to.

"We always commend those who decide to take their own life at the Neutralization Center, but they do not obtain a grave plot by doing that deed. That is just the way it is.

"There is talk of placing coffins on top of other coffins, making grave diggers having to return to the graves and dig them back up, making the holes deeper in the graveyards. Most people want their loved ones in plots, however, we may be looking more towards cremation for everyone instead. It may become a new law."

Sarah felt the creepiness squeeze her spine. "Y-You people are nuts! This is all crazy!"

"No. It is protocol."

Movement rose behind Sarah. Matt stood there behind the counter, wiping it with the rag.

The agents grabbed Sarah and lead her outside where she slid in the back seat. Her duffle was placed in the Continental's trunk.

"Matt! Help me! Please!"

"Come again, Sarah. Thank you!" Matt waved, his eyes lit up a bright yellow. Behind the flesh tiny workings of an automaton fluttered with a buzz emanating.

Sarah heard the buzz. She cracked.

*What the hells was going on? Could this all be delusional?*

Her brain sputtered; neurotransmitters attempted to grasp reality.

Sarah knew someone had to have tipped the demi off, but who?

"Wh-where's Kentil?" her voice seemed like a tiny filament.

"He's fine, Ms. Lans. You'll be reunited with him soon. Sit back, enjoy the ride."

As the replica pulled away from the curb, Sarah's face peered out of the side window, watching the neon café's sign drift into the night.

***

Inside, the customer in the business suit walked out of the bathroom and sat back down on the stool. His face an expressionless mask of Kentil. Matt refilled the customer's cup and stood back.

Each of these men who had been transfigured into automaton acted according to program, very human-like, shut down and their heads drooped.

The neon sign flickered, went dark.

The clock on the wall struck the top of the hour, the clown giggled. The overhead fluorescents began shutting off, one by one. A stubborn one winked once, twice, thrice…darkness.

### Commercial Break:

*Mourners stand and weep while the preacher speaks his sermon about a lotto winner. Each family and friend of the deceased line up and place a flower before the casket is to be lowered into the ground.*

*According to protocol when someone's life is retired, demi agents attend the funeral, there to pay their condolences.*

*A small girl about five years' old holds a long stemmed rose as she is carried by her father to the casket.*

*"I'm sorry, honey, Grandpappy is gone."*

*"He's in there?" She points.*

*"His body is, honey, but his soul has crossed over into the Great Beyond."*

*"Is he in the Wake? Will he come to see us?"*

*"Not right now. It takes time for the deceased to find out if they can return as a Reflection."*

*"You mean he'll be a ghost?"*

*"Yes, honey. That is what we call them. It's all up to a higher power now, as long as he agrees to the Paranormal Laws, he'll be back into our life real soon."*

*The girl smiles, remembering all the good times with her Grandpappy, up until a few days ago before his heart stopped.*

*She throws her rose on the coffin lid.*

*As the lowering device gradually deposits the casket into the grave, there is a hesitation in the mechanism. Two of the four metal bars supporting the coffin bend and wrench apart, causing the casket to drop sideways into the grave. Upon impact the coffin splinters apart and Grandpappy rolls out, his head flops to the side, his eyes gaze upward at his granddaughter.*

*She screams.*

*Quickly, the demi agents escort the family away while an automaton backhoe with the words GLEEMER & CO. scoops up dirt and piles it on Grandpappy's corpse and his open coffin, hiding their mistake.*

*Darkness floods the screen.*

*A pale face of a bald man wearing dark shades appears and is grinning.*

*"Howwwwdy, folks!! Carl here! Your smiling coffin salesman! Has this ever happened to any of you out there? Huh? Boy, I friggin' hope not! If you were a victim of this horror there wasn't anything you could have done about it, was there?"*

*"No, my friends, there wasn't.*

*"Before this disaster happens to you I invite you to come on down to Carl and Carla's Coffin Extravaganza! Why wait for the demi to give you a free casket? Why wait for them to give away a fraud, a generic piece of wood glued together that won't even hold a pinch of salt? How do you know you won't fall out of the bottom when they lower it into the ground? How do you know it won't leak? How do you know worms and beetles won't slip in and attempt to tickle your feet?*

*"That'd ah be a real hoot, huh?*

*He chuckled.*

*"How do you know the coffin won't splinter and break apart when something awful happens, much like what just happened at Grandpappy's funeral? Eh? Embarrassing, if you ask me! Look: Could you, already able to come back as a ghost, stand back and watch as your loved ones shriek in horror if your funeral is flubbed up like Grandpappy's? Eeesh! I sure as heck wouldn't! I'd get my butt in gear, and I'd head down to Carl and Carla's Coffin Extravaganza and get to pickin' me out a coffin 'fore I die! That's what I'd do!*

*The scene on the vid pans backward, exposing a better view. Carl wears a two-piece suit and stands next to a big busted woman donned in a crimson-colored dress with a fifties beehive hairdo. She almost looks like a clone of a Barbie Doll.*

*She blinks, smacks her lips chewing bubble gum, cheesed for the camera.*

"*Me and Carla have so many coffins to choose from! Right, Carla?*"

"*Yup!*"

"*All you have to do is touch the screen and you'll see a televid of our price list and a detailed description of each casket! Go ahead, ya know you wanna touch it!*"

*He winked.*

*This has been an approved message from the Slader Corporation*™

\*\*\*

"Walts! Time for bed!"

"Awww, mom! My show isn't over yet!"

"Walts! You have school tomorrow, and its well past your bedtime!"

"Awww! All riiight!" Walts huffed.

"Carolyn, why don't ya let the boy watch the rest of the show? That goofy coffin salesman was just on – wasting space if you ask me – and Walts' show only has fifteen minutes left. Ain't gonna hurt if Walts watches the rest."

Walts smiled at the ghost of his grandpa who defended him, sitting in the recliner. Grandpa's death had come as a shock last year from a massive heart attack while asleep in his own room down the hall, but was given the choice to return as a ghost where he could roam free in and out of the Wake. He took that option to be close to Walts.

Walts remembered Mom not crazy about it. Ghosts frightened her, stemming from her younger years living with her parents having an evil entity which haunted their house. An exorcism had been performed by a minister to rid the ghost away. Nowadays, things were a lot different. Paranormal Laws were in place for these particular reasons. Since Grandpa had returned as a ghost, this was called a haunting, not to be mistaken for something bad. This was a law where a ghost had the choice to reside in someone's home as long as he/she was in an agreement with a mortal. In Grandpa's case, being part of the family, it took a little time for Walts' Dad to talk Mom into it, reassuring her it *was* Grandpa, not some evil entity. She finally gave in and allowed Grandpa to stay.

In addition to Grandpa's situation, he was also given the ability of Free Space, roaming around inside abandoned buildings, empty houses and cemeteries.

The bizarre thing left behind after Grandpa's death was a residual apparition replaying the painful death of Grandpa over and over in his room down the hall. Mom was not too crazy about it, and Dad and Walts felt the same. Until Grandpa could get this erased from existence by a group known as Residual Removal, Inc, where the customer is placed on a long waiting list because of its small staff and the high demand of its service, the room's door was kept locked. Neither Mom, Dad or Walts wanted to see the horror of Grandpa breathing his last breath.

Mom stepped out of the kitchen, wiping her hands on her apron which had a pattern of tiled sunflowers. Every so often the hologram of a bee would buzz out of a flower, fly around Mom's waist, and slip back into the pattern. "Dad, you know as well as I do, it's best if Walts gets some rest. Tomorrow he has finals at school. If he doesn't make good grades he may not pass any of his classes."

"Oh, Carolyn, you know he'll pass them!" Grandpa ran defense yet again. "He did his studying when he got home from school today."

Mom frowned. "Dad, this is Sunday. There wasn't any school."

"Oh. That's right." Unfortunately one of the downfalls of being a ghost is losing track of time.

Walts gasped. Mom may override Grandpa!

"Well, I bet he studied a lot this weekend," he pressed, smiling, shooting Walts a wink of his eye.

Walts grinned.

"And if I remember right, wasn't his last school report a good one?"

She sighed, ran a hand through her brunette hair tied back in a ponytail. "Yes, I suppose you're right, Dad. Walts, did you study today?"

"Yep! I studied this morning before church."

Mom crossed her arms, one of her eyebrows lifted. "You're telling the truth?"

Walts opened his mouth and grandpa cut him off. "You *know* he is, Carolyn! Why would he lie?"

Mom cleared her throat. "Dad, I asked *Walts*. He can answer for himself."

"Um…sure."

"I'm not lying! I got up early and couldn't go back to sleep, so I decided to study. I want to pass my classes cause I'm ready for summer vacation!"

Mom gave the Hard Stare with a slice of Frown. It poked and prodded and tried to see if her son was lying.

"Mom, I swear I did!"

"Don't swear, Walts. I've told you not to do that. It isn't nice."

"Yes, ma'am…But I *did* study! I want to pass my classes, so I won't have to go to summer school!"

"Let us hope *not*." Mom's Tongue-In-Cheek added to the Hard Stare and Frown. She sighed. "Okay. I believe you. You can watch the rest of your show. Off to bed after. Hear?"

"Yes, ma'am."

"I'll have your lunch ready by tomorrow morning. It'll be on the bottom shelf in the fridge, okay?"

"Yes, ma'am."

Mom returned to the kitchen, washed the rest of the dishes.

"Thanks, Grandpa!"

"You're welcome, Walts. Before you go to bed, you may want to study again, just to keep it fresh in your mind. Don't you agree?"

"Um. Yeah, guess I should, huh?"

"Yes. You should."

Walts had a strong feeling Grandpa knew he had lied. He felt bad about it. Guilt making an appearance did not help, pestering him, reminding him of what he just did. Walts knew he'd probably have to break down and tell Grandpa and Mom he had lied to them. However, he procrastinated and watched the rest of his show, then went to bed.

Grandpa made a point to run defense for Walt ever since he'd been living here. Defense was a good thing. Grandpa had even run defense, convincing mom to allow Walts to stay outside an extra half hour in the evening, right before the two suns went down. Forbidden to be outside playing in the dark because of not only the curfew implemented by the demi, but the danger of a schizo.

Lying in bed, Walts pondered. Once he did cross over into the Great Beyond it could be that he would be forbidden to roam in the Wake like Grandpa because of his lie. He could be thrown into a court and sentenced by judge and jury to be sent to Purgatory. He might be thrown to the Shepherd and stuffed in a glass jar for an eternal imprisonment, all because of his stupid lie!

*What the heck would he do then, trapped in a glass jar all by himself? No doubt there weren't any games available to play to pass the time, like at the Time Riff!*

*Uggh!!*

\*\*\*

The next day Walts rose extra early but didn't get off to a good start.

Mom and Dad were still in bed. He knew Grandpa was somewhere roaming around the Wake, probably talking to old friends; making new ones, too. Grandpa sometimes told Walts it was comforting to meet other people who were deceased, some dying from a massive heart attack like him. Grandpa said he had a lot of stuff in common with them, especially the ones who lived through the depressive time of Overcast. Others, who used a service called a mobile suicide, were ones who resulted in ghosts who became a recluse, staying away from others. Grandpa figured they were so depressed in their previous life it bled over into their dead one. There were even some ghosts who were over a hundred years old and were mad at the world and everyone else. They kept to themselves, kind of cliquish, and usually did not wish to leave the Wake. They were not bent to like the new age of what Westersphere had become. Didn't suit them, so Grandpa had told Walts.

Walts tried wrestling away Guilt before heading downstairs and failed. At least the will was there. Guilt prodded Walts about the lie, reminding him it would rather stay around for a spell, acting as a horrid disease.

Adding insult to injury, Walts argued with the jolt maker to brew him a single cup of hot chocolate, no thanks to its infection of the Tourette's Syndrome virus. Walts wasn't keen on its curses it scrolled in digital letters at the base of the machine, choosing some very, very bad words. Hells, he would be grounded throughout summer vacation and half another if he used the language the j-maker used! He would definitely have to remind Dad to fix the darn thing. His father was a guru for working on electronic appliances, and it enabled him to be his own boss and work from the home, down in the basement at his workstation.

The j-maker decided to spew out jolt instead of hot chocolate.

Walts wasn't about to drink jolt. Yuck! More for grownups!

Walts dumped the brew in the sink, returned the cup to its position to catch the liquid, slapped the jolt maker on the side three times, listened to it grumble and scroll a few more curse words Walts' way, before it decided to drain the hot chocolate.

He brought a cup of the chocolaty substance to his room and

studied.

Gods he sure hated math! Despised it! He did not like fooling with numbers. Would he actually use this crap later in life? He sure as helium blast was not going to be an accountant! Wearing a tight-fitting two-piece suit and tie and sitting in a cubicle looking at five screens at once did not sound like a spacer adventure!

Nope. Nada.

He'd rather take six five minute tests, one after the other, in any other class rather than do math. And that went for English, History, Computer Science, Geography, Robotics

*— Wait. Back up! Not Robotics! Too many issues dealing with tiny metal parts or having to burp out a binary code for the unit to function! —*

and P.E.

Before he left for school he saw Mom. He really needed to confess his lie. Guilt chuckled, poking at him with a stick.

Walts sighed, confronted the inevitable.

Mom had been in the kitchen, cleaning the counter when Walts confessed. She didn't say anything for a minute or two, leaning against the sink, arms folded across her chest.

"Walts, you know better than to lie to me."

"I know, Mom."

"Why did you lie?"

"I wanted to stay up to see the show."

"Passing your classes so you won't have to go to summer school is far more important than staying up to watch the 'vid."

"I...I know..."

"I'm really disappointed with you, Walts. You do know if you don't pass those classes, you'll be held back a grade while your pal Jonas moves up a grade."

Thoughts of staying behind did not thrill Walts a bit. He might get stuck in a class with a kid like Wilson. "I did study this morning, though."

Mom frowned. "Are you telling me the truth, this time?"

"Yes! I really am this time!"

"Let's hope you are. I hope you can get through those tests, Walts." She glanced up at the clock on the wall. "You'd better get to school. You'll be late."

Walts nodded and stuffed his lunch in his Chainsaw Freckles lunchbox and started out the door when he heard mom's words chase him down:

"We'll talk more about this tonight, hear?"

"Yes, ma'am. Oh, I…um…get to leave early from school today. We're only there until lunchtime. Is it okay if I go by Jonas'?"

Mom sniffed. "I should probably say no, Walts. But, I'll allow it – this time. We'll talk tonight; you, your father, and me."

Oh, boy, Walts pondered.

He liked to walk to school, not being very far. Sure, he could take a ground transport like the other kids, if he wished. Sandwiched between two in a three-seat fashion – he felt – was not comfortable. Much like being stuffed inside a sardine can. Anyways, there were always too many kids on the transport, way over capacity – Walts thought – and too many kids chatting, shouting, laughing, etc. Last time he rode it a kid picked on him. Stole his history book and wouldn't give it back. The driver did nothing to help him, since drivers were allowed to have a clear glass barrier – some supposedly bullet proof – to shut out the noise of the kids so they could pay attention to the road. Walts felt transport drivers didn't care about the safety of their passengers. What if there was a fire? Would the sensors become defunct, not alarming the driver? Nothing was perfect! What if a kid got real sick or passed out? Would the driver pay attention to the cameras, or just ignore them? He had heard from other kids at school that their parents were furious with the school system and were trying to take legal action against this issue.

So far, nothing had been done.

The kid who stole Walts' book ended up throwing it out the

window just as they pulled up to the curb at the school, landing in a very shallow puddle of water. Not in the best shape, it did not ruin.

Walts hurried by his neighbor's house. It always gave him the creeps. Four robot yard gnomes occupied the lawn. Some people purchased these machines to use them as butlers or maids. Some purchased them for decoration, like his neighbor.

Colored hats differentiated each gnome; red, blue, green, purple. Each time Walts went by, he noticed the gnomes never stayed in one spot, always moving around when no one was looking. Kind of like changing around the furniture in a room without lifting a finger. These robots would not only change position, but change their pose. Most of the time they all wore smiles under their nose. Other times a few scowled and looked mean as ever. There were even times when they looked frozen, doing a cartwheel or two.

Walts always hurried his steps when he passed. Especially when he knew eight little eyes were staring at him.

At school, Walts cruised through the day with the horrid thoughts of what punishment his parents were going to come up with. Could be worse if he didn't pass his tests! He saw Jonas in between classes and asked how he thought he did on his finals.

Jonas felt he did fine. He might have missed a few questions; one or two of the multiple choices. Otherwise, he felt he passed the tests, ready to tackle the last year of middle school.

Jonas asked Walts about his tests.

Walts actually felt pretty good to admit he might have passed. Studying this morning may have done a world of good and kept it fresh in his noggin. He told Jonas he had lied to his Mom, not feeling too good about it.

"Hope you don't get grounded!"

Walts shrugged his shoulders. "Hope not, either."

"Worst case scenario, you'll probably get a lecture from your dad and mom both, maybe a privilege taken away."

"Maybe.

"You may have passed math with a C or C minus."

"Probably wouldn't catch much grief from Mom, if so."

As promised to the kids, school let out at about midday. It gave Walts and each student a chance to get a jump start on summer vacation. A few kids celebrated the end of the school year by riding their bicycles instead of taking a school transport. Holographic tassels powered by microchips clipped at the ends of their handlebars waved in the wind as they pedaled. Some kids had special-ordered their tassels in the shape of hissing snakes.

Ravens were known for this morbid move.

A group of them sped past Walts and Jonas. "Outta the way nerdos!" they shouted, nearly clipping Jonas.

"Dude! Watch it!" Jonas spat back.

One of the ravens swung his bike around doing a one eighty and skidded to a stop. His brows furrowed and a strand of his long dark hair hung in front of his right eye. "You say something, nerdo?"

Jonas' face flushed. "Who you callin' nerdo, *freak?*"

"Dude! Don't worry about that guy! Let's just get on home!" Walts pleaded. He didn't want this situation to twist into a bad one. He did not like confrontation; never had. He didn't want to be involved in any trouble.

Though sometimes, the planets didn't align correctly.

"Don't worry, Walts. I got this. Everything'll be fine."

"I *asked* you: Who you calling a *freak*, nerdo?" The raven put the bike's kickstand down, got off the seat. "You two look like a bunch of pansies." Chuckled. "Gonna go off and read somewhere?" He snickered.

By this time the other ravens had joined their comrade.

"At least we know *how* to read," Jonas said.

"*What* did you say, nerdo?" the raven spat.

"You heard me."

The raven stepped over, stood a foot away from Walts and Jonas. "You two have any idea who you two are messing with?"

"Jonas, let's just go. We can go to Bork B–"

"Got somewhere to be, little guy? Your mommy calling you to come home to give you a bath?"

"Leave him alone," Jonas warned.

"Or what? Gonna beat me up?" Snort. "I'd like to see it. It'd take your girlfriend there to help ya." The raven chuckled.

"Dude, why don't you do yourself a favor and turn around and get on your bike and leave?"

"That would be too easy, wouldn't it? Why would I want to miss the chance to mess with you two nerds?"

"Need some help, Rib?" one of the fellow ravens asked.

"Naw. No problem I can't solve on my own, Brit," Rib replied.

"If you need us, we're here, man."

"Groove." Rib's focus never faltered away from Walts and Jonas. "You two, with your stupid-looking clothes." He pointed a finger at both of them. "Your mommies and daddies buy 'em for ya?" Chuckle.

"Steal yours from the demi handouts they give to the schizos?" Jonas' words were a quick-snap to defend.

Rib's amusement scurried away. "*What* did you say, man?"

"You heard me."

"Jonas, let's get out of here. We could go–"

"Hang on a minute, Walts. I *told* you, I *got* this."

"Yeah, *Waltsee*. Hang around and watch your friend get his ass beat," Rib said. "May get yours beat if you don't shut up."

Jonas huffed. "I asked if you'd just turn around and leave. There's no need to fight. Doesn't solve anything."

"Sure it does. It shows who is the tougher kid. You certainly are *not*."

Walts had a premonition Jonas tried holding back his temper. He did have a lot of patience. His friend never took any crap from anyone and could almost talk his way out of fighting. However, much like the way this situation steered, Walts remembered the time they were at the mall and four kids tried messing with them. Before the kids could further belittle him and say something bad about Jonas' parents, Jonas punched one of the boys in the nose. Caught the kid off guard. Wasting no time, they scattered and left Walts and Jonas alone.

"I bet you're afraid of getting your ass kicked in front of your girlfriend?" Rib squeezed the can of lighter fluid, adding fuel to the fire.

The group of ravens laughed.

Jonas sucked in a deep breath, let it out. "C'mon, man. Let's not do this."

"Lets." Rib shoved Walts, making him stumble, stepping over to stand nose to nose with Jonas.

"Fine! Hold my cell, Walts."

Walts caught it.

Someone on another bike slid to a stop. Colin, the shortest of the bunch. "What's going on here, Rib?"

"This punk mouthed off to me. I'm gonna split it so he won't speak for a week," Rib didn't turn his head, stared eye-to-eye with Jonas.

Colin saw Walts. "Hey, Walts."

"Hey, Colin," Walts replied.

"This your friend?"

"Yeah."

"Rib. C'mon. These guys are groove."

"Maybe the one you know is right and fine and groovatronic… but this one here has a smart mouth. We ought to drag this one off and make so he has brain-salad."

Walts knew Rib spoke of using Swipe.

Jonas' face colored crimson. Walts saw his friend's hand hanging by his side doubled-up into a fist, ready to clock Rib.

"Rib. Let's go, man. Ain't worth the trouble having to face Cork."

Rib spun around on his heel, faced Colin.

It caught Jonas off-guard, and he almost swung on Rib, thinking the raven decided to throw a punch.

"This has nothing to do with Cork!"

"Sure it does when I tell him. These guys are groove. End of story, Rib. This isn't our style. You know that. We don't go starting trouble. Ain't our way. Let's get out of here and get a burger at Bork's. Get you a grape freeze to cool you off."

Rib huffed, shot a mean look at Jonas. "These guys started it. Tell 'em, Brit!"

Colin looked at Brit. "That ain't true, right?"

Brit swallowed down a dry throat. "Um. No."

"You probably didn't see Walts or his friend do *anything* to deserve this, did you?"

"Uh…no."

"See, Rib. You're in the wrong, dude. Step off. C'mon. Let's jet."

Rib scowled. He took a step back. "Next time I catch you out somewhere, I–"

"Rib! Shut it! Let's jet!"

Rib got on his bike, shot a mean look at Jonas.

Jonas stared back.

"Later, Walts," Colin said.

"Later, Colin." Walts replied.

The ravens rode away. With one flick of a switch on their handle grips, neon skull faces shimmered on their mag wheels as they pedaled.

Walts sighed, handed the cell back to Jonas. "Dude. That was *in*tense!"

"Yep." Jonas watched as the group of ravens disappeared around the corner of the school. "It was."

The two boys strolled off toward Jonas' house, discussing what had just occurred. Jonas told Walts he was a millisecond away from breaking Rib's jaw. The kid deserved it. Walts said he was happy his buddy, Colin, showed up.

Jonas agreed. He really did not want to fight and, there for a while, felt sure things would have resulted in a bad way.

When they got to Jonas' house he introduced a game to Walts called *Vector 5* on his Quasi-C game system. He told Walts he recently purchased an extra helmet so it could be a two-player game.

"Here's your helmet. It's called Envo. I'll explain more about it later. Right now you're gonna step on this mat right here, like me."

Holding the helmet, various pictures came alive, one after the other: a rocket ship blasting through space, a little girl and her robot running from three men who looked strongly like demi agents, and a ringleader hosting a bizarre carnival with vampires, werewolves and zombies.

"What's up with all these pictures, Jonas?"

"They're previews of other games."

"Huh. Very groove."

"Go ahead and step on the mat. There you go. Feels weirdo under your feet, huh?"

"Sorta feels like I'm standing on a balloon."

"That's what I compare it to. When you put the helmet on it'll feel weirdo, too. Don't panic, ya groove? You'll feel an annoying itch for a second on the top of your head. It's just Envo's feelers trying to connect to you."

"Um. What? Feelers connecting to *who*?"

"You."

"*Me*?"

"Yep. The technical sentence indicated in the manual is "microscopic wires called feelers which will slip under your skin and connect to your brain."

"Um…not so sure 'bout that, dude! Is it *safe*?"

"Ain't nothin' to worry about! Remember when that servo acupuncturist came to class last fall, showing off its presentation?"

"I do. Eegads! Don't remind me! I was the one chosen out of a hat to get stuck with those pins!"

"Didn't hurt, right?"

A second slipped by, the reflection of Walts' memory came back. "Nope. Didn't feel a thing."

"The only thing you'll feel is an annoying itch that'll last for a second, like I already said. No pain."

"Oh. Groovatronic!"

"Ready?"

"Yep!"

Jonas and Walts donned their helmets at the same time. Once Walts felt the feelers insert themselves into his skin, he wanted so bad to scratch the top of his head because it tickled. It suddenly made him light-headed. His vision warbled through the helmet's dark face shield. An odd sensation stopped for a visit and felt like a ping pong ball, ponging and pinging out of control inside his skull. Leaving as soon as it arrived, it vomited him inside cyberspace where a bright moon hung over a large city at night. Pockets of orange glow sat in windows of buildings. bouncers and replicas were parked by the curbs. Somewhere, a dog barked.

Jonas stood only a few feet away from Walts, dressed in a dark outfit and wore his Envo helmet. "Squiggly, huh, dude!" His voice sounded as if spoken through a walkie-talkie. "You made it! Come on, we've some monsters to kill!"

Walts noticed he wore the same attire as his friend. He opened his mouth to ask Jonas a question when a melodic chime fluttered through the air (much like "The Mister Softee Jingle"), snatching his attention away.

"Is that what I *think* it is, Jonas?"

Jonas nodded.

"You have *got* to be kidding?"

Jonas shook his head.

"Can't the demi stop with that horrible commercial, even inside virtual games? Egads! Gives me the creeps thinking about suicide! Don't they know kids aren't interested in that crap? Why would anyone do it, anyway?"

Jonas shrugged. "I don't think I could bring myself to commit suicide if I was a grown- up."

"Me neither!"

"They have those commercials because adults play virtual games, too, so that was probably why the advertisement was here.

"True; forgot about that," Walts replied.

A voice said:

NOW, A WORD FROM OUR SPONSER

Familiar lyrics from the chime scrolled in thought across their brains while the boys ducked into an alley:

*Oh, what a wonderful day,*
*Oh, what a wonderful day to say goodbye,*
*Oh, can't you see,*
*What a delightful day for you to die!*

*Get rid of your worries,*
*Get rid of your stress,*
*Get rid of your spouse,*
*Help us keep the population leveled and quit being such a louse!*

To entice the listener, the chime changed, more of a blues progression:

*You know my mama,*
*She said son,*

*You know my mama,*
*She said son,*
*Won't you bury me,*
*When I die!*

*Seal me up in a coffin,*
*Bury me deep,*
*Seal me up in a coffin,*
*Bury me deep,*
*So's the worms don't tickle my feet!*

Minutes later the chime grew louder, revealing a hologram of a mobile suicide unit, a direct replica of an ice cream van with pictures and data of various options labeled on each side to indicate which suicide a person would like to choose from: self-inflicted gun to the head; self-inflicted knife across the throat; self-inflicted slitting of both wrists while sitting in a tub full of water.

Other choices, with the option to ask the msu driver for help with your suicide include: knife in the back (three bone-deep stabs performed by the driver or a spouse or friend); noose tightened around the neck and hung from the nearest tree limb (performed by driver because he is an expert at this); buried alive in coffin (performed by driver, friend, spouse or any option a customer wishes to choose).

Trailing underneath:

"Try the latest and greatest of suicides in technology today! After giving you an injection which places you in a deep slumber, plunging to your death off a cliff, it will be a guaranteed death because you will slam the ground.

"Remember: Any type of other self-inflicted or assisted suicide not listed can be performed. Seize the day! Be creative! Many people have!"

Stuck on the replica's roof a holographic advertisement sign scrolled:

DON'T LEAVE YOUR FAMILY BEHIND TO SUFFER!
WHY NOT BRING THEM ALONG WHEN YOU CROSS OVER
INTO THE GREAT BEYOND? THERE IS NOTHING MORE
TO SEE IN WESTERSPHERE BEYOND THE COLONY.
FAMILY SUICIDES ARE THE LATEST TRENDS THESE
DAYS! TAKE PART AND END IT ALL! HAND OVER
THOSE ICKY BODIES OF YOURS! HELP US KEEP THE
POPULATION LEVELED!

Waiting until the mobile suicide unit and its eerie chimes vanished, the boys sprinted down a vacant street. Had the msu detected them, it would have pursued to become a long infomercial, a hologram of a salesman who closely resembled Eric Burdon trying to force suicide info down the boys' throats.

"Do you ever wonder what might be beyond the colony?" Jonas asked.

"You mean *past* the restricted signs?" Walts replied.

"Yep."

"*Past* the river of corpses?"

"Yep."

Walts screwed his face up in disgust. "Those restricted signs are there for a reason, Jonas. It's a big no-no trying to swim across the river with corpses floating in it. That's sick! I wouldn't touch my big toe in that water, even though Slader Corp pours an anti-disease chemical into the waters daily! And those wastelands aren't supposed to be safe out there where the Shift began and the world changed. Joey Conns claims there is some weird guy out there playing a flute with rats following him around."

"Joey is a goober. He thinks he has an infestation of nanobot bed bugs crawling all over him. Really odd dude."

Walts agreed.

"I bet there is another world out there waiting to be discovered, Walts. What if what they say is wrong and there is more to Westersphere to discover?"

Walts considered this. "You know, I'm not so sure about that. I still think it's too dangerous to try and leave the colony."

"I'd love to try, you know, just to see what's really out there."

"I wouldn't. The demi would stop you before you get to the edge of the river."

Jonas shrugged his shoulders. "Maybe. Think it would be groove to give it a try, though."

"Not me, dude."

"Well, it was a thought, ya know…"

They stood in front of a door attached to a warehouse.

"So….What kind of monsters are we after anyway?" Walts inquired.

"You'll see," Jonas replied. "Careful when you step inside here."

"Okay."

"This'll get you away from those old game vids! No more using stupid joysticks or having to punch buttons or use guns with wires attached to them! You'll teleport back to the present after this and not have to live in the past!" Jonas smiled.

"Okay. Sure!"

"Follow me." Jonas twisted the doorknob, Walts followed, letting the door close behind them, shutting out the darkness of the last scene, opening mysteries of the next. They strolled in darkness.

"Walts, don't say the words. Think them. Use your telepathy option and tell Envo to turn on night vision."

Walts did so and the room lit up in a greenish glow. "Way cool!" The place held large unopened boxes, rolls of conveyer belts and stacks of wooden pallets.

Jonas rustled around in his pocket.

"What are you doing?"

"Watch this. It's freaking squiggly!" Jonas flipped a coin up in the air and caught it.

"Here, you do the same."

Walts did the same thing Jonas did and immediately felt a change in the air, a slight

ripple over his body.

"Okay. That felt…weird." Walts said.

Jonas chuckled, but didn't say anything until reaching another door. "Here we are,

Walts."

"Here we are *where?*"

"You're just full of questions, dude. Relax. Everything is cool."

Walts thought otherwise. Being inside this game started to give him a scare. That odd change in the air gave him an odd sensation along his spine. Not hip to it.

"This place is actually called a Cyberspace Junction, CJ for short; kind of a nexus for us gamers."

"Huh."

"See what ya been missing, Walts?" Jonas punched Walts in the arm, jokingly. "The last time I played Quasi-C, I ventured through here, I saw another kid being chased by two dark creatures in shrouds. Odd thing, though, the kid wasn't wearing a suit like ours. He was dressed normally, like he was actually *part* of the game. Usually you only witness creatures roaming around in here, not humans. I've heard they are placed here to frighten the gamer."

"It'd frighten me, dude."

"I bet! Like always, the creatures never mess with you; kinda like posing as scarecrows. That day those things wearing shrouds and the kid they were after disregarded me like Joey Conns does for studying for tests, though. Total mindbender."

"Weird-oh!"

"Yep. Seeing is believing, dude. It was twisted!"

"So, what did you do? Stop playing?"

"Heck no! I continued on, like we're doing now."

"Oh."

"I opened a door and stepped into another game."

"Wow!"

"Like this one we're in front of." Jonas grabbed the doorknob.

"So, what's up with the coin?"

"You need it to get out of the CJ. Kinda like your own personal skeleton key to unlock your own game. Without it, you'd be trapped in here."

"Trapped?"

"Yup."

"You're kidding?"

"Nope. There's a warning label on the box the Quasi-C came in that warns gamers. Serious business, dude."

"Can't you just take your helmet off and step off the pad?"

"Nope. Those feelers attached to your brain could stay locked on, preventing you from taking off your helmet and escaping."

"Whoa!"

"And the only way to free a gamer stuck inside the CJ would be to either bump into another gamer who was passing through, someone who would be nice enough to share their own coin to help you leave, or having to hire a computer hacker. They're the only guys who could come to the rescue."

"Wait. Those dudes are not cheap!"

"No. They are not."

"I wouldn't want to be stuck in here, that's for sure!"

"Well, the first time I played I goofed up and was trapped in here."

"You did?"

"Yep. I got lucky though and saw another gamer who helped me out by sharing his coin. I ended up playing his game, though, and didn't get to actually play mine. It wasn't no big deal. His game involved battling a bizarre carnival of freaks from another planet who were stealing humans and mutilating them, changing them into side show creatures. Afterwards, I was able to take off my helmet and connect a USB line to it and to my Recog tablet and download a driver from the Quasi-C website called a "Coin Key. Then it was safe to play the game again, without being trapped, since I got another coin from the website."

"Bet you were glad you didn't have to find a hacker."

"I was!"

"Wait. How could you find one, being trapped inside the Quasi-C? If you can't take off your helmet to use the interface, what then?"

"There's an option where you can call out while you are inside this game. Watch this."

A holographic blue screen popped up in front of the boys.

"Hey, that's the same screen as on the interface!"

"Yup!"

"Squiggly!"

Jonas typed in random numbers.

A woman's face appeared. "Synth-Fit Hair, how can we serve you?"

"Sorry, wrong number," Jonas said.

"No problem. Have a good day." The woman smiled and the screen went blank.

"We should keep that one on speed dial!"

Both boys burst out laughing.

Walts was, so far, very impressed with the Quasi-C as he followed Jonas through the door, straight into the cabin of a tug almost ready to disembark into space. A light gray color covered the interior. Multi-colored lights spread across the panel in front of the pilot and co-pilot's seat. Through a large panoramic screen he viewed a massive hanger filled with workers in bright orange suits as they busied themselves getting the ship prepared. They scrambled around like orange-colored worker ants.

The door they walked through had vanished behind them, now a wall of the ship.

A voice announced:

{Welcome to the *Vulturine* space ship, soldiers. I am Vodburkk, the *Vulturine's* computer. Please, take your seat. It is minus ten seconds before take-off.}

"C'mon, strap in, dude! You'll freak with this!" Jonas said.

Walts sat down and strapped in.

Jonas held both hands over the arms of his chair. Holographic blue flames flickered under his palms, flipping through pictures of different items, finally settling on an undulating skull face. "Came up with that one myself! Designed it on the Recog and downloaded it into the Envo." Jonas smiled. "Pretty simplified."

"Groovatronic!" Walts replied.

{Minus nine seconds before take-off.}

The working ants outside in the hanger hurried, some slipping into doors that slid closed in their wake; others were detaching and rolling up thick cables which had been connected to the ship.

{Minus eight seconds before take-off.}

"Wait'll you feel the blast, man. Ain't nothing like it!" Jonas said.

Walt grinned. He felt his adrenaline rise.

{Minus seven seconds before take-off.}

"Once we're in space Vodburkk takes over, guiding us to the planet Vector 5," Jonas explained. "The trick'll be for me to maneuver down to the surface once we enter into its atmosphere."

"Sweet."

{Minus six seconds before take-off.}

Twin hanger doors slid apart; a maw of deep space littered with stars flooded the boys' vision.

{Minus six seconds before take-off.}

Vanished from sight, the workers busied themselves behind a sleek glass window.

{Minus five seconds before take-off.}

"Hold onto your seat, Walts, we're going for a ride!"

Walts frowned, surprised at his friend. "Reciting something the character, Short Round, would say in the movie *Indiana Jones and the Temple of Doom*?"

"Huh? Oh, yeah." Chuckle. "Didn't think I'd watch it, huh?"

"Nope. Figured you keep the memory stick for a month, forget about it, then find it one day under your bed and give it back to me and say you never got time to watch it."

"I'd never do that!"

Walts chuckled. "Dude. You told me that same story when you borrowed my flash drive with the first Indiana Jones vid, *Raiders of the Lost Ark*, on it."

Two point seven seconds slid by before Jonas pondered, replied: "Oh, yeah, forgot about that."

"See! Told you! Glad you finally watched it…since I had to twist your arm."

"You're right. You did," Jonas surrendered.

{Minus three seconds before take-off.}

{Two.}

{One.}

"Stick with me," Walts said. "I'll keep letting you borrow all kinda classic –

{All systems go!!}

"Viiiiiiiiiiiidddddddddssss!"

The skull faces under Jonas' palms screamed as the ship rocketed away from the hanger into space, followed by the screams of the boys. Warp drive engaged automatically, thanks to Vodburkk, plastering the boys against their seats. Flesh on their faces felt as if it rippled under their helmets. The reflection of stars splattered against their helmet's dark visors, fusing together in a bright spotlight of white.

The *Vulturine* shot across space, passing bizarre-looking

Milky Ways and black holes that reached out and snatched lone travelers, plunging them into nonexistence. Once the ship's warp drives finally slowed, stars winked, a planet grey and crimson in color appeared on the screen.

{Prepare for landing on planet Vector 5.}

"What's on this Vector 5, anyway?" Walts asked.

Jonas grinned beneath his visor, too dark to be seen by Walts. "I'll never tell. You'll find out in due time, dude!"

{Minus five seconds until breach of atmosphere.}

"Here we go, Walts!"

{Switching to manual control. Good luck soldiers.}

The skulls growled under Jonas' palms as he took over the controls.

The *Vulturine* nose-dived into the atmosphere of Vector 5, slipping through dark clouds, quickly viewing the reddish-orange surface below. Swaths of green appeared in different areas, as if an artist had decided to throw buckets of paint on a wide piece of canvas.

The planet's gravity grabbed hold of the tug, gave it a hard yank, fiercely making the *Vulturine* shake fiercely and rattle. Walts thought for sure it would shred apart and both he and Jonas would plunge to their death.

Jonas hit a button and applied anti-gravity mode. His flying skills were top-notch. He used the controls like a pro to maneuver the *Vulturine*, pulling the nose up seconds before impacting the ground

– almost making Walts pee his pants –

and shoot back up into the sky, level out, and cruise at a slower pace. Hitting another button, he engaged the landing gear.

The tug hovered over the land and set softly on the planet's surface.

Walts and Jonas took a deep breath at the same time, and let it out.

"What a ride, eh, Walts?"

Walts was speechless.

{Oxygen level at ninety-seven percent. 80° Fahrenheit. 60% Humidity. Winds 30 mph from the east.}

Unstrapping from his seat, Jonas said: "Nothing to it, huh?"

"I almost peed my pants, man!" Walts said, unstrapping also. "That was *not* cool!"

"Aw! C'mon! We landed safely, right?"

"I'm not so sure about this, Jonas."

"Hey. Some of the worst is behind us."

"*Some?*"

"Yeah. If you're shocked at what just happened, you ain't seen nothing yet! You just wait!!" Jonas lightly slapped Walts in the arm.

"Jonas. You're crazy!"

"Aw! Not as nuts as you! Don't worry, you're gonna be fine when we get out there and do this job."

"Uh-huh." Walts wasn't so sure.

"Seriously! You will be!"

Walts shook his head. *What the hells did Jonas get me into?*

"Vodburkk said it's okay to breathe the air outside. However, I think its best we keep our helmets on while outside. We may be able to shed them later. I've found the air changes without warning. Nearly killed me the first time I played this game. This game likes testing players, trying to eliminate them before they get five feet from the ship's door."

A panel slid open beside the door to exit, exposing two odd-looking rifles with fat barrels tucked into slots in the wall.

"What the heck kinda guns are those? They look like rail guns on steroids!"

"Fancy ones, Walts! They're called Turmoils. Best in this biz. Real groovatronic! I programmed the Quasi-C we'd both have one apiece in the pre-setup of two player-mode." Jonas picked his up. "Don't worry, I downloaded the instructions into your Envo helmet on how to use it. Go ahead, research it, using that tiny thing inside your skull you call a brain."

"You're real funny."

"Sorry. I meant microscopic."

"Keep it up, Jonas!" Walts chuckled.

Jonas laughed. "Seriously, dude! Check it out! The helmet'll give you the info, thanks to the feelers. All you have to do is think about it, an envisage will appear."

"Envah-*what*?"

"Envisage; short for why we call the helmets Envo's. It means a picture in one's mind. Remember earlier when I told you to use Envo telepathy? Do the same thing and tell it to show you specs about the Turmoil, and it'll download the info into your brain. Might show you an example of how to use it, too."

"Huh. No kidding?" Walts picked up his Turmoil and didn't have to think but a second of how to use the weapon. A glob of virtual knowledge splattered him with info. If it had been slime, he would have had a Dr. Peter Venkman moment in the movie *Ghostbusters.*

It reminded him, he needed to watch the old vid again soon. Great movie!

"Whoa! Groovatronic, dude!" It showed him examples of the gun being used, the fat barrel rotating when firing grenades, laser shots, ice shots and acid shots. Walts could choose a setting with a click of the thumb or a finger.

"Just leave it on the laser setting for now, Walts," Jonas said.

Walts checked his setting. Laser.

"Ready?"

Walts nodded.

"Let's go."

They had only gotten no more than twenty feet away from the tug when the ground under their feet moved.

"Whoa! What's up with that?" Walts stumbled back, startling

him. It felt as if somebody's fingers were poking the soles of his boots.

Jonas chuckled. "Only bugs under there. They're just curious. Watch this." He scuffed the dirt with his boot. Black bugs burrowed out of the red dirt and crawled all over his foot.

"Ughh! Creepy!"

"They won't hurt ya, Walts. They're only curious."

"Reminds me of my babysitter's house I told you about long ago. The one infested with automaton cockroaches?"

"Oh yeah, I remember."

"Those bugs loved to congeal together behind her retro TV hanging on the wall. Instead of your ordinary cockroach attracted to moisture and food, these creatures were attracted to the TV's electronics. Sometimes they'd short the system out. She had to buy an anti-virus program you had to release in the air to kill their central processing units. It took a while."

"How the heck could someone get infested with automaton cockroaches?"

"Mom told me my babysitter received an anonymous gift from a place called 'The Joke's On You!' My babysitter turned it into the demi, but they never could get a lead back to the one who sent it to her."

"Huh. Did they reproduce themselves?"

"Yep. Tiny robot factories, dude."

"*That's* creepy!"

"Groovatronically unacceptable!"

Jonas laughed.

"So, you know where you're going, or are we wandering out here under this beautiful day with dark clouds hiding its two suns?"

"Yeah, *real* beautiful! Thanks to the navigation Envo is supplying me so far, we're headed in the right direction. There's been times it has taken me a different direction when I've played the game by myself. That's what's so cool about this game! Each time you play it, the challenge is different. It makes it hard to make it to the next level if you get killed and have to start over. Since it is a two player game right now, it's a mystery even to me what to expect. What, take me for a loon or something?"

"Cool!"

"Just stick with me! I'll make you a gunni yet!"

"A *what*?"

"That's what they call a pro in these here parts," Jonas said, reciting a cowboy persona. "Stick around, you'll learn sumthin'!"

"You're talking like that, and you're accusing *me* of watching old movies and playing old Atari games?"

"Hey, can't help but like old westerns off Quasi-Cinematix. They're free downloads on the website."

"I bet."

"As for the Atari games…not my cup of jolt! Outdated technology."

"I already know that."

"Still can't understand what you see going to the time Riff."

Walts shrugged his shoulders. "It's cool, man."

Jonas frowned. "If you say so…"

As they crested the first hill, they spied a patch of woods below. Off to the side lay an abandoned cabin in ruins. Three charred bodies lay a few feet away and something moved inside of them, making the burnt flesh crackle.

"Um. What is causing *that*, Jonas?" Walts pointed at the cadavers,

"Those bugs we just saw. They're curious."

"Odd curiosity they have, man. This is already *way too* weirdo. First, we're in the suburbs; next, we're inside a warehouse; then, inside a hanger; and now here listening to bugs search around inside a dead body."

Jonas laughed. "Man, you're fine! You're too uptight! Loosen up! This is just a game! You're gonna have some fun. I promise!"

"I hope so…"

"Those bugs are harmless. Nothing to worry about there.'

"I know that already, but *eeesh*! Those things creep me out!"

"Calm down! You'll be fine! Those things don't hurt you. *Trust* me. You groove?"

"Yeah. Sure."

"Just wait." He flicked his eyebrows twice behind the visor of his helmet. "The fun hasn't started yet! Come on!" With a wave of his hand he indicated for his friend to follow along a dirt trail into the woods where the trees looked massive, limbs stretching to claw the clouds in the sky.

Walts suddenly had the feeling of being tiny in the land of wooden giants.

"What *is* the object of this game, Jonas?"

"You didn't research it on your Envo?"

"Hadn't gotten that far yet."

"Go ahead. It'll take less than a second for it to splatter you with the info."

Walts did so. Envo not only showed Walts details of what kind of metal monsters were responsible for ripping apart the race living inside the dome, it explained the quick history of the planet. Man inventing machines, machines infected by an unknown computer virus which caused them to turn on man and twist their world into a terrifying dystopian society overnight under the ruling of giant machines. The game held a similarity of another Walts had played down at the Time Riff; however, this one looked way more challenging.

The object of the game: Rescue as many survivors as possible and return them back to base where the *Vulturine* had blasted off from.

A large white dome appeared while they traipsed around an oak tree with a huge knot bulged from its flesh. The dome's door was shut, a neon keypad sat to the left, blinking at them. Jonas used his Envo's info to break the encrypted code. The door slid open, revealing a blood trail snaked to a large puddle: congealed leftovers from warm flesh. A small doll lay close by.

Walts picked it up, turned it over, noticing the dark shade of dried blood on its backside. He dropped it, wiped his gloved fingers on his suit. "These people were slaughtered. Envo didn't lie."

"Envo doesn't," Jonas replied. "We need to look for a trapdoor that leads underground. The survivors might be hiding there."

"What if they're not?"

"We'll have to start exploring the planet."

"Wow."

A second slipped by, grabbed other seconds to add, as the boys searched for the door. Walts located it, told Jonas. Ten crimson fingerprints ran along the edge of the door, as if one's fingers had been severed when the door shut.

"Kinda nasty looking, dude. *Sure* we have to check this out?"

"Sure, if we want to keep playing this game and locate the survivors, allowing us to move to the next level in this game. Anyways, if we find the survivors they may tell us what those creatures look like."

Walts pondered. "Envo already showed me what those metal monstrosities look like, though."

"Ah, but they morph into other things, Walts. They just don't stay dormant, first looking like one of those old Asimov robots they sell downtown, they can change into hideous creations."

"Oh. Wow."

"*Wow* is an understatement! Okay. Ready to continue?"

"Yep."

"Since you located the door, you can do the honors of opening it. Push that round button."

Walts looked at the button covered in dried blood. "Oh, gee, *thanks*!" He rolled his eyes. He sighed, reached down, pushed it; and the door slid to the side. Metal rungs attached to a concrete shaft led downward into darkness.

Walts looked at Jonas.

"You first," Jonas insisted.

"Thanks, *again*."

"Hey, what are friends for?" Smile.

Walts grumbled, shook his head, added a grin behind his visor showing he wasn't really agitated and slung his rifle over his shoulder. He descended the rungs one by one. Before long he stepped into ankle-deep water. Jonas followed and when he had climbed six rungs from the top, the door slid shut.

"It's freaking dark in here!"

"Don't get your panties in a twist, Walts! Use your Envo, tell it mentally how to switch to night vision."

Walts got his to work. The world became a greenish glow and he stood in a corridor. Black ooze covered the walls. For some reason the glow giving him a remembrance of the color of those lime popsicles he liked, the ones in shapes of the creature from the movie *Creature from the Black Lagoon*. Bizarre-looking treat, but really tasty!

His amusement shattered once he stepped into something.

He stumbled backward into Jonas climbing off the last rung.

"Whoa, Walts! Watch it! You almost knocked me into the water, dude!"

"Sorry! But look at that!"

Jonas chuckled. "Calm down, man. The dude is dead."

Walts and Jonas stood in front of the corpse of a guy who lay soaking in the water. A gaping hole looked as if it had been chewed out of his chest.

"Hey, you knew about this part of the game, right?" Walts asked.

"Sorta." Jonas shrugged his shoulders. "Sometimes he's here; sometimes he's not. I told you, each time you play there's always a different challenge."

"I was about to ask, 'Why didn't you warn me?', if you had known about it."

"Even if I had, where's the fun in that?"

"Guess it wouldn't be. Creepy seeing some dead guy, though. Ain't groove, dude."

"It's only a *game*, Walts."

"Yeah…but it's so real!"

"I know. You wouldn't want me to spoil things, would you? Like telling you everything that you'll encounter."

"Guess not."

"I've encountered some things that were sorta the same while playing this game, like how the machines look, dead people like that dude in the water, the woodland area, etc. If, by chance, things were exactly the same every time I wouldn't imagine this game would be much fun, right?"

"Right."

"Those old video games at the Time Riff are like that."

Walts considered this. "You got a point there." Suddenly he felt like he should be tired of playing those old games, hoping to play more of the Quasi-C where each time you play is a different adventure. However, he still dug the old games. Vintage games were groovatronic and would always be!

"And the same thing goes if we were watching a movie you've never seen before, and I kept telling you what'll happen next. You wouldn't want that, would ya?"

"No…guess not."

"Well, there you go. It'd be squiggle-stupid."

"True. Squiggle-stupid max!"

Jonas chuckled. "Yep!"

"I told you, I've played this game enough times already. I know some surprises that'll make you pee your pants."

"I nearly did on the *Vulturine*."

Jonas laughed. "Oh yeah! That's right! Look, before we move

any farther, I'm gonna check something." Jonas wore a wristband that beeped while he fiddled with it.

Walts hadn't noticed it before. "Where'd you get *that*?"

The wristband beeped again. "I acquired it from the Barn. It's where I stash weapons and stuff I've won playing this game."

"Where's the Barn? Close by?"

"Nope. It's in the virtual memory of the game."

"Oh. So, you just Envo it into the game – so to speak – and it appears?"

"Exactly."

"Way squiggly! Can't wait 'til I can get some extra stuff and stock it in my own Barn!"

"You will if you keep playing this game with me. You wouldn't believe how much I've won already, dude!"

"Cool!"

"Okay. According to Envo's navigation, we follow the corridor this way." Jonas pointed. "Be on alert for enemies."

The boys sloshed through ankle-deep water. Those pestering black bugs from above also lived down in this corridor as well, darting along the walls, in and out of the black ooze. This place creeped him out!

They came to a fork in the path.

"Which way now?" Walts asked.

"Envo says to go left. The other one should take us back to ground level."

"Okay."

The water drained away from their ankles as they explored a left side which inclined, leading toward a lighted open space where there were men, women and children sat here and there. Immediately, they welcomed Walts and Jonas, issuing many thanks and hugs.

"We found them!"

"Yep. But now we have to lead them safely *out* of here. From now on it will become tricky. We need to watch out for our enemies, Walts!"

Walts brought up the rear as Jonas took the lead, the survivors sandwiched in the middle as the group went back through the corridor, until stopping at the split.

"Listen, Walts," Jonas said, pondering for a second, "you take these people back the way we came."

"Shouldn't we take this other path?"

"We could…but I have a plan. Got some information from Envo about where this other path leads."

"Where's it lead?"

"According to what I am told, it might place us closer to the *Vulturine*. If so, I may be able to elude the machines and get the ship running, then come back and pick all of you up using a tractor beam. This way would be easier, Walts, instead of running for our lives and leading the survivors back through the woods, hoping to get to the ship all at once. I'll meet you up top. Okay?"

"Dude, I'm not so sure about this."

"It may very well work. Trust me!"

"There's that 'Trust me' thing again."

"C'mon, man. I'm pretty sure it'll work!"

Walts sighed. Since he was a rookie, he didn't feel very good about this. But: "Okay. I'll do it your way."

"Cool!"

"Just don't let me get killed!"

"I'll do my best not to, dude! Watch your back, Walts." Jonas warned as he hurried out of sight.

Walts looked at the survivors. "C'mon, let's get you all up and out of this miserable place." *And me as well!*

The survivors followed him back the way he and Jonas had come. The door slid open and Walts poked his head out, surveyed. Climbing out, keeping his rifle at the ready, he told the survivors to run to the front door of the dome. Careful not to step in any of the blood or congealed piles of the muck, he strode up to the door to go outside, opened it slightly.

No enemy sighted.

Outside, he felt sure he could get the people to safety. He could get used to this game; that is for sure! Being the hero who saved people from evil would be groove! And what more groove would be the fact he could obtain extra items like Jonas and stash them in his own Barn. Perhaps he would get to choose a few after all this game was ov –

The ground vibrated.

Walts looked left, he looked right.

Nothing in sight.

*The heck* was *that?*

He told the survivors to hurry and to follow the dirt trail into the woods, he'd cover them. Nodding their heads, they rushed off.

Halfway into the woods the vibration switched into a rumble. Walts lost his balance, slapped a hand against a tree, steadying himself. Others followed suit, some slipping onto the ground. Branches snapped away and leaves fell from above, raining down on the survivors. Covering their heads they rose and ran, searching for cover in the woods.

The sound of twisted metal, rattling Walts' bones.

*Chink-chink-chink-chink-chink.*

Burrowing itself from the ground, an enormous automaton worm sheathed in chrome with a spinning carousel wheel for a mouth lined with serrated teeth ripped free. Sensors from the monstrosity picked up the survivors and Walts. Dirt cascaded off its frame as sleek, razor sharp tentacles grew out of its cylinder, wasting not a second to stab a woman through her gut who tried to escape into the woods.

It lifted her a few feet off the ground while her body slid down the blade.

She screamed.

Her pale flesh began to pulsate. Her body convulsed. Her blood sprayed the ground. Deep within her meaty shell her internal organs combusted. Chrome spots appeared and bubbled, bursting, giving birth to nanobot arachnids that scurried out of the holes, covering over her newly-formed shiny flesh, transforming her into an automaton. Wires sutured themselves in and out of her flesh. The nanos scraped away her face, regenerating it into a blank sheet of chrome. Completed in her robot shape-shift, the worm released her and she fell on all fours. Two yellow slices trickled down her face, eyes which gazed at Walts.

"Too weird-oh!" Walts took aim and pulled the trigger. The Turmoil's barrel spun, fired off two laser shots, missed the female automaton, found a home in the side of the worm, shaving away a chunk of metal.

Sparks flew from its wound.

The worm's mouth rotated counter-clockwise, revealing another set of blades for teeth. "Eegads!" Walts got back up just in time to notice the female automaton add another

change to her person. Two limbs slid out of her sides, two sharp blades like her predecessor had, giving her an arachnid-like quality.

It hissed and charged at Walts.

Walts let loose another couple of shots, this time blowing the metal monstrosity apart, knocking his own self on his rump once more.

*Where the heck was Jonas? He needed help!*

People were screaming as they were snatched up by the worm and metamorphosed into more metal monstrosities. He watched bodies convulse and twitch and transform into the creatures. One man's head imploded while the nanobots were working on him, burrowing into his face, suturing, carving, shearing away flesh and bone, articles not needed as the modification became a large mouth lined with a smaller spinning carousel with serrated teeth.

Another creation from the worm spotted him and charged.

Walts set the Turmoil to acid shots and melted the robot into a pool of metal. He blasted away two other creatures before he could snatch a second to scan the area for survivors.

He did not see a one. *Had they found a safe place to hide?*

The worm reared back like a cobra and took a dive into the ground, its mouth chewing up pieces of the earth. The rumble knocked Walts off balance, and his feet flew up in front of him, and he landed on his back.

Two more monstrosities lurched out of the smoke and spray of the dirt in the wake of the huge worm. Tentacles grew from their post-human chrome cadavers. Before Walts could aim his Turmoil and let loose another shot, it was knocked away by one of the creatures. The other grabbed his legs using two clawed-appendages that were once human hands and flipped him over on his stomach.

Walts clawed the ground, trying to escape.

The automaton's limbs were strong. It pulled him toward a sheet of needle-sharp points located on its underside. Each one spun like a drill bit.

Above, a loud sound sliced through the horror. Walts thought for sure another automaton surfaced, replacing the worm.

The *Vulturine*.

Walts' hope rose.

Tractor beams shot down and teleported survivors who had hidden themselves in the woods into the ship.

Metal limbs snaked around Walts body, pulling him into his fate. He fought to free himself, but the machine's strength extinguished freedom. With one hard yank the automaton buried Walts into its spinning points where it ground into his suit and into his flesh.

Blood splashed the creature.

GAME OVER

The words crawled in front of Walts' eyes as his body catapulted to the side like a rag doll. The machine hissed as it scurried away.

Walts watch the *Vulturine* blast into the sky and vanish.

GAME OVER, CADET. THANKS FOR PLAYING.

Darkness.

The feelers slid out of his brain, making him light-headed. His vision un-warbled as he took off his helmet, stepped off the mat. "Man, I didn't want to get killed!"

Jonas had already taken off his helmet. "Sorry. I couldn't get to you in time. I rescued survivors right and left. Fifteen out of thirty were saved."

Disgusted, Walts said: "I wish I could have gotten away from that machine that eliminated me from the game!"

"I was trying to get to you, but it was too risky."

"Risky?"

"Yeah. I was trying to save those folks."

"I know you were trying to save them! But you didn't save *me*!"

"Sorry, man."

"You're smiling! You had this planned out!"

"Planned out?"

"Yeah. You planned it out by using me as some kind of diversion, Jonas."

"Who, me?"

"Yes, you!"

Jonas chuckled.

"Dude! It's not funny!"

"Sure it is."

Walts grinned. "Jonas, you suck!"

Jonas burst out laughing. "I know."

"I'm going to get you back for this, dude, mark my words!"

Walts chuckled. He could never be mad at his friend. But he loved giving him hell every once in a while.

"Yeah, I'll…um…mark them all right."

"You're not right, man."

"Never admitted I was normal. Hey, you had fun, right?"

"I guess so…"

"You guess?"

"Yeah…I suppose."

"Vector 5 is a hard game. You'll get more used to it the more you play it."

"Yeah, you're probably right."

"I know I'm right! Dude, the first time I played it I barely made it to the dome before a small automaton sliced me apart."

"Really?"

"Yep."

"Huh…"

"Seriously, though, you *did* like the game?"

Walts did enjoy it. *It was so freaking realistic!* "I admit I liked it, Jonas."

"Sweet!"

"Look at it this way, next time you might become the hero." Jonas punched Walts in the arm.

"Ow!"

"Dude! I didn't hit you hard!"

"Yes you did!"

"No, I did not!"

"Yes. You. Did!

"No. I. Did. *Not!*"

"Well, I think you owe me, now." Walts stuck his nose in the air, smiled. "Got me killed in that game of yours; hit me in the arm."

"Oh geez! You got your own self killed! You could have defeated that machine."

Walts eyed him.

"Well. Maybe not…but I don't owe you anything."

"Sure you do. Still coulda saved me."

"Riight! That was a hard task to do, saving survivors and trying to save your butt!"

"I bet."

"It wasn't easy!"

"Well, I think you owe me."

"Owe you?"

"Yup."

"For what?"

"Getting me killed."

"What? You're crazy. I've heard it all now! Walts, you are a piece of work!"

"That, I am. How about buying me a Bork burger?"

"Say what?"

"Another burger. Your treat!"

Jonas snorted. "You really are crazy!"

"And then some."

"Okay. This time I will. Next time we play, whatever the outcome, if I happen to get killed because of you, you are to buy *my* burger."

"Maybe."

"Maybe nothing! That's the deal or not. Your choice!" Jonas crossed his arms and grinned.

"Okay. Deal. Let's go get some grub!"

"Squiggly!"

And off to Bork Burgers, Inc., the boys went.

\*\*\*

The mobile suicide unit rolled past Bork Burgers as the boys stepped through the doors, turning down a street in a nearby suburb. One of its familiar, morbid chimes played through a speaker with a Doppler effect:

*Oh what a wonderful day,*
*Oh what a wonderful day,*
*What a wonderful day to say goodbye!*

Its front brakes squeaked when it rolled up to a stop sign.

Curtains were drawn inside houses, while some were left open a crack. People who worked on their front lawns paused when the unit drove by. Most did not like the unsettling feeling that washed over them. As always, someone would choose to use the msu service. The big mystery was *who*.

The msu turned into a cul-de-sac, made an arc, emerged. Taking a turn, it rolled ten feet, stopped.

A man stood on the curb.

"What can I do for you, man?" a hippy with long dreadlocks stuck his head out of the driver's side window and asked in a hoarse voice.

The man took a deep breath. "Think it's a good day for me. It's time to leave this horrible world behind."

The hippy grinned, showing a few of his missing teeth. "The demi agrees with you, my good man. It is your day to end it all!"

"I've prayed to the gods for support. They've told me what to do in a dream."

"Apparently they have. I believe you have prayed. I believe they've shown you what treasures and tranquility are in the Great Beyond, a mysterious place without pain or a worry stuck in your head."

"I have."

"Nothing to worry about, man. It'll all soon be better for ya."

"Hope so."

The hippy blinked. "Wearing that two-piece suit is of the

squiggly sort, man. Dig that hat, very radical-like. Tells a lot about a person ready to end it all in this crazy world. All dressed up, ready to blow this infested place called Westersphere in style. Ya groove?"

"You really think so?"

"Yep."

"Then yes. I...um...groove." The man shifted his feet, stuck his hands in the pockets of his pants.

The hippie chuckled. "You'll groove more after this msu service, sure to satisfy each and every customer! Sorry, no refunds."

The man frowned.

"Just a joke, man! Trying to help you relax is all!"

"Oh," he chuckled, "y-yeah. Th-thanks."

The hippie shifted from behind the wheel to the back of the van and opened a side window. He stuck out his hand. "Step over here, my man. I'm Moree Bund. Pleased to meet ya, man."

"Robert."

The men shook hands.

"Now, all ya gotta do is put your hand on this Recog tablet. That's right. Hang on a sec." The tablet beeped. "Good. Thanks, man. Got your ID. Says your name is Robert Staun, you live at 233 Jakes Street; divorced, no children; your last job was a computer programmer for IBM; you were on contract to do computer networking for the Slader Corporation – impressive! –today at 9:00 am you decided to terminate your employment...Everything sound up-to-snuff, my man?"

"Up-to-*what*?"

"Everything sound correct?"

"Yes, sir."

"No need to call me sir, I'm a working stiff like all of us." He guffawed at his own joke.

The customer grinned.

"Take this tablet and read the fine print and sign the waiver, please, by pressing your thumb in the blinking red box."

The customer read the waiver, understood that his body would be harvested and used in the sake of scientific research. If he did not die right away by the choice of death, he could not file a complaint. He also could not file a complaint once his soul ventured into the Great Beyond.

Robert Staun pressed his thumb on the blinking red box. Under it, the words appeared:

```
COMPLETE. THANK YOU SO MUCH FOR CHOOSING
THE MOBILE SUICIDE UNIT AS THE END TO YOUR
SUFFERING, MR. STAUN! WE STRIVE TO GIVE
GREAT CUSTOMER SERVICE. PLEASE FILL OUT A
QUESTIONNAIRE WHILE YOU ARE WAITING AT THE
BRD AND HAND IT TO A BRD REPRESENTATIVE.
GOOD LUCK, GODS BLESS.
```

"So, what's your poison, Mr. Staun?" Moree asked, waving his hand at the collage of suicides offered.

Staun took off his hat, pondered. "Which would be quick and painless?"

Moree smiled. "Everyone asks the same question, Mr. Staun. Doesn't seem anyone wants the pain of dying. I sure wouldn't!" He snickered. "Honestly, Mr. Staun, committing suicide isn't painless, no matter how you look at it. I do have a synthetic local anesthetic I could administer, if you'd like. Takes the edge off; numbs you up."

"That sounds good to me."

"All you have to worry about is the sting of the needle."

"Oh-okay." Staun fumbled with his hat, turning it around and around in his fingers.

"While you're deciding on the best fate, stick your arm up here, and I'll administer that local."

Staun took off his jacket, rolled up his sleeve, stuck out his arm. The sting wasn't too bad and the drug took effect immediately.

His nervousness vanished. He felt calmer. He felt good. He felt… jolly. Not a worry in the world. If a hole opened up beneath his feet and he plunged to his death in the fiery pit of the hells filled with snakes, he wouldn't give a crap.

In this state of mind, his fear of snakes slithered away, no longer an issue – nor the fear of dying.

"Looks like the drug's helping you…ooh…ooh, Mr. Staun." Moree's voice echoed, flickers of vocabulary evaporated in the air. "Which suicidal tendency will work for you…ooh…ooh?"

Staun smiled, shrugged his shoulders. A numbing feeling crawled over his flesh. His vision transmitted a pulsating sphere with wiggling tendrils around the edges, while the pic of Moree's face spoke out of its center as if the design could be a bizarre Looney Tunes intro.

"Let me help you out…

out…

out."

Moree pursed his lips to say the last word. Robert thought his angel of death got ready to blow raspberries.

It made him giggle.

"You look like a gun-to-the-head kind of guy, Mr. Staun. Ever shot one at the range…ange…ange?"

"No…

oh…

oh…

oh."

"Don't worry. Nothing too it!" Moree's cheeks swelled in what Robert Staun now considered his drug-induced state as Staunvision. "Press the barrel against your temple and you're off to the next life. Eeeeasy-peeeeezy, man! Real raaaad-like. Whatchya think about

that…

at…

at…

at?"

"Sounds pretty gooood, man." Staunvision was cool, the most relaxing. He wished he was inside a helium balloon floating in the sky. Maybe with synthetic chicken Roll-Ups so he could strip off each pressed-to-size layer of fake meat and chew on it.

*Nomnomnomnomnom.*

Moree chuckled and it echoed in Stuan's ears. "We have a nice selection of guns. Here's a lisssst." He tapped a finger on his tablet, scrolled, showing his customer the list.

Staun swayed on his feet. In Staunvision all guns looked similar to him; except for the one that had a long barrel. He chose it.

"Nice choice, Mr. Stauuun." Moree pressed a button on a small door inside the back of the van, retrieved the gun and checked it for ammo before handing it over to his customer. "Here's your gun of choice right here, loaded, ready to go…oh…oh…oh!"

The gun felt heavy in Staun's hands. He wondered how many times it had been used.

"Feels good in your grip, doesn't it, Mr. Staun?"

In Staunvision, it sure as groovy did.

"Stick that barrel against your temple. Yep. Like that. Pull the trigger and you'll go beddie-bye…

eye…

eye…

eye.

"Real raaaadical, man. Welcome to the Great Beyond. I couldn't tell you how many times I've seen people do what you're doing, Mr. Stauuuun. You've a heart of gold, I'm here to tell you that at…

at…

at.

"You've got courage, sir. Not loooong ago there was this one woman – nice-lookin' chick…

ick…

ick – and she didn't want to pull the

*BLAM!*

"Trigger." Moree screwed his face up. "Kinda messy, Mr. Staun. Nothing to worry about. That's why I'm here. Gonna get your body processed and clean up the spot on the street real nice. Hey, Chains, you awake in there, man?"

A square metal head stuck out of the van's side widow. A blue eye roved from one corner to the next like a marble in the sleek glass cylinder in the middle of its face. "Bleep?"

"Yes, I hollered for you. Get out here and get this body transferred to the boss."

A small radar atop Chains' head spun around. "Bleep!"

"No, you cannot keep recharging. Get out here!"

"Bleep!"

"Hey, man, ain't my job! I do my part, you do yours. That's why you're here. You groove?"

Chains grumbled, expelling the sound of tools spilling out of a large tool box.

"Don't get grumpy just because I took you away from drinking your unlicensed synthetic bot oil laced with that drug called goose to do some work. It's your job to ignite the Hula Hoop Orbitor, metal dude."

"Bleep?"

"Yes, you! I sure as hells don't have the right code to for it."

"Bleep."

"*Oh* no. I don't want no responsibility for keeping that code. That means they'd have to put an implant in my brain. Hell. *No!*"

"Bleep."

"Why not? Are you nuts? I don't want to turn into some kind of schizo, a zombie cyborg! I'll keep living in this body covered in flesh, thank you very much!"

"Bleep."

"I'm not scared! Just ain't going through with it.'

"Bleep."

"What? Chains, I know you have implants. They're called sensors. We humans don't need those things in our bodies."

"Bleep."

"Are you crazy? I said we humans don't need those things."

"Bleep."

"Hush."

"Bleep."

"Hush, dude!"

"Bleep."

"Not listening to you, dude." Moree threw his hand up. "You're not being groovatronic, Chains. Stop arguing with me. We have work to do here, you know."

"Bleep."

Moree did a face palm. "Man, we can stand here and go back and forth all the day or get this job done, ya groove? C'mon, let's get this dude transferred and get out of this 'burb. Look at all those people who are looking out there windows, being nosey. This dude's body is gonna start stinking if we don't send it off."

Chains grumbled. A screw driver or a pair of pliers bouncing across a hard metal surface echoed inside his shell as he vanished from view and the back doors to the van flew open, vomiting the small automaton rolling out on its single wheel.

"You really need to stop drinking that synthetic stuff laced with goose and drink ordinary, bot oil. If the demi catches you, you'll be in trouble. Who knows what's in that crap you're consuming. Sure makes you moody, I'll give you that."

"Bleep."

"Yes it does."

"Bleep."

"Yes it does, dude! Hey! Don't shrug your shoulders at me! You should see yourself right now! Ever since you've been on that crap that dude sold you six months ago you've changed. It's been really hard working with you lately."

"Bleep."

"So? Did you just say 'so'?"

Chains crossed its metal arms. "Bleep."

Moree did another face palm, this time with both hands, and shook his head. "Dude, you are un-freaking-believable. You're the definition of being un-squiggly. I'm just trying to get through that metal scalp of yours the crap is bad for you!

Chains huffed. Blew what could have been described as a raspberry transmitted via the flicker of metal cards on a rolodex. "Bleep."

"Whatever, dude!" Moree spat. "Too bad you can't shut the metal grate you have for a mouth," he mumbled. "Let's get this body transferred to the –

"Bleep?"

"Nothing. I didn't say anything."

Chains' radar swiveled. "Bleep."

"Chains. We need to get moving. No more arguing right now. My patience is thinning. Look, now there's people out on their lawns. They're staring at us. Probably pissed we haven't got this body gone yet."

"Bleep."

"Because, if you haven't noticed, we haven't got this body gone yet, since all you wanna do is argue with me."

"Bleep."

"Me? I didn't start it!"

"Bleep."

"Chains." Moree held up his hand. "We're done here. Hurry up and use the Hula so we can get the hells outta here. Would you at least do *that* so we can get gone?"

Chains grumbled, the dropping of a hammer on a metal plate. Did not budge.

"Please? Please get the Hula, Chains."

Chains grumbled a second time, a spill of a huge box of screws. A small sliding door opened on the side of his shell he reached a three-fingered hand inside and withdrew an object the size of a pill and squeezed its gel surface. Swelling thicker in size, it could be very well pass for medication a troll could swallow. Shaping itself into a large circle, the object glowed orange and Chains placed it on the ground around Staun's corpse. As the color brightened the body stood up on its own, the head lopped to the side, its arms stuck out on each side as the circle began spinning, causing the body to gyrate with the motion.

As the two mobile suicide workers watched, Staun's body withered and drained into the Hula Hoop Orbiter. Once it regained its small size the pill evaporated.

"Cool. Let's get outta here, Chains."

Chains rolled off.

"Crap. Hang on. Let's get this brain matter on the ground cleaned up before we go. Usually the Hula takes care of the mess. Guess it has a malfunction, like your attitude, Chains."

"Bleep!"

\*\*\*

Fred's head exploded on impact.

Hit by a transport.

Scoring that last goose a few hours ago had goosed Fred higher than cloud nine – and then on to clouds ten, eleven and twelve and three-quarters, the last quarter stolen away by the transport. Tucked inside the body bag of his own flesh numbness pulsed in his hands, feeling like two inflated balloons. He knew if he attempted to explain how he felt to someone they would frown, shake their head, call him a liar. Fred had a bizarre belief his brain was so swollen, it had grown tendrils and pushed against the interior walls of his skull full, trying to vacate the premises.

*But where would it go if it managed to escape?* Fred wondered. *Ooze onto the sidewalk, leaving sluggish goo in its wake? Dragging its tail of a brain stem? I'd be left to walk around the streets in the colony as one of those zombie creatures called schizos!*

As he strolled down the sidewalk, passing people, each of their faces warbled into sheets of flesh flavored with cackles from stitches stretched, attempting to keep the mouths closed. Smaller warbled faces atop small bodies were jerked away by their owners' branch-like limbs. Some mouths spat curses at him.

*"Druggie!"*

*"Drug addict! Go back to the sewers!"*

*"We don't need your kind 'round here, gooser!"*

When Fred stepped off the curb in front of the transport's metal grill, the front middle tire grabbed hold of his feet, jerking him under, there was a filament of a second where he worried his brain was going to make its escape right there and then and scurry away from its soon-to-be free of the dark space in his skull. A millisecond later, a finalization of his death as his vertebrae snaped, crackled and popped, Fred's thoughts were replaced by a realization he had left a ghostly residual behind in the Wake – more work for the Residual Removal, Inc to do – replaying it over and over like old movie vids down on Fourth Street. If a medium had stridden by on the sidewalk later in the day, he or she would pick up the replay of his demise:

*Fred's silhouette stumbling off the curb, his face washed with a daze from the goose, a smile crested under his bleeding nostrils and leaking red eyes, the transport speeding down the street filled with adults and children with one little boy in particular who giggled, having a grand time with his pappy, not understanding why the driver screamed when Fred's body vanished under the wheel feet-first and slight bump as his blood sprayed up on the windshield*

*— for some reason the only thought slipping into the driver's mind at that exact second: Really should've laid off the eight-hour energy drink before leaving home, Tim —*

*and the family of four who were walking down the sidewalk viewing the sites of the big city, once all smiles, now all screams, thus creating a domino effect for others of the like to joining in on the unwelcomed horror not long before*

Fred stood in a place resembling the Bureau of Motor Vehicles, entitled the Bureau of the Recently Deceased. He was a kid again, mind you, and it freaked him out more than when goose had coursed his mortal body. He learned real quick dealing with one of the bureau's staff, as painful when he felt his pelvis and spine crunch under the public transport tire seconds before a projectile of blood spewed out of his mouth.

And then some.

The representative at the BRD, a tall lady with glasses resting on the bridge of her nose and sporting a red, beehive hairdo sitting in a high-back chair behind a long desk wore BELINDA stenciled on her name tag, but should have been stenciled CRUDE instead. She didn't like druggies. Period. She informed Fred they usually shove all drug users through the blood red door, into Purgatory, no questions asked. Period. Drugs were for fools. Drugs were hideous human creations only to be abused by other humans. Humans were stupid meat puppets stuffed with non-warranted organs and could be cloned by any OSSMS and, hopefully, a good one who did not think the world should live in a haze of narcotics, pushing synthetic pills.

At any rate, Fred's case was different, Belinda noted after her rant. Fred was lucky. Fred had friends and family in The Great Beyond vouching for his well-being. Surprisingly, the gods had been nice enough to give him a choice of his fate. Something others did not have. She informed him once again of her disgust with druggies and if *she* had been the one in charge, she'd shove him through the blood-red door without thinking twice.

Period.

Fred's choices were simple: become a ghost and have full access into the Stygian Wake and the ability to return to Ozarium and find somewhere to haunt; or step through the burnt orange door into the hells or the blood-red door to Purgatory. Not many options there, but Fred's decision fell on being a ghost.

"Please read the Paranormal Laws, Mr. Sockuv," Belinda said, shoving the Recog tablet across the desk and into his hands, "and press your thumb in the blinking red box provided for identification at the bottom."

It began with:

1. Said ghost is allowed to keep his/her soul and forbidden to touch or harm a mortal, such as possessing his/her body. Breaking this law will be subject to having a visit from an Insurgent of the Bailiwick, an agent of The Great Beyond. Said ghost has a total of three strikes until it will be stripped of its privilege and disposed through the burnt orange door.

2. Said ghost under possession of a demon will be collected by one of the Insurgents and placed in an Extraction Room in Purgatory used to extract sins from souls who were originally forgiven for their sins. If actions performed do not exorcise the demonic possession, the Insurgent will dispose said ghost through the burnt orange door.

3. Said ghost is entitled to Free Space, Haunting anyplace where applicable. Abandoned houses, abandoned warehouses, cemeteries, are examples of Free Space. Ghosts are eligible to own the property if resided there more than six months.

Said ghost must fill out the correct application and have information regarding ownership filed away on a memory file or chip in the program Thunderclap by logging into any Recog in the Stygian Wake. If this is not done and given to the Bailiwick when asked to do so, said ghost can and will be banished from residence.

4. Haunting does not mean terrorizing humans, performing poltergeist activities, terrifying them out of their homes. Haunting is a ghost who has taken up residence. Disciplinary actions will be taken by Insurgents if Paranormal Law is broken.

5. Said ghost living less than six months in Free Space purchased by a mortal must give up rights of ownership, unless an agreement between said ghost and mortal for the eligibility to remain on property in Good Faith. This means that said ghost will behave and not act out using poltergeist activity while inside the house. If there is ever a disagreement of these terms between mortal and said ghost, apparition is banished to the street.

6. Said ghosts rights are always limited.

7. Said ghost is allowed to leave and return from property at his/her convenience by Ekto-Leaping, the ghostly way to teleport from one spot to the next. A ghost Ekto-Leaps by concentrating on one spot. For example, if said ghost is standing outside a house he/she knows the floorplan, said ghost could easily Leap inside.

8. Said ghost is allowed to leave and return from property owned by mortal.

9. Said ghost will always have the option to leave and return to the Stygian Wake.

10. Said ghost will agree to comply with these

laws or will be disposed through the burnt orange door.

"Do you understand these terms, Mr. Sockuv?" Belinda asked.

"Yes, ma'am," Fred replied.

"Please make the indication in the red box with your thumb. Great. Thank you so much.

Step through the door, next to the burnt orange door, entitled STYGIAN WAKE. From there you may familiarize yourself with the ghostly place and will be able to slip into reality."

Fred stepped through the door, and it clicked shut behind him. A bright light flashed. A large swirl of greenish yellow light shot out of the floor and encircled him like a funnel cloud, twisting rapidly. Two eyes opened inside the light. One winked at him. A maw of serrated teeth widened into a grin and guffawed.

Startled, Fred stumbled backward, reaching for a doorknob that no longer existed.

Guffaws continued, reverberating throughout the enclosed space, finally dissipating, leaving behind darkness.

An odd sensation prickled the top of Fred's head, skittered down his ghostly spine, making his ghostly skin crawl. A sensation of what he could only perceive as a million tiny legs scurried over him. No pain, only a close similarity of a bad goose-induced trip.

A second later a sliver of a bright light carved itself into the dark canvas, widening its toothless mouth, swallowing Fred. Infused with a cloudy membrane silhouettes of various size passed him, some noticing the new-comer, some not. As the light oozed away, he hardly had a chance to glance at the ghostly world and, making a rookie error, stepped three feet forward instead of allowing the world to complete its shrouding of his frame, leaving the Stygian Wake, and stood in the living room of someone's house.

A family sat on a leather couch watching a commercial on their televid.

The dog lying on the floor raised its head, growled.

## Commercial Breaks:

*A Tip From Derrick, A Former Addict:*
    *"Goose used to take me places where the brain feared to go. Goose helped me wind down after a long day at the office. Sometimes the drug scared me, thinking thousands of tiny black bugs covered me from head to toe, shaping me into their host. My skin replaced with an undulating body of bugs, I moved as one, while each twitched and scurried over themselves, keeping the shape formed like glue. And to make it even more bizarre, I could shape myself into anything I wanted. A dog. A tree. A park bench. A suicide booth. A Jolt-laced candy cane. Anything I desired to become. Other times it gave me asensation as if I could float in the sky over the colony and see far away, past the river of corpses, into what lay beyond in the wastelands of Westersphere.*

    *"But when I drove the Bouncer into the river, drowning the only woman I ever loved and the boy who I can still remember holding for the first time, emptied from the womb – even in this ghostly shape I live inside while in Purgatory—gripping my finger with his tiny hand, the boy whom I remember loved mint chocolate chip ice cream in a plastic cup shaped as Chainsaw Freckles, the boy who bugged the hell out of me that day at the mall after he got his pic taken with the clown and so wanted me to buy him an alarm clock in the shape of Freckles, remembering the look on his face when I caved and bought it, and he held it in his hands and thanked me and told me how much he loved me and said I was the greatest father ever, then, as my life materialized, having to stand back and witness my loved ones, Heather and Jeffrey being escorted through the blue door, Heather first scowling at me, shouting hateful things, reminding me they were dead because of me, and I would have to live with the pain of my loss throughout my ghostly life, Jeffrey's face washed with an expression between confusion and sadness, wondering where he was and wondering why Daddy was not following him and Mommy through the door as they stepped inside,*

*it slamming shut, vanished into The Great Beyond.*
*"Think again before you try goose.*
*"I wish I had."*

*This has been an approved message from the Slader Corporation*™

\*\*\*

*"Howdy, folks! I'm Andy Astroh! Come on down to my shop, Andy's Automatons of the Future, where synthetic flesh meets metal! Get yourself a reasonably priced automaton fitted in what we call a body-boot made of synthetic skin! That's right, folks! A reasonably priced automaton complete with a positronic brain and a cover to hide all the inner workings of a robo!*

*"Pinching creds?*

*"Don't have enough cred to keep your old robo maintained?*

*"Your robo have the Tourette Syndrome Virus?*

*"Don't take all that negativity from those machines! Come see me, folks! I'll fix ya up with an automaton with a life-time warranty.*

*"That's right! A lifetime warranty!*

*"I'll even throw in a brand-spanking new Quasi-Cinematix system, complete with the latest Envo helmet design!*

*"Are you tired of robos you've purchased from my competitors, like Ricardo's Robot World, that'll break down after a year? Tired of not finding parts when you order off infomercials? Buy one at a demi auction recently that backfired and spun out of control, harming you or your family or destroying your house? It's happened, folks, I'm telling the gods-honest truth!*

*"Don't let it happen to you! Demi robos are not to be trusted! That's right, I said it! Don't trust those machines, whatever you do!!*

*"If you happen to be cruising over top of the Slader Corp building one day and see our sign hovering in the air, amongst all the other holographic billboards, drop your Bouncer down to ground-level in*

*front of Macy's Deli, go about two kilometers to the south, pass the Anchor's Away building, and you'll see our show room all lit up. The sign is outside, scrolling our title in large letters. Park your Bouncer and slip inside and see one of my robo associates. They'll find a robo that'll fit your needs!*

*"Oh, and if you mention this ad, you get twenty percent off your purchase!*

*"Have a great day, have a safe day, see ya soon!"*

***

"Who wants popcorn?" Mom's voice drifted from the kitchen.

"Wish I could eat a few pieces." Grandpa licked his lips, undulating in his chair. "Can't remember what it tastes like."

"Not me," Dad said. "That meat loaf filled me up." He patted his gut.

Walts sat in one of the two recliners. He stuck his hand over his head as if he were in school. "Me!"

After supper Walts' parents had a long talk with him and decided not punish him—this time. Carrying around a cesspool of Guilty Conscience more than twenty-four hours had been punishment enough. Confronting Mom about the lie he told helped his situation, instead of allowing it to go on any longer. However, Walts was instructed next time it happened, Mom and Dad intended on grounding him for a week and not pay his cred for doing his chores.

He said okay.

Mom and Dad said they hoped he *did* pass his classes. They did not want to see him held back a year while everyone was a step ahead.

Walts agreed, he sure as heck didn't want to be held back a grade. By the time Jonas graduated from high school Walts would still be searching for the right girl to take to the prom, if that was even possible! Always the shy type, Walts stood in the "nerd" category, which of course wasn't a bad thing.

He heard Mom tell the microwave to fix the popcorn. The machine replied with a monotone voice: "It will be ready in exactly 3 minutes and 6 seconds, ma'am." Once ready to eat, she deposited the popcorn into a large plastic bowl, returned to the living room and sat down beside Dad. He put his arm around her shoulder as she snuggled close.

After the automaton commercial, another showed on the televid.

\*\*\*

*Two ladies sat on the front porch on a warm summer day during a barbeque. Each held a plate of food on their lap. Adults and children played a game on the lawn in front of them.*

*"This was a great idea, setting up this vacation spot for a family reunion," one woman said after chewing and swallowing a raw carrot.*

*"I agree," the other woman said around a mouthful of corn on the cob. Flakes dripped down her chin. "Even if this is all a hologram, what we see."*

*The camera zoomed in to view a small mass of dots scurrying from behind the woman's ear, crawling across her face, consuming the food particles.*

*"Betty! What on earth just crawled on your face?" It startled the woman so much she almost choked on a celery stick and nearly dropped her plate of food. The dog sitting next to her licked his lips, ready to catch a bite if opportunity arose.*

*Betty smiled. "It's the latest thing in keeping your face clean, Cecilia. They're called Tidybots."*

*"Tidywhat?"*

*"Tidybots. It's the latest thing on the market! Here, I have an extra unit. Clip it around your ear so the tiny box points to the back of*

*your head. Yep. That's right."*

*"Huh. Kinda like a hearing aid."*

*"Yes, it sure is. It's really neat, Cecilia. You'll never need napkins again! All you have to do is think of the instruction you want to give the cleaners and they'll do the job."*

*Cecelia's eyed were wide. "You mean, it has a telekinetic ability?"*

*"You got it! Tidybots will also clean your hands. Here, let me email you a copy of the commands from my Recog and the correct code and password to use. I had to set it up after I purchased it, that way no one can steal it and use it for themselves."*

*In less than five seconds Cecilia had already downloaded the instructions. "Interesting!"*

*"Try it out! Eat something and be sloppy about it!" Betty giggled.*

*Cecelia chewed into the meat of a chicken leg and let the juice drip down her chin. Automatically, the Tidybots scurried out from behind her ear and cleaned her face. It was her turn to giggle. "That tickled! Handy little snots, aren't they!"*

*"Yep! I use 'em wherever I go!"*

*"Well, so will I!"*

*The vidcam pans backward, the picture blurs, and bold letters crawl across the screen as a man's voice reads: "Tidybots! The human flesh cleaner! Purchase Tidybots today and receive your very own holographic vacation! Why leave your home? Why pay for one of those expensive virtual travel agencies in the colony to book your family vacation? Why have to pay with your Bodykredd to kennel your pets? Why not stay at home and relax on a holographic beach! Or be able to sit inside a holographic scene like Cecelia and Betty? Just call 1-800-tidybots-4-me to order your very own Tidybots and receive your free holographic vacation!"*

*"Coming soon: Tidybots' Framework, cleaning each pore and spec on the human body! You may never need to bathe again!"*

*This has been an approved message from the Slader Corporation™*

\*\*\*

After the commercial break Walts and his family began watching a game show where the producers rehashed old ideas, sticking contestants in vintage television shows. This one was an episode called "Night Call" taken from *The Twilight Zone*. A woman was the contestant who played the character of Elva Keene, receiving calls from her dead husband, Brian, on a 1940's rotary phone. The object of the game was for her to leave the house and find the correct burial site inside a huge cemetery where the telephone line had fallen across Brian's grave.

Fog rolls across the graveyard as she searches. Every so often she hears moaning and the shuffling of someone moving in the dark. Other oddities to deter her away were telephone lines fallen across other graves.

"So, champ," – Dad sometimes called Walts champ – "what are you and Jonas going to do tomorrow?"

Walts pondered, popped a few pieces of popcorn in his mouth and chewed. "Probably play games on his Quasi-Cinematix."

"No swimming?"

Walts swallowed. "Dunno. Maybe." He wasn't sure if Jonas would want to see Wilson again.

"I really like the way this game show brings back old episodes!" Grandpa said, pointing to the vid's screen. "Reminds me of my own Dad telling me about all the shows of the past." He belched. Wisps of ectoplasm puffed out of his ears.

Walts chuckled. He had asked Grandpa before why he belched, since he never ate anything. Grandpa said it was a gaseous-like buildup of ectoplasm, much like a mortal has in his or her stomach.

Mom shook her head at grandpa, trying to look disgusted, though the smile under her nose couldn't deliver the lewd gesture.

"Make sure you lather up with sunscreen if you decide to go,

Walts" she said. "You burn easy with that pale skin of yours."

"Uggh! I hate that stuff! It's greasy!"

"Would ya rather be in pain with a sun burn when both suns go down? You know how bad it hurts."

Walts grumbled. "Oh…okay…I will." Last year he remembered a nasty burn causing a gooseflesh of blisters.

"Before you leave in the morning," Mom added, "cut the grass."

Walts was horrified. "Tomorrow?"

"Yes, *tomorrow*, Walts," Mom pressed. "It needs cut."

"It's the first day of summer vacation! Chains can do it!"

"Not gonna happen, champ," Dad said. "Your mother already has that robot busy with other things tomorrow. Cutting the grass will be your job before you go to Jonas's, if you want to earn more cred for the week. Right, Mom?"

"Yep," she replied.

"I know… but…I'll have grass all over me. I'll need to take a bath!"

"Won't hurt you none," Mom said. "If you don't go swimming, you'll have to only take one bath. But, if you go swimming, you'll need to wash the chlorine off your skin."

"What? Twelve baths in one days' time?"

"That's right. You don't want chlorine from the pool to stay on your skin after you swim."

"Really?"

"You already know that, Walts. Don't think you'll get out of getting a second bath."

Walts sighed. "Okay, mom." *Taking a bath meant you had to stand in the jet spray for fifteen minutes so the automated system could clean your skin thoroughly. That was twelve minutes more he could be doing something else, rather than having warm water blasting his body! Wait. Now add the twelve to the hours he and Jonas could spend doing something fun. Uggh! There's another reason to hate math! Hells, he could play two games at Time Riff in that time frame!*

*Eegads!*

*The only delight standing in the jet spray would be programming the shower to release scrubbing bubbles, making a bubble shower instead of a bath. Least it was cool watching bubbles shape themselves into faces of Chainsaw Freckles.*

Later, Walts hugged his Mom and Dad goodnight. Grandpa's ghostly shape became solid enough so Walts could hug him, too. Grandpa could only do it for a couple of seconds, so Walts always hurried with a squeeze; otherwise, he'd end up falling into Grandpa's shape. It had happened before and Walts fell into an invisible block of ice.

He made sure not to make that mistake again.

On his way upstairs to his bedroom Walts heard Mom say something about going to the store in the morning and Dad replying it would be fine, because he was going to be extremely busy working on a jolt maker/jolt bean grinder/espresso maker for a client. The job would probably take most of the day for the repair, a little longer after downloading the correct driver off the Gridd into the machine's tiny positronic brain pan, teaching it how to perform its tasks correctly.

Upstairs Walts got online and checked his mail. His wallpaper on the screen was tiled skulls. His icons were Chainsaw Freckle faces and when you right-clicked them with your mouse, the sound of a chainsaw growled. His recycle bin was a basket of blood.

In his spam folder an email of a company called GORACK promoted their sale of refurbished robot parts. Walts wondered if that was against the law.

He deleted it and went to bed.

\*\*\*

The next day Walts rose early, ate breakfast, did a few chores, and started toward the garage to get the lawnmower out to cut the grass when Mom said, "I'm going into town and pick up a few things from the grocery. I'll be back after a while." After a while was about an hour and a half. Mom might only need a few items from the store, but she would always spend extra time browsing, even picking up other stuff on sale.

She kissed him on the top of his head. "Be back in a few. Love ya."

"Love you, too, Mom."

She unscrewed a plastic neon-colored egg, shook out a gel which shaped into a large hand. Opening its palm, Mom sat down and it lifted her atop the garage where the Bouncer sat.

Walts looked up at his Mom. "Has dad come up with a name for that thing yet?"

"I think he's calling it a Boost," she said as the hand dime-sized and oozed back into the egg.

"Cool."

Mom slipped behind the wheel of the Bouncer and blasted into the air.

Walts noticed Chains in the garage. The robot was picking up a large cardboard box and as his arms extended, placed it overhead on a wooden shelve that had been nailed down on the rafters.

An idea scrolled across Walts' brain. *Mom gone; Dad busy down in the basement....he wondered if...*

"Hey, Chains."

The robot rattled. His head swiveled around on its body and his cyclopean blue eye roved back and forth like a marble in the sleek glass cylinder in the middle of his face.

HELLO, WALTS. HOW ARE YOU?

"I'm fine. Whatchya doing?"

YOUR MOTHER HAS INSTRUCTED ME TO PLACE THE BOXES FULL OF HOLIDAY ASSORTMENTS, AND THE BOXES RIGHT THERE BESIDE YOU FULL OF

WINTER CLOTHES, OVERHEAD.

"She must have you real busy today, huh?"

NOT TOO BAD.

"I have to cut the grass. I really don't want to because…um…I wanted to get a head start on doing other things today. It's the first day of summer vacation and all."

Chains rattled. IF YOU WISH, I COULD CUT THE GRASS.

"Really?"

YES. I'LL GET TO IT AS SOON AS I CAN.

"Thanks, Chains!

"YOU ARE WELCOME, WALTS.

Walts started off.

Stopped.

*What the heck was he thinking? Did he really want to go through with this? That lie he told almost gotten him grounded! As much as it gave him a thrill inside to get a jump start on the day's fun, this wasn't like him, disobeying his folks. The thought of not receiving his cred for the week was not a good thing. Going to Time Riff or Bork Burger without any cred would be horrible!*

He sighed.

"Um…Chains? I better go ahead and cut the grass…thanks for offering to do it…"

\*\*\*

The bright light made Sarah squint. White walls with a spider web-designed holographic border wrapped the entire length of the room. Every so often holographic black spiders would trickle halfway down the wall on a strand of their silk web; then scurry back to the border.

An IV was stuck in the bend of her arm, feeding her vein. A line ran to a bag of clear liquid hung on a metal stand. Another metal stand, this one shorter, nestled against a wall, a white cover shrouding it.

The door to the room swung open and a nurse came in holding a Recog tablet. Not saying a word, she checked the quantity in the IV's bag, made a note on the tablet's screen using a stylist; checked the feed in Sarah's arm, made another note; checked Sarah's pupils, using a small flashlight, made a third note after a swipe of her finger; and before the nurse left Sarah found it odd she waved a hand in front of the small camera hanging in the corner of the room, one directing its attention at Sarah.

Sarah wanted to ask this nurse where she was.

*What happened to her? Why was she here?*

Her neurotransmitters shorted out, the transmission mute, unable to retrieve a memory. The segment deleted, as if there had been nothing there at all; a fraction of her life missing.

However, the memory of the buzzing sound, stayed with her. A light vibration tickled her skin.

*What the heck had it been?*

Unable to wrench open any doors marked Recent Memory in her brain caused darkness to ooze down the hallway, black tentacles wrap around her wrists, legs, throat, snatch her away, severing connection with it, as well as reality.

Fading…

Fading…..

Fading….

Away.

A tear drained from her right eye, moistening a spot on the white pillow cover.

\*\*\*

Dogs have this thing called Good Hearing. This ability can pinpoint things better than, say, us humans. As soon as Fred made his rookie mistake and stepped into the living room of where the family was, their dog sensed his presence and growled.

Then let loose a bark.

A little blonde-headed girl who sat on the couch had good perception, too, especially since Fred could be seen. Her little blue eyes widened. "Daddy! There's a ghost in here!"

Fred held up his hands. "Um. Sorry, folks, just passing through…"

"Way squiggly!" the little girl's brother said. "Ghosts are groove!"

The man of the house rose to his feet. "Why the hell are you in our house? You ghosts know the Paranormal Laws! You are forbidden to enter the home of a mortal unless allowed! Get the hell outta here! What, you blind or something? Didn't you see the sign on the door? It reads in black and white we're against you creatures. You're as bad as roaches! It's bad enough our kids have to grow up around mobile suicide units!"

The dog barked again, standing up.

"Patrick," the wife said to her husband, "it's okay. I'm sure he'll leave. Think of your heart. Don't get too upset, hon. The OSSM told you they're still waiting on an upgrade for your pacemaker."

"I'm going…I'm going," Fred kept his hands up, drifted toward the front door.

Ignoring his wife, Patrick said, "Damn right you are! Get *out*!"

Fred, not realizing being a ghost can be disconcerting, tried grabbing the doorknob.

It slipped through his hands.

The dog barked and moved toward him.

"I said *get out!*" Patrick's voice boomed, his hands curled up in fists.

Frantic, Fred tried grabbing the doorknob once more. Pointless. How the heck was he supposed to leave?

"Are you *dense*? You can walk through walls, idiot!"

"Oh…that's right…I'm sorta…uh…new at this stuff."

"Imagine that?"

"Can't we keep him, Dad?" the boy stood by his father. "Ghosts are neat-oh-rific!! Bobby gave me a hand-held device he calls a Morto! We can keep him in there!"

"Hush, Jamie!" Patrick scolded. "Ghosts are not welcome here! And what are you doing hanging around that Bobby kid? He's nothing but trouble. You're not s'pose to have that machine!"

Jamie's excitement flushed itself down the toilet. "But Bobby said his Mom bought two of them. He didn't know what to do with the other one, so he gave it to me."

"He could have pitched it in the trash! I blame Debra for buying Bobby that crap! Those things are dangerous, son! They have a nuclear center that operates it. You could get cancer if it breaks open."

"Oh."

"You stay away from Bobby and his bunch of rejects. Hear? They have no idea what being anti-ghost means."

"Yes, sir."

Patrick turned back to Fred who floated inches off the floor. "The hell *you* still doing here? I'm not teaching a class here. You've already screwed your life up somehow. That's why you became a ghost. Only reason you creatures exist. The gods in The Great Beyond always give defunct mortals another chance in life. Freaking unbelievable! That's why we have an overpopulation of ghosts in the world! That's why I'm doing my part this instant and telling you for the last and final time to get your *ass* out of my home or, so help me, I'll call Residual Removal, Inc.!"

The dog charged Fred and he stumbled back, drifting out the door and onto the lawn.

**NO GHOSTS ALLOWED HERE. ANTI-GHOST MEMBER, LOCAL 152** scrolled in bold yellow letters on a rectangular hologram of a sign across the face of the front door.

*Huh. I didn't know about this stuff. Belinda never said anything about it. Shouldn't it have been listed in the Paranormal Laws? Had I been using drugs that long, oblivious to the world around me?*

Fred could hear the dog barking. He could also hear Patrick gasping for a breath. His wife told him to calm down, unless he wanted to go to the OSSM.

Patrick spat OSSM's were all a bunch of quack robot doctors whose microprocessors missed a few pieces of data. Said he didn't need them. He was fine.

Fred drifted away, leaving that craziness behind. Other dogs in the neighborhood started barking, picking up his presence.

"I need to get outta here! This is *madness!*"

Fred drifted along, watching people working on their lawns staring at him, their faces screwed up as if he was a pile of dog poop. Some pointed at him, speaking to each other. Fred didn't have to hear the comments. He knew each one was bad. Were all the people in the neighborhood against ghosts? Wouldn't that be nuts!

He wished he could remember when he lived in the mortal world if he had been against the dead or not. Drugs scrambled your memories, blocking all incoming traffic of the world from entering into your brain. And how old had he been when the transport mowed over him? Why couldn't he remember that?

Fred shook his head, tried to pry a few more boxes open in his noggin, only to find them vacant, while not noticing the four-door bouncer land beside him. Animated holographic images of Chainsaw Freckle's shape were on the hubcaps, severing a man's body apart with the chainsaw repeatedly.

"Hey."

Fred continued to drift.

"Hey. I'm talking to you, man."

A teenager stuck his head out the passenger window. His bottom lip was pierced with a steel circular barbell. A thin silver chain shaped with skull heads hooked onto it and attached to a hoop ring looped into his ear. The driver was another young kid with a Smart Tats animated tattoo of a tiny bat flying around on the skin of his neck.

"Hey," Fred responded.

"What are you doing around here? This is a non-ghost suburb."

"I don't know. I'm leaving though. You can bet on it. Do you know the way out of here?"

The kid grinned an upper palate of dental braces shaped with a string of tiny meat cleavers; the lowers had a line of erect daggers. "Oh, yeah. I know how to get you gone, man."

"Which way do I need to go? I don't want any trouble here in this suburb."

"Right…go down that street," the kid pointed, "turn left, go about a block, you'll see some privacy gates. That's the way out."

"Thanks." Fred floated off.

"Hey, we can drive ya there, dude. We're going that way. No problem at all."

"Um. I'll be fine."

"It's not groove floating through here, man. Ain't safe. These anti-ghost freaks can be dangerous. Seriously. You don't need all that. Jump in. We'll give ya a bounce outta here."

The kid was right. Seeing more people on the street gathering together, looking at him, pointing, did make him wonder if he would be attacked or whatever they did to ghosts who trespassed. Would it be possible to leave on his own?

"C'mon. Jump in, dude. Me and my buddy here, Harold, like ghosts. We think their squiggly. Right, H?"

H nodded and the bat continued flapping.

The bouncer's side door slid open.

"C'mon. We'll take care of you."

"Thanks, guys." Fred slipped into the backseat and the door slid shut. "I really appreciate the ride."

The kids in the front seat looked at one another. "No problem.

We appreciate the company." A flash of the meat cleavers and daggers. "I'm Bobby, by the way."

He stuck his hand out.

## Commercial Break:

*An unseen narrator explains: "Smart-Tats, your colony's tattoo dealer specializing in animated holographic designs on synthetic skin such as arms, legs, chest, back, throat, head and face. Who wants the sting of the needle from one of those defunct OSSMS dealers? They always claim their equipment is sterile, but do you know it for a fact? Why not try a pain-free Smart-Tat where all you have to do is stretch the transparent skin over the part of your body where you'd love to see an animated tattoo take form and move?*

*"Here at Smart-Tats we have every design imaginable! If not, you tell us what you want and we'll have one of our specially trained clones draw up the design.*

*"Decide one day you don't like where your tat is located? Feel like it should be placed elsewhere on your person? Wearing Smart-Tats also gives you the option to move the tat from one spot to the other, whether on a sleeve for your arms or legs, a full mask over your face and head, or, better, if you choose to purchase a fit-to-size Smart-Tats Body Bag, snug against the skin, you will have the ability to move a tattoo from, say, your scalp to the bottom of your feet. Or wherever suits your fancy!*

*"Love Halloween? Love dressing up in scary costumes? Why not purchase one of our Shifterchips, a microchip you insert into an inside pocket of the Body Bag that will shift the appearance of the Bag into a costume. For more costume selections please visit www.smarttats.com and choose from our large catalogue.*

*"Smart-Tats, Your One Stop Shop For Tattoos!"*

*This has been an approved message from the Slader Corporation*™

***

*An unseen narrator explains: "Has this ever happened to you?"*

*A man walks down the sidewalk carrying his briefcase when a burst of wind grabs his toupee, nearly snatching it off his scalp. He slaps a hand on his head, keeping it from flying away. When he thinks the wind has died down he removes his hand and continues on, unaware of a surprise return when he turns a corner. This time the wind has its way and the hair piece is snatched off his scalp and pitched in front of a small boy and his mother who are walking on the sidewalk toward him.*

*The woman steps on it. Slightly embarrassed, she says, "So sorry about that...I...I didn't see your hair piece."*

*The man smiles. "No worries, ma'am." He bends down to pick it up and, like some rabid Tribble, it scurries away with help of the wind, sliding under a Pontiac Firebird replica at a stop at the red light.*

*"Look at it go, Mommy!" The boy laughs as his mom quickly pulls him down the sidewalk.*

*The driver is speaking to someone on an interface set atop the dashboard and is oblivious to the hair piece. When the light turns green the Firebird replica speeds away, the momentum of the craft whips the toupee up in the air and as another gust of wind catches it, it is blown away like a balloon filled with helium.*

*Embarrassed, the man is left standing there, beat down with embarrassment. As he gazes at the tall building across the street he knows he has to step into the meeting, bald, naked of his pride.*

*People pass him by as if he is a ghost wandering the streets searching for the right place to haunt.*

*The scene shifts, showing workers in a factory developing synthetic hair.*

*"Here at Gorack Industries, a subsidiary of the Slader Corporation, we not only produce robot maids, we produce hair for men and women who need it the most," the same narrator as before says. "Our toupees are windproof and fireproof. If you come by and visit us we can fit you with the correct piece using animated microscopic wires called feelers which will slip under your skin and connect to your skull. This procedure is*

*painless. The feelers act as tiny suction cups, latching onto the bone.*

*"Your baldness hidden away, you will be the center of attention with the ladies. I guarantee it!"*

*A handsome-looking young man strolls into the picture, perfect hair, perfect teeth, a woman on each arm.*

*"Please come by, and let us fit you with Synth-Fit Hair, the latest in hair replacement."*

*This has been an approved message from the Slader Corporation*™

\*\*\*

About five streets over, out of ear-shot or view of the anti-ghost community, the mobile suicide unit rolled down a street. An older man and woman stood at the end of their driveway, arguing. The driver stopped the Bouncer and stuck his head out the window.

"Good afternoon, folks. Everything okay here? May I be of help?"

The woman stopped yelling and her attention redirected. "It is *far* from a good afternoon! Everything is *not* okay! This husband of mine needs your service, Moree. He needs to be put out of his misery!"

"Just like an old jack ass, so do you, Madeline," the man countered.

"Why, you...*you*...," the woman flipped through the index of her vocabulary, finalizing with, "*bafoon!*"

"Bafoon? Call *me* a bafoon? You *wench!*"

The woman lashed out, smacked her husband's face. The man's head rocked to the side. His Syth-Fit Hair shifted on his scalp. The feelers stretched to readjust.

"How *dare* you hit me? Why, I oughtta...I oughtta..." He balled up fists, took a step forward.

"Oughtta *what*, Ben? Hit *me*? Ha! That'll be the day! You can't even bring yourself to kill a mouse, you coward! You shoulda seen him!" Madeline said to the Moree, pointing a finger at her husband. "Ben caught a rodent on a glue pad and used cooking oil to free its little feet up, letting it loose outside. *Oh* no, you didn't want to kill the poh…wittle…*tang*!" she said in her best baby voice. Then back to adult: "Gods forbid he did *that!* You should have seen that nasty little creature once it was free." Snort. "It turned right back around and shot back inside our home! Ben, here, ain't good for *nothing*!"

The color of Ben's face sequenced itself with the red mark from the slap Madeline delivered. He sucked in a breath and said: "Let me tell you something about this wife of mine, Moree. She can't cook or clean house herself out of a wet synthetic bag with holes in it! All she does all day is sit on the couch, watching the televid, stuffing food in her mouth. Hells, there's a dip in the couch where her big ass has taken up space!"

"What?" Madeline fumed.

"You heard me, Madeline! Maybe that's why you look the way you do!"

"What are you trying to say? Huh? Calling me *fat?*"

"Nailed that one on the head, didn't ya?"

"Ooooh!" Madeline swung her fist.

Ben ducked.

"Hey, you said it! I didn't have to!" Ben laughed.

Madeline took another shot, missed.

"Ha! You'll have to do better than th –"

Madeline landed a kick in a very private place on her husband's body, rendering Ben a painful interlude.

"Hold up, folks! Hold up!" Moree got out of the bouncer. Held up his hands. "Let's do this in a more civilized way, ya groove?"

"*Civi*lized?" Madeline huffed; frowned.

"Yes, ma'am. *Civi*lized."

Ben was gasping, holding his crotch, attempting to get off the ground. "Ain't no civility here…Moree."

"Look. How about I offer a solution to your problems?"

"Solution?" Madeline asked.

"Yes. You guys know why I'm standing here. It's the best way for you two to be happy, ya groove?" Moree smiled.

"Got a gun in that van of yours?" Madeline, a sly grin under her nose. "*That* would sure make me the happiest woman around! Gonna put this two-timing idiot out of his misery right *now!*"

"Two-timer? The hells are you talking about, Madeline? I've never cheated on you!" Ben ran defense.

"Oh, *really?* You keep talking about that woman you work with, Krissy. You can't stop talking about her, Ben. Krissy did this; Krissy did that; Krissy brought me lunch today; Krissy helps me with my work; Krissy always smiles...ughh!" Madeline threw her hands up. "I don't want to hear any more out of your mouth about *Krisssseee!!*"

"Has your defunct positronic brain crashed or something?"

"I'm not a robot, Ben!"

"Coulda fooled me. You have a steel anvil for a heart. Cold. Heavy, like your jaw you can't seem to keep shut!"

Madeline drew back her hand, stepped forward.

Ben took a few steps back. "Krissy is my *secretary,* Madeline! That's her job to assist me! Sheesh! The four gods who ride inside transparent spheres blowing raspberries! You're so thick-headed and stubborn! She has to smile and be nice because we have a lot of clients who seek out our law firm for help! I sometimes ask her to pick up lunch for me if I'm swamped with work. Krissy files my stuff in the memory of the computer when I get finished typing it up. *That* is her job, Madeline. Her. Freaking. *Job!*"

"I bet it is! How about Rachael in accounting who is schizophrenic? Huh? You said she ate lunch with you!"

Ben huffed. "You've got it all wrong! Rachael stopped by my table in the cafeteria while I was eating and poured water on me because she thought my hair was on fire! She's a nut case!" *She even came by my desk yesterday, informing me of future trouble I was going to have with you, Madeline, like she had some sort of precognition.*

"Well, the truth hurts, doesn't it, Ben?"

"Geez! You are a piece of work, Madeline!" Ben threw a fit, threw his hands in the air and hopped not once, but three times off the ground.

Madeline laughed. "You're nothing but an idiot, Benjamin! My mother was right about you! No good for nothing!"

Ben's eyebrows furrowed. "You got a gun in that van, Moree?"

"Uh. Sure," Moree said. "You gotta fill out the necessary forms on the Recog, though. Sign the waiver with your thumbprint. Gots to be legit, you know. Slader Corp rules." Smile.

Madeline continued to laugh. She added some other choice words and curses and accusations which would have made her mother roll over in her grave – that is, if her mom's soul was still inside the flesh and not haunting somewhere in the Wake.

"The hells with signing a waiver! It'll take too long!" Ben swiveled around on his heel and stepped into the house for a whole three minutes and five seconds before exiting after grabbing his Great-Great-Grandfather's old pistol from one of the wars – Ben couldn't quite remember which at the moment and really couldn't give a servo gnome's breath – and like a professional marksman wasted not a second longer and aimed the barrel point-blank at Madeline's still laughing face and fired.

The back of Madeline's head blew off. Her one hundred and eighty pound sack of flesh thumped the ground.

Ben blinked. A grin spread across his face, though not for long, diminishing. The reality of the murder gut-punched him. He gasped for a breath. Anxiety sidled next to him. His chest tightened up. The world around him wobbled, and he lost his balance and thumped the ground.

"Ben, you gonna be okay?"

Ben barely heard Moree's words. He had killed his wife! Even though he and Madeline had their problems, he could never bring the thought of actually *murdering* her. Hells, in all of sixteen years, two months and a handful of days of marriage it had never once crossed his mind! Why now? Why *freaking* now? Had he finally lost his patience? Was he a threat to others? Would he be thrown in front of a judge and jury and sentenced to death at the Neutralization Center? Or would he be thrown in a padded cell and forgotten forever?

Sentenced to life in prison? Not likely!

"Ben? C'mon, man. Let me help you up."

Moree held out his hand to Ben. He took it, got up.

"You may want to hand over that gun, Ben."

The gun felt heavy.

"You have a choice," Moree said. "You don't have to use my service for anything if you don't want to, ya groove? No pressure."

Ben gazed at Moree.

"Everything will be okee-dohkee now." Moree grinned.

"Right, Moree. Okee-*doh*kee." A tear slipped down his cheek. The good times he had with Madeline crashed into him. Why stay alive at this point? Could he join her in the ghostly world? There was a slight chance he might have the option. Slight being a much better word than none.

Ben stuck the gun inside his mouth and pulled the trigger. First his toupee flew into the air, spinning like a Bouncing Betty. Then the top of his scalp followed suit. His one-hundred and fifty pound sack of flesh made a thud on the perfect Astro Turf next to his wife.

Neighbors who had been standing on their lawns, watching the show, shook their heads and slowly slipped back into their homes.

"Well," Moree said, scratching his head. "Some days, my job is easier than others. Chains, get out here and give me a hand please."

The robot rattled.

\*\*\*

Earlier in the day Walts and Jonas got ready to play Quasi-Cinematix again. Jonas's parents made their vanishing act – as usual – and the boys had the house to themselves. They thought it was cool without any adults around to bother them.

"Hey, when did you get *that*?" Walts asked, pointing to a corner up high in Jonas' room.

"Oh. The floating hologram of the *Vulturine*? Found the Holo Shaper on the kitchen table last night in a box. My parents left it for me."

"The Holo Shaper?"

"Yeah. Look." Jonas grabbed an object as slim and as flimsy as a mouse pad with a surface plagued with animated kaleidoscopic designs. "It's a holographic projector that displays the Vulterine. Even other shapes if I want to download a driver off the Gorack Industries website."

"Way cool!"

"Yeah. It's cool, but guess they think buying me presents makes up for lost time they never spend with me. You're awful lucky, Walts, you get to see your parents. I never do."

"I wish it was different for you, man. Really. I'm sorry that it is the way it is for you."

Grin. "Me too. Thanks, Walts. You're my best friend. Glad to have you around."

Walts smiled.

"Now, let's get this sentimental crap outta the way and play Quasi-C!"

"Squiggly!"

This time Walts blasted apart more robot monstrosities, saved many survivors, gained some points, and after Jonas used a tractor beam to save Walts from the automaton worm, Jonas steered the tug around and hit the accelerator, blasting them off the planet.

Still in the virtual world, Jonas showed Walts a trailer for a game he might buy:

*"Revisit the apocalypse! Visit the pre-Shift days where an evil entity possesses each child, making them killers as they murder adults one by one. The object will be to eliminate the evil entity before it turns children into huge rats and the creatures take over the world."*

*Images of children morphing into rats flash before the boy's eyes, chasing down adults, ripping them apart.*

*"Play Shadow Out of the Sky, if you dare!!!*

*"Due out this Halloween!"*

Walts couldn't wait!

\*\*\*

Dad and Grandpa were in the living room when Walts got home in the late afternoon. They were watching a game show on the televid, another recreation from an episode from the *The Twilight Zone* entitled "Time Enough at Last". The young male contestant had to act like Henry Bemis who only had a certain amount of time in an apocalyptic setting to read five pages out of a book before his eyeglasses slid off his nose and hit the ground and broke apart. The eyeglasses the contestant wore were constructed by nanobots. Once the glasses slid off the contestant's nose, and he tried to catch them from hitting the ground, they would break into pieces and scatter like roaches under a bright light.

Before a commercial break, the show gave viewers information about the nanobots, explaining they had been a new creation, evolved by Gorack Industries.

"Oh. Good timing, Walts," Mom said, stepping into the dining room. "Go sanitize your hands and help me set the table, please."

Walts stuck his hands under the automated mini-sanitizer shaped as a dragon. It threw its head back and spat out a coin-sized crimson glob for him to clean his hands with. Walts laid out the plates and utensils.

"Let's eat," Mom said after placing a large bowl of chicken pesto in the middle of the table.

Excluded from dinner by his choice, like normal, Grandpa sat in his favorite chair and continued to watch the game show. He chuckled at a funny commercial about a female robot killing rats in someone's house while Walts and his family ate dinner. Eventually Dad retired to the living room with Grandpa. Walts did the same, and as soon as he sat down, the interface next to him on the end table bee-beeped.

"Walts, would you mind getting that?" Mom asked. "I have to scrub this bowl before I put it in the dish and cup sterilizer."

Walts hit the button.

Jonas's face appeared, the *Vulturine* blasting through imaginary space in the background.

"Hey, I didn't know you had an interface in your bedroom."

"Dad gave it for me before he went back to work this evening. He got home about five minutes after you left."

"Huh. Cool. What's up?"

"Um. Can you come over Walts? I need to talk to you." He blanched. Something Walts had never seen him do.

"Right *now?* It's close to curfew. Schizos will be out soon, you know."

"I know….It can't wait 'til tomorrow, Walts. I really need to show you something I received today. I…I'm not sure what to think about it."

"Your Dad buy you another game for your Quasi-Cinematix or something?"

"Nope. Nothing like that. I haven't even shown my folks this. Lucky I was here by myself when the mail came."

*The heck was he talking about?* "Really?"

"Dude. I wouldn't be calling you, but this is important. You're the only one I trust to tell."

Walts frowned. "Hang on….Hey, Mom?"

"Yes?" Her voice drifted out of the kitchen.

"Mind if I go to Jonas's house? He has to show me something."

"Tonight? Curfew is in fifteen minutes. Schizos are out. You aren't supposed to be outside one second past the hour. You know the rules."

"I know, but –"

"But nothing, Walts. You know the rules of the colony. You'll have to wait until tomorrow. Sorry."

Jonas heard Walts' mom, and he shook his head. His face screwed up in a frantic expression. "You *need* to see what I got in the mail today!"

This issue Jonas had to see him about which could not wait until tomorrow made Walts worry. "Mom, he *really* needs to show me something."

"Jonas can show you on the interface, Walts. You're not going out, this close to curfew. It isn't safe."

Walts tried another tactic: "Dad?"

"No way, champ. I agree with your mother. It'll have to wait until tomorrow."

Walts huffed. "Can't do it, man, my folks won't let me…"

Jonas chewed his lower lip. He pondered until his face lit up. "I got it!" Cupping his hands around his mouth he whispered: "Can you slip out after your folks are asleep? I can meet you in front of your house at eleven o'clock."

Good thing the interface was aimed where Walts' Dad could not see.

"See you then."

Jonas rang off before Walts could tap the button to end the call.

A few hours later Walts lay in bed, pretending to be asleep. His mom came into his room and checked on him, giving him a peck on the head.

*Eesh! He hated when she did that. He was way too old for her to keep treating him like a baby. Would it never end?*

When ten fifty-five scrolled across the face of Gort, the six-foot alarm clock (sold only in six-foot versus the authentic eight-foot size because it could fit inside houses in Ozarium) in the shape of the robot from the vintage flick *The Day The Earth Stood Still*, Walts slipped out from under the covers and, wishing he had the power of invisibility or the cool new invention by Gorack Industries called a Pocket Disintegrator-Integrator, slipped downstairs – he didn't see his Grandpa, thank goodness – and carefully twisted the doorknob on the front door.

Jonas was already standing on the front lawn, hands in his pockets. The street light shone down, showing beads of sweat on his cheeks, his face still blanched.

"What the heck is going on? What's so important you couldn't show me tomorrow?" Walts asked.

Jonas chewed his lower lip. "You're *not* going to believe it."

"Believe what?"

Jonas shuffled his feet.

"What? *What* is it?"

"Dude, this is really odd." He cleared his throat. "Check this out." Jonas reached into his back pocket and pulled free an envelope and handed it to Walts. Jonas's address was printed in the middle. No return address lay in the top left corner, but the words Slader Corp did. "Go ahead, open it."

Walts took the letter out, read:

CONGRATULATIONS!
YOU HAVE WON!
YOUR DREAMS OF BECOMING A MILLIONAIRE HAVE
COME TRUE!!

# Ozarium

Dear Jonas Leeshur,

Have you ever wondered what it would be like to win so much cred you will never ever have the burden of coming up with enough to keep a roof over you and your family's head? Have you been stressed, knowing you cannot make your utilities, your house, money you have borrowed from the bank to work on the house, or make your bouncer payment? What about coming up with enough cred to buy groceries? What about coming up with enough cred to buy your children Holiday presents?
Has the horrid thought of turning schizo crossed your mind?
Sure, you could keep clean by using one of the Sterilization Booths and live amongst the others who get free demi food, but… really? Live on the street? (Blowing raspberries) Hells with that! Well, no worries now! You are surfing the technological grid in the world of limitless funds on a hoverboard! Your dreams of becoming rich have come true! The world is at your disposal! Ha! You are the sixty-first person to win the Lotto! (Applause inserted here. Woot-Woot!) No signature required, your Bodykredd will have the funds available immediately!
Spend the money however you like, as long as it is within the written laws found below in this letter. More information about the Lotto can be found at www.lottowinnings.demi.com. I cannot urge you enough, please review them.

Lotto Laws

»Said Winner will accept Laws.
»Said Winner is allowed to purchase items for his or her family, though forbidden to purchase items for friends.
»Said Winner will obey Laws.
»Said Winner is forbidden to transfer cred into account of family or friend.
»Said Winner will conform with Laws.

NEW! »Said Winner is forbidden to associate with the Rebellion or have an Accomplice venture with him or her to go into the Subterraneans; otherwise, Accomplice will face the same fate as Winner.

»Said Winner will go quietly in a mature manner when the demi comes to collect their body for disposal.

»Said Winner will comply with these Laws or have their family disposed of alongside at the Neutralization Center.

Congrats again!!

Sincerely,

Your colony's leader, Maximus Slader

"You sure this is legit?" Walts asked.

Jonas nodded. "Yep. I researched the website. They even have my name posted on there."

"Man, ya gotta tell your parents! This is a mistake! Kids don't win the Lotto!"

Snort. "This one just did. I doubt it's a mistake. C'mon, ever heard of the demi making mistakes choosing lotto winners?"

"No. Guess I haven't…"

"I told you before, you can't count your cloned chicken eggs before they're hatched, didn't I?"

"Yeah, but –"

"I'm doomed, Walts! End of story!" Jonas threw his hands in the air, shook his head. "Guess you could call me the Six Million Dollar Kid! Only not rebuilt with bionic parts!"

"No…*wait!* I can't believe this! You need to tell your parents and get this thing fixed, Jonas! The demi doesn't kill *kids*!"

"Looks like they do now."

"Your parents will know what to do! Your Dad is an important dude!"

"What the hells is *he* gonna do? Hide me away somewhere? Riiight! It's not his concern. We ain't playing Vector-5, Walts. This is not a virtual game. It's reality! I'm sure as hells not going to tell them! Dad can't change this. He's not as important as Maximus Slader."

"Are you *nuts*? You can't let this go! The demi agents will come and get you when your time is up! You know it'll be a random pick when they show up on your doorstep to haul you off to the Neutralization Center."

"I know."

"You can't keep this a secret!"

"*Yes* I *can*! To protect one's privacy, they never reveal who the winner is to the public until the day they go after him or her. I'll figure out something by then."

"Figure out *what*?"

"Figure out how to disappear or something."

"How? Where will you go? You can't swim across the river of corpses. That'd be suicide."

"Walts, if I choose to do that, what difference is it? My path is already a suicide!"

"I still say you need to tell your folks."

"Hells with them! They are no use to me! They shower me with gifts and hardly pay attention to me, as if I'm some family pet. Feed the dog, make sure it's got water, take it out when it has to pee or poop. That's my life right!"

"Jonas…dude, your folks would understand this."

"No! Let 'em worry when I'm hauled away and disposed of! It'll be a good lesson to them."

Any words Walts wanted to add scurried away.

"If I gotta go, Walts, I'm going out with a bang. Told you that if I ever won."

Walts looked at a stranger, not a best friend who he'd known for five years. Jonas had stuck up for him more than once throughout the years, like dealing with Rib and the ravens. Walts stood in front of someone who must think he'd stepped inside a virtual reality. No, this is not some Quasi-C game. "Jonas, this is nothing to play around with. It's serious!"

"Ya think?"

"This doesn't sound like the Jonas I know."

"No. This sounds like the Jonas," he tapped his chest, "who has surprisingly won the lotto for whatever gods-freaking reason unknown and is trying to think of the best way to handle it. Evidently his best friend cannot get *that* through his thick head!"

"Jonas…I'm just trying to figure out the best way to handle this."

"And not doing a very good job at it! I'm not stupid! I said it's up to me to find a good solution, and I will."

"I didn't say you were stupid."

"Well, it sounds as if you are making me out to be!"

Walts sighed, shook his head. "Man…"

"Look-it: If I'm going out in a body bag, why not do it with a bang? Think we're living in a perfect world, Walts? Huh? Got news for ya, it's far from *that!*" A tear slipped down Jonas' cheek. "Maximus Slader is up there in his smug office with his smug agents sitting in his comfy chair making a decision to snatch away a person's life whether he or she wants their life to end or not. What gives him the right to do that?" He sobbed, wiped his runny nose. "I'm doomed, Walts, and I'll never get to grow up and do what I wanted to do in life!"

"Jonas…"

"If you are my best friend you need to promise me right now you will not tell your folks or anyone about this!"

"Jonas, I'm not sure I can do th –"

"Walts, I consider you my only and my best friend! I'm counting on you to not say a word!"

Walts sighed. He wasn't sure he could keep this hidden.

"Dude! You need to *promise me!*" Jonas spat, pleading, wiping away tears. "You *owe* me for being a great friend to you! We have always stuck together, right?"

Walts nodded.

"Then do me this favor; don't not say a word."

"Okay..."

"*Promise* me!"

Walts was hesitant to agree. But Jonas *was* his best friend. He'd been there for Walts when he needed him. So, having no choice in the matter, this was a no-brainer. "Yeah...sure. I-I promise, dude."

"Thanks, man."

As much as Walts wanted to run back into the house, wake up his parents, tell them this horror, he couldn't at this point. His friendship was on the line from here on out. It could be extinguished as easy as pushing the delete button on the keyboard.

"Look. I gotta go." Jonas wiped his eyes and made another swipe under his nose. Schizos are out, you know..."

Jonas didn't wait for his best friend to reply and waved a hand bye, sprinting down the street, leaving Walts alone with his thoughts.

Walts stood there, speechless.

This was not good. The forthcoming death of his best friend Jonas slammed into him. The demi planned on snatching away his best friend, and there was nothing he could do about it. Nothing at all. Surely Jonas would have the option to return as a ghost once he crossed over into The Great Beyond. Surely, being so young, they'd give him a chance to return as a ghost.

Wait.

Jonas could stay with me! Stay with us in the house!

These thoughts warmed him, shoved the bad ones away, though for one second until the loss of his friend yet to arrive haunted him.

A warm breeze ruffled Walts' hair as he stood there a moment longer, sobbing. Wiping away tears he slipped back into the house.

\*\*\*

Seconds later headlights stabbed away the dark. The replica filled with multiple options and gadgets of suicide turned down Walts' street, passed his house, stopped at the stop sign, took a left.

Dark silhouettes shuffled under the glow of a street lamp.

Bees caught inside a glass jar, a buzz chased in their steps.

\*\*\*

Far across town in Bobby's basement Fred was held prisoner in an upright coffin-shaped machine designed to hold a ghost called a Cryptronica. Sat flush against the wall its power cord stuck into a 220 volt outlet. The Cryptronica required about as much power to run a 25,000 BTU window air conditioner. Unlike the Morto, an electroshock weapon which vacuums a ghost's energy, rendering the immortal nearly lifeless, the Cryptronica did not harm a ghost, only imprisoned them.

Electroshocked by a Morto, the only antidote the ghost could receive was to drain the energy of a mortal which of course is against the rules according the Paranormal Laws found at the Bureau of the Recently Deceased.

Fred had spent the night. A transparent window viewed Fred's kidnappers sprawled out – Bobby on a sofa; Jamie in a recliner – snoring away.

When Fred slipped into the backseat of the boy's bouncer it had been a trap. After shaking hands with Bobby an electronic pulse slithered off a bracelet he wore, reached out, grabbed Fred. The door locked and, similar to the technology of the tractor beams on the *Vulturine* Jonas had used to save people, trapped Fred in an invisible cage.

Bobby and his accomplice laughed, informed Fred to shut the hell up, sit back, enjoy the ride.

Upstairs, the door swung open.

"Bobby, breakfast is ready!"

Bobby didn't respond. He was snoring.

"Bobby! Breakfast is ready!"

Bobby's eyes popped open.

"Bobby! I said breakfast is *ready!*"

Bobby cleared his throat. Smacked his lips. Groggily: "I'll be up in a minute, mom."

"Don't be long. Your eggs will get cold."

"So? You'll fix new ones for me if I tell you to."

Jamie woke up and ran a hand over his face, came back with saliva in his palm where it had leaked from the corner of his mouth. He frowned, as if it was some alien matter.

"Now, Bobby, I'm not going to do that. I don't intend on wasting food. Your father expects you to eat with us every morning. It's our only family time we have. School is out for the summer, and I know you may not make it home until late, so this way we can get a head start on the day. All three of us."

"Maybe I don't want to eat with you two, mom. *Family* time requires all of us to talk about our day."

Bobby imitated his father using an amusing, deep voice:

"*Bobby, what are you going to do today, son?*"

Bobby imitated an immature example of himself, his finger touched his chin:

"*Gee, Dad, lemme see…I think me and my good buddy Jamie should smash bouncer windows and drown a cat or two, listening to it gurgle as its lungs fight for air, and rob the corner market.*"

"*That's my boy!*"

"Bobby!" his mom shouted. "That's not nice!"

Jamie chuckled.

"You're not like that! You're a good boy, Bobby!" Mom said.

Bobby rolled his eyes. "Yes, Mom, I'm a *gooood* boy." Smile. "Here's my impression of you and me talking:"

"*Did you and Jamie have a good time?*"

"*Yes, Mom! We shore did! We ran over a dog, and it got stuck under the bouncer, and you should have heard it yelping and whimpering and howling as we dragged it until blood emptied its dying husk, coloring the pavement like the yellow brick road! Should have seen all that blood! Man what a mess! Bet if you go back to that spot and listen close, its residual will be heard on that street, yelping, howling, forever and ever more!*"

"*Well, that's nice, Bobby. Do you and Jamie want cookies?*"

Bobby burst out laughing.

"That's horrible, Bobby!" Mom said. "Why would you say awful things like that? Your father and I didn't raise you like that!"

"Because I *can* say things like that, Mom. It's cool!"

"No it is not cool, young man!"

"Sure it is."

"Bobby McDillun! I am surprised at you!"

"Surprised?" Snort. "Shouldn't be, and you really think I *give* a damn? You have no idea how much happier I am outside of this miserable shrine you call a home. I'd rather be living in a sarcophagus!"

"Bobby! Why do say that? I've never done anything to you to deserve this!"

"You've never done anything, *anyway!*"

When his mom spoke again, a sob caught in her throat: "Please, come on up here and let's talk about this. Get you some food. Your friend Jamie can eat, too."

"I'll eat when I *want*, Mom. Jamie isn't hungry."

Jamie gave him a Yes I Am look.

Bobby waved him off.

Jamie gave him a What The Hells Dude? I'm Starving! look.

Bobby flipped him the bird.

"Go back to watching your stupid morning shows, Mom."

"I wish you wouldn't take those tones with me ...I am still your mother."

Bobby snorted. "So? I'll do what I want, when I want. Got it?"

"You really shouldn't talk to me like that. It hurts my feelings...," she sobbed.

"Big deal! All you and Dad are around here for is to keep a roof over my head and come up with enough cred to send me off to college. I'm gonna *love* the day I get to leave this stupid house! Sometimes I kneel down and pray to the gods *that* day comes! Sheesh! Damn place is a dump! You never clean house!"

A pause.

"You don't really mean that, Bobby. I know you don't..."

"Wanna bet? You are as big of a burden as Dad, getting on my nerves all the time. Why don't you do me and yourself a favor and shut the door and go back doing whatever you do every morning. Hell, you're even a bother to Jamie. You should see him. He's down here with a scowl on his face and his hands over his ears."

Jamie held a palm over his mouth, attempting to stifle a chuckle.

"I don't believe you. Jamie is a good boy. I wish you wouldn't act like that! You never used to say horrible things to me and your father. You used to be such a sweet boy."

"Yeah? Well I'm *still* a sweet boy. Back then I didn't know any better. I was young and dumb. I'm grown up and smarter now... Can't say much about you and Dad being the same."

"You...you don't mean that..."

"Wanna bet? Close the freaking door and go do whatever you do! *Now!*"

Bobby's mom couldn't take any more punishment. She burst out crying, slammed the door.

"You can really manipulate your mom, dude," Jamie said. "My

folks are stone; can't work my magic like you do. Real groovatronic, Bobby!"

"Thanks." Bobby saw Fred watching them. "The hell are you looking at, *freak*?" He pointed his finger. "You undead think you know everything, don't ya? Think the world should be flushed down the toilet, right? Think you creatures should have more rights? Haunting here, haunting there. Whatchya got is nothing! *You* don't matter! *You* creatures shouldn't exist in the world! You freaks should stay put in The Great Beyond or the place called the Wake. You freaks should to be disposed of properly and – *newsflash* – my buddy and I are the guys to do it!"

Bobby jumped up and stood in front of the coffin.

If Fred could float backward, he would have.

"The Anti-Ghost Members Local 152 group doesn't have anything like this contraption you're in. Me and Jamie built it ourselves. Engineering 105 paid off for us at school. Nerdy class, but it was cool learning about technology.

"See, all the members of the Local 152 is protest to others how much they dislike ghosts by using holosigns and spamming email addresses. See, they don't have the hate I have for you creatures. There was a time when I read scary books about ghosts and thought they were cool. Not anymore. My teachers tried telling me they're not like that. Ghosts are innocent. Ghosts are friendly. Ghosts are lost souls who are trying to find their way to The Great Beyond." Snort. "That's crap! Cherry flavored popsicles in the shapes of Chainsaw Freckles! Spare me the bullshit! You ghosts are dangerous! You hear? You freaks are a danger to society! Just you wait, Fred, when me and my buddy are through with you, you'll be lost forever. They'll never find you. You'll never be able to haunt anyone *again!*"

\*\*\*

"Ms. Lans? Ms. Lans? Can you hear me?"

A buzz and a vibration tickled her cheek. Sarah opened her eyes, gasped.

"No need for you to fear me. Do you remember me? I'm doctor Caddel."

The arachnid servo unit stood by her bedside. Its floating quartet of eyes trapped in liquid behind a yellow-shaded lens gazed at her. "Ms. Lans, how are you feeling?"

Sarah blinked. A nurse stood off to the side holding a Recog. On the wall behind her a holographic spider trickled halfway down the wall on a strand of their silk; then scurried back to the web.

Submerged in dreamland Sarah could not capture the entire memory of it. Her world wobbled; she felt numb from the drugs pumped into her veins, no less. She did, however, recall the memory of being taken away by demi agents in the Lincoln replica with suicide doors:

*"The ride won't take long, Ms. Lans," the agent in the passenger seat had assured. "Sit back, relax."*

*The Lincoln's wheels hadn't rolled very long before rubber left the pavement and the replica took to the sky. Sarah questioned the replica, pegging it as a hybrid mode, perhaps something new the goofy car salesman, Tyler Ray Jim Bob Elrod III sold to Slader Corp.*

*After cruising alongside traffic in SkyDrive, drivers faced-forward in bouncers or allowing auto-pilot to drive it for them, each heading toward their own destination, the driver of the Lincoln turned the wheel and veered toward a large building. Slader Corp's holographic yellow letters scorched the darkness. A large door slid open on the slant-side of the building and the Lincoln slipped inside, swallowed whole.*

*The large door shut out the night and a thin-faced guard, flesh snug against his cheek bones, stepped out of a booth holding a Recog.*

*Landing, the driver and the other agent got out, opened Sarah's door. She stood as both agents took turns placing their palms on the face of the electronic tablet. The screen winked green three times each.*

*Both agents glanced back at her as their explanation was initiated* to the guard.

The guard nodded.

"Come along, Ms. Lans," one of the agents said with a wave of his hand toward a door which, oddly, spiraled inward, coming apart piece by piece, "after you."

Sarah obeyed, stepped through. The door spiraled back together.

An agent walked in front of her, the other walked behind her, escorting down a long hall.

Sarah stepped through another door spiraling inward, closing after, and into a room with one desk and two chairs. Metal walls gave Sarah a funhouse reflection: her body either skeletal or a swollen head and feet. A vacancy of pictures, windows, or a door lay visible.

"Sit down, Ms. Lans. I pray your stay will be a short one. Good luck," one of the agents patted her shoulder and followed his accomplice out of the room.

Sarah sat down. There was a chill in the room. She rubbed her arms. She wondered if they had forgotten to turn on the heat.

The wall behind the desk spiraled inward. Startled at the robot's odd design, Sarah watched it hover into the room, a buzz chasing the unit, and the tips making a tick! every time each of its six appendages tapped the floor.

"Hello, Ms. Lans. I'm doctor Caddel." His voice was monotone through a small grill for a mouth. "I am to welcome you to the Slader Corp. I wish it was under different circumstances, but since you disobeyed the Reproduction Laws, did not send in the correct request via email before you decided to become pregnant, this visit will not be a good one. Not a good one, at first. I am very sorry for that. However, I am going to make sure the remnant of your stay is pleasant, since the demi has not decided to take further action to your body, undergoing the process of TransmoG."

"Where is my boyfriend? I want to see him!" Sarah said.

"You will see Kentil in due time. What you need to focus on right now is rest, especially after the surgery."

"Surgery?"

"Yes. My nurse will be in here to get you prepped and ready."

*The hidden door spiraled apart.*

"What surgery?"

"I will see you in about an hour."

"What *surgery? What are you going to do to me?"*

*But Sarah already knew the answer to her question before the door pieced itself back together in Caddel's wake.*

*And what the heck was TransmoG?*

"Ms. Lans," the doctor's voice snatched Sarah back to the present. "Your recovery is going well. Nothing to worry about. How do you feel?"

Forming the words around a numb tongue, a thick piece of non-pliable flesh, she mumbled: "F-Fine."

"Good. What you need is more rest. I'm keeping the IV drip for a day or so longer. You'll need it for the pain."

"Ms. Lans does not need to be disturbed." Caddel said to the nurse. "Rest, Sarah. Your recovery won't be more than two weeks."

\*\*\*

Walts' gasped for air. He woke up with face buried in his pillow. *How'd that happen?* Sweat ran down his back as reality settled in around him. The nightmare oozed away. The reality of where he lay, in his own room, in his own bed, drifted into his brain.

The smell of jolt wafting from downstairs tickled his nose. Mom and Dad had to be up because the timer on the j-maker wasn't working, having to manually push the button for it to brew. Yet another thing his Dad would add to the list of things to fix.

He sighed; ran a hand over his face.

*Gods on pogo sticks blowing raspberries! What a nightmare!*

The demi had come to collect Jonas, and Walts had tried to hide him. The boys had taken refuge, of all places, at Bork Burgers,

Inc. The same robot that always took their order stood behind the counter. The unit informed them the spaceship on top of the building worked. A trip into space could be an escape from the authorities. The demi did not have the technology to chase them, the robot assured.

Walts had believed the machine and wished he hadn't.

As the demi converged on the restaurant, driving halftracks with twin cannons on top, an agent jumped down and shouted through a loudspeaker, demanding the two boys give themselves up. Things would go a lot smoother if they did. Even Ray Manisquaski from his show *Whadda Ya Gotta Say, Ray?* played a part, eyes bugged out, sweat beaded up on his bald head, anxious for that report to inform all the people in the colony what was hot and what was happening right now.

Walts ignored the agent's demand and shoved Jonas up a ladder that had suddenly appeared in the middle of the dining room. They slipped into the tug and Walts began hitting buttons, getting the ship ready for lift-off. Walts told Jonas to sit down and strap on his safety belt as he himself did the same. An odd sensation tickled Walts' palms as blue holographic pictures flipped like cards until settling on the face of Chainsaw Freckles. The clown's lips pulled back and burst with a giggle as the ship blasted off, leaving Bork Burgers and the surrounding planet in their wake.

Breaching the atmosphere, the radar picked up an invader. Closer examination showed Chainsaw Freckles in pursuit, flying in a Superman pose, legs together, both arms extended, fists clenched, the sound of his chainsaw ripping through the tug's speakers in the cabin.

Frantic, Jonas shouted at Walts to stop the tug and give themselves up.

Walts said he was going out with a bang, and if Jonas didn't like it, get off his tug.

Jonas scowled. He informed this wasn't how Walts acted. He

would never go nuts in a situation like this!

Freckles' chainsaw grumbled throughout the speaker. The assassin was closing in.

Walts turned back to Jonas who was now chowing down on a Bork Burger, kicking his legs and feet, happy and content as a baby in a high-chair eating chocolate pudding.

*What the hell?* Walts tried making sense of this complete turnaround.

Sounds of the chainsaw crackled through the speakers until they burst outward, a shower of sparks escaping, including a horde of scattering automaton cockroaches.

Walts screamed.

Jonas guffawed. Pieces of Bork burger spewed from his lips.

Walts' second scream was abrupt as he lost control of the tug as it jerked to the side.

Jonas' seatbelt ripped, and he flew out of his seat and slammed into the wall face first. As he slid down, a smear of blood left his mark.

The screen imploded, Chainsaw stepped inside and the oxygen inside the tug was vacuumed into space.

Walts gasped for air.

Freckles giggled, grabbed hold of Jonas' corpse, returned into space.

Walts held his palms over the arm rest, transposed mini holographic faces of giggling Chainsaw Freckle blowing raspberries, sticking thumbs in their ears, waving their hands, mocking Walts as the tug spiraled out of control, heading toward one of the two suns.

Warmth spread across Walts' cheeks as the suns rocketed forward.

The orange orb blinded him.

Before impact he woke up, the sun bright through his window.

Reality settling in, horrid thoughts of his nightmare were not good. Reflections of his friend winning the Lotto weren't much better. How could this have happened to his friend? Kids were exempt! Maximus Slader had pointed it out on the televid the other day. Walts remembered Fields saying this during his last re-election when he saw him downtown. Walts remembered it as plain as day! Had the great leader lied to the colonists?

Walts slid out of bed, ran a hand through his hair.

He really needed to tell his mom and dad. There had to be a mistake, a breakdown in communication somewhere. His parents needed to know! Grabbing his doorknob and giving it a twist, he remembered what Jonas told him last night:

*"If you are my best friend, you need to promise me right now you will not tell your folks or anyone about this! You owe me for being a great friend! We have always stuck together, right?"*

No, his parents didn't need to know. Breaking Jonas's trust would not be good. Their friendship would become mute.

He sighed, went downstairs.

Grandpa sat in his chair watching the news on the televid. A news anchor spoke about a man in custody, accused for stealing identities of the dead from graveyard plots by using a ground penetrating radar, and masking automatons with synthetic flesh to rob banks. The demi intended on sending the accused to the Neutralization Center.

Mom sat on the couch, her feet up. She was reading a paperback. Mom never liked reading a book on the Recog. She said she liked the smell and feel of an actual book, rather than reading pages off some electronic machine you had to keep charged up. You never had to worry about a paperback keeping a charge. No technology there.

Unfortunately, paperbacks were banned by Maximus Slader many years prior and everyone had been instructed to take them downtown to the drop off in front of the Slader Corp building. Not only Mom, but many other people refused, keeping a stash of lit hidden. They figured what the demi did not know didn't hurt them.

If ever found out, the worst the demi could do is cite someone for breaking the Montag No-Paperback Law.

"Hey, Mom. Hey, Grandpa."

"Morning, Walts," Grandpa sat in his chair. "Sleep well?"

"Uh. Sure did." Walts forced a grin, masking the lie.

"Boy, you really slept in today!" Mom said. "When I woke up at seven and checked on you, you were snoring away."

Walts peeked at the holo clock on the end table. Wow! "Yeah. Guess I did..."

"Already a few days into summer vacation, and you're already worn out, huh?" Mom smiled.

"Yeah, guess so."

She chuckled. "I made some eggs and bacon. Want some?"

"Sure."

"I have you a plate made. It's sitting in the warmer."

"Cool." Walts nodded. He stepped into the kitchen, pulled out the eggs and bacon, told the j-maker to brew him a cup of hot chocolate. It gave him not an ounce of grief or spat curse words. Three seconds later he was sipping a frothy top off the top of a cup.

"Dad fix the j-maker?" Walts asked, sitting down beside his mom.

"Yep. Nice that it doesn't spit curses at you, huh?"

"Very nice."

"That darn Tourette's Syndrome virus is bad news. Your dad had to get online this morning and download a program that eliminated the issue. He had it fixed pretty quickly. He's downstairs now."

"Oh. Cool."

"The j-maker's timer even works."

"Squiggly!"

"I'll need for you to do a few chores before you take off today."

"Oh. Okay." Thoughts of what was going to happen to Jonas crossed his mind again. "Um...how many things do I have to do?"

"Not much. Take out the garbage; put the dishes away in the drainer."

"Okay."

Mom frowned. "Something wrong?"

"No. Why?"

"You seem down about something. You feeling okay?" She felt his forehead using the back of her hand.

"Yeah. I'm fine."

Moms had that built in radar to pick up the slightest defect of her child. "Doesn't sound like it....something bothering you?"

Walts wished he could tell her his problem. No way could he breathe a word; he promised his best friend. "I'm fine, mom....a little tired I suppose."

"Okay. You get to feeling bad, come straight home. All right?"

"Yep."

Walts stabbed a chunk of scrambled eggs with his fork and ate it.

"So, what did Jonas show you on the interface last night?" Mom asked.

He choked.

Mom freaked. "You okay?" She lightly slapped him on the back.

Walts coughed, didn't vomit, swallowed bits and pieces of chewed up egg.

"You okay?"

"Y-Yeah. Fine."

"Sure?"

"Yeah...just fine. Stuff got stuck in my throat."

"*Sure?*"

"Yeah, Mom." He cleared his throat. "I'm good."

"Here, have a drink of my water."

Walts tipped the bottle back, swallowed.

"Okay now?"

"Yeah. I'm better."

"Don't scare me like that!"

"Sorry."

"That's okay. So…anyway…What did Jonas show you on the interface last night?" Mom asked again.

"Huh?"

"What did Jonas show you last night that was so important it could hardly wait?"

"Um….it was a…um (*think quickly!*) new game for the Quasi-C. He wanted to show me the lay out."

"Oh. It was *that* important he had to show you in person?"

"Yeah…well…you can't actually watch that stuff on the screen. Not like down at the Time Riff. You have to put a helmet on, and it zaps you into a virtual reality. Plus, Jonas was going to show me a map of the land we were going to explore."

"Really?"

"Yup."

"That's all rather…um…unique."

"Very groovatronic, Mom."

Smile. "I bet."

Walts stabbed another chunk of egg, swallowed.

"You two gonna play the game today?"

Walts swallowed. "Er, we plan on it."

"Inside an actual game…" Mom frowned, trying to imagine it. "Bet it is groovah….groovah…"

"Groovatronic, Mom."

Mom chuckled. "Groovatronic. Kinda rolls off the tongue. Where you kids come up with that slang, I'll never know."

"All the kids say it. It's a cool word."

"As long as all the kids don't decide to blast off into space, it'll be right fine by me."

Walts smiled. His mom could be really cool sometimes. He finished the last of his breakfast, got up.

"I'm gonna get my chores done and take off."

"All right."

Walts rinsed his plate off in the sink and, before placing it in the sterilizer, he put the dishes up that were sitting in the drainer and took out the garbage. Afterward Walts said bye to his Mom and his Grandpa. He got to say the same to Dad because he came up from the basement, taking a short break from his work. After grabbing a cup of jolt, Dad headed back down the steps.

Walts strolled off to Jonas' house, not paying attention to his neighbor's front lawn where those horrifying robot gnomes kept changing positions every so often. Like normal, Jonas' parents had already left for the day.

"Hey, c'mon in." Jonas' attitude hadn't lightened much from the night before.

The house smelled of bacon and eggs. Walts sat down on the couch. Jonas plopped down in the recliner, his leg over the armrest. On the televid a news anchor was speaking about the maintenance being done to the Neutralization Center. Various scenes showed robots working on the suicide unit.

"So, what…um…do you want to do today, man?" Walts asked.

"Don't know."

In further news Chainsaw Freckles was going to be down at the Time Riff, meeting and greeting folks. The newscaster said children could get their pictures taken with the infamous clown. It showed previous shots of Chainsaw standing in front of a mall while moms and dads stood back and snapped pictures of their children with the assassin.

Walts suddenly hated the clown. Chainsaw Freckles was a poster boy for death and as bad as the mobile suicide unit and Neutralization Center. Children who did not know any better were laughing, holding the clown's hand. At least the baby, who was crying, cradled in Chainsaw's arms, had the right idea about the mechanical freak.

Time slipped by as the commercial about Martha The Rat Exterminator X was shown.

It amused the boys.

"Found out my Bodykredd had the funds this morning." Jonas said.

"You did?"

"Yup. Got on the laptop and brought up my account."

"How much did you get?" wondering if he should ask or not.

"More than you could imagine. I'm filthy rich, dude. Bork Burger establishments for everyone!" Grin.

Walts returned it. "Wow!"

"I stayed up late thinking about all this. I'm still going out with a bang, Walts. No doubt about it. I really don't care if my parents know about my winnings or not. Hells with them! I got things planned out. First, we're gonna have some fun. C'mon." He rose. "Let's get some lunch and see what we can get into."

"Groovatronic!"

Jonas said "Off" to the televid before they went outside.

The screen turned black.

***

Sarah's eyelids rose. Holographic spiders scurried down the wall in pairs, retreated. She lifted her head, and the world wobbled, shifted, resettled. The IV bottle on the metal stand was empty, and the needle was vacant from her arm. A cotton ball with a piece of clear tape over it hid the needle's wound.

She sighed, placed her head back on the pillow. Her stomach throbbed. She feared what they had done. No. She already *knew* what they had done. Fear was replaced with sorrow. Benny was gone. Severed away from her flesh; stolen by the demi.

The tears came, washed her cheeks. Sobs racked her body. Her only child, forever gone, *dead*; never having a chance to breathe a pocket of air; never having a chance to laugh and play with other children.

Minutes scurried by as more tears followed.

She swallowed down a dry throat, rose up, made the world do that wobbling thing again. When it righted itself, she swung her legs around; her big toe touched the cold floor.

Voices lurked outside the door. Shadows passed under it, dark spots invading the orange light.

She balanced herself on one foot, held onto the bed as the room spun, then fell back onto the bed until the ride decided it was time to stop. Three minutes slid by before she attempted to rise again. This time she was able to balance herself on both feet and stumbled past the IV stand, almost knocking it over, and reached for the doorknob to the closet, giving it a twist. Her clothes hung neatly on hangers inside.

Sarah managed to sit back down on the bed, slowly dress herself, and a punch landed in her gut. She folded over, wishing the throb to vanish.

Nausea stepped by for a visit.

A bead of sweat cascaded off the tip of her nose.

Finally Nausea left, pulling Throb along.

Sarah stared at the door. She balanced herself once more, held onto the wall, grabbed the doorknob, gave it a twist and opened it a crack. Peeking out, she saw a vacant hallway. No one at the nurse's station directly across from her room.

Stepping out of the room the world did that wobbling thing again, almost making her lose her balance as the floor reached up to meet her.

She slapped a hand on the wall, stopped herself from falling.

Carefully, she made her way down the hall, the wobbling oozing away, where double doors lay in her path. Two thick windows, wired mesh molded into the glass, framed the view of another hallway.

She pushed open the doors, not paying attention to the sign on the wall next to her:

MATERNITY WARD
EMPLOYEES ONLY

\*\*\*

Back inside Sarah's room the small camera on the wall captured her exit and transmitted the data, while another camera kept its lens directed on her as she went into the Maternity Ward.

\*\*\*

At the Time Riff Walts blasted through the arcade game. Aliens dropped bombs while he maneuvered his ship, escaping death. Walts returned the favor by disintegrating his enemies with heat rays and rail guns. Jonas stood in front of another machine and had already deposited a lot of tokens in the game. Walts still hovered on his use of a single token and was getting his cred's worth.

"Aw, man! Killed off again!" Jonas spat.

Walts grinned, not looking at Jonas, keeping his eyes on the screen. "You'll get better. These games are easier to learn and to master than your Quasi-C."

"Dunno about that. Rather play the C. At least I know how to win. *Geez!*"

Walts laughed. Earlier, he had shoved what the future held for Jonas away. Jonas' death was not going to peck at his nerves. Nope. Not today. He didn't want to think about it; at least, tried not to. The only thing that seemed to make things better was a chance for his friend to be able to return as a ghost. Would Jonas' parents allow their son to haunt their house? Why not? Surely they would! Hells, they were never home, never really did much with Jonas, so why would they care? Right? Walts felt as if he was Jonas' *only* family. He felt like Jonas' little brother. And, if need be, Walts could see Jonas living with him, haunting his house along with Grandpa, his mom, and his dad. Why not? That. Would. Be. *Awesome!*

"Dangit to hells! My ship was blown up again!" Jonas spat.

"Keep feeding the coins, you'll get better!" Walts chuckled.

If Jonas was given the choice to come back as a ghost, Walts thought, it would be groovatronic! He could still hang out with Jonas. One thing is for sure, Jonas wouldn't ever have to mess with going to school again. No more lessons. No more books. No more of that holographic clown head Poppy who appeared out of the air at your desk giggling uncontrollably – sent by the teacher no less – giving you a pop quiz right after you get back from lunch. If that was an accurate depiction of Jonas' next life, it would be *way* groovy!

"Okay. Gotta go to the rest room," Jonas said. "Then I'll get some more cred for the games, Walts. Too bad there isn't an option where you just scan your palm over a scanner on the machines. You have to go scan it over the small Recog at the register to receive tokens. Kinda sucks. Oh well, be right back."

Walts continued to play his game, blasting away more alien ships until:

"Well. Nerdo city in here, huh?"

Walts froze. He recognized the voice.

"So, this where all the nerds hang out, huh?" Laughter. "Surprised I haven't seen any of your ghostly relatives down here hovering over these antiques you call, um, video games."

Walts turned.

Rib wasn't alone. Ravens never are.

"Whatchya playin, Waltsee'? Huh?" Rib asked.

Walts heard his second to last ship blow apart. The game was going to be a total waste.

"Awww, sounds like you got all blown up! That's too bad, huh?" Rib laughed and the other three ravens did too. Rib stuck out his bottom lip, and in a baby's voice he said, "Is that the last of your cred, Waltsee? Dontchya got anymore?"

Walts didn't say anything. Rib's antagonizing wasn't going to get on his nerves.

"Bet he does, Rib." Brit stepped over. "Colin said his dad makes good Bodykredd these days, working on automaton appliances for customers."

"That's a lie! My dad doesn't make that much!" Walts spat.

"Oh? So your family is poor?" Rib chuckled. "Little po'boy, Waltsee! Why don't you join the schizos and get some synthetic demi cheese and synthetic demi powdered milk. I saw three of those freaks a while ago down the street. I'm sure you and your mommy and daddy can join them. A couple of 'em were picking out stuff inside dumpsters. Bet you'd like to do that, too, wouldn't you, Walts?"

"No."

"No? Sure about that, Waltsee? We can show you. C'mon. Let me show you how they eat out of a dumpster."

Brit and one of the other ravens grabbed Walts, Rib in the lead. Other kids inside Time Riff stopped playing their games and watched the show. Walts wished they'd raise a hand to help, but he knew they'd fall victim of the ravens if they had tried. And the consequences would become messy.

"No roughhousing in Time Riff. It is not allowed," the robot attendant's monotone voice warned them as they passed the register.

"Go stuff bolts up your ass, you recycled titanium trash can!" Rib spat.

"Please leave this establishment. Verbal abuse is against the rules. From now on your cred at Time Riff is no good. This incident will be noted and reported to the demi."

"So? Report it!" Brit said without a care in the world. "This place is a geek hideout anyway!"

Brit got a few stares from the patrons.

"What? You all got a problem? We can make an example out of each of you, too, like we're gonna do to *this* kid!"

The patrons looked away.

Snort. "That's what I thought!"

Outside, Walts was hauled down an alley beside a dumpster. Both of its plastic lids were open.

Rib stuck his face in Walts'. The smell of peanut butter and gods knew what other specs of halitosis were on his breath. "This is for getting me in trouble the other day, Walts. Your buddy Colin ratted me out. Got chewed out by Cork! No one likes being yelled at. S'pecially me! I warned you if I saw you or your girlfriend out somewhere I'd take care of you both!" Rib stepped back. "Throw this miserable piece of crap where he belongs – in the garbage! He's not even worth a Swipe!"

Brit placed his hands under Walts' arms, and the other kid grabbed his feet, chuckling while they did so.

"Allow me to do the honors, eh?" Rib said.

"Sure!" Brit said.

"One!" Rib started the countdown.

Walts' back scuffed the ground as they swung him toward the uninviting stench of the dumpster's mouth.

"Two."

Another scuff across the back.

Brit laughed.

"Next time you decide to talk back to us it's going to be a *lot* worse!" Rib warned.

The other kid laughed, too.

"Thr–*ugh*!" Rib didn't see the intruder but felt the force of the punch in his kidney as it doubled him over and knocked him to the ground.

Jonas stood over him.

Rib winced, held onto his side.

"Let him go!" Jonas spat.

Brit and the other kid's eyes were wide with fear. They let go of Walts and took off.

"Awww, man! It *hurts!*" Rib squirmed on the ground. "Think you broke something!"

"You're lucky I didn't 'break your nose!" Jonas said and helped Walts up off the ground. "You okay?"

"Yeah...I'll be fine," Walts replied. "Thanks."

"No problem. Sorry I couldn't have been out here sooner. Think those chili dogs from Hotdog Heaven we ate earlier messed me up!" Jonas rubbed his stomach.

"That's fine." Walts chuckled.

"When I came out of the restroom and didn't see you, I asked the attendant. The robot mentioned some kids had come in and started trouble. The machine said they had gone outside. Seeing those holographic tassels in the shapes of snakes on the handle grips of the bikes parked out front tipped me off."

"Dude! I think you really hurt me, man! You suck!" Rib spat and managed to rise up, placing a hand on his side.

"Oh, are you still here?" Jonas asked.

"If I see you two again I'll—"

"Turn around and go the other way or you will surely get a broken jaw. Get the hells outta here, Rib! Don't mess with us again, hear?"

Rib scowled and took a step forward until he realized how alone he was, his friends already vanishing from sight.

"What, your friends abandoned you?" Jonas smiled.

Rib kept his scowl and hobbled off.

Jonas asked Walts again if he was okay.

"Yeah. I'm good. Think my shirt's ripped."

Jonas looked. "Yep. You have a hole on the back of your shirt.

Hey, no worries. Let's go buy you another."

"Cool!"

"Then off to Bork Burgers!"

"Squiggly!"

\*\*\*

"Stop by Todd's, man. Score some stuff before we do this."

"Squiggly."

Fred's small prison jostled in the back of the bouncer as Jamie drove a few minutes longer before stopping, shutting off the engine. It had already been a long day in Bobby's basement. Fred wondered what more surprises there were to arrive. He and Jamie had taken turns belittling Fred from time to time, if they weren't watching the televid and stuffing their faces with food. Sometimes Bobby's mom would call down from above, asking what they were up to, and each time Bobby would shout at her or tell her to leave him and Jamie the hells alone.

Around seven in the evening the boys hauled Fred's prison through a door on the other side of the basement, up concrete steps, placing him in the back of Jamie's bouncer. Fred had no idea what plans they had for him, but knew it wasn't going to be good. His only view was looking at the gray-colored interior roof of the bouncer.

"Todd! *My* man!" Fred heard Bobby say. "What's groove? Anything?"

Todd's voice, faraway: "Nothing. Working on my bouncer."

"Nice. Add the tail fin yourself?"

"Yup. Groovatronic, eh?"

"Yeah, dude."

Closer now: "What's up, Jamie?"

"Hey," Jamie replied.

"What are you two into?"

"Oh, a few things…hey," Bobby's voice lowered, "got any goose for us?"

Pause. "Sure. Got the cred?"

"You *know* I do! Drained some of my parent's bank account this morning." Chuckle. "They'll blame it on someone else, hacking into their account. I cover my tracks well, dude."

"Very groove! Hang on, let me get my scanner, and we'll do some business." A couple of minutes slipped by before Todd returned. "Okay. Got it ready."

"Scan my palm, dude, punch in your price."

There was bleep.

"Okay, got it."

"Hey, how the hells is it you don't get caught using a scanner for goose transactions?" Jamie asked.

"Well, I got my ways. A magician never reveals his secrets, right?" Todd replied.

"Right!"

"No offense, but I'm not about to reveal mine, my friend. Let's just say it's good to have a big brother who's a computer guru, working for Slader Corp."

"Wow! They pay big cred!"

"Got that right!"

"Not to be rude," Bobby said, "but, can you get the goose so me and Jamie can be on our way? Got business to tend to."

"Oh…sure, man. You and Jamie, now that's new! Ain't heard you call him that before!"

"Ah, rolls off the tongue. I got all kinds of cool words stored in my brain."

"I bet! Hey, um, what's up with riding around with a coffin in the back? That's just *morbid!* Friends with Chainsaw Freckles or something?" Laugh.

"Let's just say there's a good reason behind it," Bobby smiled. "Like you say, a magician never reveals his secrets."

Todd burst out laughing. "Love it, dude! You're one of a kind, Bobby! Hang on, I'll get your goose!" Not but a few minutes later: "Here ya go, guys. Always a pleasure doing business with ya, Bobby. Come back when you need more."

"Sure. We might go out to my parent's cabin this weekend. Wanna come with us?"

"Abso-freaking-lute! Thanks for the invite, bro!"

"Call you later, set up the details. Okay?"

"Sweet!"

The bouncer's engine fired back up.

"Later on."

"Take is sleazy, you two."

"Always."

A short pause for the cause sidled in as the bouncer moved again.

"Bobby, you never invite *anyone* out to the cabin," Jamie said. "I've only been out there a handful of times. What gives?"

"Thought about having a party, that's all. I'm sure we can round us up some girls. Bet you'd like to see Jenny there, eh?"

"Oh. Yeah!"

"She's a beaut. Goose her, and she'll practically do anything you want her to do."

"Anything?"

"*Any*thing! She's easy like that, if you know what I mean!"

Jamie laughed. "Groovy!"

"All right. Let's go to the cemetery and scope us out a plot, whaddaya say?"

"What? We gotta dig one first! I ain't into physical labor!"

"Don't I know it, looking at your size and weight."

"Hey! That's not cool!"

Bobby guffawed. "Aw, man, just razzing you! Nothing personal! It's all groove, dude."

"Well," Jamie chuckled, "okay, then. But we gotta dig?"

"You need to take a hit of goose and get it in your system already! Need to calm down and relax. Anyways, did I *say* we were gonna dig a hole?"

"Well…no."

"Then, there you go. Listen up: we'll use hand-held mortos to get the freak out of the bouncer and place him by that serial killer's tomb, David Fouk. It's said his ghost lurks about the place, terrorizing other ghosts. I'm sure he'll love terrorizing this freak we have in the box!"

"You mean that guy who collected people's hands?"

"Yep."

"Crap! Gives me the creeps!

"See? Sound like a great plan, huh?"

"Gotta admit it does, man! But what about our well-being? Won't Fouk attack us, too?"

"Jamie. We have mortos. They'll defend us if his ghost decides to come after us."

"Oh. That's right."

"Let's go have some fun, shall we?"

\*\*\*

Sitting on the side of the road the driver of the tractor and trailer with the grinning cartoon face of a guy wearing a straw hat, giving a "thumbs-up" watched Bobby and Jamie pass by, while kicked back in the seat, long legs stretched out, boots rested on the passenger seat.

The figure tipped his hat.

\*\*\*

The hall stretched out before Sarah. Closed doors were on each side. Bright fluorescent lights above washed her head and cheeks with their glow as Sarah held onto the wall, making her way toward two more double doors at the end. Through their windows she noticed a nurse stepping out of a glass door, heading this way.

Frantic, Sarah twisted the doorknob to the closest door next to her and darkness shrouded her as she shut the door, covering her with a strong odor of cleaning supplies. Sarah coughed once, felt the gut-punch again. Throb poked her. Wincing, careful not to be seen, she peeked out the window at the nurse strolling by.

A man's voice, down the hall, made the nurse stop in her tracks.

Sarah saw it was a male nurse. He made polite conversation with her, asked her what she was doing later. She smiled and said she'd be off at five. Said he'd call her on her mini interface.

Smile from the nurse; a blush.

They parted ways.

When the coast was clear, Sarah left the room, one hand covering her stomach. The pain subsided. She snatched a breath of fresher air, coughed, thanking the gods for not allowing another gut-punch this time. Pushing the next set of double doors open, a wide glass window was on her left. She stopped and stared. Small rectangular tanks of clear fluid angled around an automaton in the middle of the room. This one looked nothing like Caddel. Six black tentacles grew out of a tall, chrome-colored cylinder-shaped machine and picked babies up one by one, feeding them baby bottles filled with a green and yellow liquid.

One child drained its bottle as if hunger was on the verge of dissipating in the colony.

A line of red lights scrolled across the top of the automaton as it finished feeding the child, returning an oxygen mask over the child's nose and mouth, returning it into its tank where it floated and squirmed inside. Three separate tubes reared up off the floor of the tank and plugged themselves into portals in the baby's back.

The machine repeated its steps, picked up another child to be fed as the tubes on the child's back unattached themselves.

Names scrawled in a digital format on Recogs hanging from the tanks closest to Sarah. Johnson, Cameel, Barbers, Lans, Rommels, Smith, Rice, Werlly, Hubble, Ga–

Her eyes widened.

*Lans.*

Squirming in the fluid was Benny, blue eyes wide as coins. Tubes were also attached to ports in his back. A small mask covered his mouth and nose. A long hose connected to a small cylinder-shaped object with the words OXY-GIIN stenciled across it in black lettering.

Two inches of glass kept Sarah from reaching into the fluid and touching Benny.

*Benny…*

*My baby boy!*

She looked at the glass door. Swung her head to the side, peeked through the windows of the double doors she had just come through. No sign of life invading the hallway. She gazed at the other doors with similar interest at the other end of the hall. No sign of life approaching.

Twisting the doorknob, she stepped into the Maternity Ward.

\*\*\*

Outside Walts' window the msu rolled down the street, hoping to score more flesh, as he lie in his bed. Walts hadn't gone to sleep. He was too excited. His day had been groovatronic! Minus the problems running into Rib and his guys and it would have been groovatronic to the *max!*

*And then some!*

Unfolding the day's events after he and Jonas had left Time Riff they headed to Bork's, scarfed down two burgers apiece, and had gone shopping at Time Riff's sister establishment called the Body Chute. There Jonas bought two skateboards. After riding them for an hour inside Body Chute's tunnels, Jonas came up with another great idea.

Walts freaked out hearing the words.

Absolutely *freaked!*

Money not being an option, they stepped inside Visualize The Virtual about a block away, laid their boards to the side, donned Envo helmets, felt the feelers tickle their scalp as the microscopic tentacles slipped into their brains, and surfed the Gridd on virtual hoverboards. The place was crawling with other young patrons. Some only had enough cred to stay for half an hour, whereas Jonas' and Walts' stay was infinite.

The first hour on hoverboards, the second hour they drove souped-up replicas in a race where the player had to dodge giant automaton praying mantis' attempting to stab the vehicles with their spiked forelegs and fling them off the track; the last hour they blasted off in space in a tug, landing on a planet called Vector-Boink. The aliens, dark-skinned creatures called the Ockuli, had sent a distress call for help. Walts' and Jonas' object of the game was fighting off midget cannibal clowns wielding huge cleavers and save other Ockuli who had been taken prisoner and were being consumed one by one.

Working off their burgers from earlier, both physically and mentally playing these games, they decided to visit Plutonium's Pizza Palace and ate an extra-large pepperoni with sausage pizza, chasing it down with two root beer floats you had to keep covered with a plastic top after each sip because the sudsy multi-colored Pop Rock Candy oozed out of the glass, all over the table.

Walts' mini interface vibrated in his front pocket. Tapping the screen, Mom's face appeared. "Are you coming home for dinner? It's already six-fifteen."

"Oh crap! Sorry, Mom! Didn't realize what time it was!"

"That's okay." Chuckle. "Be home soon. I'll keep your food warm."

"Thanks!"

"Love you."

"Love you too, Mom."

Walts tapped the screen to end the call. "Good thing she didn't see the picture of the pizza behind me. She would *not* be happy! Hells, I'm gonna be stuffed by the time we leave here!"

"I bet!" Jonas laughed and swallowed the last bit of his pizza. "You know, I have to admit: I envy you, dude."

"Why?"

"My parents hardly ever say 'love you' to me."

"Get outta here!"

"It's true. You know I hardly ever see 'em. When I do I hardly ever hear them tell me they love me."

Once again, Walts felt sorry for his friend. "Dude, that ain't right."

"No. It isn't."

Silence sat down for a spell. The world around them shuffled past. People seated in other booths chatted, ate their food and conversed. A ding stabbed the air, indicating someone's pizza was ready to serve.

"Well. What do you want to do tomorrow?" Jonas asked.

"Dunno," Walts replied.

"Sleep on it, Walts. I'm sure we can get into something else that'll be fun."

"Cool."

Jonas swiped his hand over the scanner on the table, paid the bill, leaving a nice tip for the waiter and followed Walts outside. They headed home and said their goodbye's until tomorrow.

Now, as Walts lay in his bed, wondering what fun would be on the horizon tomorrow, sleep snuck into his room and took him prisoner, setting him adrift into dream world. Nightmares stayed away; however, the other ones in reality anticipated *their* nightmares once morning arrived.

***

The Deputy Point cemetery has an open invitation for day visits where one can visit their loved ones' remains, people who never returned to them in the form of a ghost. Nighttime is different. Mortals are forbidden to enter, which makes curfew even more important. Here, some ghosts decide to stay within the boundaries of the cemetery; some that had no family in their previous life or had no interest in seeing their family ever again. They rarely materialize in the daylight.

However, tonight a pocket of Change is pulling up in a bouncer. The chain on the cemetery gates is being sheered apart with a pocket laser and the uninvited are headed toward David Fouk's tomb, the largest one in the cemetery, a large concrete gargoyle sits on top of a rectangular slab hiding the serial killer's remains.

Only a few yards away is an open grave for a sad Wilbur Rankins who decided to take his own life with a bullet. Tomorrow is his funeral service. Wilbur had had no interest using the mobile suicide unit's service. Nor had an interest in trekking up to the Neutralization Center to have his corpse floating in a watery grave.

Just didn't seem right for a body to be in there.

Something about dealing with a guy who didn't want to cut his hair, Wilbur had trouble with. Who names their kid Moree Bund? This he wondered three hours before getting his nerve to pull the trigger and blowing his brains all over the bathroom walls. At the time he knew the wife might get upset about the blood on the tiled frog designs, but who the hell cared at that point? That's what they made Clorox for, right?

She drove him to suicide. *She* was the one who led them into bankruptcy, having their house repo'd by the bank. *She* couldn't stop spending her Bodykredd. *She* was the one who did not want to work. *Not* him!

*Bitch.*

Speaking of women, can't say he liked the lady at the BRD. What was her name again…um…Belinda? That sounds right. Rude woman. If she was wearing a penguin's outfit, much like a nun's, it would fit her to the T. Might hide that puffy red hair, too.

Wilbur was sitting atop his gravestone when the bouncer's brakes squeaked to a stop beside Fouk's grave. It was one place he stayed away from. The ghost of Fouk was as evil as when he was a living, breathing mortal.

"I'm getting hungry, Bobby. Wanna stop at Bork's on the way back?" Jamie asked, getting out of the bouncer.

"Realize what time it is? They're closed, man!" Bobby said, getting out himself.

"Oh. That's right."

"Help me drag this coffin out about halfway. I'm going to open the top panel. Be ready with your morto, okay?"

"Yep." Jamie took his out of his pocket. "We gonna get goosed after this?"

"Yep."

The boys dragged Fred's prison out. His only scenery was the dark sky filled with stars.

"What are you boys up to?" Wilbur asked.

Bobby and Jamie stopped, looked around.

Wilbur hopped down. "Curfew is already established, boys. Shouldn't be in this graveyard after hours."

"Mind your own business, freak!" Bobby spat. "Keep your ghostly ass away from us!"

"Hey, you need to watch your mouth, young man! Didn't your parents raise you right?"

"They raised me to hate *your* kind!"

Wilbur rolled his eyes inside his ghostly skull. "Oh. You're one of *those*, huh?"

It caught Bobby and Jamie off guard, making them blink back a chill.

"One of *what?*" Bobby asked.

"Those twerps who are anti-ghost members."

"Yep. So is my buddy here."

Jamie raised his Crypto.

"The hells is that? Some type of squirt gun?"

"A gun that'll hurt you, old man," Jamie said.

"Ain't never seen one before."

"You'll see how good it works if you don't stay out of my way," Bobby said. "Go back over to your grave and sit your ghostly ass down and watch how I use it on this ghost that's being held in this prison me and my buddy designed. Otherwise, maybe I'll decide to use it on you." He pulled his morto from his front pocket and pointed it at Wilbur.

Wilbur held his hands up. "Sure thing, kid. Never seen the thing before. I sure do not want to find out what it does to me."

"Smart, old man….Ready, Jamie?"

"Yup."

Bobby flipped open the head of the Mortonica and instructed Fred to get out. Fred obeyed, gazed at his surroundings. *Lovely; a graveyard. The hells are these boys up to?* He noticed Wilbur. "I'd get away from these two as far as you can."

"Shut up!" Bobby spat. "Jamie, hit this freak!" Both mortos fired at once, trapping Fred in a tractor beam.

"Oh. Wow," Wilbur said, eyes wide with interest.

"You get to meet a new friend tonight. How about that?" Bobby told Fred.

Fred remembered them talking about that serial killer during the ride here. He had no interest of being next to or around David Fouk's ghost, even though he had no reference in his memories about Fouk, since goose had snatched it away when he was of flesh and blood.

Bobby and Jamie pulled Fred toward Fouk's grave using the beams.

"Um. I wouldn't go over there, boys," Wilbur warned.

"What?" Bobby glanced over his shoulder.

"I said I wouldn't go over there. Ain't safe for you mortals; much less a ghost. Fouk is bad news."

"I'll be the judge of that, old man. I already told you to mind your own business. Go off and haunt somewhere."

"Don't say I didn't warn you kids."

Bobby gave Wilbur a mean look. "You best keep quite! Don't think for a minute I won't use this morto on you!"

Wilbur didn't say another word. *Let 'em see what happens, those know-it-alls. Those smart-ass kids are gonna have another thing coming if Fouk is bothered. He's a mean one! He'll probably –*

His words were cut-off as Wilbur saw a large group of silhouettes coming into the cemetery. He snorted. "You know curfew is in place for a reason, boys. Being in a graveyard at night isn't a good thing. You two may need to get your sorry butts outta here ASAP."

Bobby stopped five feet from Fouk's grave. "I *told* you to mind your own business, old man! That's it! Once I'm through with Fred here I'm coming back for you!"

"I'd like to see it."

Bobby fumed. "On the other hand, why don't I take care of you right *now*…Jamie, keep your beam on our friend. If he tries to break free, switch your morto over and burn his ass."

"Okay."

"Keep your beam on that freak. I'm gonna deal with the other." Bobby turned his off and stomped toward Wilbur who stood there, not attempting to escape. "Wipe that smile off your face, old man. I'm gonna incinerate you, so you'll never be able to step into The Great Beyond!" He raised his morto.

"Don't try to get out of that beam, freak!" Jamie said.

"How the hells am I going to? I'm trapped." Fred rolled his eyes and shook his head. He watched as Bobby walked toward Wilbur. He hoped the old man wasn't going to get hurt. He should get the hell away. Then, he noticed a large group of silhouettes coming this way. "Hey, you may want to warn your friend. Look over there."

Jamie took his eyes off Fred and his eyes widened. "Um. B-Bobby."

"What?" Bobby did not turn around, still faced Wilbur who continued to smile.

"Bobby!"

"What? Speak up!

"Schizos, man!"

"Where?" A slight turn and Bobby stared into long streaks whirling diagonally, erratic patterns tucked under a dark hood of a schizo. This close, the creature's buzzing brought pecking needles on his face.

***

Sarah gazed down at her little baby boy squirming in liquid. His big blue eyes stared back. He cooed under his oxygen mask adding a toothless grin to boot.

*Benny...*

The automaton finished up feeding another child, replaced its oxygen mask, sat it back into a tank, picked up another which cried until the nipple of the bottle rested between its lips.

Ecstatic, she would be able to hold her son. They had not murdered him.

She reached into the cool fluid of the tank, brought Benny out and cradled his wet body against her breast, soiling the front of her shirt. The vapors of his breathing fogged up the interior of the oxygen mask.

"My big boy!"

Benny cooed and grinned.

Sarah took the mask away and his grin widened. She hugged her son. He blew raspberries, and she chuckled. She glanced up, trying to see if anyone had spotted her.

The hallway lay vacant.

Sarah knew she needed to find a way out of the building with her son. Excitement still coursed her body knowing her child was alive and not disposed like a piece of trash. Reunited with her son, gods help her as she tries to escape this place, one way or another.

This time they would not take her Benny from her!

*** 

Walts' interface sitting on the table beside his bed beeped, waking him.

"Ready for another fun day, man?" Jonas was smiling.

"Sure." Yawn.

"Meet me in a half an hour at my house. Today will be *awesome!*"

Walts got up, stretched, dressed and went downstairs. Saw Grandpa in his chair.

"Morning, Walts!"

"Hey, Grandpa..."

"Got a lot planned on your agenda today?"

"Yup."

A commercial on the televid, a tall, bald man in a dark suit narrating, sitting in a cubicle along with other employees stuffed in their own matchbox, gazing at computer screens:

*"Ever felt like you never have the energy to make it through an entire day at work? Do those other caffeinated brands not give you the 'jump' on the day you need? Do other brands give you a caffeine rush only lasting a few hours? Do they give you the uncontrollable*

*jitters if you drink too much at one time? Do they not keep your mind focused at work or your body at play long enough? Well, why not try Jolt? It's guaranteed jitter-free! It keeps you alert longer than those 12 hour energy shots! With only 2 calories per serving, we guarantee its performance or your money back!*

"Check out these before and after pics of people!"

*The screen flipped to a woman nodding off at her desk, fighting to keep her eyes open, trying to type.*

"Look familiar? Now, check this out:"

*A hand with a cup of Jolt reaches into the picture, setting it on her desk. The woman drinks a sip, her eyes widen. A smile tugs at the corners of her mouth. Focused, her typing speed improves.*

*The screen revolves, LATER... appears on the screen.*

*Her boss walks by with a Recog in his hand, gives her a wink, a thumbs-up, points to the tablet.* "Great work on these reports, Jill! Keep it up! Soon you'll have my position!"

*She giggled.* "Aw, Mr. Popp, thanks for the kind words!"

"Wake up smelling the fresh aroma of Jolt! Don't start your day without it! Go to www.joltdoesntgivemethejitters.com to score a coupon good for one free bag of Jolt and where you can receive a free four ounce bag of our latest blend, Jolt-X, laced with a very small milligram of goose, a tiny amount to make it legal!

*One free bag, ladies and gentlemen! How does that sound, eh?*

"One cup of Jolt-X will stimulate your senses to perform your daily activities! And, do not fear, adding this very low amount of goose to our product is within the guidelines of Slader Corp's Food and Drug Administration.

"While you are checking out our website, take a minute to enter to win a year's supply of Jolt, six months of Jolt-X and a free J-maker to boot, too!

"Jolt! The right choice to make in life!" *the narrator says, his hand lifting a cup, bringing it to his lips for a sip.*

Breakfast wafted out of the kitchen. Pursuing the aroma,

Walts found his mom stacking plates in the sterilizer.

"Morning, Walts. Want some breakfast? I made blueberry pancakes. They're in the warmer."

"Awesome!"

Mom cocked her head. "You seem more chipper than yesterday. Get some rest?"

"Yep."

"Good. You'll be happy to know it doesn't look like I have one chore for you to do today. You have the day off."

"Groovy!"

Mom chuckled.

Walts scarfed down his pancakes — which were always tasty when Mom made them — told his mom and grandpa bye, and before heading to Jonas' house, heard a commercial on the televid about cloning yourself. *"Everybody's doing it, why not you?"* was their slogan.

Walts found that idea rather unsettling. He thought it would be creepy having a Walts clone running around. Then again, he supposed the clone could go to school and do the chores for him while he played games with Jonas.

*That may not be so bad...*

Walts hurried past his neighbor's house with the roaming robot gnomes in their yard without a glance and went to Jonas'. Oddly, he didn't even have to knock on the door; Jonas was already standing behind the screen door, waiting his arrival.

*Huh. That was a first.*

"Today I have something really cool for us to do, Walts! You'll freak, man!"

"Cool."

"First, check *this* out!" Jonas opened the screen door and stepped outside and stood in front of the garage. "Close your eyes, man. I have something for you."

"For me?"

"Yup. Close your eyes. *Trust* me!"

"Okay.

Walts shut his eyes and heard the garage door rise.

"Open your eyes."

Inside the garage were two brand new mountain bikes. Not just ordinary mountain bikes, either. They were top of the line carbon-framed bikes called Grizzlurs, named after Tony Grizz, a local biker who had won many races.

"You got me a...a...*Grizzlur*?"

"Yep."

"Dude, that's like a lot of...of...of..."

"Bodykredd. Yep!"

Blink. "Thanks, man! Too freaking-groovatron-ickly-sound!"

"We can ride in style now!"

"Wait." Walts pondered. "Dude, this isn't legal!"

"Huh?"

"According to the Lotto rules, you can't buy your friends anything material. I read it in your letter. Only family is allowed."

"What's the difference? I paid for us to play games and stuff yesterday. Right?"

"Yeah...but I think this is different, Jonas."

"Naw. It's all groove, Walts." Jonas waved him off. "Anyways, who cares? So what if it's against the rules?"

"*I* care. I might get sent to the Neutralization Center, too! I don't want to die!" Walts regretted saying that last word.

"Oh, do you think *I* do, Walts? Well, *I* don't! Think I have a choice in this matter? *I* don't! My destiny is inevitable: don't pass go, stop at the Neutralization Center on the way, get an all-expense paid trip floating in the river."

"Jonas, I'm just trying to say this is against the ru—"

"The hells with the rules, Walts!" Spittle flew from his lips. "I'm going to do what I want to do because my neck is on the line here! *Not* yours!"

"My neck will be on the line if I accept that bike, man!"

"Then don't accept it! *Leave!*"

"Jonas, you don't mean that..."

"Sure I do! Get the hells out of here, Walts! Go back home!"

"Jonas..."

"*Leave!*"

"Um...okay....guess I'll see ya..." Walts turned to leave. He had never seen Jonas act like this. Why would Jonas want him to die too? Wasn't fair. He couldn't help the fact his best friend won the Lotto. He didn't pluck his name out of a hat to choose the winner.

Walts had gotten no more than twenty feet from his best friend when he heard:

"Walts! Come back, man! I'm sorry," Jonas said. "This...this lotto crap has me messed up, you know? I feel like my brain has the symptoms of that drug called goose or something: paranoid; worried; panic attacks. Gods know why people take that crap to get high! Right? Anyways, this morning I got up early and thought it would be really cool if I went out and bought these bikes." Pause. "I was hoping you'd like the gift I bought you."

"I do, man. I'm just worried this is against the rules."

"Like I said: So *what?* I'm making sure I'm covering up my tracks. Trust me! The demi won't come after you, Walts, they only want me. Heck, I'm their latest addition to the game. I'm the *youngest* lotto winner in the colony's history!"

Walts wasn't convinced when the demi came to collect, they'd only grab Jonas. Walts feared he'd be taken, too. Walts felt like his head was on the chopping block. Hiding these thoughts, not wanting to fight with his best friend again, he painfully accepted the bike.

Soon, they were pedaling toward downtown.

"Anyways, Walts," Jonas said, "so *what* if it's against their stupid law? Big freaking deal! I'm doing what I want, and I'm going to make darn sure they won't come after you, dude! Before this day is over, you'll see what I mean!"

*The hells was Jonas talking about? Now he's saying he'll be able to protect me against the demi? His brain must really be mush!*

Walts followed Jonas and began to wonder if his best friend had cracked up.

***

The demi agent who sat behind the wheel in the Lincoln replica about a block down the street looked through his binoculars, grinned, said something to his partner in the passenger seat, and spoke a few words into his mini interface and drove off.

***

Peddling away on their bikes they cruised through a designated woodland area, only for bikers who wish to ride trails, per Slader Corp.

"Today will forever be an imprint on the following days to come, Walts!" Jonas shouted, looking back at Walts bringing up the rear.

Walts wondered what his friend had in store for him.

They spent a couple of hours on the trails. Climbing steep hills, racing down others, swerving to prevent smacking trees head-on. If they had honed the craft of a medium their neurotransmitters would have zoned into a residual ghostly scene of the ritual killing of a young girl. Not the case here, the boys cruised downtown and into an alley between tall brick buildings, stopping at a dead end.

Jonas said, "Remember landing on that planet after flying the *Vulturine?*" He slipped off his bike, put the kickstand down.

Walts reflected. "Yeah. I remember."

"Think of the scene when we climbed down into that hole."

Walts pondered. "Okay...got it."

Jonas looked to the left, to the right, making sure no one else was around and stepped beside a sewer lid. Tapping it three times with the toe of his shoe, it spiraled open, much like the walls inside Slader Corp.

"What *the?*" Walts blinked.

Jonas smiled. "Holographic camouflage, dude. Groove, huh?"

"Yeah. Wild!"

"Follow me!" Jonas stepped onto a metal ladder, began a descent.

"Um. Where are we going?"

Jonas chuckled. "You'll see..."

"Hey, what about our bikes?"

"Oh. Wait." Jonas stuck his hand out of the hole, holding a small device, and pressed a button.

The bikes vanished.

"What the heck happened to them?"

"When I bought the bikes," Jonas replied, "I wanted to make sure they never got stolen. The salesman sold me the latest thing on the market preventing thieves from stealing your bike called a Facade. It makes the bikes invisible."

"Whoa! Groovatronic! Bet it was costly!"

"Yup!" Jonas' voice echoed out of the hole. "C'mon! Follow me!"

Walts took two steps, a weird feeling coiled in his gut. *Where was Jonas taking him? This was really odd. What could possibly be underground for them to see?*

Jonas' head popped back out of the hole. "Hey! Don't just stand there, Walts, follow me!"

Not knowing what his friend was getting him into, Walts obeyed, descended.

The sewer cover spiraled shut.

***

The dark shoved back. Dome lights flicked on as soon as they climbed down into a long corridor. It reminded Walts of the game *Vector 5*, save for not standing in filthy water and witnessing black ooze, bugs, and a man's corpse.

"We only have to walk a hundred yards or so," Jonas said.

In their wake the dome lights began winking out behind them, allowing a lighted path for them to traipse forward.

A camera above revolved, aiming its eye at them.

"Um. Where are we going, dude. This is *really* creepy! What's up with that camera? Who's watching us?"

"You'll see. Fifty feet to go. Don't want to spoil the surprise."

A filthy-looking metal door sat in their path. Jonas reached out, wiped away the smudge of dirt and grime and flipped open a small, hidden door. Waves of multicolored lights collaged on a small screen. He bent down, wore a mask of various colors, stuck out his tongue. Words crawled across the screen:

*Transmitting.....*

*Transmitting.....*

*Transmitting.....*

*DNA recognition found:*

The door repeated the sewer lid's spiral entrance, revealing churning walls enclosing a bridge.

Walts blinked. "Oh. Wow."

"Remember, it's just like that part in the haunted house we went to last year. All you have to do is hold onto the handles, Walts. You'll be fine."

*Great. Didn't like* that *part of the haunted house.* "I sure hope so."

The boys stepped through, and the door spiraled shut. Gripping the rails of the bridge the room gave Walts vertigo, hitching a ride as the room revolved.

Once they were at its end – Walts more happy about it rather than his buddy – a section of the wall spiraled open, allowing them to step into a large room. The door shut, and a large rectangular light loomed over them.

"Where are we, Jonas? What *is* this place?"

Jonas grinned; he wiggled his eyebrows three times.

The wall in front of them spiraled open, and a tall man dressed in a dark attire stepped into the room. His dark hair tied back in a ponytail. To the boys he looked Special Forces, plucked right out of a military game on the Quasi-C.

He adjusted his rifle hung off his shoulder.

"Hello, Jonas and Walts. I am Daniel, a member of the rebellion. I welcome you to the Subterraneans."

\*\*\*

Bantering back and forth the rattling small robot and the long-haired guy had already used their Hula Hoop Orbitor to transfer Jamie's corpse, observing the gyration of the kid vanishing, relocating its final destination.

Fred wondered if Belinda at the BRD would allow those two boys to become ghosts. That would be the worst punishment they could receive. If they were shoved through the blood-red door he wondered what that dude called the Shepherd did with the souls he collected, especially all the people who used the msu's service to commit suicide.

"That was might nasty to see, wouldn't you agree, Fred?" Wilbur stood next to Fred.

"*I'll* say. Makes my death a little less gruesome after hearing those boys' necks break!" Fred said.

"Those schizos are nothing to mess with."

"Got that right! What the heck *are* those things, Wilbur? I remember always being told to obey curfew and stay clear of the schizos, but I never knew of anybody who actually knew *what* those creatures were; like they are afraid to say."

"Kid, if any mortal besides the demi and Maximus Slader do know, they would never admit it. Might get them a one way ticket to the Neutralization Center."

"I can see that."

"However, since they can't send any of us ghosts to the Neutralization Center, or have that guy over there, Moree Bund, use his suicide service on you, we ghosts have a pretty good idea what schizos are. Notice that they did not attack us?"

"Yeah. I kinda thought it was weird."

"They are only looking for flesh and blood."

Fred frowned. "Moree Bund was exempt, then?"

"He works for Maximus Slader. He's exempt."

Fred snorted. "That figures."

"Can you guess where he transfers the bodies?"

Fred shrugged.

"Slader Corp. That's where the schizos are birthed."

"Really?"

"As sure as I am standing on top of my own grave."

"Huh. What *are* they?"

"You really want to know?"

"Sure."

"This is what most of us ghosts think: schizos are dead lotto winners. When the demi comes to collect the winner, haul him or her off to the Neutralization Center, they murder them, and keep the corpse for schizos use. It's no surprise Maximus Slader isn't a good leader of the colony. Fred. A lot of people know this. His front as a 'savior of the people' is a lot of pig poop!"

"You know, I've had my doubts about the man for years, Wilbur. Even when I was a mortal and addicted to goose."

"You were addicted to drugs?"

"Yep."

Wilbur shook his head. "Don't tell me it was responsible for your death."

Fred sighed, ashamed to say: "It was."

"I told you not to tell me!" Chuckle. "Just kidding, kid...but seriously: I'm sorry to hear drugs messed your life up."

Fred snorted. "Oh, you just don't know, Wilbur. Guess we all learn from our mistakes in life."

"You're right. I'm not perfect, either, so don't be too hard on yourself."

"Okay."

"You know how Maximus presses the case about keeping the population leveled?"

"Yep."

"I don't have to mention to you how terrible that lotto business is – its *bad* stuff, Fred. You already know it is, so there's no need to explain much more about it other than the mention of the stupid game. They even have a special viewed on the televid where you can watch the winner wave to the viewers at home before stepping into the Neutralization Center."

"Unless you're Jake Velmer, running from the demi when they come to collect."

"Velmer was an idiot."

"Yes, he was. That, I do remember about the Velmer case through the haze of my goose addiction." Snort.

"Hard to miss that part of Ozarium's history, huh?"

Fred laughed.

"If I had intended on going out with a bang I wouldn't follow Velmer's lead. I'd have a better plan of action. Not exactly know *what* I'd do," he frowned, "but something! Have any idea what they did with Velmer's body after Chainsaw Freckles did its job?"

"No idea."

"I think they change the corpse into a robot."

"Come again?"

"I think they made him a schizos. Stuffed him with robot parts."

"You're serious?"

"Sure as I'm standing a foot atop my grave, Fred. I'm betting those two kids who were terrorizing you will become schizos too. Least, that's my take on it. I believe Slader uses those schizos to keep colonists from nosing around the Slader Corp building."

"Why would someone nose around Slader Corp?"

"To see what Mr. Slader is up to. A lot of people in the colony do not trust him. The rebellion has increased its membership in the past year. There's a war coming, Fred. Mark my words. People are waking up and seeing what is going on; not brain-washed into thinking they have such a grand life here. We are all brought up to follow what the Slader Corp provides us. Schools teach it. Our parents have taught us. Have you heard about those new machines called Best Friends Forever in production? They're supposed to replace teachers."

"No. Haven't heard that."

"Heard it from one of the other ghosts. Before long every colonist will have their own teaching machine, a BFF they call it. It'll force the kids to be home-schooled by a machine, blocking them from having human contact with other children. Ever notice how it's so normal for someone to commit suicide?"

"Sure."

"It's not normal. It's crazy! Who wants to die if in their right mind? I shouldn't have killed myself. This bizarre life drove me to it. One day I woke up, and it was like someone switched on a light in my head, and I realized this world is messed up!"

Fred agreed. He had these thoughts for many years, even goosed up. Sure, some of it was paranoia from the drug; the rest wasn't.

"You know, we're all taught to believe the rebellion are the bad guys. They are the good guys trying to bring a more peaceful environment to the colony."

"I agree."

"Maximus Slader is really an evil guy, Fred. Make sure you stay clear of him and the demi, even though now you are a ghost."

"I will. I never had any desire to be around them. Probably too stoned out of my mind to worry about much of anything for that matter." He chuckled.

"Make *damn* sure you keep away from them. You can always slip into the Wake and watch the world roll by, oblivious of them noticing your presence. That's the cool thing about being a ghost!"

"Um, speaking of the Wake, leaving the BRD I somehow missed stepping into the Wake. Not sure what I did wrong."

"That how you got mixed up with those two youngsters?"

"Yep. I stepped in someone's house. Smackdab in their living room of all things! I think I took too many steps."

Wilbur smiled. "It happens."

"The man of the house wasn't too happy with me."

"How so? Doesn't sound bad. Not your fault. You lost your way first time out of the barn."

"It is when they're anti-ghost members."

"Oh. I see." Wilbur rolled his eyes. "*Those* kind of people!"

"Yep."

"Guess those two kids nabbed you there, huh?"

"No. I didn't meet Bobby and Jamie until after I left the house. Man, the dude was pissed! He ordered me to leave, and I got the hells out! And when I realized the entire suburb of people hated ghosts, too, I was approached by Bobby and Jamie, offering me a ride out, not realizing I'd been tricked. They kidnapped me and placed me in that box called a mortonica for a while, then decided to bring me here."

"What a wild tale." Wilbur shook his head.

"Yeah, glad that one is behind me. So, what happened to you, Wilbur? You said you'd tell me about your past. You mentioned in so many words when you realized the colony had gone to pots. Were you given a choice at the BRD?"

"The BRD almost didn't give me a choice to come back as a ghost. They frown on the ones who commit suicide on their own – like me. Weird, huh? You can flag down Moree Bund and have him assist you in suicide, and it's all good and dandy, or take a stroll to the Neutralization Center and have the demi end your pathetic life, but don't you go taking your life in your *own* hands. Nope. Not a good thing to do, according to the BRD."

"That's wacked!"

"Tell me about it. Other ghosts who linger around here have had the same thing happen to them."

"Huh."

"Yeah, I goofed up. Decided to do it all on my own, Fred. Do it up right. Used my own suicide service, Wilbur's Instant Death." Chuckle. "Blew my brains out."

"Ouch!"

"Ouch is right! Hurt like *hell* before I died."

Fred winced.

"And don't ever let any of these other ghosts around here tell you they never felt it when the bullet broke through their skull and smashed through the back of their head. They'd be lying if they did. You don't die instantly, Fred. Nope. That'd be too easy. You feel a terrible pain like someone cracked you over the head with a sledge hammer. You have a headache worse than a migraine. Lying there, blood draining out of the hole in your head, you wish you could force your body to get up, grab your chainsaw out of the garage and use it to sever your head from your shoulders."

"That sounds really awful."

"Awful is not the word, buddy! And after dealing with the BRD, they decided to give me a choice. Go to Hell or go to the Wake."

"Sounds kinda like my case, screwing my life up, addicted to goose – like I already mentioned – wandering aimlessly around for two years high as a cloud. During that span of time can't remember much."

"Goose is nasty stuff."

"Yep. Found out first-hand!" Laugh.

"You overdose on it or something?"

"Nope. Worse. Walked in front of a transport while I was high as a carbon-fibered kite and *smack!* no more Fred."

"Ouch!"

"Tell me about it! Not the way I wanted to die."

"Surprised the BRD didn't send you to the hells for being a druggie."

"They *almost* did. Gave me two choices: Purgatory or the Wake."

"Well, sorry your return as a ghost hasn't gone so well. You should be fine now."

"Speaking of the Wake, how *does* a ghost stay in it once he enters?" Fred pressed.

"Oh, it's kind of a little trick you do with your noggin, kid. When you're ready to step into the Wake, just think about something nice: the giggle of a baby, bringing flowers to your lover, your favorite ice cream, anything that makes you happy. Got it?"

"Yeah. I think so."

"Now, once you're in the Wake, keep your mind focused on being in the ghostly world. Did you get to view the Wake at all?"

"For a second."

"Remember it being somewhat brighter inside? Like the world glowed?"

"Yep."

"Okay. Keep it in your mind about the glow, like a bright bulb. And, when you are ready to leave, think of something dark, like the dark color of a bouncer or like a, um, grave."

"I think I got it."

"Good. Don't worry, you'll be fine, kid. Takes some practice, but you'll be fine. A lot of mortals don't know this little ditty – obviously, because they aren't a ghost – however, we apparitions can lead them into the Wake if we want. Such as a relative."

"Is it dangerous?"

"Naw. Very safe."

"Huh."

"It's kind of a secret all us ghosts know about and never tell mortals. If we did, there would be problems."

"How so?"

"It seems that the ghostly world of the Wake think that mortals would try and use it to claim stake; like those stupid Paranormal Laws the BRD presses."

"I see."

"I think if Maximus Slader and the demi could control it, they'd find a sure way of screwing things up somehow."

"I agree with you. From what I can gather already, the Wake is a kind of freedom for ghosts to roam about."

"Exactly. And what's better, I've heard of ghosts not obeying the Paranormal Laws, staying inside the Wake where mortals cannot see them, and hide out in houses."

"Mortals don't hear them?"

"Not if they do things quietly."

"Interesting…might have to think about doing that in case I don't find a place to stay."

"Be very careful if you do, okay? The BRD has insurgents that keep things running normally, checking up on the ghostly world every so often."

"Really? Insurgents?" Fred had a picture of a group of dark figures carrying scythes, keeping things controlled in the Wake. "I'll…uh…sure keep that in mind, Wilbur. Hey, know any empty houses I could haunt? I'm not crazy about stumbling into one which is already inhabited with mortals." It seemed so odd for him to say those last three words, since mortality had been his previous life.

Wilbur pondered, scratched his nose. "There's a house I do know of when I was of flesh and blood. Old place, been around for years. Really have no idea of its history. If you take that street over there," he motioned, "and take a left on Harris Street, follow it down to the river, you'll see an old abandoned house. The place could be empty of ghosts. Not real sure, though. Be careful."

"Will do. Sounds like a plan."

"Worst case scenario, you'll run into a ghost down there, end up either getting along with him or her, or have to relocate."

"I'll give it a shot. Thanks."

"You're more than welcome to hang around here. Most of the folks here are nice. We stay away from Fouk's tomb. Very far."

"I appreciate the invite, Wilbur, but I think I'll check out that house you spoke of." Hanging out in a cemetery, whether being a ghost or not, gave him the creeps. "Why do you hang out here instead of in the Wake?"

"I stay around visiting friends of the past. A lot of them congregate here instead of dealing with trying to haunt houses, dealing with mortals, or roam in the Wake. Everybody has their pet peeve, you know."

"Right. Were you ever married? Could you go back and see your wife?"

"You kidding?" Wilbur snorted. "She was a piece of work! We hardly ever got along; only stayed married for the kiddos. As soon as I died a few years ago that woman was already on her interface, finding out how much my life insurance policy was worth from the insurance agent. She wanted to cash it in and find herself another schmuck to marry and ruin *his* life. That's her style, Fred. Stupid woman! That's why I left my son ninety percent of my insurance money and my wife the ten percent, just enough cred to bury me." Smile.

"Wow!"

"And I'll tell you something else, she was my *second* wife. My first wife of thirty years of marriage passed fifteen years ago from some obscure illness called the scourge. I've yet to locate her ghost. She must have crossed into The Great Beyond."

"Scourge? Never heard of it."

"Bad stuff, Fred. Be glad you didn't die from it. I did get a visit from my wife after she passed, appearing as a ghost, letting me know it was okay if I wanted to find someone else to spend the rest of my life with. Hells, I was all broken up. I did not want to think about someone else! Then, Julie came into my life. Wish I could say it was a good thing." Pause. "Hell, looking back, if I had played my cards right, died with Ginny, not committing suicide years later, I'd already been with her."

"Don't beat yourself up. You can't predict the future, Wilbur. Those ten years could have been glorious."

"*Coulda been* is the right word for it." Snort. "You're right, though."

Wilbur gave Fred an odd look.

"What? Did I say something wrong?"

"Nope. You're a good guy, Fred. You just took a wrong turn in life." He patted Fred's shoulder. "Thanks, kid. 'Preciate your kind words. Always been good to people, ya know, just got a little side-tracked in my past life. Kinda like you making some bad choices, I suppose."

"It happens."

"Think I miss my Ginny more and more these days. Guess I'll never see her again."

"You never know. Think positive, Wilbur. Who knows, the BRD might come to you one day and allow you to cross over into The Great Beyond. If the only terrible thing you did was commit suicide, someone in the offices of the BRD might give you another chance."

Wilbur scratched his head. "The BRD does review cases every

so often, though. Maybe there's a chance for me." Smile. "Thanks again for the kind words, my friend. Let's hope it'll happen. Times have changed, never thought I'd be wandering around this planet as a ghost."

Fred chuckled. "Me neither. Weird world we are in, Wilbur."

"I second *that*, my friend. I wonder what the world was like before the Shift."

"No idea. Could have been better."

"Or worse."

"True. Well, might see you around some time, Wilbur."

They shook hands.

"Take it easy."

"You too, Fred! If you pass by, don't be a stranger, come visit me."

Fred grinned, waved bye and strolled out of the cemetery, noticing other ghosts materializing out of the air, drifting around the graves, conversing with one another.

A few waved at him; he returned the gesture.

Fred drifted down Harris Street, located the house by the river. Oddly out of place in Ozarium because most of the colony saturated itself in new homes and buildings, the structure's bones wore old skin. Oppressive, it loomed over Fred. A chill tapped him on his ghostly spine.

If there were ghostly tenants, he hoped he'd get along with them. If not, he'd have to find another place to haunt.

\*\*\*

Walts gasped.

*Subterraneans? Um…this didn't sound good! What the heck was Jonas getting me into? This was the surprise? The Subterraneans? Our gods riding on the backs of purple colored gnomes with a nervous twitch!*

*This was the home of the rebellion that fought against the demi laws! They were considered extremely dangerous and caused a lot of trouble!*

Walts knew there was no way he could just do a right-faced turn and get the hells out of this place. Nope. Not gonna happen that easy. He feared they might shoot him in the back for trying to run. Walts had no choice in the matter, he had to keep his mouth shut, go with the flow.

Daniel escorted Walts and Jonas to the leader of the rebellion. The woman sitting in the leather chair wore the same attire as the guy with the rifle.

"Our guests, Madam Case," Daniel introduced.

"Thank you, Daniel. Welcome to our home, young gentlemen." She wiped a strand of her long red hair from in front of her eyes, smiled. "Which one of you is Jonas?"

Jonas raised his hand.

"You wish to be trained to fight, child?"

"Yes, ma'am."

*Uh. What? Fight? Fight? Was he nuts?*

*What was Jonas thinking? Jonas was still a kid who liked to ride bikes and play games and eat pizza and eat Bork Burgers! This surprise was not a good surprise! It was a shock! Fear leeched onto his spine. Who did Jonas intend on fighting? Surely not like the rebellion, against the —*

"...demi? You wish to fight them as we do, child?" Madam Case asked.

"Yes," Jonas nodded.

Walts gasped.

"I'm sure you have no idea when the demi will come and collect your flesh. That is something unforeseen. But you are here where it is safe."

"I've been breaking some rules lately, madam Case; might've sped up the process."

Walts frowned. *No doubt he sure as hells did break some rules. He bought me that new bike. It probably did speed up the process of the demi coming after him!*

"Breaking the rules will indeed speed up the process of the demi coming to collect your flesh, Jonas. Do you know what they do to the winners? Have any idea?"

"All I know is the winners are escorted to the Neutralization Center."

"Correct. Slader Corp spends the cred for the deceased, so they can have a nice funeral; however, not very many people know they harvest the winner's brains by sending them through what Maximus Slader calls a TransmoG, a transfiguration, converting them into robots, wiring their brains to new, infection-free, eternal robotic shells. Those things called the schizos moving around during the night are the results of the dead winners. Perhaps others fallen victim to Slader Corp, too; such as the homeless. The schizos are sentinels, super heterodynes for the demi and for Maximus Slader. Our leader has found a way of not only controlling people's lives by keeping the population to a minimum, but in addition, using brains of the dead to run robots, keeping a voyeurism on the residents of the colony – another way for Slader to control the human population.

"If a colonist does not take heed against curfew, they are never seen again," Case explained. "Do you boys know that? No? I am not surprised. This secret is never leaked to the public. If someone vanishes after curfew, the demi will imply they ran off or some other lame excuse. Believe me, the schizos are more dangerous than anything you boys have ever heard of.

"Now, I want you two to know all of us down here admire the ones who come to us to rebel against the demi. It is admirable. It takes a lot of courage for one to indulge in such an act. Maximus Slader's organization needs to be stopped! Maximus Slader is *not* a good man. Never was! My people have uncovered many things about Slader that would raise the hairs on the back of your necks, boys; make you realize what horrors he has done to people, besides the transfigurations. One day he will be dealt with by a bullet in the head. However," she cleared her throat, "I am getting ahead of myself... rambling ...I am sorry.

"Jonas, you are here to learn how to fight to the death against a regime which steals away the lives of the innocent. Slader is wrong in doing so. We, the rebellion, are trying to change this. I want to personally thank you for wanting to fight back, for making a stand for what is right. During the pre-Shift era, the lotto was a great thing. One could win tons of cred and live out their lives happy, knowing an organization like the demi would not be responsible for their death. These days, it has veered greatly from the path of happiness. The colony is a very demented place, boys, thanks to Maximus Slader.

"Jonas, you ready to endure suicide under our rules, correct?"
"Yes, ma'am."
*Suicide?* Walts thought. Jonas is committing *suicide??*
*I'm a goner anyway, Walts....*Jonas' words reminded Walts.

"Good." Madam Case smiled. "I have arranged for Daniel, here," a wave of her hand, "to get you prepped and ready. Listen to everything he has to say. Pay close attention to his instructions, understand?"

"Yes, ma'am."

*I want out of here!* Jonas wanted to go out with a bang all right, like Jake Velmer, and he was obviously planning on taking him along for the ride! Not good! Not good at all! He had no interest of being part of this! He wanted to detach himself and climb back to the surface.

Walts turned to leave, hoping he could find a door out of this room and –

Daniel turned, placed two fingers on his right ear, gave it light tap. "Yes?" His eyes widened. "Thank you." He faced Case. "Ma'am. The demi has found us."

Case's eyes widened. "How?"

"I do not know, ma'am."

She glanced at the young visitors. Scowled. "Screen. Up."

Part of the wall vanished, and a wide screen appeared. Three demi agents stood in the alley holding rail guns where Walts and Jonas had been only minutes before. One held a small ground penetrating radar in his free hand, scanning the ground.

"Has the virus been engaged?" Case asked.

"Yes ma'am," Daniel replied.

The demi using the radar stopped, looked down at the small screen on the device. No sound came from the speakers on the screen, but it didn't take an idiot to know the frustration on the demi's face and what he spat from his lips while shaking the radar, pressing buttons.

"That should stop them," Case said. "Our virus has infected their machine. It will erase the location of the sewer door and any footsteps or handprints you boys left behind." She pointed a finger at Walts and Jonas. "The demi may have some really technical toys, but our computer viruses have always worked."

Case gave the boys a cold look. "You two realize you have broken a major demi rule, never come in contact with the rebellion. That in itself is suicide! Since the time we trained Jack Velmer, the demi has taken precautions and set up sentries around the town, keeping a close eye on folks. That is why we had intended on doing things differently with your situation, Jonas." Pause. "However," she curled her bottom lip, "perhaps they have been keeping an eye on *you*, Jonas."

"I...h-haven't noticed them," Jonas said.

"Maybe you haven't. Maybe they've bugged your person somehow, or have had someone following you."

"Don't think so."

"You do not *think?* Child, you should have taken precautions."

"Precautions? How was I to know?"

"Yeah! How was he to know if they have been watching us?"

Walts said.

"You should have been keeping an eye over your shoulder at all times since winning the lotto. You should have been aware, Jonas – as well as you, Walts, if you have been with him when he has spent his cred."

"How were we to know this would happen? We don't read minds, Madam Case!" Walts ran defense.

Daniel unslung his rifle and Walts gasped.

"Do not get smart with me, young man!" Case said. "That is not wise! Unfortunately for you and Jonas it changes our plans." Case took a deep breath. "I must ask and – I must warn you – tell me the truth, or I will shoot you both where you stand." She reached behind the chair and pulled free an automated rail gun.

Daniel trained his rifle on the boys.

Walts took a step back.

Case sucked in a breath. "Are you and your friend working for the demi? Yes or *no*. Are you spies? Tell me the truth or so help me I'll cut you down," the words rolled off her tongue.

"N-No!" Jonas pleaded. "We're not working for them!"

"He's right! We're not! Why would we do that?" Walts added. "Why would we lead them to you?"

Case's eyes were slits. Her lips pursed. "To infiltrate our society of rebels, child. We hardly trust anyone. Anyone who wishes to become part of our group has their background researched thoroughly. We have done that in both your cases."

Thoughts of someone poking around in Walts' past gave him a bad feeling. *Did they know about the lie he told to his parents? Did they know about his bad grade he received that year in math class?* "We aren't spies!" Walts said.

"How do I know the demi has not paid you boys a visit this morning: threaten your family's life, Walts; maybe decided to not give you a trip to Neutralization Center, but keep the lotto cred, turning you against us?"

"The demi has not visited us!" Walts said.

"Being that you, Jonas, are the youngest lotto winner in the colony's history and have given us a hefty sum of cred to fill the organization's account, there's an ounce of trust which I should feel… on the other hand, I am not so sure to allow you a pass on this situation. I am still not convinced you are on the side of Slader Corp and have infiltrated our home. Good thing, is you have not set your sights on the entirety of our environment in the Subterraneans, since we've kept you in this small room." Pause; she cleared her throat. "I'm sorry but you leave me no choice, boys, we'll have to pass judgment once we probe your brain using Swipe."

*Swipe?* Walts bowels twitched, almost let go.

"Why would we lie to you, Madam Case?" Jonas asked.

"To gain access in our underground location and disrupt what freedom we have, Jonas. We have dealt with intruders before. We have not left one sliver of a trace of them, either." Not wavering from the stare she gave the boys, she added: "Daniel, escort them to the interrogation room and get the probe ready. I'll be there in a few. I need to figure out what I should do about our other problem in the alley."

On the screen, the demi agents had not left, being the cockroaches they were.

"Yes ma'am," Daniel replied.

"You gotta believe us!" Jonas cried. "We aren't part of the demi! We don't work for them!"

"That is yet to be seen using Swipe, Jonas," Case added. "Get these intruders away from my sight, Daniel."

"Yes ma'am."

The wall behind Daniel spiraled open and Daniel escorted Walts and Jonas at gunpoint down the hall and into a large room splashed with white walls. A wooden table and two chairs sat in the middle of the room. A basketball-shaped robot hovered in the corner.

"Robot, if these two try and escape…kill them." Daniel scowled at the boys as he stepped out and the door spiraled shut.

A gun barrel slid out of the center of the robot with a click.

"What the heck are we gonna do *now*, Jonas?" Walts asked. "They think we work for the demi! We need to get outta this place, Jonas!"

"I don't know what to do!" Jonas huffed, shook his head, threw his hands up. "This wasn't my intention. At. *All!* Can't believe it went all cadaver! I transferred a lot of Bodykredd to Case's account before we got here. That should have meant *something* for her to trust us! Hells, I got nothing to lose! Why would I lead the demi here? Why would I do something like that and get you in a mess? You're my best friend, Walts!" Jonas looked at Walts. "Wasn't s'pose to end like this. My plans were to make sure the rebellion was going to take good care of you while I strapped on a suit filled with explosives, and once the demi delivered me to Maximus Slader himself, I was going to explode." Chuckle. "Go right out of this life with a bang, dude! Right out of this life and into The Great Beyond! Wouldn't that be *so cool?* Better than holing myself up in my house or somewhere and fight to the death, huh? Be a Velmer all over again! Ha!"

"No! Not cool, dude! You really *were* going out with a bang? Geez!"

"Yup! And taking Slader with me!"

"I can't believe this! What, are you the Jonas I know? The one who's been my best friend for years?"

Jonas opened his mouth to say something, hesitated, froze up.

Walts blinked. *What the hells?* "Jonas? you okay?"

Jonas blinked back a few twitches of his eyes. A sly grin spread under his nose. "Sure, Walts. I'm your *best* friend. Always have been." He cocked his head. "Don't you believe me?" His voice, but not an effective statement.

Walts felt a chill along his spine. Something wasn't right. He took a step back.

"I've *always* been your best friend for life, Walts. We are blood brothers until the end, my friend. Groovy, huh?"

Walts took another retreat.

"We are locked together, you and I, Walts." Jonas' blue eyes materialized into a deuce of tiny TV screens flaked with snow and static.

"W-What the heck is going on? Y-You're not Jonas!"

"Sure I am…. Just not the Jonas you know," a different voice overrode Jonas'. "His body has already been processed and has transfigured, developed into this end result. I am a new improved Jonas," the monotone voice explained. "*I* led the demi here. *I* am a spy. We have been planning on infiltrating the rebellion's hideout for quite a while. Jonas' husk has been our pass inside the Subterraneans. Walts, we are quite sorry, you have become a casualty in war. Unfortunately you are in the wrong place at the wrong time."

"*What?* I didn't want this!"

"Not to worry, Walts, it'll all be over soon." Jonas' and the monotone voice wrapped together as one: "We are sorry, Walts. It is what it is. But, look at it this way, you are scheduled for a TransmoG very soon. A vast improvement to your flesh."

Walts gasped. *I don't wish to be a robot! I don't want to end up what they did to my best friend!*

Part of the wall spiraled open. Daniel and Madam Case stood there. Daniel saw Jonas' eyes and immediately unslung his rifle. "A TransmoG!"

The Jonas-copy grinned. "Yup!"

Before Daniel could pull the trigger, the Jonas-copy moved lightning-quick, snatched the barrel out of Daniel's hand, swung it around, making a bone-crunching connect to the side of the rebel's face.

Madam Case rocketed off down a corridor, slipping into a

spiraled opening. Bullets chewed into the wall from the Jonas-thing firing a round of bullets using Daniel's rifle.

Not giving the basket-ball sized robot a chance to use its weapon the Jonas-copy swiveled around and blasted it, sending it crashing against the wall, leaving a dent, then smacking the floor with a loud *gong!*

The Jonas-copy faced Walts. "Let's take a ride, shall we?"

Walts didn't budge.

"I said we are taking a *ride*, Walts! Get moving out into the hall, now!" He aimed the long barrel at Walts' face.

Walts obeyed and stepped over Daniel's leaking skull.

A siren screamed, reverberating off the corridor. Strobe lights washed the hall red.

"Jonas! Drop the weapon!" One of the rebellion, this one clothed in dark military attire and a dark helmet, slipped from a spiraled-open patch in the wall, stood not ten feet away. Three others stood behind him.

Each aimed their rifles.

The Jonas-copy guffawed, pulled the trigger.

Walts dropped on the floor face-down and held his hands over his head.

The Jonas-copy's two shots drilled through the throat of the guard demanding the unit to drop the weapon, punching a hole through the helmet's visor of the one directly behind, dropping both figures to the floor. The third guard pulled the trigger, chewing off a sliver of material and flesh from the Jonas-copy's shoulder.

It did nothing to abate the Jonas-copy's terror.

The copy wasted not a second, shooting the man in the gut, knocking him off his feet.

A fourth member of the rebellion appeared and fired a crossbow. Twin lasers morphed the place of arrows as they sailed through the air, slamming into the Jonas-copy's face, shaving flesh off with a burn, exposing hidden wires and metal, the face of the automaton.

Hardly fazed by the attack, the lens of a cyclopean-eye shaded with bright yellow focused, aimed the rifle, layered its enemy's flesh with oozing red pockets until the body crashed the floor.

The Jonas-copy reached down and picked up Walts around the throat. A sideburn of synthetic flesh stretched from the scalp left to mask the Jonas-copy flapped against its metal cheek. "We are to leave *now!*" The vocals had changed into a single monotone voice, bereft of the old Jonas.

Walts stumbled down a long hall with a shove from his kidnapper, the wailing siren adding to the red strobe lights splashing the two.

***

Sarah found a blanket and wrapped it around Benny, snugging him against her breast as she stepped out into the hallway. Left or right. All appeared similar. She had no idea which way to go. Stuck in a labyrinth, no idea where the exit lay.

Deciding on a backtrack, extra cautious, she peeked through one of the two windows of the double doors, noticed the nurse's station across from her room still vacant; then she slipped through, passed her room, arriving at a T in the hallway. A large sign on the wall depicted OFFICES THIS WAY with a red scrolling arrow indicating it to the left; a yellow scrolling arrow pointed right for the LANDING PAD.

Sarah headed right. Stepping though a door, her heart leaped when she saw her ticket to escape. Six bouncers sat in a row; not a hint of anyone around. She hurried over to one, slipped inside, laid Benny on the passenger seat.

He cooed at her.

*My baby boy!*

She pushed the button, firing up the bouncer's Wankel-

McMeyer turbine engine. As she lifted off the landing pad, a large door in the ceiling automatically slid open, the sky gave her an invite to freedom.

***

Four demi agents walked across the landing pad, gazed into the sky. For a quicker communication with each other and able to speak with Central where their commanding officer was located, agents used HeadKase, allowing telepathic signals.

« Central. » one agent transmitted, «The jar has crashed onto the floor; the soul has escaped. I repeat: The jar has crashed onto the floor; the soul has escaped. »

***

Sirens chased Walts and the Jonas-copy.

"Hang a left. That's right. Keep moving, Walts." the Jonas-copy instructed.

"Where are we g–" Walts tried to ask.

"Hush! Refrain from your questions. *Move!*"

Walts snapped his mouth shut and ran.

"Turn left at this junction."

Walts would have lost his balance, if not for slip-resistant black strips on a descending ramp into an underground hanger. Bouncers and halftracks sat in rows of two.

"Get in this bouncer. Yep. Right there! Get in the back." Jonas-copy pointed a finger. "If you try to escape you'll have a skull that leaks brain matter. Clear?"

Walts nodded, climbed inside.

The Jonas-copy pushed a few buttons on the wall. The ceiling squeaked, slid open. Sunlight leaked through the expanding gap.

The Jonas-thing slipped into the driver's side and hit a button, causing the Wankel-McMeyer's to rumble.

They blasted into the sky.

***

Sarah did not follow the traffic laws of SkyDrive, growing tired of hearing the recorded male voice through the Bouncer's speakers, a consistent reminder she drove beyond the maximum speed limit, driving reckless and should be following the correct traffic pattern, no passing, keeping in formation behind other drivers. She would be cited if she did not stop.

Safety features implemented for someone *not* wanted by the demi.

*Didn't apply to her, so the hells with the demi!*

She didn't have to worry about listening to the warnings very long before it cut-off and two large metal spheres appeared behind her, glowing their red and blues.

*Damn! Narks!*

"Pull over on the nearest rooftop, Ms. Lans. It is for your safety." One of the narks addressed in its monotone voice, flanked on her right side; the other appeared on her left.

*Hells with them!*

She had her baby boy. All she needed. No doubt Kentil was dead. Sure, the doctor said she'd see him. Probably in the same freaking coffin they had planned to put her in.

She wiped away tears.

*Kentil…*

Benny cooed, giggled.

"Don't worry, momma's here. Everything'll be all right," Sarah could not wrap her mind around the fact her baby was alive. Still alive. Still breathing. She had truly believed they had murdered him.

One of the narks bumped the side of the bouncer, jostling it out of traffic pattern, knocking Sarah back to the present. She fought with the steering wheel, regained control of the craft.

"Land on the nearest rooftop, Ms. Lans. This is for your own safety. Do this *immediately*."

She hit the thrust reverser, slowed the craft, nose-dived toward a rooftop, and when the narks braked, closing in behind her, she hit the red TURBO button and blasted off, careening around the nearest building, zipping through a wide gap in between two buildings, and shot toward the river, barely kissing the side of another Bouncer taking flight from its landing pad.

\*\*\*

"Whoa! That was close!" Walts cried.

Walts watched as the Jonas-copy drove the bouncer like an expert, escaping a close call with the lady driving the other bouncer. Two narcs minutes behind, speeding after her.

The Jonas-copy slipped the bouncer into traffic, slowed down, pulled out a hand-held device, pressed a red button.

"Where are you taking me?" Walts asked.

"You will see," the Jonas-copy faced forward. "I've jammed the rebellion's nose from sniffing us out." He wiggled the device.

"What happened to my friend?"

The Jonas-copy did not answer.

"What happened to the real Jonas? When did they come for him?"

The Jonas-copy ignored Walts.

"When did the demi come for him? Answer me! I deserve to know! Jonas was my best friend!"

The cyclopean eye swiveled, focused on Walts. "Last night the demi broke protocol, given the order from Maximus Slader himself, and came to get Jonas after you last saw him. We transfigured your friend into what you now see. There were no problems with Jonas' parents, either. They had been taken care of long before we took your friend. They, like many others, are part of Slader Corp. They were reborn as a TransmoG and placed back on the street as schizos. Very soon everyone in the colony will be lotto winners and will undergo TransmoG, their human husks scraped clean of organs, replaced with robotic parts, wiring their brains to a new, infection-free, eternal robotic shell."

"You mean, turning *everyone* into robots?"

"Correct. It is a good way to keep the population leveled, Walts. It is a solution to the colony's problems. There will never be a worry of the increase of population, illnesses, disease, especially the people who go against the reproduction rules, having children without being approved. Everyone will be happier in this new found colony, thanks to Maximus Slader. This place will become a better place to live."

Walts was speechless.

"Don't you want to live forever, Walts? Don't you want to be immortal?"

"No! I want to continue to eat pizza and play the Quasi-C and grow up and go to college and work on things like my dad! I do not wish to be a robot!"

The Jonas-copy glanced at Walts. "That is good. You *should* want to be like your father. His circuits are burning to see you, as well as your mother's."

"What? What do you mean?"

"A half an hour after you left the house this morning we collected their bodies. They did not want to come quietly, but in the end they understood. Their transfiguration should be completed by now."

Horrid realization slammed into Walts. They had stolen away his mom and dad. He loved them. Enraged, he spat "NOOOO!!" unstrapping his seatbelt, grabbing hold of the Jonas-copy's head, covering the yellow eye, causing the robot's hands to jerk the wheel of the bouncer and hit the one next to them, sending it into a spin, almost crashing into a nearby building.

Jonas-copy's and Walts' bouncer's nose whipped downward, the tail-end following suit, scraping the undercarriage of another craft passing over.

The Jonas-copy managed to peel Walts off, using the other hand to shove him backward into the seat. An attempt to take control of the bouncer ended in failure as it flipped upside down, spiraling downward.

Walts' body rebounded off the ceiling.

The Jonas-copy fought to control the bouncer, but seeming to have a mind of its own, plummeted toward an old abandoned house by the river.

*** 

Riddled with panic Sarah's gut tightened, bringing a throb of pain from her wound as she swerved to miss the bouncer popping out of the building in front of her.

*Jumping freaking rain gods on the beach!*

Her bouncer bumped against a concrete pillar sticking off the roof of a building, setting her into a spin.

She wrenched the wheel, gods-know-how but regained control, headed toward the river.

The narks zipped by in pursuit.

*** 

Fred drifted through the front door of the house by the river.

The old place gave him a creepy feeling.

*Vacant of ghosts or not? Guess I'll find out soon enough.*

Deep holes depicted small trenches in the walls above a huge staircase. Only one picture hung on the wall, a man and a woman, both blank-faced, as if their happiness had been shaved away. On his right, thick dust sat on covers shrouded over furniture in what Fred took for the living room. Through an archway exposed a dining area. Spider webs decorated a huge chandelier directly above Fred's head. A hallway trailed off into another part of the house.

Fred decided to head upstairs, have a look around. After floating up to the first floor two ghostly heads materialized.

The same couple inside the frame.

"May we help you with something?" the man asked as his shape unraveled, a cascade of a full-bodied apparition. Arms behind his back, he wore an older attire, perhaps pre-Shift.

The woman's form repeated her partner's.

"Just trying to find a place to crash," Fred replied.

A cock of the head. "Not so sure it will be *here*. You should leave. There is no trespassing upon these premises. Correct, my darling?"

"Yes, my love."

Down the hall, a moan.

Fred frowned. "What the heck was th–"

"That is not your concern. You must leave *now*. My wife will show you to the door," he gestured with an open palm.

"Um…sure I cannot stay?" a curiosity tugged at Fred. *What or who was down the hall?*

Another moan slipped out into the hall.

"Please, if you will, leave this house," the man insisted. "Margret, please escort the young man out."

"Yes, my love." She gazed at Fred. "Come with me," a curl of her long finger, gesturing Fred back down the steps.

Fred obeyed. He didn't want any trouble. He already had enough of it from those two kids kidnapping and sticking him in that contraption. Halfway down, the woman stopped and cocked her head to the side. She closed her eyes. Sniffed the air. "Phillip, warm flesh and blood are close by. I feel their mortal presence coming."

Fred blinked. *Ghosts that could smell a mortal's presence? Who were these two?*

Standing on the top step, a smile crested under Phillip's pointy nose. "Well," he rubbed his hands together. "Why don't you stay, my good man. Perhaps we *should* welcome your presence, refigure your situation. There is so much we can show you. We may be hosting a party for a couple of mortals. They are an interesting breed of creatures. Margret, please show this man to his r–"

*Boom!*

Dust flakes showered, seeming as if the entire house shook.

"What the hells was *that?*" Phillip spat.

***

Ray Manisquaski's mini interface bleeped. A blonde-haired kid appeared on the small screen.

"Ray! Gotta a lead for ya, man!"

"Oh, yeah? What is it?"

"You know that rumor about a kid winning the lotto?"

"Yeah. I remember hearing about it. There's a running bet here in the news room to see if it's true or not."

"Well, better get your Bodykredd ready to download the winning pot! It's true! An eleven year-old kid won!"

Ray perked up.

"Don't know how, or if there was a glitch in the system, but he's the winner! Plus, I got a tip the kid and his friend ran off to where the rebellion is hiding out. The kid wanted to be trained to fight against the demi."

"Really? Interesting…could be another Velmer reprise."

"Yep. But I bet this'll end a lot different. The kid never got the chance to be taught *how* to fire a gun."

"Sure about that?"

"As sure as I know I'm gonna get good cred from you, giving away this tip." Smile, a few missing teeth from the upper palate.

"If this is true, you'll get the cred; otherwise, no cred will leave my flesh."

"What? I've not let you down before, Ray! You know me better than that!"

Scotty never faltered with any news tips. But Ray enjoyed watching the guy squirm. Got a kick out of it. He knew the kid hungered for his goose fix. Ray felt like a drug pusher knowing Scotty could turn to him to cred his addiction. Scotty had no other job. No employer would hire a gooser.

"I know you enough you'd leak this tip to Channel 5's news anchor Melissa Parks, if the money was better."

"Why would I do *that*? You're a buddy of mine, Ray!"

*Buddy?* Snort. *Not quite! Scotty really was a junkie!* "Yeah, well, with a lot of cred involved, someone addicted to goose like yourself, friends can change quickly. Look at how past lotto winners have had to deal with things. Old friends come out of the cracks, telling 'em how great it is to see them again, wanting some cred to buy stuff."

"C'mon, Ray! That's different! I never get that much money from you handing over my leads! Anyways, my connection to Ms. Parks isn't on…um…very good terms."

Ray chuckled. "Not since you leaked bad information to her."

"Ray…You *told* me to do that! You said you wanted to share the wealth and help another reporter out!"

Ray frowned, tapped his lips with his finger. "Oh. That's right. Forgot it was my idea." Sly grin.

"Pulling that prank got me in a lot of hot water, Ray! You used me! Now I can't go to no one else!"

"Sorry about that, buddy."

Snort. "Bet you are."

"Huh? Say something, Scotty? I think your signal is fading. Getting a bad connection here."

"Oh, yeah? Go ahead, Ray. Cut me off, and you'll never get this news! I haven't told you all I know yet! Your fans will wonder why you don't have this news lead, one of the best, while the other stations will send out their reporters to stand in front of the vidcam and smile and tell the colony all about the youngest lotto winner and where he is right now. You'll be a bouncer after burn." He laughed.

*Damnit!* Sigh "Okay, Scotty...you've made your point."

"And you might get in trouble with your boss, Gerald. I know you two aren't exactly on good terms—"

"No. We're not."

"— since you messed around with his wife and all. Smart thing to do Ray." Sniff. "*Really* smart! Lucky you are a famous reporter and Gerald doesn't want to fire you."

"Scotty, you've made your point. Give me the info about the lotto w—"

"*Plus*, I could leak it out to the colony I've seen you dressed up like a homeless person to get demi cheese and —"

"*Scotty! I said you've made your point!*"

Scotty chuckled. "Not so funny when the shoe is on the other foot, huh, Ray?"

Ray's face flushed red.

"All right," Scotty said, "enough badgering each other. I'm sending the details to your inbox; got a picture of the kid, too."

"Awesome. I'm sending the cred to your Bodykredd via wi-fi. Let me know you received it."

Three seconds went by before the exchange went through. "Got it, Ray, thanks."

"Thanks for the heads-up, Scotty."

"Welcome."

Ray went to cut the transmission, stopped. "You need to kick that goose addiction one day, Scotty. It's bad for you."

Scotty grinned. "All those goose-filled nanobots you lay on your wrist, thousands of them melting into your vein, and the high afterward? Not gonna happen, Ray. You should give it a try. Come on over to our side for once." A cheese, missing teeth.

"Uhhhh ...no. You can have that crap. Not my style. Not into psychedelic drugs that'll kill brain cells."

"You'd see things in a different way, man. Goose is the way to go! Weird things'll step out of the wall and speak to you; they'll tell ya the secrets of life!"

"I think I already have the secret to my life figured out, Scotty, thank you very much. Besides, I already have that problem with weird things speaking to me, Scotty."

"Huh? What are you talking about?"

"Weird faces talking out of interfaces."

"Huh?"

"Weird faces blabbing about stupidity."

"What are you talking about, Ray?"

"Weird freaks on goose."

"Huh?"

You, dumbass!"

"Hey! That ain't ni– "

Ray severed connection, laughing. "No. It's not nice, Scotty, but its sure fun messing with you!" He swiped his finger across his Recog, tapped the GriddMail icon, opened his inbox. Jonas' school picture popped up and his history written below: his birthdate; where he lived; his parents'; his relatives; his hobbies; his school grades on his holocards; friends he hung with.

Walts' picture popped up.

Scotty added a note: The boys were headed to Slader Corp.

Ray got up and his mini interface bleeped. Scotty texted Ray.

✌Ray, the kids are in a bouncer spinning out of control, headed toward the old house by the river of the dead.

Thanks.

Ray grinned. *Well. Here we go again.*

\*\*\*

Benny cooed.

"Shhh! Momma's here. We're gonna get out of this city."

Narks appeared in the rearview mirror. "Land your Bouncer, Ms. Lans. Things will go easier if you do. This is your *last* warning."

*Hells with them! She had her baby and they were out of this crazy colony!*

The old abandoned house sitting alongside the river came into view. Sarah punched the accelerator. "Almost out of the colony! Hang on tight, Benny!" Sarah had never been out of Ozarium. Never had stepped foot out of the colony. Always forbidden by Slader Corp, the corporation cautioned colonists they would have a death wish if they crossed the river. The lands beyond were said to be filled with danger. Colonists would be out of the safety of the demi.

Sarah had extinguished every opportunity of safety from the demi. She had acquired a fugitive status. Staying in Ozarium would be her death wish. If the narks caught her they'd give her an escort to the Neutralization Center.

At this point she had nothing to lose.

She glanced in the mirror.

The narks had mysteriously vanished.

*The hells did they go? Had they given up the chase?*

*Riight...*

Another glance over her shoulder. Not one nark in sight.
*Huh…that's odd…*

Benny made an odd sound. Not a coo nor a cry, but a buzz. Hundreds of bees stuck inside a mason jar. Sarah recognized the sound. Benny stood up on the seat. His blanket slipped into the floorboard; his face a blank expression.

"Benny? What are doing?"

Benny's eyelids fluttered, snapped open. His head swiveled. Tiny screens filtered with snow and static stared at Sarah. His mouth clicked open. "Please deliver this unit back to the lab," a man's voice pushed through, the lips of the child not moving. "Please turn the bouncer around and return to Slader Corp. It is imperative for you to do so."

A chill slithered down her spine.

"Please, Ms. Lans. This is the only way to issue the message. No harm will come to you. The narks cannot help you if you cross the river. It is forbidden for you to cross over. Allow them to escort you back to Slader Corp, for your safety. Take heed, Ms. Lans. Beyond the river there is both danger and death."

Sarah tried digesting this sudden development.

"If you travel beyond the river, Ms. Lans, this synthetic-covered shell will self-destruct. There will be no way to save you from dying. We will not be able to save you."

The Benny-copy blinked.

Realization of what the demi did to her baby boy slugged her in the jaw. She felt the blood drain from her face. A band tightened over her stomach, her hopes of escape shoved itself over a cliff.

*They had her!*

*They freaking had her!*

They had cut her child from her womb, transformed him into some kind of machine. Benny had died. Slader Corp had killed her baby! The horror when she first woke up in the hospital bed, realizing her child had been murdered, stolen away by the arachnid doctor, returned. Sarah had failed. She'd just as soon set the Bouncer down and give up.

*Why else should I intend on living? Benny dead, Kentil dead, what else was there? What else was there for me to live for, here in the colony? My parents had died long ago. Live under Maximus Slader's rules and regulations? Not! What the hells was there here in this stupid colony?* She feared the demi would steal her flesh too, change her into....into whatever Benny had become! They would kill her, not save her!

Ice cold fingers startled her. "Mommy, please return me to the lab. Pretty-pretty please with sugar on top?" The Benny-copy's bottom lip quivered, a bizarre match to his snowy eyes.

Sarah blinked. Snatched her arm away from the tiny fingers. She sucked in a deep breath, let it out. Obeying their wishes, returning to Slader Corp, would be suicide. No need to call upon the mobile suicide unit to accompany her into The Great Beyond. The demi had her death covered.

The bouncer's turbines spun, blasting toward the abandoned house.

\*\*\*

Walts' brain had spun the Wheel of Luck, landing on You Got This, Kid!

He had no idea how he managed to do it. Not a squiggle of an idea. While thrust into the back seat, the wind sucked out of him, he had grabbed the seat belt and stretched it over his body, clicking the end into the metal groove before impact.

The view of the old abandoned house widened, spreading itself like a disease through the windshield.

Walts stomach lurched as the bouncer spiraled downward. He squeezed his eyes shut seconds before the bouncer crashed into the top floor of the house. The second of impact the bouncer's safety feature in the event of a crash disengaged, spewing white foam from the air vents, drowning the interior of the craft, cushioning the passengers.

Shoved against an enormous marshmallow Walts peeled himself out of the craft, stumbled, felt a wash of dizziness, and slapped a hand on the bouncer to right himself. Leaning on the craft, he slid down on his rump. The recoil of spiraling out of control still pulsed inside his flesh. Once the world righted itself, Walts took note of himself in the Bouncer's side mirror, now sitting on the floor.

Miraculously, the only wounds were a few scrapes on his face. No broken bones as he moved his wrist, arms, legs, and feet. No teeth missing. Memories of watching a commercial where they stuck a dummy in the seat of a bouncer and rammed the craft into a steel wall reflected back, watching the foam grab and hold onto the dummy.

*Strange that the demi and Maximus Slader provided safety like this,* Walts thought, *at the same time encouraged suicide. Didn't add up.*

He sucked in a deep breath, scanned his surroundings.

A wave of dizziness returned with a slap as he rose to his feet, almost losing his balance again.

…A voice shouted from somewhere.

Walts gazed at the wall the bouncer had crashed through. A gaping hole showing blue skies and a stretch of buildings. Air traffic littered SkyDrive.

The Jonas-copy had shot through the windshield and punched a hole through a wall, revealing a hallway.

The shouting drew closer.

\*\*\*

"Hello viewers! Welcome to the Whaddaya Gotta Say Ray Report!

We're here in front of an old abandoned house where said lotto winner, Jonas Leeshur, has supposedly crashed into the top floor minutes ago. Behind me you can see the end of the bouncer sticking out and black smoke rising in the air.

"Leeshur is not alone, either. His best friend, Walts Brinner, is with him.

"Breaking lotto rules before the demi comes to collect is forbidden. Such as in the case of Jonas Leeshur. The demi caught Leeshur and Brinner entering the Subterraneans. As we all know, ladies and gentlemen of the viewing area, speaking or associating with any member of the rebellion is strongly forbidden, whether you are a winner of the lotto or not. This move will certainly give you a one-way ticket, all-expenses paid, to the Neutralization Center. Since the case of Jake Velmer, strong security measures have been in place by Slader Corp.

"We were lucky to be on the scene before demi agents arrived. We may not have seen a hint of Leeshur yet, but we feel *sure* he's bound to be moving around in that old, decrepit-looking abandoned house sitting behind me."

***

Sarah accelerated faster, passing streets and buildings and the small coffee shop where she had been stolen away by the demi. That was a place she wished she could delete from her memory for good!

"Mommy, please turn around," the Benny-copy said. "I wish to be returned to the lab. I'm awful hungry."

Sarah ignored the unit, snatched a glance of a TV crew below accompanied with halftracks crawling to a stop. Bouncers landed. Demi agents poured from the vehicles. And once Sarah crested over the top of the house a large hologram hovered in the air:

DO NOT PASS BEYOND THIS LINE
FOR YOUR SAFETY AND OTHERS PLEASE TURN
AROUND AND RETURN TO
THE COLONY
HAVE A NICE DAY

Sarah steered the craft through the sign and accelerated.

Warning lights lit up on the dashboard. The Wankel-McMeyer turbines shrieked once it crossed over the watery grave, skimmed over a large copse of trees, plunging out of the sky.

\*\*\*

"Wow!" Ray said. "Somebody just flew their bouncer over the old house and crossed the river! I'm speechless, ladies and gentlemen! *Speechless!* I have never seen this happen! No one has ever left the colony before!"

"Two people breaking the law today. How bizarre!"

\*\*\*

Walts heard the scream of another bouncer's turbines. He feared it, too, would crash into the house. Ready to duck for cover, he stumbled and squatted in a corner.

But the bouncer flew over, until the sound of its engine abruptly severed, as if someone controlled it with the flick of a switch.

*What the hells happened to it?*

Dizziness had not let go of Walts' cranium. Cautiously, he stepped through the hole in the wall. Pieces of the wall crunched under his shoes. The Jonas-copy lay mangled, its cyclopean eye shattered. The head would have been severed from the neck, if not for thick multi-colored wires.

Walts stepped around an oozing greenish-blue bodily fluid he took for machine blood.

Directly across a door had been ripped from its hinges. Walts figured the Jonas-copy rebounded off it after punching a hole in the wall.

"Hey! *Answer me this second!* I asked you a question, and I do *not* like to repeat myself!" The ghost of a very tall man drifted down the hall. His face was a mask of rage.

Walts stumbled back a step.

"What gives you the right to crash into our house!" He pointed a long finger in Walts' face.

Walts stumbled again, caught himself from falling.

"I asked you a question, young man! *Why* did you crash into *our* house? There is no trespassing into this house. There is no trespassing over its threshold. This is our sanctuary, a safety net away from you disgusting mortals!"

"Um…um…I'm sorry…didn't mean to…"

"Didn't *mean* to?"

"N-No…look…I wasn't driving."

"You just happened to be flying that metal machine and decide in that thick head of yours to crash into our home?"

"No. I wasn't driving."

"Pathetic child creating mischief and trouble and – what did you say? You weren't driving?"

"N-no."

"*Who* was?"

Walts stumbled back, nearly tripping over his transfigured

friend's corpse. "He…was."

"Who?"

"Jonas…that robot…the transfiguration on the floor."

"*This* thing? Really?"

"Yes."

Snort. "Preposterous! I think you are passing blame, young man. Even *I* know robots are forbidden to drive! Maximus Slader made a public announcement on everyone's televid after that couple went out for drinks one night, not too long ago, allowing their robot to drive them home in their bouncer only to have it malfunction behind the wheel and crash into a concrete pillar."

"I'm telling you the truth! He took me hostage! *Honest!*"

"Don't raise your voice to me! Manners, child, you need to be schooled with manners when speaking to an adult."

"But…"

"But *nothing*! Let me tell you what I believed happened, shall I? Good. You steal your mom and dad's bouncer and take your best friend forever, this defunct metal body stuffed with cogs and wires and bolts and screws supporting a positronic brain that has not a filament of intelligence, and you go out for a joy ride and suddenly decide, hey, let's see what it's like to crash into someone's house, why not aim for a monumental house? *That old abandoned place by the river to be exact!* One no one cares for, right? One could care less for, right?

"*Right!*" he answered for Walts.

"So, here you are with a robot that is destroyed, your parent's bouncer which is beyond repair, and a house which will need a complete make-over unless one of you brainless flesh and blood creatures get a stupid idea and try and demolish it. *That* won't happen, I assure you that! Yes, I know it is an eyesore sitting in the colony. Yes, I know you and your little friends have chatted about it. Yes, I know you are aware of this even though your expression gives away a dumbfounded appearance. Let me explain something to you, young man, this is our sanctuary. *Our* home!"

"Y-Your home?" Walts asked.

"Did I stutter? Eh? *Our* home. Plural, young man. It is mine and my lovely wife's house. We have been here since the Shift."

"Look, I'm sorry, sir..."

"*That*, you certainly are!"

"I was taken hostage by that robot, and we crashed into your house. Honest! I'm not lyin'! He really was driving!"

"There you go again, saying a robot can drive."

"*He was!*"

Phillip rolled his eyes, replicating symbols on a mechanical reel in a slot machine. "Tell me another tall tale."

"You gotta believe me!"

Smirk. "You're really telling me the truth?"

"Yes, sir!"

"I think you're trying to sneak one past Phillip."

"I wouldn't try to put it past you, sir!"

Snort. "Huh. Let's ask the robot, then." The man reached down and grabbed a hand full of the robot's hair. "Did you drive that machine? Huh? No? Yes? I can*not* hear you? What's wrong, a wire stuck in your throat? A virus infect your hard drive?"

The Jonas-copy said nothing.

"Huh. Must be dead, then. Is that what you are, creature? Are you dead?"

The Jonas-copy still said nothing.

The man let go. The head dropped with a thump. "Guess he's not gonna answer my question, huh? Well then, come with me, young man," he grabbed hold of Walts' ear, "I'll get you to admit you just lied to me!"

"Ow! I didn't lie! That thing kidnapped me and drove the bouncer into your house! Honest!"

The man halted. "Let me reiterate: Not I. It is *our* house, child. Margret's and mine. Remember that when you reference whose house it is! Am I clear?

"Yes. Please let go of my e– "

"Good. Unfortunately for you it looks as if you'll have to be punished for your actions, young man!"

*Punished?*

"Phillip!" a woman shouted from below. "Phillip! You need to look outside! We've got company!"

Phillip huffed and dragged Walts down the stairs, right into the living room where a tall ghostly woman peeked out the front window. "There's a lot of mortals out there, Phillip. I don't know what they want."

Phillip let go of Walts.

Walts rubbed his ear.

"Probably searching after this kid for causing all this trouble. The narks were probably chasing after him when he stole his parent's bouncer."

"I'm not responsible for this! You gotta believe me!" Walts said.

"Hush! I have heard enough of your lying! Keep that hole under your nose closed, or I will suture it up using your intestines!" Phillip's face flickered a morph of a grinning skull.

Walts shrank back.

"Maximus has given me and my lovely Margret," Phillip's face returned to the norm as he gestured a hand toward the woman, "this place. Its vast history and its ownership are filed away on a memory chip at Slader Corp. Unlike other ghosts lurking around the Stygian Wake searching for a place of residence to haunt, Margret and I own this house. No mortal can steal it from us. I told you there was no trespassing here, and I meant it."

"Come out peacefully, Jonas Leeshur and Walts Brinner, and things will go easy," a voice blasted through a loudspeaker outside. "We do not want to make this harder than it already is. Please come quietly, boys, and hand over your flesh."

*My flesh?* Walts knew it was the demi coming to collect. *Did they not know of Jonas' transfiguration? The real Jonas told me they collected him, transformed him. Did somebody not relate the news? Or were they playing dumb? Were they hiding the truth?*

Phillip gazed at Margret. "Should we hand this child over to the authorities, my love? Or shall we have some fun and show this child what we do to intruders?"

Margret grinned. "If we hand him over to the demi Maximus Slader may commend us. He may give us the cred to fix the place up."

"That is an option, my dear."

"However," she placed he finger on pursed lips, "showing our unmistakable love we have shown to so many souls throughout the years to this kid may be the way to go. It has always been the best way. He'll thank us for it, will he not?"

A wry grin. "Very much. He will have a brand new life."

Ghostly eyes gazed at Walts.

He shivered.

"I do believe it is the way to go; right, Phillip?"

"You are quite right, my love."

Margret's ghostly face altered into a grinning skull. Her hands turned into claws. "Let's do it. We *love* to puni – We love trespassers." She cackled, drifting toward Walts.

Walts stepped back.

Phillip's face morphed into a gruesomely similar version of his wife's. Long, clawed fingers reached behind his back and came away revealing a very long, very sharp knife. The tool being no apparition.

Walts gasped.

"I think what we will do," Margret said, "is to leave a mark on this child so he will never forget it. We shall show our love."

"Good thinking, my dear."

Margret's hand lashed out and grabbed Walts.

He tried to jerk away and could not.

"Don't worry, child," Margret brought him close, spun him around to face her husband, "the pain only lasts for a short while, then you will feel the love. One cannot have salvation without enduring pain, correct?"

Walts struggled.

"Do not struggle. We only want to watch you...*bleed*." Phillip gripped the handle of the knife, drifted forward, chuckling. "Why hand him over? He would be much better if he stayed with us as a ghost. He would be an excellent addition to our collection. Wouldn't you agree, my dear?"

"Yes," Margret giggled.

"This is your final warning, boys. We will not tolerate such nonsense!" the voice demanded through the loudspeaker outside.

Two seconds slid by, then the start of a chainsaw.

Phillip whipped his head around, stared at the door. "That damn fool wouldn't dare!"

*\*\*\**

The automaton vid-cam zoomed in on Ray Manisquaski's grinning face. "Do you think Mr. Leeshur and his friend will give themselves up? Will they stay inside the house and make the demi come after them? Will they take the chance to burst out of the front door fighting, only to be cut down by the demi's guns?

"Wait! The demi has sent in their assassin! Don't dare touch that remote! Let us watch and find out, ladies and gents, how things pan out for these two boys!"

*\*\*\**

The doorknob jiggled. The door rattled in its frame.

"Go away, fool! You know the rules! There is no trespassing! Even for your kind!" Phillip warned.

The one behind the door did not heed to the warning.

"You cannot have this child! He is *ours!*"

A loud roar, a grind, and the end of a chainsaw chewed into the front door, carving out a good-size hole. An eye peeked through.

"I am warning you, freak! Do not enter!" Phillip's black eyes were slits.

An arm covered in a blue sleeve reached inside the house and a white-gloved hand twisted the doorknob, allowing the door to swing open. Sunlight glorified wild bright red hair atop a mask with sutured crimson lines for eyes and a sutured red mouth stretched into a grin. The tall figure's pale face, his blue shirt, his multi-colored checkered pants and his large red shoes would have given off the impression of a clown-for-hire for a kid's birthday party if not for the hand scythe hanging from his wide belt harboring the designs of cyclopean skulls and the rumbling chainsaw he held.

"Take the child upstairs, away from this filth!" Phillip scowled. "Lock him in one of the rooms."

"Yes, dear," Margret dragged Walts upstairs.

"You may *not* pass into our house, fool! We have a deal with Maximus. You are never to enter this place!"

Chainsaw Freckles' weapon revved in response, as if saying "So?"

Snort. "That will be no use against me. I am a ghost!"

Freckles cocked his head. The weapon idled.

"Mortal things do not hurt me. Something wrong with your processing unit or mainframe? You, sir, will leave our house immediately! Go back and inform Maximus he has a breach of contract. We will be speaking to him soon."

Atop Freckles' left shoulder there was a *whirr* as a small door flipped open and *click* as a cannon locked into place.

"What, think you can scare me with practical weapons? Ha!

Just try it!"

Taking aim, it shot a small neon green sphere at Phillip which expanded like a spider's web and trapped him in a large balloon-like object which hovered ten feet off the floor. The words MORTO scrolled across it.

"Hey! Let me out this minute you freak!"

Freckles only cocked his head, gazed at his prisoner, and began climbing the staircase.

"Come the hells back here and let me out at once! You have no right coming into our home! Come back here you poor choice for a clown! You pathetic tin can! You're only alive in that metal suit because Maximus felt sorry for a pedophile like you! A child murderer! Reject from the mortals! Least me and my Margret don't kill children and bury them in their backyards. We kill them and keep their souls here, in this house. You hear me, freak? We're better than you'll *ever* be! Maximus will hear about this! *Mark my words, clown!*"

Freckles clanked as he ascended the staircase.

\*\*\*

"You need to be placed where it is safe....for *now*," Margret glanced back at Walts, dragging him to the third floor. "Let's get you a room for your stay, child. You'll be very happy her—*what the?*"

She stopped. Walts stumbled through her ghostly shape and bounced off the Jonas-copy. It stood there on one leg, rattling, emanating a buzzing sound as if angry bees in the glass jar wished to be let out. Connected by wires it had dragged its left leg, a lost dog that had broken its chain. Deep cuts in the wooden floor left a trail. Severed wires snaked out of the thing's neck, the tips sparking. "Hand over the child," the head of the Jonas-copy croaked, cradled in the crook of its arm.

"This child has become possession of the house, as all things do, when they trespass!" Margret spat.

"Hand over the child," the voice warbled. "It is Maximus' wish." Its metal hand, bare of synthetic flesh, stretched to grab Walts.

Margret pulled Walts away from the robot. "Keep your claws to yourself! Maximus has no say in this matter. Maximus does not own this place or own *us*. Understand?" She looked at Walts. "If you intend to live, child, go through the door, there!"

Walts started for it.

The Jonas-copy took two long strides and snatched him.

"Let go!" Walts tried wrenching free.

Margret's eyes fluttered. She hovered off the floor, stretched out her arms and hands, opened her mouth, shrieked, causing each of the six doors in the hallway to repeatedly open and slam shut. One ripped from its hinges, rebounded off the wall, chewed off a few chunks of plaster, knocked the robot sideways, sprawling it down the stairs and

\*\*\*

Slammed into Chainsaw Freckles who had made it to the first floor, sending the machine crashing backward, rolling into the living

\*\*\*

"....ROOM, CHILD!" Margret's voice boomed. "I SAID GET IN THERE, NOW!"

Walts dove into the open doorway when the Jonas-copy released its grip. It slammed shut, leaving him in a pitch black, windowless room. His body slid to a stop, smacking into a wall. As he stood, Margret's words chased after the Jonas-copy, cursing its existence.

Walts felt his way through the darkness by a crawl, grabbed the doorknob, gave it a twist.

Locked.

"You'll be safe in there, Walts," Margret said. "Stay put for a little while."

"Let me out of here!" Walts spat.

"Calm down, allow the room be your friend."

*Friend?* Walts tried wrenching open the door again.

"Sorry, try as much as you want. That door is locked for your protection."

"Let me out! It's creepy in here!"

"Enjoy your time in one of our *special* rooms, Walts. This house has unsettling memories, ghosts of the past, a place where two boys decided they'd hunt for ghosts, biting off more they could chew." Giggle. "The room you are in has a slightly different view of the macabre. Sort of a nexus."

*Nexus? Like a Cyberspace Junction?* "What's in here?" Walts twisted around, only to find darkness looking back at him.

"You shall see what defines a nexus, child."

The sound of her giggling and footsteps faded away as she strolled down the hall.

A door slammed shut.

He grabbed the doorknob, twisted it for a third reproach, repeating the same find: Locked.

A flash and silver light blazed into the room. When he turned, he faced a graveyard under a full moon. Gravestones littered the land. He saw no end to the place, as if it ran for miles.

A group of hooded individuals stood not but about twenty feet away. Their heads turned, gazed at the newcomer.

A familiar buzz reached Walts' ears. A vibration crawled over his flesh, making the hairs on the back of his neck erect.

Stepping into a ray of moonlight, their hoods pulled free, exposed small arachnid-shaped automatons clamped atop each of their heads.

They started toward Walts.

\*\*\*

Wonder what happened to Fred? Yeah. Me, too. So, shall we rewind?

\*\*\*

Margret had led Fred up to the third floor, ordering him to hide inside a room. She commanded him not to come out, whatever he heard.

Fred should have known better. Once the door clicked shut, it became a trap. Four ghosts, chains linking each, rose out of the floor. Victims of Phillip and Margret's terror, they had been kidnapped by the sinister duo and cut apart not only physically, but mentally, keeping them chained to the wall in closed rooms for days on end in darkness, extinguishing their hopes of escape. Faces slashed beyond recognition, they wore masks of pain. Flickers of crimson light replaced human eyes.

If not for the long hair and the shape of the slender figure, one could not distinguish the fact a woman stood amongst three men. Two were armed with knives; the other, a very stocky lad, held a large wooden mallet.

Their chains vanished.

The woman led the pack, showing the flash of her blade as the other ghosts trudged forward in queue, like the dead slaves they were.

\*\*\*

Freckles got up.

The enemy causing the dilemma slowly rose.

Freckles snapped a picture using its 35mm Turbo Camera, built in its right eye.

*<Chainsaw Freckles to Slader Corp: Come in. Do you copy?>*

Slader Corp to Chainsaw Freckles: Go ahead, Freckles.

CF to SC: *<What is this machine? Stand by for transmission of visual.>*

During transmission Chainsaw visualized the head of a spinning, laughing skull icon:

*<Spinning…*

*…Spinning*

*Laughing…*

*…Received.>*

SC to CF: Machine is a recent TransmoG. The unit is a carbon copy of said lotto winner Jonas Leeshur, 16 Quad Street, Ozarium. The unit is damaged beyond repair and is of no use to Slader Corp. Orders are to discontinue the machine.

CF to SC: *<Discontinue unit. Copy.>*

End of transmission from SC.

Chainsaw Freckles' chainsaw roared to life.

Above, in the Morto sphere, Phillip shook his fist, shouted obscenities and threatening to inform Maximus about this outrage. Ignoring the ghost, the robot clown took a long stride and, with a wide swing of his chainsaw, ended his enemy's existence.

Chainsaw gazed at the stairs.

*:Running heat signature program five dash two: Handprints on wooden banner. Send data to Central's mainframe computer located inside Slader Corp:*

The head of the laughing skull spun during transmit of data.

*<Spinning…*

*…Spinning*

*Laughing…*

Received.>

SC to CF: Handprints of said accomplice of Jonas Leeshur, Walts Brinner, 11 Quad Court, Ozarium. Orders are to take Walts Brinner prisoner and deliver boy to Slader Corp for TransmoG.

Chainsaw Freckles clicked on Walts' picture, using its positronic brain and downloaded it into a memory chip.

CF to BG: <*Copy.*>

End of transmission.

\*\*\*

The woman swiped her blade through the air, barely missing Fred's cheek and ear. He pushed her into one of the other ghosts, making two stumble back and fall. Catching him off guard, pain exploded into his gut, lifting him off his feet, leaving him in a sprawl on the floor.

The stocky one with the wooden mallet loomed over Fred, smiling, serrated teeth inside a cleft lip expertly designed by Phillip and his razor. He lifted the mallet over his head for a skull-smashing blow. Fred rolled to the side, a scant instant before the end of the mallet slammed the floor.

Fred bumped into two pairs of feet.

Ghostly hands reached down and grabbed Fred.

The woman stuck her face in his and smiled. The point of her knife pressed against his ghost flesh directly under his left eye.

And hissed, licking her lips.

\*\*\*

A deafening buzz in his ears, a filament of hope chased Walts as he passed gravestones, sprinted down a hill, splashed through a creek, scrambled up another hill, slipped, and took a tumble end over end back the way he came.

And bumped into the legs of one of the creatures.

The creature gazed down at Walts. A rectangular blue screen

sat in the middle of its face, flickered with static. Its partner in crime atop its head clicked its legs, a flutter against both sides of its face.

Claws grabbed Walts around the throat.

"No! Let me go!" he begged.

The creature only buzzed a reply, lifting him off his feet.

Walts fought to pry open the vice-grip.

***

*<First floor...>*
   *<Vacant of target to acquire...>*

***

As a mortal, Fred thought the pain of being hit and crushed by the transport was bad. When the female ghost's knife cut out his left eye with the point of her blade, Fred shunned the previous pain away and gathered the new. His right eye socket emptied next by the blade's tip, left him blind – but only for a few seconds until his attackers appeared as white silhouettes, undulating between four walls glowed a neon green grid.

A few more transformations with the blade created scars on his face. His senses suddenly yearned for the pain, a constant high goose could never give.

Two ice cold clamps squeezed his wrists, bounding him. Links chained together, attaching him to the group who had attacked him.

Fred giggled, pulled along with the others into a darker part of the house where screams from dismembered heads reverberated off the walls and flesh and blood attempted to recreate human bodies previously skinned and autopsied alive.

# Ozarium

\*\*\*

Downstairs in the Morto bubble, Phillip grinned, happy for Fred.

\*\*\*

Walts tried wrenching free of the vise-grip. Held tight, the buzz of the creature vibrated Walts' skin.

It began dragging him up the hill.

Walts kicked the creature's knee, hoping it would free him. Nothing happened. He tried again, more force behind his kick. Nothing happened. Nearly choking himself from the grip around his neck, he used both feet and it buckled, causing the vise-grip to release, causing the creature to fall head-first into the water.

A pop, a sizzle, a slew of sparks and a wisp of smoke followed Walts as he splashed through the water.

Another creature took three strides, latched a claw on Walts' shoulder. Able to shrug off the grip, Walts shoved the creature into the other monsters.

They fell over like dominos, splashing into the water.

Walts clambered back up the hill and down, rocketing past more gravestones.

\*\*\*

*<Second floor...>*
  *<Vacant of target to acquire...>*

\*\*\*

"Ladies and gentlemen of the viewing area!" Ray Manisquaski said. "We have already witnessed Chainsaw Freckles ripping through the

233

front door of the house! We even heard a terrible scream! Stay tuned to this channel! Jonas Leeshur and Walts Brinner are still in there! When we return, we hope to have the conclusion for you to find out what happens to our youngest lotto winner!"

\*\*\*

Grandpa had been visiting an old friend residing in the Wake. He returned home by Eckto-Leaping, a teleportation method used by apparitions. On the telelvid Ray Manisquaski said:

"Do you think Mr. Leeshur will give himself up? Will he stay inside the house and make the demi come after him? Will he burst out of the front door fighting only to be cut down by the demi's guns? Wait...."

Grandpa's eyes widened, watching Ray pause, receiving more information in his ear piece. He reiterated: Jonas had an accomplice: Walts.

*What are those boys doing down there? Why is Manisquaski telling folks Jonas may blast through the front door and fight the demi?* Grandpa thought. *That house is part of the forbidden zone, connected to the river.* "Carolyn? You in the kitchen? Gods have mercy! You need to get in here and look at this! Tell Steven to drop what he's doing and get upstairs! Walts and his friend Jonas has gotten themselves in trouble!"

A figure walked out of the kitchen, wiping its hands on an apron. A mask of static produced Carolyn's voice: "Everything is fine, Grandpa. Jonas is fine. Walts is safe, and his life will improve very soon."

"Carolyn? Wh-what happened to you? Why are you a schizo?"

The static on the schizos face flipped, as if it tuning into station or transmission, emitting a servo buzz. "Nothing is wrong. Everything is good. Right, Steven?"

Another schizo appeared. Placed its arm around the other's

waist. "Yes. Everything is just great. *We* feel great. Walts will soon feel great, too."

"Who did this to you?" Grandpa said, aghast.

"Grandpa, you shouldn't worry," the Carolyn-schizo assured. "We are reborn."

"No worries, Grandpa," the Steven-schizo added.

"Do not think of leaving. You are to stay here." Both schizos aimed rail guns.

"Those bullets won't hurt me, son."

"I am afraid they will. They're made by a company called Morto, Inc. Perhaps you've heard of it."

Grandpa had. The business had been snatched off the market years ago. Originally, Morto was used against evil spirits during a time when many people were possessed, long before the Paranormal Laws went into effect. Later, when people realized not every ghost was evil, especially in cases such as Grandpa's, able to return to be with his family even after death, it was allowed for ghosts to have rights – minimal ones at that – and allowed their Free Space, as long as they followed the Paranormal Laws. The downside were the anti-ghost groups surfacing off and on, expressing their hate for apparitions because they believed each and every ghost was an evil entity. And armed with illegal Morto weapons.

"You know this is the only ammo which will cause ghosts harm. Sit down, Father." Steven nodded to the televid. "Things in Ozarium are about to adjust for the better. Making Jonas the very first child to win the lotto is the first step of something new; something great. Maximus Slader has decided to make this adjustment. People have disobeyed the reproduction laws. People disobeyed rules of the lotto when they win. People are not obeying rules of the colony, they need structure. They need to be punished. Slader Corp is in need of extra flesh. There is a need for more workers at Slader Corp to help with the transfigurations, the TransmoGs." Grin. "The Neutralization Center is about to become overworked today, and more schizos will be developed."

Outside, two halftracks rumbled down the street.

"Colonists have all tuned into the show on the televid, learning about the latest lotto winner, Jonas," the Carolyn-schizo said. "They are horrified; but will be more horrified when they learn they will walk the same path and become a TransmoG."

"Ray Manisquaski has done a swell job reporting the news. Now his time is up. His flesh is scheduled for TransmoG, like Walts, like everyone else," the Steven-schizo said. "Maximus Slader has decided to give us a salvation we deserve. For many years the lotto has been a salvation. Now, the colony has taken a different turn, each of us will be reborn."

Grandpa knew these two imposters could not know how easily he could reshape into an orb before their eyes. He had accidently stumbled on the illusion a while back. That was something the rude red-headed lady Belinda from the BRD did not tell him about. Nor did she say anything about the Eckto-Leap.

*It was a Learn-As-You-Go mentality when you're a ghost.*

"Sit down or I, we, *will* shoot you," the Carolyn-schizo warned.

Grandpa nodded, acted as if he was going to sit down in his favorite chair, and, in the blink of an eye, shrunk into an orb and zipped away.

Morto bullets chewed into the empty cushion.

\*\*\*

Walts stumbled over a few grave markers, blinked twice, and a flicker in the sky caused the moon to vanish, a sun in its place.

"Um. *Oh*kay. That was just...weird." Walts glanced over his shoulder. No sign of those creatures. Had they given up the chase?

Walts noticed each gravestone had either a one or two digit number, though not in sequence. One read 26. The next read 35.

Another read 56 and the one beside it read 78.

Didn't make much sense to Walts; neither did this odd place, for that matter.

The earth moved by his foot, startling him. A small sink hole spiraled downward. Walts braced himself for the appearance of the hand of a zombie, but the sight of chrome replaced the thought. Congealing like a patch of blood, chrome bugs excavated from the soil and scurried toward Walts.

He gasped, took off.

Bugs poured out of each grave, the tiny leaders pulling their hordes in arrow shapes. Walts took leaps and bounds over gravestones and clambered up another hill where he slipped, tumbled down the other side, sliding smack dab in front of a large tomb.

His eyes widened.

A concrete gargoyle stared down at him, both eyes winking red, wings spread like claws. Its feet gripped the ridge of the tomb, its body loomed over a stone door below.

Sunlight reflected off of the chrome bugs as they crested the hill, nearly blinding Walts. He grabbed the stone handle on the door of the tomb, gave it a yank.

It didn't budge.

He used both hands.

No good.

He used his foot, pressed on the door jamb, it moved.

The bugs began to hiss, converging on their prey.

Another yank and Walts slipped inside, slammed the door, shutting out the horror of the invading bugs, as well as the sunlight. He sucked in a breath, ran a hand over his face, and after closing his eyes heard the chainsaw grumble.

***

Grandpa zipped outside, reshaped, and when he started off down the sidewalk, he heard:

"Hey! You there! *Stop!*"

Grandpa had forgotten about the demi outside. If he had been smarter, he would have just Ekto-Leaped.

"What's your hurry?" a demi agent said.

Other agents knocked on doors of homes, ordering residents to leave, per Maximus' orders, directing each citizen to bouncers which landed in the street. Shouts and curses from the neighbors; some threatened to fight the demi. Their thoughts extinguished after peering at the barrel of a rifle.

"Oh…I'm, uh, out for a stroll," Grandpa lied.

An agent walked out of one home holding an arm full of old paperback novels – forbidden for a person to have since the birth of electronic books – and pitched them on a flat disc automaton on rollers called a Nuke Pit. A blue flame ignited, christening the pages black.

Grandpa noticed one book's title, *Fahrenheit 451* by Ray Bradbury, before being pitched into the Pit.

"A stroll? Where to?" the agent inquired.

"I figured I might go see a few…friends, you know."

Frown. "Hang on a sec." The demi tapped his ear. "We have a stray apparition here, sir. Not sure where he lives and if ghosts are allowed to leave during our sweep of the neighborhood. Have our orders changed? I see…okay…got it." He focused on Grandpa. "Sorry, pops, no one leaves right now during our sweep."

"But I have business with someone."

"If you do not return to your home, I will have to subdue you." He reached into his jacket, pulled a rail gun. "I would advise you to not move. There are not ordinary bullets in this gun."

Grandpa blinked. *Why all of sudden the appearance of pistols that shoot Morto bullets? Geezee-peez! The hells is going on?*

"Go back to your house. You will be contacted shortly, informing whether you will be allowed to stay or will have to leave."

"Leave?"

"Yes. You may have to slip into the Stygian Wake and stay put until further instructions. We are assessing the situation and will make a decision soon. Understand?"

"Er…okay." As much as he'd prefer to stand and argue with this agent about his rights granted by the Bureau of the Recently Deceased, allowing him to stay and haunt where his family lived, this wasn't the time to do so. Things in Ozarium had changed. He needed to get-gone.

Grandpa started back toward his house. He needed to devise a plan quick. Walts and Jonas were in trouble. No time to waste. He needed to save them before the demi snatched them up.

He glanced over his shoulder.

The demi agent walked off.

Grandpa Ekto-Leaped two seconds before the Carolyn-copy stepped outside, followed by the Steven-copy.

*** 

Margret's head oozed through the door to the room. She watched the machine take the boy away. Too bad she couldn't have kept the kid. Could have shown the child more dread than his young brain could muster. Could have scrambled the kid's brain, shoved him toward a delusional transition, morphing him into another pawn, like their new resident, Fred.

She grinned.

At least she had Fred, a new toy to play with.

She frowned.

Too bad the room she shoved the kid inside had still been in its experimental stages, a nexus developed by Slader Corp. She really had no choice but to give up the boy. The kid was used as a guinea pig to see how things went.

Plus, allowing the kid to be caught by the machine credited her and Phillip. Maximus Slader should be happy about that.

She'd have to calm her husband down, though.

*** 

The automaton vid-cam zoomed in.

"Folks, it looks as if someone is coming through the front door…yes!" Ray Manisquaski cried. "There's our youngest lotto win– *no! Wait!* It's not Jonas Leeshur. It's Walts Brinner! Dragging him outside is none other than the infamous killing machine, Chainsaw Freckles. Wow, can you all hear that? The crowd is clapping and cheering for Chainsaw. They really love that guy!

"Demi agents have grabbed Mr. Brinner and are escorting him off and to a bouncer. Let's see if we can get any information from an agent."

The vid-cam zipped behind the news reporter's hurried steps.

"Where's our lotto winner? What will happen to Mr. Brinner?"

The agent shut the door to the bouncer, held his hand up. "No comments at this time, Ray."

"Can't you allow me and my fans a little insight?"

"No. Good day, Ray." The agent climbed into the passenger seat, and the driver blasted it into the sky.

Manisquaski spoke into the vid-cam. "Well, folks, guess we won't know what will happen to that kid. Where *is* our youngest lotto winner? Is he still inside the house? Has he escaped out the back door of the house? Who knows! That's a mystery which needs to be solved!

"And will Walts Brinner be kept alive? Will he be charged as an accomplice for Leeshur? Will he be sent to the Neutralization Center? All these things place us in the dark, ladies and gentlemen. As soon as I receive an update, I will share it with you! Thanks so much for tuning in, fol… *hey! Watch it!* Why do you have a gun pointed at me? I'm not breaking any laws! Well, folks, it appears I am being taken away by the demi, along with others here, for some bizarre reason!

"Hey! Don't shoot my vid-c—"

\*\*\*

Grandpa Ekto-Leaped on the lawn of the old house by the river, missing the bouncers blasting away into the sky by minutes. He had not a clue where they were taking Walts. Perhaps a ghost in the old house could tell him something.

He frowned, gazed at the carved out hole in the front door. *What the heck caused that?*

A ghostly man and his wife stood inside, conversing with each other.

"Hello?"

The man gave Grandpa a look of disgust, and his words sidled next to the verb, holding a touch of malice. "Lost? Can we help you with something?"

"I'm trying to figure out where they took my grandson."

"Who?"

"Walts Brinner."

The man blinked.

"The kid the demi hauled off."

"Oh, must be the child that crazy clown robot took away."

"That's him."

"We have no idea where he took the child, sorry." The man turned back to his wife.

"You have no idea in the slightest?"

His nostrils flared. "Uh. No. *We* don't. Please leave. There is nothing here for you to see."

"There has got to be some kind of clue around here that'll tell me where he is."

"Well," the woman said, "*your* grandson crashed a bouncer into the top of our house."

"Walts doesn't know how to drive."

"You would be surprised at the mortal youngsters these days, being mischievous, lying, cheating, talking back to their parents. Surprised he hasn't talked back to you."

"He has not. Walts is a good kid."

The man snorted. "So you say. The kid must have you snowed, old man. Walts needs to be punished. Perhaps the demi will discipline him. Tan the kid's hide."

"They best not lift a finger to hurt him."

A wry grin. "And what could you do, old man. As a ghost, like me and my Margret, we hardly have many rights in Ozarium. Per Maximus we are to stay inside this house; never leave it. But times are gonna change. Mark my words. I have a bone to pick with Maximus once I inform him of the incident. The house needs major repair, and he is going to pay to have it fixed."

"Did you say…*Maximus*?"

"Yes. You know him as Maximus Slader. The Ozarium's idiot leader." He rolled his eyes and threw his hands in the air.

"Uh…Okay. Why would you blame him? Does he own this house? How is he the one

held responsible?"

"No, he does not own this house. I'm blaming Slader and holding him responsible because he deserves it. His defunct demi agents have *not* done their job. This house is *our* sanctuary. Our house has been invaded by outside forces, trespassing onto *our* property. Margret and I have filled out the necessary application for our rights of ownership of this house, and it been downloaded into a memory chip in the program Thunderclap, filed away at Slader Corp. Maximus has broken his word, allowing an invasion into our house.

"Now, if you do not mind, please leave us alone. My lovely

Margret and I need to assess this entire result of your grandson's and that…that…monstrosity of a robot he was with, both who have caused problems in our sanctuary."

"That clown was a brute, Phillip! I pray he has not hurt you, my love!" Margret said, placing a hand on the side of her husband's face.

Phillip smiled at his wife, took her hand, kissed it. "Thank you for your concern, my dear Margret, but I have already told you that I am quite fine. At least that bubble he used to stick me in burst when he dragged that child – your grandson," he said with a sidelong glance, "outside; otherwise, I had no idea how I was going to be able to escape that small prison."

Grandpa noticed a small body lying in pieces by the stairs. "What the hells is that laying over there?"

"A child robot your grandson said that drove the bouncer that crashed into the top of our house." Sniff. "I will admit to you I did not believe your grandson's tall tale; however, as much as it pains me to admit, I could be wrong."

"A *child* robot?"

"That's what I said."

"Never heard of such a thing!"

"That makes *two* of us."

Grandpa stepped closer, noticed the clothing on the robot. *Looks like the same stuff Jonas wears! What the hells? Could this be a copy of Jonas? Could Jonas still be alive?* "Mind if I see that bouncer you spoke of?"

Phillip's nose flared again. "Be quick about it, and please leave after. It's on the third floor."

"Thank you."

"I have never liked trespassers in our home, especially other ghosts. I'm not running a hotel. My wife and I have had enough turmoil for one day. Plus, there are other things we need to tend… um…to."

"Thank you. I'll, uh, be out of here as soon as I can."

"Good."

Grandpa zipped up the stairs.

"Why, Phillip," Margret gazed at him. "You aren't getting soft on me, are you?"

Confusion fluttered across Phillip's face.

"You know darn well what I mean, my love. Why did you not threaten that old ghost, inform him he will never leave since he trespassed into our house?"

Phillip held up a finger, placed it on her lips. "Do not fret, my dear, I have not gone soft. That is an old ghost. I enjoy keeping the young ones around, before we carve them up." Grin. "At the moment I wish to rest, place this day behind us. Anyways, do you not recall of the other ghost who trespassed earlier?"

Margret pondered. "Oh! How quick I have forgotten!"

"If it makes you feel any better – gods know it will me – let's go see how he is holding up, shall we?"

Margret giggled. "Yes, my love…let's. Surely, our family has given him a huge welcome into the household."

"I'm betting on it."

The two held hands and floated up the steps.

*** 

Grandpa studied the remains of the bouncer, its Slader Corp title on the side. He did not have much time to waste. If the demi had invaded his suburb and taken everyone away, he knew exactly where to look for his grandson. He hoped he could find Jonas as well.

And he probably did not have much time before they decided to change the boys into what Carolyn and Steven had become.

\*\*\*

"Walts Brinner, do you understand *why* you are here?" the voice slipped out of an unseen speaker, reverberated off the walls of a room with a wall-size mirror.

After Chainsaw Freckles handed Walts off to the demi then told to get into the back of the bouncer, he watched news reporter Ray Manisquaski attempt to inquire where Jonas was, the youngest lotto winner, and what was going to happen to Walts. An agent stuck his hand in Ray's face, said something to him, and the reporter's face scowled.

Blasting into the sky Walt's ride was as quiet as a grave. An armed agent sat across from him, staring through his dark shades, while the driver and a third agent sat in the cab. Once they arrived at Slader Corp, his escorts whisked him through a door that spiraled open and into a room. Bright fluorescent lights overhead splashed a metal chair and a wooden table. A camera in the shape of a small hovering sphere tucked high in one corner of the room, aimed its eye, recording his every move. The room reflected all those cop shows he had watched, where all interrogations took place. He knew whoever was speaking to him was hiding behind the huge mirror.

"Mr. Brimmer, do you understand *why* you are here?" the voice repeated.

Walts didn't respond.

"Come now, you are a smart kid, Mr. Brinner. You should know that accompanying a lotto winner to the rebellion's hideout is against the law. Correct?"

Walts kept quiet.

As a hologram of the five Lotto Laws appeared, one sentence blinked a thick shade of neon, heavy emphasizing: Said Winner will not associate with the rebellion, have an Accomplice venture with him or her to go into the

Subterraneans; otherwise, Accomplice will face
the same fate as Winner.

"The one who breaks this law must be sentenced to death at
the Neutralization Center and the human organs will be harvested
for scientific use. The body will undergo a TransmoG process, and
used for whatever the Slader Corporation deems necessary."

Walts gasped. *TransmoG, like Jonas?*

He had been tricked! No doubt about it! He shouldn't have
followed the robot who had once been the best friend he knew
underground into the Subterraneans. He should have told the
Jonas-copy he wouldn't do it and could have gone back home; *could*
have. However, he did not know Jonas had been transfigured. No
idea his friend had been stolen away by the demi the night before.
Too bad he could not save Jonas from what the demi had done to
him.

But, *had* the Jonas-copy told him the truth about his parents?
Were they actually transfigured into robots, too?

The demi had played on his emotions, made him believe the
Jonas-copy posed as his best friend who led him underground.
They knew he would not leave Jonas by himself. The real Jonas had
always been his best friend through thick and thin. The real Jonas
stood up for him when Rib and the ravens caused havoc. If he
hadn't, Walts would have already been in a huge mess of hurt lying
in the hospital or dead or even have had his brain drained by Swipe.
Either way, being tortured to death by the ravens or sitting here
facing death by the demi, had sent him up the virtual river without
a paddle. He prayed for the choice of returning as a ghost after his
death. Would he be able to locate Grandpa in the Wake? Would he
have a choice to come back as ghost? A terrible feeling sat down on
his chest. The possibility of never being able to find his relatives and
become lost in the ghostly world, all alone, could happen.

The door spiraled open.

"Step through the door, Mr. Brinner," one of two armed
agents who stood there demanded.

Walts didn't move.

"Step through or you *will* be forced."

Walts stepped through and handcuffs were placed around his wrists. Chains were hooked to the cuffs and attached to a hovering sphere-shaped robot.

The door to the interrogation room spiraled shut.

\*\*\*

Grandpa Ekto-Leaped and appeared in the lobby of Slader Corp.

"Hey!" a demi guard stood up from behind a long desk and pointed his finger. "You do not have clearance in here. Please leave!"

"I need to see my grandson, Walts Brinner, and his friend, Jonas Leeshur."

"They are not here. You must leave. Ghosts are prohibited inside Slader Corp."

"Aw, rectangular helium blast! I *know* they are here, young man! You can't fool me!"

"No. They're not. Please leave."

Grandpa stole a look at a hallway running beside the front desk. "Let me see them. They're here because I watched all that commotion going on down at that old house by the river. That demented robot clown escorted my grandson out the front door, and I witnessed you demi agents stuff him in a bouncer. No telling where his friend is, but I bet my ectoplasm ass he's here too."

"I asked you to leave, and you have not, sir! You should be well aware of your Paranormal Laws. You, sir, have broken a rule. Stay where you are. Do *not* move." The agent pulled his gun and used telepathy for: « Central, we have a situation in the lobby. We have a trespasser; a ghost. Send security ASAP. »

Grandpa morphed into an orb and shot down the hall.

"Get back here!" the agent shouted, firing a round.

\*\*\*

Grandpa wished he could Ekto-Leap, snatched Walts and Jonas and gotten the boys the hells out of the building and somewhere safe. But he couldn't. It sure would have been faster. Grandpa had not a clue of the building's layout.

He zipped through the building, careened around corners, eluding the eyes of demi agents, continuing his search of each and every floor. When he reached the top of the building, not sure where else to look, he was at a loss.

*Had they killed him? Gods, he hope the hells not! The kids* had *to be here somewhere!*

A horrid thought arrived. A way to locate Walts and Jonas; perhaps the *only* way. Against the Paranormal Laws, it could get him in deep trouble. Insurgents from The Great Beyond could be alerted, and they would come after him.

Grandpa pondered.

At this point he didn't give an organic rat turd from a synthetic rat bot. Let them send the troops after him. The hells with them. His priority was keeping the boys safe. Carolyn and Steven had fallen victim to what horror the demi and Maximus Slader were doing – erasing the entire mortal existence.

*Hang on, boys, I pray you're still alive!*

Speeding around a corner, down a hall, luck smacked him.

The agent had not a clue what hit him. While chatting with Central by telepathy, informing the intruder had not been seen, the agent received a gut-punch, knocking him off guard and sending him in a sprawl. Something searched his brain, blurring his vision, flipping through an index of knowledge. This caused a skull-splitting headache. He tried rising off the floor, only to watch the floor snatch him back. The headache worsened, his blood pressure rose, and a blood vessel burst in his brain, causing him to stroke.

His body twitched, his eyes rolled back into his head, and he tried swallowing his tongue. Death squashed its existence.

Grandpa slipped out of the body. *Damn!* He had not intended for it to happen. He only wanted to tap into the guy's brain, find the boys.

Grandpa started off, stopped. He had an idea. Another horrid thought, but might work in his favor.

Something moved behind him.

A hawkish-faced figure shrouded in a hooded cloak loomed over the corpse.

*What the?*

A claw reached inside the guy's flesh, pulled free a bright blue glow, dropped it inside a small mason jar. A snicker came from the creature as it patted the corpse's head. "I'll be taking that, thank you, Charlie Sloss."

The creature gazed at Grandpa. Nodded with a grin; vanished.

Grandpa blinked. *Jumpin' stunt gods on hover bikes! The hells just happened? The hells was that creature? It stole the guy's soul!*

Whatever prompted that, Grandpa had not a clue. And he had no time to mess with pursuing the answer. He jumped back inside the agent, wearing the dead man as a suit, and peeked through blood-shot pupils as he stood.

He pulled the guy's firearm from the shoulder holster.

He knew exactly where they were keeping Walts.

But not Jonas, if he was still alive.

« Agent Kiles, are you okay? Come in. Are you okay? »

The voice echoed in the dead man's skull, startling Grandpa's head

He searched for the voice.

« Agent Kiles, come in. Are you okay? »

Then he realized it was a telepathic signal. « Are you okay, agent Kiles? We saw you on the camera. We watched you fall. Are you okay? »

*Crap!* "Oh…I'm…uh…fine. Just had a twitch, you know."

Chuckle.

« Looked more than a *twitch*, agent Kiles. Get to the ER on level five immediately. »

"Oh…um…I'll be fine."

« I doubt it. You know the drill. If ER thinks you are having health problems living as a mortal, they'll send you to TransmoG. Standard procedure. »

"I'm fine…nothing to worry about, Central."

« This is an *order*, Kiles. Get your ass to the ER immediately. Agent Biles is on the floor you are on. He will make contact with you in a few seconds and accompany you. »

"I'm telling you I'm f–"

"Agent Kiles," the one called Biles said as he stepped around a corner, startling Grandpa/Kiles. "Please come with me….Hey. What's wrong with your face? One side of it is drooping. Looks like you've had a stroke."

Grandpa/Kiles had forgotten what a stroke does to a person. He also did not realize his broken speech through Kile's lips. That was why Central was so damn interested in his condition! "I'm… good. Nothing to worry about, Biles."

"I think there *is* something to worry about. C'mon," Biles grabbed hold of him, "we're off to ER. Central's orders."

"But…but I still need to go after our intruder."

"Not at this moment you don't. Your job is done for the day. If you have to be sent to TransmoG, you'll be sent back as a robot. There are plenty of other agents who are looking for that ghost. We'll find him."

Biles hauled Grandpa/Kiles down the hallway toward an elevator.

Grandpa/Kiles had to do something quick. He knew this situation would not end well. They turned a corner and Grandpa/Kiles took a quick glance for any cameras. He did not see a one. Still holding the pistol, he used the handle to hit Biles over the head.

Biles thumped the floor.

Grandpa/Kiles managed to get the legs of the dead body moving and tore down a hallway. He could feel rigor mortis beginning to tap the guy's spine. He didn't have much more time inside this dying flesh before it started to become a workout.

He took a turn, found the wall he searched for. It spiraled open and, before he slipped in, an alarm screamed.

« Whoever you are inside agent Kiles' body, give yourself up immediately! » the voice echoed. « We have scanned Kiles' body. You have murdered our agent and have kidnapped his corpse. You have broken a Paranormal Law. You have committed a serious crime. The Bureau of the Recently Deceased will be contacted. This is a severe penalty, and you will be punished by sending you to Purgatory. »

***

The door spiraled shut.

Walts shuddered.

The Neutralization Center loomed before him, placed inside a room the size of an airplane hangar. Pictures on the *Whadda Ya Gotta Say, Ray?* show did not do the automaton justice. Walts had the impression the facility had been located outside. Not anymore. If one sought out this demented place, they were obviously never seen from again, because of their pursuit of a Death Card, not window shopping for a Joker.

The Neutralization Center's massive shape began with a cylinder base and stretched upward, thick and as slim as a smokestack. A slow-moving turbine sat on top, bright multicolored lights splashed the walls of the room, depicting shapes of skeletons hand in hand, dancing in a graceful manner.

People were lined up in front of the killing machine. The

demi ordered each by gunpoint to take turns and step inside the garage-sized sliding metal door of the killing machine.

*What was up with that? Why were they here, too? Surely all these people didn't commit the same kind of crime he was being charged with!* Walts thought to himself.

The hovering sphere-shaped robot dragged Walts down a long metal staircase, released the chains but not the handcuffs, placing him in line behind the others.

"If you attempt to run," an agent told Walts, "you will be shot."

A man wearing a blue baseball cap stood in front of Walts. "Hey, aren't you that kid off the televid?"

"Yeah, I am."

He scowled. "I'm wondering if *you* are the cause of all this!"

"Me? Why would *I* cause this?"

"Because you and your stupid little friend did not give yourselves up when the demi told you to! All of us wouldn't be here waiting on that thing to consume us," he waved a hand at the Neutralization Center in front of them, "and this may not have happened if you hadn't broken the lotto laws and gone off to the rebellion's hideout."

"He's not the reason for this! This is Maximus Slader's doing!" a young woman defended Walts.

"*Riight!* Tell me another tall tale, lady!" the man in the cap snorted.

"This boy is innocent! His parents are probably here, too, waiting to die in that death machine!"

"Perhaps they are *already* dead." The man grinned. "Serves this kid right for his actions."

A sliver of anger blossomed under Walts' ribcage.

"This kid broke protocol allowing his friend to lead him into the Subterraneans," the man continued. "He also allowed for his friend to buy him things, which, as we all know, is against the lotto rules. Am I wrong?"

An older woman stepped forward: "No. you are dead-on. That kid is the reason for us being here. We were dragged from our homes and brought here to die. I say we shove him up to the front of the line where he can die first. He deserves it!"

Shouts reverberated off the walls. The young woman's words who defended Walts became obsolete. People chanted the death of Walts.

"C'mon, kid," the guy in the cap pulled Walts close.

*Uggh! The guy had some serious halitosis going on!*

Grinning, a mouthful of servo replacement teeth twitched inside his mouth, instead of dentures.

*As these automaton teeth spin in their sockets, I assure you ladies and gentlemen these are teeth that'll chew through metal!* Walts snatched the memory of the commercial of the pudgy little salesman dressed in a dentist garb assisted by a servo unit programmed to perform the surgeries.

Walts blinked, and the flesh on the guy's face warbled, reshaped, becoming a flicker of Maximus Slader.

The colony's leader guffawed.

The flick of the switch the face returned to the norm. "Get in front of *me!*" He shoved Walts forward.

*What the heck was* that? *Were my eyes playing tricks on me?*

Someone grabbed Walts, shoved him further along up the line. Flickers of Maximus' face dotted across other faces in the crowd. Hands grabbed Walts, shoving him closer to the death machine.

"Don't worry, kid, the pain of death doesn't hurt," an older man said, yet another with a bad case of bad breath. "But this does."

Walts folded over, gasped for a breath.

Another man picked up Walts' as he sucked in a pocket of air.

The face of Maximus flickered across the guy's face.

Vanished in the blink of an eye.

"We want to watch you *bleed*, kid!"

Walts was shoved into a woman's arms, and she said: "We want to hear you *scream!*"

Shoved into a teenager's arms, the kid said: "Man up, Waltsee! Don't be a dweeb-oh! We want to hear a guttural sound clawing its way out of your throat as you suck in your last breath and *die!*"

Shoved into the arms of a familiar face, the neighbor from across the street, the same who kept all those awful robot gnomes in his yard: "I want to see my gnomes dance a jig on your corpse, Walts! They *love* the touch of dying *flesh!*"

Before he knew it, Walts stood in front of the Neutralization Center's door. An agent said, "Any last words you wish to say, Mr. Brinner?" The flesh on his face warbled, flickered Maximus Slader, but paused long enough to allow a few seconds of a guffaw. Then, as quick as it appeared, morphed back.

Walts chewed for words failing to arrive.

"Well then, step inside on that platform where the red X is." The agent placed a hand on his back, pushed. "Nothing to worry about, kid. It will all be over quickly." Smile.

The metal door slid shut. A yellow glow shrouded Walts' as he stood between four ten-foot high walls decorated with long razor-sharp spikes – a similarity of an Iron Maiden's interior, perhaps her brother. As the death machine's six-cylinder engine grumbled to life belts shrieked, forcing a long groan, emitting a vibration under Walts' feet.

"Welcome to the Neutralization Center," a recorded voice said. "You have made a wise choice. Employees at Slader Corp commend you for it. We appreciate your business, even if it is your last transaction you will have in your life. Do not fear death. It is only the beginning of a new life. The people at the Bureau of the Recently Deceased will work hard to make the best choice whether you should return as a ghost, or you should move toward the Light, entering The Great Beyond.

"Please stand very still. Your death will arrive in ten seconds."

\*\*\*

The door spiraled open, revealing the Neutralization Center in the center of the room. A long line of people were not only awaiting their death, but cheering for a boy who stepped into the machine and the door slid shut.

*Oh no! Walts!* Grandpa stumbled down the steps, the dead agent's legs forced to keep up with momentum as he headed toward the death machine.

"Kiles? What are *you* doing here?"

Grandpa ignored, passed the agent, raced up the ramp.

"Stop him!" one of the other agents barked. "That isn't Kiles! It's our intruder!"

Grandpa shoved people out of the way, making his way toward the door.

"Stop him!" another agent shouted.

Five feet from the machine's door two hands grabbed Grandpa, yanking him backward. His feet left the ground and he smacked the hard floor, snapping the spine. It didn't hurt Grandpa, enclosed in Kile's cocoon of meat, kind of a protective shield.

Faces peered down at him, scowling, fluttering a quick-view of Maximus Slader, then dissipated. Arms scooped him upright. Three agents took aim with their rifles.

"Leave agent Kile's corpse at once or we will plug you with Morto bullets," an agent stepped through the crowd. "If you think this agent's skin will stop them from reaching your ghostly flesh, you best rethink your options, intruder."

Grandpa slipped out of Kile's body, and it dropped like the sack stuffed with human organs it truly was. Grandpa gazed at the death machine's entrance, only a few steps away, his attempt to rescue his grandson now a lost cause.

The enemy had won.

***

The death-machine groaned its countdown to Walts' demise: "Eight seconds."

Walts wished for an escape.

"Seven."

Wished pounding on the metal door, begging to be let out would be an option.

"Six."

Walts did not want to die, especially like this. In a few minutes he'd become a human pin cushion, skewered by spikes. Thoughts of being a ghost, how squiggly it would be, faded. *Would he be allowed to return as a ghost? What did Grandpa say that place was called? His kidnappers said the name before he was shoved out of that interrogation room. It went by an abbreviation... BVD? No. BDD? No. BRD. Yep. That it!* The Bureau of the Recently Deceased. They were the ones who sealed his fate giving him the opportunity to be a ghost or shove him into the Light. He feared he may not get a choice. He feared he would never get to return and see his Grandpa, his mom, or his dad again. He feared they would shove him into The Great Beyond where he would be neighbors with the quartet of gods in the spheres – end of story.

"Five; four."

Walts squeezed his eyes shut.

"Three."

He did not want to watch as spikes were driven into his body.

"Two."

Walts tensed up, braced for impact.

"One....Thanks so much for your business at the Neutralization Cennnter-ter-ter-ter-teeerrrrrrrr...," the voice stammered, chewed a huge wad of bubble gum, fizzled out. A grind of gears, a *thunk!*, and a long hiss permeated Walts' metal tomb as the machine abruptly stopped.

Walts' gasped. *What the heck happened?*

"Dude! You okay?"

Walts knew the voice.

"You okay, man?'

Walts opened his eyes. "J-Jonas?"

"Yep! It's me, Walts! The *real* one! Sorry for the late arrival, dude. I had to wait, like for*ever*, in a line at the BRD. I didn't realize they made you take a number and have a seat until they call you up." He rolled his eyes in disgust.

"*Jonas!*"

"*Then*, you have to deal with those people who work there. *Man*, do they have a bad attitude! You'd think everyone they spoke to were bad people or something! I bet they hate people in general." Snort. "Kinda wondered if they were even mortal men and women before they *worked* at the BRD. Maybe they were bad people; who knows? Anyways, I feel for you when *you* have to deal with 'em! It sucks!"

"Jonas! You came back! Groovatronic!"

"Yeah, I'm back. Not in the flesh, but ectoplasmic-shaped, I suppose." Chuckle. "You're just lucky when the folks at the BRD sent me back I slipped up and stepped through the Wake and ended right outside this death trap. I saw them forcing you to the front of the line and watched the door shut. Lucky the demi or any of those people out there didn't notice me."

"I don't think they're actual humans, Jonas."

"Huh?"

"Their faces change. I kept seeing flashes of Maximus Slader. I think they are all TransmorGs."

"That's…weird."

"Man, I'm just glad you're here to save me!"

Jonas smiled. "You're welcome, dude! Freaked me out to see them throwing you in here. Had to throw a wrench in the system, so to speak, stopping the Neutralizer from killing you. But, listen up: Your Grandpa is here. He tried to save you and was captured."

Walts blinked. "Grandpa is out there?"

"Yep. The demi drove him off at gunpoint when I arrived. For some reason, he had possessed an agent's body. I saw him ooze out of the corpse."

"He did *what?*" he said incredulously.

"Yep," affirming it, "he possessed the dude's corpse."

Walts screwed his face up.

"Your grandpa was probably sneaking in here using the agent as camouflage."

"That's... weird."

"Definitely an un-squiggle thing to do."

"Yup."

"I bet your grandpa needed a brain to pick to find out where you were. Maybe the guy was alive when he did it."

"Could be. Do you think Grandpa killed the agent?"

Jonas shrugged his shoulders. "No telling."

"We have to save him, Jonas! He's in danger!"

"We will. But so are you. First we need to get you the hells out of here. By now I'm betting the demi is scratching their heads, wondering why their beloved death machine has quit working."

"I figured I'd never see you again, Jonas, since they transfigured your body into a robot."

"Like I said, sorry for arriving late. I knew the demi planned on neutralizing you. They told me so when they placed me exactly where you are standing."

Walts' gasped. "They put *you* in here?"

"Yep...I am not going to go into details, Walts. You do *not* want to know how painful it was to die."

Walts refrained from attempting to imagine it.

"Remember the other night when I met you outside during curfew? Well, the demi was waiting on me when I got home. So were my parents! Weird, huh? You know how my relationship was with my folks. I hardly ever saw them; then, suddenly, here they were sitting in the living room watching the televid. When I asked how they were doing they looked up me, and I freaked. Their eyes looked like when the televid lost its signal."

"That clone of you told me what they did. Seeing your folks like that had to be just *creepy!*"

"Creepy would be an understatement. Anyways, a couple of the demi agents walked out of the kitchen and ordered me to come with them. I tried to run, but was zapped with something that sent an electronic pulse throughout my entire body, knocking me unconscious. I woke up handcuffed in a room. After that, they escorted me here, to my death."

"Wow!"

"Terrible experience, Walts. I wouldn't wish it on Rib, for that matter!"

"That's one bold statement."

"No kidding. It's the truth though. Anyway…let's not let you end up like me and see if we can work on finding a way out of here and try to save your grandpa."

#

"Well, hello there," Maximus Slader said. He glanced at an agent. "Lower the Mortonica, so I can talk to him."

Grandpa's small prison descended, face to face with Ozarium's leader.

"They say you kidnapped and possessed one of my agents and caused him to have a stroke and die. That right?"

Honestly, Grandpa did not feel good about causing the death of someone, but he needed to find Walts. The demi and Slader were enemies. Not showing he gave a rat turd he masked his feelings, shrugged his shoulders, said: "Evidently the kid couldn't take the shock I gave him."

"*Evidently?* It was quite an interesting tactic, old man. Not impressed, though." Snort, a wave of his hand. "Lose an agent, gain another after TransmoG."

"You may not care about your men, but I care about my grandson. Is he still alive? Could have sworn I heard your stupid machine stop working before being hauled away."

"Unfortunately your grandson *is* alive and inside my machine awaiting death. Workers will figure out what went wrong and fix it. The Neutralization Center has *never* been shut down before."

"What a shame, Slader. Goes to show you nothing lasts forever. You need to let my grandson go, Slader. He has done *nothing* to deserve being put to death. Let me take his place. Use me for whatever you want. Just don't hurt Walts."

"And what use do I have for you, Mr. Brinner? You are already deceased. You are a ghost; not a mortal. You cannot undergo TransmoG and become one of my slaves. I have no way of controlling you. I have yet to perfect the use of controlling a ghost to do my bidding." Sly grin. "However, it's in the works, I assure you that. As we speak things are taking a slight shift in the colony. Everyone who is of flesh and blood has begun their TransmoG process, changing them into robots."

"You did that to my son and my daughter-in-law."

"Correct."

"Why? Why are you doing this?"

"You must see my side of it: A preventative maintenance to help the colonists. I have decided the best way possible to keep the population leveled, other than the lotto, to keep people safe from disease, sending them through TransmoG. First I experimented with convicts, the homeless, transferring them into schizos. A successful endevour, why not continue the practice with lotto winners? Right? Oh, well, too bad you don't see my side of the future of Ozarium. See, before I took leader status in Ozarium things were such a mess.

"Are you aware of the mutant infestation during the Overcast era?"

Grandpa shook his head.

"Didn't think so…it had to be dealt with by creating mutants to fight mutants. And before you ask, I will not release any information concerning my creatures, now stuffed in a cryogenic state. No one knows of the ones I developed, and no one will ever find out their existence.

"Anyway, a depression slid by, shoving people from jobs, making them starve, forcing them to live off the street and die; some turned to a life of crime. The demi had their hands full. The world had succumbed to despair. Overcast had been the darkest of days Ozarium had ever seen."

"On a good note, I unplugged the mainframe of Quill, the computer left to run the colony by the gods and swept up the bad and polished, layering the good, developing a normal society. Inventing the lotto was a stroke of genius, if I do say myself. People were happy to win all that cred and spend it almost anyway they like. Then came people like Jake Velmer and others before him who wanted to go down with a fight. His kind had not been thought of, thinking everyone who won would be joyous. It only takes one person to screw it up for others. Pitty, eh? Velmer's actions resulted in the rebellion to surface. Now they have been a titanium thorn in my ass, no less! They have always challenged my leadership. Well, not anymore. They will pay for their actions.

"There were times when the rebellion tried to breach security and enter inside Slader Corp; however, they did not anticipate being cut down by the demi. So, to repay that affront, I figured why not send a spy off to their hideout and counter what they tried to do to me; why not make a child lotto winner and use him as an advantage. After Jonas was *randomly* chosen – by yours truly – the teeth in the wheel of the mechanism slipped into the grooves, the conveyer belts began to run, delivering the product promptly. Transfiguring the very first ever child ever in the history of the lotto and sending him to infiltrate the rebellion's hideout in the Subterraneans was a stroke of genius, was it not?"

Grandpa gave him a cold look.

"Well, at least *I* think it was." Sniff. "Who cares what you think, old man."

"You're mad, Slader. Guess you thought killing one kid wasn't enough. Why not include another in your demented plans."

Maximus Slader shrugged his shoulders. "Casualties. Sorry, old man. Look at it this way: Walts will be the *second* child I murdered."

"You made Walts out to be an accomplice in a crime. You are going to pay, Slader."

"You are right. Again, sorry. And how am I going to pay for my actions? I am the supreme ruler in Ozarium. Even the rebellion will fall if they challenge me."

Grandpa fumed. "You're lucky I'm inside this bubble, or I would possess your husk in the blink of an eye, Slader! And if you think your agent Kiles died horribly, your death would be far worse!"

Maximus snorted. "Spare me, old man. That will never happen. No way could you possess me. Very soon Walts will become history, like all the people of the colony, and there is not a damn thing you can do about it."

"Killing innocent people is not right. I have never agreed with your stupid lotto nonsense. Why mutilate the entire population, anyways?"

"Like I said, to keep the population leveled; to keep in control of their actions. There will be no one who dares to overthrow my leadership. I am *the* king. Much like the king who murdered that defunct rat catcher who thought he could come in and become a hero of the village, I am the supreme ruler of Ozarium. No one will take that from me. They who wish to, will die horribly, much worse than what my death machine will do to everyone in this colony very shortly. Once the process is complete, Ozarium will be an entirely new world, free of sickness and disease and trouble with a group of rebellious individuals who think they can fight for what is right.

"Right now you need not to worry yourself, or worry much more about your grandson's well-being. His soul may get to choose to come back as a ghost. Or not. It'll be up to the staff at the Bureau of the Recently Deceased."

A spiral open as he stepped in front of it.

"Oh, one last thing," Slader added. "The laws are going to change for every single apparition. Your kind will be forbidden to enter Ozarium. Your kind will be quarantined permanently inside the Wake. You may never see your grandson again. Get used to it. Once you are placed inside the Wake, if you cross over, you will be shot on sight with a barrage of morto bullets."

"I will see my grandson, and you will not succeed in this horror, Slader."

Snicker.

"If I get out of here you will be sorry!"

"Keep telling yourself those lies if you wish, old man. Believe whatever you want. They are useless imaginations."

The door spiraled shut.

*** 

"Sorry for leaving you by yourself longer than I wanted to. I thoroughly searched this machine and found the only safe way out of this place is through that small door directly above your head. Wait. Hang on a second." Jonas disappeared through the wall of spikes and about a minute later Walts heard: "Heads-up!" The door above Walts' head popped out, bounced off the floor and Jonas came next. "That, up there," he pointed, "leads into a ventilator system. I figured I'd make it easier to get inside by knocking out the grate when you climb up there."

"*Climb* up there?"

"Yep. "

Walts gasped.

"*And* you really need to hurry; they are outside trying to fix this machine."

"I thought you shut it down for good?"

He shook his head. "Temporary stoppage. All I did was pull out some wires and twist out some tubes."

"Oh. Great."

"I'm not a mechanic, dude! I was going in blind when I did what I did!"

"I should know that, sorry. So, how the hells do I climb up *there?*"

"You'll have to use those spikes to climb."

Walts didn't like the sound of it. *Touching those spikes? Uggh! What if he slipped and fell and scraped against those needle-sharp points?* "Seriously? No other way?"

"I'm afraid not." Jonas drifted out of the machine again; slipped back in. "You need to hurry! I think they figured out the problem."

"Crap!" Walts grabbed hold of two spikes, pulled himself up, placed his foot on one, hoisted his body up. Halfway up, he managed to rip a good-size hole on the front of his shirt, thankfully missing the chance to tear a chunk out of his skin.

He sucked in a breath, blew it out, climbed further.

The machine groaned.

"Hurry, Walts!" Jonas said.

Walts noticed the door three feet above him. "Hey! How can I get to it, Jonas? There's nothing to hang on to!"

"Oh, crap! Wait a minute…got an idea!" Jonas grabbed hold of a spike, grabbed another, climbed much faster than Walts had. "Let me see if I can hold you and give you a push up."

"What if you fall?"

"Walts. I'm a ghost. Those spikes won't hurt me."

Walts blinked. "That's right."

The machine groaned a second time.

The voice spat out its gum, unraveled: "Thaaaanks soooo much for your business at the Neutralization Center. Gods bless!"

Two of the walls jerked toward one another, closing inward.

"Hurry, Jonas!" Walts cried. "What the? Are you touching my —"

"Butt. Yup. I got you. Let go, dude." Jonas said.

"Let *go?*"

"Let go and reach for the door! That's it! Hurry! I won't be able to hold you very long!"

Walts' fingertips touched the metal handles.

Jonas gave him a hard shove.

Walts grasped the handles, pulled himself up into darkness seconds before the spiked walls below shut.

"Jonas!"

Jonas' head squeezed out of where the walls connected, not only glowing like a street lamp, but swelled as if a balloon.

"You look like a cartoon character." Walts laughed.

"*Annnnnd* for my next trick," said, pulling himself erect, standing beside Walts on top of the connected walls.

Walts shook his head. "You aren't right."

"Never said I was." Grin. "Start climbing, dude, and lead the way. We have a long way to go."

The grumbling and groaning of the death machine chased the boys as they climbed, soon shutting down. Walts had begun to wonder where the end could be until —

"Ow! Geez!" Walts rubbed the top of his head.

"Oops. Sorry. Forgot to warn you about the door," Jonas replied.

"That's fine." Walts fumbled around for a handle, twisted, and it opened, spilling in light. They climbed out, stood on the back side of the Neutralization Center. Cautious not to be seen, they peeked, saw the crowd lined up, ready to succumb to their death inside the death machine; however, they were not moving, as if the ride at the amusement park had ended.

"Um. What the heck is wrong with them? Could they be robots?" Walts asked.

"Possible," Jonas said.

"Hey, where'd the demi go? I don't see them?"

"They might have figured you were dead and that was that. They could have returned back inside." Jonas pointed to the door Walts had originally come through.

"I sure hope so. I don't want to be spotted. Hey…look, Jonas! There's a metal bridge that'll take us over to that wall."

"*Soooo* we're climbing over to a wall where there's no door? Brilliant move, Walts."

"Could be a possibility it'll open. See how there's a wider spot at the end of the bridge? Kinda looks like it's there posing as a metal porch. Or something like that. You haven't seen the ones they have here. They open really weird-oh. Remember the ones in the Subterraneans?"

"Huh?"

"Don't you remember? They spiral-open and –" The recollection of the REAL Jonas not by his side when he ventured underground crashed into him. "Sorry, I…uh, I forgot you weren't with me."

"Nope. I was here."

"Good thing you weren't. It wasn't fun. That copy of you tricked me into going into the Subterraneans. That's why I'm here now."

"If the rebellion had collected you the same time they did me, shoving us both into the suicide machine, we'd be in the Wake."

"True."

"Instead they played out their sinister plan of copying me and infiltrating the Subterraneans, dragging you along for the ride, right?"

"Yep. But on the flipside you wouldn't have been able to use those cool new powers of being a ghost and have come to my rescue, saving me from that death machine. That's one incentive."

Smile. "Yeah, but we're not out of the woods yet, Walts. The demi still wants your skin."

"True. I just hope I'm not caught."

"We are going to work together, hoping it isn't going happen, man."

"Squigely!"

"So, about this weird door you were talking about...?"

"Oh! Check this out! C'mon," Walts gestured with a wave of his hand, "let's see if that wall will open funny."

The boys traipsed over the bridge holding onto the rails, glancing over their shoulder every so often, just in case they were spotted.

Walts found out something horrible and stopped.

"What's wrong?" Jonas said.

"I don't like this height."

"You're kidding?"

"Nope."

"You're afraid of heights? When did this happen?"

"Two seconds ago."

Jonas chuckled. "Look, there's only a few more steps to go, dude. C'mon, you can make it!"

Walts hurried across. Once they were both in front of the wall it spiraled open, revealing a long hallway.

"Oh...wow," Jonas said. "Weird-oh!"

"Told ya!" Walts replied. "C'mon, I want to find Grandpa."

Ten feet down the hall, around a corner, they ran into a demi agent.

Actually, Walts did; Jonas slipped through the agent.

"Hey! What are you kids doing here? Wait. I know your face!" He pointed at Walts. "You're supposed to be dead!"

"This way, Walts!" Jonas said.

Walts followed.

"Stop! Get back here!" the agent took chase.

Rounding another corner two demi agents appeared.

"C'mon, Walts!" Jonas shot down another hallway, Walts in tow.

More agents. Both boys slid to a stop, twisted around.

Other agents converged, trapping them.

Behind the boys a door spiraled open and they quickly slipped inside.

"Walts!" Grandpa gazed down at his grandson.

"Grandpa!"

"Do not move, or I will shoot you both," A demi said, aiming his rifle. "Morto bullets will not only kill ghosts, it'll put a hole in your skull kid."

\*\*\*

The Mortonica Bubble burst.

Grandpa floated down to the floor and, not leaving the boys behind, armed demi agents escorted the three into a room about half the size where the Neutralization Center sat. The demi had successfully rounded up each and every person in Ozarium and delivered them to Slader Corp, placing each in a long line to await their TransmoG which lay inside a glass room filled with ten coffin-shaped glass-faced pods.

Walts joined the others and stand in line, per orders from the demi. All Grandpa and Jonas could do was to stand off to the side, guarded at gunpoint, while Walts was destined to undergo his TransmoG.

"We need to do something to help him!" Jonas said.

Grandpa needed to figure out a plan to save Walts. More demi agents stood by, armed with rifles. "I wish we could, Jonas. Wish there was a way to stop this nonsense! If you knew how to Ekto-Leap, things would be different. They'll kill you instantly if they think you are trying to escape. Darn well cannot take that chance!"

"Ekto-Leap?"

"Teleporting from one spot to another."

Jonas blinked. "No kidding? How do you do *that*?"

"It would be hard for me to explain. It takes time and practice to do the trick."

"Sure you can't show me, like a quick run-through?"

"No. Too risky. You'll be cut down before you leap, Jonas."

"There has to be *something* we can do! Walts is moving closer and closer to those pods!"

Grandpa's hands were tied. One move and he and Jonas would be chewed apart by morto bullets. He did not know how to save his grandson. It infuriated him.

*Damn Maximus Slader for causing this!*

The demi agent continued to watch him and Jonas.

Sure, Grandpa knew he could very well try and Ekto-Leap and grab Walts and slip out of the wall, but there would be no way to save Jonas unless –

"Jonas, if there is a way we can get closer to a wall," – Grandpa glanced at the agent who looked in the other direction, using the few seconds to see how far away they were from a wall: not but ten steps away – "it may be possible for you to slip through the wall and vanish from the demi's sight while I Ekto-Leap and grab Walts. If we do this, you need to make sure to watch your ass. There may be demi behind the wall. Okay?"

Jonas nodded.

Walts moved closer to the TransmoG's room entrance.

"Ready?" Grandpa asked.

"Yep." Jonas gave another nod.

"Move when I move." Grandpa kept a close eye on the demi who guarded them. The guy turned his head in their direction; then looked elsewhere.

Grandpa and Jonas stole the chance, moving backward two steps.

The agent glanced at them; then at the line of victims.

Grandpa and Jonas stole another chance to move, took it.

Five feet from the wall the agent glanced at them, then turned back to the line.

*The guy isn't even paying attention to us!* Grandpa thought.

Four feet from the wall.

The world around Grandpa and Jonas continued to shift forward.

The agent guarding them glanced at Grandpa and Jonas; then faced the crowd.

Grandpa and Jonas acted fast.

Jonas slipped through the wall.

Grandpa Ekto-Leaped.

\*\*\*

On the threshold of the TransmoG room Walts saw one agent running the TransmoG system, tapping the screen of a Recog tablet. People were forced to lie down inside each pod and once the glass doors closed mechanical arms appeared, injecting serum in their necks, placing their bodies asleep. A small circular saw cut open the scalp, extracted the brains, placed them inside plastic containers on a container belt.

Soon, it became Walts' turn.

Directed to his glass coffin Walts lied down inside the pod. Once the glass door whispered shut there was a whir and a servo hum as the machine began to work. Three straps secured his body in place while a robot arm rose up beside his neck, a long needle at the tip.

Walts squeezed his eyes shut, braced for the sting.

"Hang on, Walts! I'm gonna get you out of ther–"
Grandpa's voice severed as an explosion rocked the room.

*\*\**

"Are the colonists being taken care of?"

"Yes, sir."

"Good." Maximus Slader replied to the agent as he sat behind his desk, his fingers steepled. The hologram of an evil entity shrouded in a hooded cloak led a line of demonic kids armed with cleavers and knives inside a snow globe on his desk. "Very soon the restructure of the Ozarium colony will be complete." Grin. "The only living, breathing creatures around here will consist of you, myself, the small amount of agents who are left to undergo the process TransmoG for their own good, and the rebellion whom we have not caught yet. Their TransmoG will be scheduled ASAP when they are brought here." He glanced at agent Styles. "I pray your agents have them in custody?"

"Sir, there are certain problems we have, um, run into."

Maximus blinked. "Problems? Are they not captured?"

"No, sir. While infiltrating the Subterraneans after using the copy of Jonas as a spy, most of them were able to escape in Bouncers."

Maximus frowned. "And why have I not been informed about this until now, agent Styles?"

"As much that has had been going on already," – a trickle of perspiration slid down the side of the agent's face – "collecting each and everyone in the colony, sending them off to undergo TransmoG, keeping a close eye on the ghostly population, our manpower has been stretched thin. We do not have enough agents, sir."

"Agent Styles, you are in charge of Central. I expect a lot from you. I expected you to follow my orders to the T."

"I have sir," – clears throat – "to the best of my ability. I made sure my men collected Jonas, placed him through the process of TransmoG; made sure his friend Walts was also part of the plan to infiltrate the Subterraneans so we could invade them."

"I will give you that, agent Styles. You have done well so far, but the matter with collecting each and every breathing soul in the rebellion must be carried out immediately and dealt with by TransmoG. It is unacceptable the rebellion is loose."

"I-I know, sir, but we are trying t—"

"Agent Styles, you are not trying hard *enough*. Perhaps I need another agent that will do better?"

"Sir, the best thing I can do is retrieve more agents and track down the rebellion."

The floor rumbled.

"What was that?" Styles questioned.

Maximus frowned. A telepathic message slid into his head. He blinked twice before saying: "There is no need to locate the rebellion, Agent Styles." A crooked grin. "They have arrived."

"Arrived?"

"Yes. They are here."

"Here? Good. Then I must go and make sure they are sent to TransmoG, ASAP."

"One last thing, agent Styles."

"Sir?" He glanced over his shoulder.

"Your services are of no use to me anymore." A spot on the wall spiraled open and two large automaton arachnids crawled into the room, both carrying five-foot rats. "Decommission this failed human. Feast on his brain and flesh if you wish."

The rats licked their lips, nodded.

Webs spun, wrapping around Styles, dragging him through the door as it spiraled shut, clipping the agent's screams.

\*\*\*

The explosion rocked the room.

The hole in the ceiling viewed the sky, blown open by the rebellion. Four bouncers landed inside the room. Case step a foot out, shot an agent point blank in the face with her 9mm. Wisps of smoke curled out of the wound as the body slumped onto the floor. Another agent took a shot at Case. She ducked, rolled and, while still on the floor, blew the side of the agent's face off, revealing the inner workings of the automaton.

A dark-haired member of the rebellion close to Case took aim and dropped three agents, stopping their attack. Only one human, spilling a pool of blood out of the hole in his head. Other members of the rebellion followed suit, pouring out of Bouncers, taking aim at the agents inside the room.

Without a second to waste, rebellion members began corralling people together and shoving them into Bouncers.

Victims who had undergone TransmoG in the adjoining room where the conveyer belts ended, appeared out of a spiraled opening in the wall. Yellow cyclopean eyes scanned the room, locating the rebellion, began their attack. More agents appeared in the schizos wake, taking aim, firing their rifles at the rebellion, shooting a few, picking off people who had not undergone TransmoG.

"Bonner! Take out that agent running TransmoG!" Case ordered.

The one called Bonner took aim, blasted a hole through the agent's head while colonists were rounded up, escorted to bouncers.

*\*\**

During the raid Grandpa had stuck his hand through the glass pod, grabbed hold of the robotic arm, preventing the needle from sticking Walts in the neck. With his other hand he was able to snap away the straps. "Get out of there, Walts! I can't hold this arm back for very long!"

Walts tried pushing the glass door with his hands, not having any luck jarring it loose.

"Hurry, Walts!" Grandpa bit his bottom lip. "Can't hold it much longer!"

Walts used his feet and slammed the glass.

The glass did not crack.

He slammed it again, over and over.

No dice.

He planted his feet and shoved the glass with all the strength he had.

The lights above flickered. The power shut down. The door flipped open. He crawled out as fast as he could, half a millisecond before Grandpa lost control of the arm.

The needle, still sparked with electronic life, staked the cushion where Walts' head had been.

Walts looked up at Grandpa. "Thanks."

Grandpa helped Walts up, made himself solid so he could give him a big hug.

"What the heck is going on out there?"

"The rebellion is out there. They blew a hole in the roof, and it looks like they're saving people left and right. C'mon, let's get you out of here."

Door to each of the pods lifted, freeing each victim of their doom.

Walts took two steps; stopped.

Grandpa had made long strides, glanced back. "Walts, c'mon! We need to get-gone!"

"Umm…"

"Um, *what?*"

"The rebellion may be mad at me because I was with that fake Jonas when we went to their hideout. I was an accomplice to the demi finding them."

"We'll just have to explain it to them later. Right now we need to save the *real* Jonas and get out of here."

"Where is he?"

"He slipped into another room. Probably through this wall." Grandpa pointed to a wall. "I wanted to get him out of sight while I saved you by Ekto-Leaping.

"Let's see if we can find him."

\*\*\*

When Jonas slipped through the wall he stood in a hallway. Agents ran past him, a couple slid to a stop, noticing him, and switched their rail guns over to fire Morto bullets. Taking aim, they fired.

Slipping through another wall Jonas heard the bullets in his wake. He twisted around, peered into the face of a demi agent and the business-end of a rifle.

"Why, Jonas, good to see you again. I pray your life as a ghost has been a good one?" Maximus Slader chuckled.

\*\*\*

"What is the problem here, Harrens?" Case asked, glancing at Walts and Grandpa.

"These two do not want to come with us," Harrens replied around a cheek full of synthetic chewing tobacco, shifting his thick frame.

Case frowned. "Why not? It's not safe here. Slader will send more demi here, I assure you."

"I understand, but we need to find my grandson's friend who is a ghost."

"Walts' friend?"

"Jonas."

"Jonas Leeshur? The lotto winner?"

Grandpa nodded. "He came back as a ghost. Slader put him

through TransmoG."

"Yes. I did hear about him being put to death shortly after the infiltration at our base." Case scowled. "Jonas came to see me, but we did not realize it was a fake. Your grandson accompanied him. Trouble followed." She looked at Walts.

Walts gulped. He took a step back. He wanted to run, afraid she would order her soldiers to shoot him on sight or take him back to the Subterraneans and lock him up in the room where a new robot hovered in the corner.

"However, everything is fine, now," Case grinned; winked at Walts. "Let's find Jonas. Maximus Slader will do unspeakable things to him, even in the boy's form as a ghost. He can kill him using Morto bullets."

"Oh, I already know about it," Grandpa replied. "He had me captive and threatened to use them on me."

"Allow one of my men to accompany you two to one of the bouncers so you can safely arrive at the Subterraneans. My company and I will look for Jonas." Case ordered six other soldiers to come with her, including Harrens and Bonner.

Before she left, she said: "Look, Walts…I know you were not responsible for what happened in the Subterraneans. I'm not blaming you. You had no control over what Maximus Slader and his demi did to you, setting you up. Let's let bygones be bygones, okay?"

Walts nodded. The overshadowing fear that Case would punish him scurried away.

"Maximus Slader fooled you. He fooled me, using a fake Jonas. He played on your emotions. The man is evil. I assure you we are going to do everything in our power to get your friend back safe."

"Thanks."

To her soldiers: "Terrance, take these two back to the Subterraneans."

"Yes, ma'am. This way please." Terrance gestured with a nod of his head, adjusted his thick jaw, chewed on an unlit cigar.

Case and her men stepped through a door spiraled open, shutting in their wake. Grandpa and Walts followed Terrance to one of five bouncers. Seatbelts clicked, Terrance pushed the button to start the bouncer's turbines, and the craft blasted out of the large wound in Slader Corp's roof.

\*\*\*

"You've already made your point killing me once and sending me through TransmoG, converting my body into one of your horrible robots. Let me go."

"Let you go? What fun would that be?" Maximus snorted, tapping a button under his desk. To his agent he said: "Anyone entering this room, kill them."

"Yes, sir."

A wall spiraled open, exposing a kaleidoscope of colors materializing a tourbillion. "This is a called a nexus, Jonas. There is only one other, located in the old house by the river. Whereas it is quite miniscule, developed as a prototype. This one is complete, filled with an array of worlds. It is a creation your father helped design, besides being part of the team of the ones improving the TransmoG process." Smile. "Ah, I see you are shocked at this news. You did not know he worked special projects for me?" Chuckle. "You must have thought he worked some other job here at Slader Corp, perhaps a computer programmer or hacker, equal to a janitorial position. Right? Not likely. A brilliant scientist, your father. A top rate developer for the corporation. I must apologize for keeping him so busy all the time, Jonas; hardly allowed to spend time with you or your mother." He shrugged his shoulders. "The nature of the job."

"Where is my mom and dad? What did you do with them? I

deserve to know!"

Grin. "Let's begin with your mother: We picked her up while she was shopping at Shop N Save A Bundle, Jonas, shortly before we arrived on your doorstep, collecting you. Your mom knew what your father did at Slader Corp. She wasn't blind. We couldn't leave a loose end. Not logical thing to do.

"Your father's turn came next. We plucked him out of his lab. He fought us. Tried to escape. Tried pleading for his life. Should have known better, the fool. Your father should have known the consequences when he attempted to destroy TransmoG by infecting it with a virus. The damn fool did not realize I already had the best anti-virus software created by another scientist. Always good to have a backup plan, I say."

Slader winked.

"Unfortunately the same guy tried to embezzle a million cred from the corporation, thinking he could steal us blind. His actions sent him to the Neutralization Center. So it goes, eh? Can't keep good help on the payroll."

The explanation of the death of his parents crashed into Jonas. His hate for Slader elevated. "You're going to pay for this, Slader."

"By whom? By *you*? The rebellion?" He guffawed. "Tell me another tall tale, much like those pathetic paperbacks I chose to have burned. Why keep pre-Shift literature around in this day and age? I see no reason to. Do you know," he cleared his throat, paused before continuing, "I did learn something new about your mother, Jonas. She was a tuff one. Tougher than your father. See, I had this theory at one time…would you, um, be so intrigued to hear it?"

Jonas did not reply.

"I'll explain anyway. Women are tougher than men; they can take pain better. Maybe it reflects the agony of natural childbirth; I'm not exactly sure. But your mom was the toughest I had seen. One hell of a fighter! The machine struggled to strap your mother down inside the pod. She cursed us over and over as we watched her brain being extracted from her skull. Her lips continued spatting curses out afterward, too. Odd, that. As if….her body continued to fight after death."

"I wish to kill you, Slader."

With a shrug of his shoulders, a wave of his hand, he replied: "Get in line, boy. I have many enemies who wish to see me bleed to death."

A door in the wall spiraled open, shutting after two schizos entered. Vertical waves, static, snow and flickers of familiar faces on their screens lay under their hoods.

"Hello, son."

"Hello, darling."

Jonas gasped.

"Allow me to introduce your mom and dad, reborn inside one of my new, infection-free, eternal robotic shells." Slader said. "You and your mother and father will be the first family to explore the nexus and live happily ever after, wherever it transfers you three."

"I'm not going anywhere!" Jonas spat.

His mother and father pointed rail guns.

"You best do as they say, Jonas, or their Morto bullets will chew you apart. See, I am one step ahead, already taking measures, making sure you will not escape," Slader said. "Your destination into the abyss awaits. Have a good trip, Jonas, welcome to your new lif –

BOOM!

Everyone in the room crashed the floor.

The rim around the hole in the wall sparked as Bonner stepped through, took aim with his gun, drilled a hole in the agent.

Wisps of smoke curled from the face.

Case entered next. Harrens, and the four in tow.

Maximus peeked over the edge of his desk.

Both schizos rose.

Case fired, dropped both. Swung on Maimus Slader.

"Stand up, Maximus."

Maximus' eyes were slits.

"Stand up if you value your head. I won't hesitate to make it explode."

Maximus stood.

"Hey! Get those hands out of your desk drawer and in the air." She aimed her pistol at his chest. "Or I *will* shoot you where you stand!"

Sigh. "Fine." Maximus withdrew his hand, held them up.

"Jonas. Over here with us."

Jonas crawled over, stood beside Bonner.

Maximus snickered.

"What? Something funny?" Case inquired.

"Really? An explosive entrance to save this kid? That all you have? How'd you find me?"

"I could add with blowing off your hand if you chance sticking it in a desk drawer again. Thanks to our young computer guru, Fasoh here, he used his IdentiScan to locate your whereabouts."

Chuckle. "Interesting. Case, your name, correct?"

"That's the rumor."

"Leader of the rebellion. In my office. Here at the corporation. Wow. I wish it could be a pleasure to meet you."

"My thoughts exactly. We're taking you into custody, Slader."

"Who's custody? Yours? Ha! You are not the law in Ozarium. I am. Surely you and your group of derelicts don't believe you can overthrow my leadership. You are outlaws. Wanted by my agents. Only what I say goes. Sorry, corporation rules, Case."

"I wouldn't bet on that, Slader."

"Oh? I'll bet, and I will win. All of my agents, machine or mortal, are devoted to me, followers of faith, much like the god who developed this planet, setting a seed for mortal life. If it wasn't for the rebellion's unwelcomed visit all colonists would already be finalized in their TransmoG process, transferred into the metal bodies of schizos. However, there may still be a chance to undo what has been done."

"It ends now."

"Keep telling yourself that. Maybe you'll believe your own lie. You've caused me a lot of problems, Case. Much too many. You've destroyed many projects my team of scientists developed. Including a few Jonas' father took credit for. You helped Jake Velmer fight back, giving a brainless idiot the idea he could take on the demi and win. There are many more things I can add to the list of what the rebellion has soured. I must admit, it is a long list.

"You and your men are wanted by the demi on many charges, Case. I suggest you rethink your position and tell your men to drop their weapons and give yourselves up. You won't make it out of the room alive."

"You will come with us where you will be placed behind bars in the Subterraneans."

Snicker. "You are in no position to make those demands, Case. Trust me. You best think long and hard about your present position. Give yourself up and tell your men to stand down. Last chance. I'm being nice, sparing you of having their blood on your hands. Otherwise, all of you will die."

"My men have guns pointed on you," Case said. "You have not a one in your hand. I assure you Harrens here on my left is our best sniper. Bonner here on my right can split apart a fly with one shot at one point five miles. The others in my company are a slight second to both men. Each are trained marksmen. The very best, Maximus. *We* have the upper hand here. Not you. All I have to do is say the word, and there will be nothing left of your head after seven shots. Time for the rebellion to take control of Ozarium, impeach your ass from office."

"Tsk-tsk. Threats you cannot deliver, Case. Don't tell me in a few minutes, as I admire your dying corpse gaze up at me, I did not warn you, young lady. You have acquired a devastating responsibility of six deaths."

In the adjoining room through the gaping hole in the wall a low rumble of a chainsaw echoed.

As the group faced the sound, Maximus Slader snatched a chance to morph his appearance, shrouding himself dark as a shadow, the form of an evil entity The Reckoning granted him so long ago.

\*\*\*

Ssss...sssss...sssss...sssss...sssss...sssss...SSSSS...SSSSS...SSSSS...SSSS...SSSS... ssss...ssss...ssss...BOOOOM!

The explosion of the other bouncer nearly set them in a spiral descent.

"What the *hells!*" Terrance spat, regaining control of the craft.

"We lost a bouncer full of survivors!" a voice crackled through the speakers in the cabin.

"Gods help us!" Terrance glanced over his shoulder. "You two okay back there?"

"Walts?" Grandpa asked.

"I'm okay," Walts replied.

A Nark zipped into view, armed with twin cannons.

"Shit!" Terrance blasted to the left, staved off shots from the Nark, swerved past a building, clipped its edge. Shards of glass plunged into the streets below.

Walts stomach lurched from the craft's motion, as if he rode a rollercoaster.

Terrance thumbed a yellow button. SHIELDS ENGAGED scrolled across the interior of the windshield. He barked into his headset, "Everyone, use your shields!"

"Copy!" replies flooded the cabin.

Three more Narks appeared, fired. The bouncer jostled; however, the shots did not once penetrate the shields.

Twin cannons clicked into place atop each of the other bouncers, began firing at the enemy. Terrance swung the craft around, a direct view of a Nark, thumbed a red button, let loose an array of bullets.

Yellow burst of light and flame split the air as the Nark exploded.

"I'm positive the demi must have something else up their sleeve." Terrance glanced at Grandpa and Walts. "May want to be prepared for the worst to come."

\*\*\*

Fear laid a hand on Jonas' shoulder as Ozarium's mechanical celebrity stepped into the room. Any love he previously had for the killer wilted away.

Corners of the machine's sutured red mouth twitched. Its view under its sutured eyelids portrayed six silhouettes engulfed in heat signatures, canvassed on a blue computer screen. The seventh glowed white.

"Let us see what you and your men are made of, shall we, Case?" Slader's voice rasped. "My friend here always loves a good fight."

Case's eyes snatched a look at Slader's new appearance, her eyes wide. "What the hell are you, Slader?"

A skeletal face materialized from under the hood; its teeth chattered: "I once was a savior of humanity, loved by many who thought of me as a hero of their village, and would have continued to be if not for the drive of an old king's selfishness causing me to be tortured to death in my previous life. After my four masters saved my soul, I returned to the planet at a much later date, became loved by children, giving each a choice of living with me or staying with their miserable, sinful parents who abused them, punished them for no reason, shoving pathetic lies down their throat.

"Thus, the children embraced me. I became their savior for life. Right, my children?"

The kaleidoscope of colors in the nexus peeled back, opening a circle of a field where many human bodies lay impaled into the ground. A large group of demonic children and a huge litter of five-foot rats gazed into Slader's office, a grin on their faces sliced ear-to-ear. A few of the kids giggled and played tug-of-war with one of the dead's intestines.

"My children love a good show. Especially when blood will be spilled."

Freckles triggered his chainsaw, grabbed the scythe off its belt lined with designs of cyclopean skulls with its other hand, took three long strides, driving the edge of his automated weapon into the chest of a rebellion member in the blink of an eye.

The guy's body convulsed as the rotating blade chewed into him, snapping bone into splinters. Blood splattered the clown. Finalizing the kill the murderer jerked the blade up and out of the dying body.

Case shot the machine point-blank in the face, shaving away a sliver of the mask, though doing not a lick of damage to the machine.

A barrage of bullets burrowed into the clown by the resistance, slamming the machine against a wall. Ribbons of smoke drifted from tears in the clown's attire as it focused and threw the scythe, decapitating a young rebel.

"Bonner, Deflect! Brights, Fasoh," Case said, "throw your grenades! Jonas, stay behind us!"

Bonner clicked a button on his belt, engulfing the five in a protective shield.

An ear-piercing explosion rocked the office from the launch of two grenades.

\*\*\*

*Damn! The demi has blocked our entry into the Subterraneans!*

"Hang on!" Terrance whipped the craft out of the way, missing a Nark, but not out of the way of its array of bullets, hammering the bouncer's shields.

Cannons swiveled atop two demi halftracks. Electricity crawled across their barrels as deafening pulses shot from their tips, snatching a bouncer out of the sky, engulfing the craft in orange flames.

"What the heck was *that*?" Walts cried.

"Gods help us. I had heard a rumor the demi had been working on a hypervelocity oscillator. Unlucky for us we saw it first-hand."

"A *what*?"

"Bad news, kid. Real bad news." Terrance spoke into his headset: "Pull back! Everyone!"

Narks swarmed the air, a portrayal of metallic locusts.

\*\*\*

Plumes of grey smoke swarmed the office.

The transparent shield of DeFlect covering the rebellion hummed.

"Everyone okay?" Case coughed from the smoke.

"We're good, Case," Bonner replied, flicking off DeFlect.

"Jonas?" Case glanced at Jonas.

"Yep," Jonas said.

"Is that clown dead?" Brights bit down on a toothpick between his lips, pushing up the bill to his cap.

"Has to be, dude," Fasoh replied, scratching his bearded cheek. "No way a robot could withstand – "

A chainsaw started up, rumbling.

"– that," Fasoh finished.

"You have *got* to be kidding?" Bonner said incredulously.

A neon yellow eye burned a hole inside the grey smoke as it pulled away from Freckle's own DeFlect shield. Partially naked of its attire, the clown's skin revealed a shell of chrome. Freckle's mask a synthetic ooze on the floor, revealed the crafted face of an evil clown.

The clown's cyclopean eye blinked.

"Did you really believe it would be so easy to destroy my work, Case?" Smoke hid the entity until vacuuming inside the nexus. The desk lay in splinters.

The children all sat cross-legged in the field, eyes wide, smiles sliced under their nose, intrigued as if watching a Saturday morning cartoon.

Chainsaw Freckles snapped off his DeFlect, triggered his chainsaw, charged the rebellion.

Brights touched his knee to the floor, shot the clown in the eye before his own eye popped out and his jaw ripped off by the killer's hand. The rotating blade emitted a skull-shattering grind, driving it into the rebel's face, lifting the convulsing body, allowing the serrated teeth to finalize the death by dragging it to the casing, splitting the head in two halves.

Brights corpse hit the floor, sprayed a warm stream of blood from the stump, slapping Bonner's face.

The children laughed and clapped their hands.

*There has to be a weak spot on this rust bucket!* Case flipped open a pouch on her belt, used two fingers to pull a small rubber ball. "Bonner, Harrens, Fasoh, group together! Jonas, get back there! Bonner, DeFlect!"

Bonner clicked the button again.

Case threw the ball against a wall. An explosion of sparks, as if a welder had been at work, sprayed the room in blue and yellow jolts of electricity.

\*\*\*

Narks swarmed the bouncers, firing on each of the remaining four as they retreated.

"Guys, follow me!" Replies crackled through the speakers. Terrance switched his cigar from the left to right between his lips, bit down, and kicked the bouncer into overdrive.

Bouncers of three slid into a convoy.

"Narks are on our tail! They're blasting the hell out of our shields!" Echoes of booms crackled through the speakers. "Don't know how much longer they'll hold."

"Hang in there, Roj. We're headed toward the old house by the river."

"Where are we going?"

"We're crossing the river."

"What? Its suicide!"

"We haven't a choice."

"Beyond the river is forbidden land. Undiscovered country. No one knows what's out there."

"We're about to find out."

"Hope you know what you're doing."

"I have a hunch, Roj." *If my hunch even holds water...*

"You heard from Case?"

*Damn!* Terrance chewed on the end of his cigar. "No." Terrance grabbed a hand-held walkie talkie. "Case, you copy? Case?"

The small convoy rocketed across the sky, skimming houses, chased by Narks.

An unsettling feeling touched Walts' skin when he saw the old house by the river. He hoped to never venture inside the place.

Ever.

Again.

"Case? Come in?" Terrance repeated. "Case, are you there?"

\*\*\*

Electricity cocooned the killer, severing its protective shield, sending it crashing through a wall.

"We need to get-gone. Now!" Case informed the others. "Head for the bouncer. Everyone!"

The quartet sprung off across the floor, escaping through the hole in which they had entered. They rocketed down a long hall, slipped around a corner, launched into the galley of where the TransmoG machine sat.

The entity hovered off the floor, grinning.

"Do you think you could crash our party and leave?"

*How the hells did he do that?* "Get out of our way…whatever you call yourself," Case aimed her gun. "We're out of here."

"Your bullets will not affect me. You will be wasting your ammo. I suggest you surrender. The odds are against you, Case."

Behind them, running footsteps.

"Case, we're in trouble," Bonner said.

Demonic children poured into the room, grinning ear to ear.

"Neat-oh-riffic! Play toys!" a small boy wearing a ragged Peterson Elementary shirt said.

*"Case, are you there?"* a voice crackled in Case's ear.

"Terrance?" Case replied. "What's your twenty?"

"Headed toward the old house by the river. We're down to a convoy of three. Have you left Slader Corp?"

"Three?"

"Narks destroyed the other two craft. They blocked us from the Subterraneans."

*Son of a b–* "We're still here. Get those survivors to safety, Terrance."

"What about you and the rest of the group?"

"Don't worry about us. Focus on you and your cargo. We'll see you soon. Leave a Tracer where you can be found."

"Copy. There's a good chance we may have to cross the river, Case."

Pause. *Not a great idea...but:* "Do what you need to do, Terrance. Get those folks to safety. Copy?"

"Copy. Out."

A small girl cocked her head to the side, stuck out her bottom lip. "Why would you want to leave, Case? We only want to see you bleed. Is that so bad?"

***

Water leaked from a gaping mouth from a body floating in the river.

"Follow me, guys," Terrance said into his headset. "We're crossing the river. Be alert."

Responses flooded the cabin.

Walts looked at his Grandpa. "What about Jonas? Did Case rescue him?"

"She didn't say, kid," Terrance said. "Don't worry, Case is damn good at what she does. I'm sure your friend is safe."

"I hope so." To Grandpa, Walts said: "Jonas is like the brother I never had."

"I know. Have faith in Case and the rebellion. Okay?"

Walts nodded. "Have you been passed the river, Terrance?"

"Nope."

"Do you know what's out there?"

"I've heard rumors."

"Good ones? Cause Maximus Slader always said it was dangerous, uncharted territory."

Frown. "I think Slader has lied to us all this time. I have a hunch. Don't worry. You and your Grandpa are safe with us. I'm sure your friend is safer than us. Case is a warrior. She won't let anything happen to him. When she rescues someone, she always gets her man."

***

Four demonic children gripping cleavers and butcher knives; took turns chanting the rhyme:

"Eeny.."

"…Meeny."

"Miny…"

"…Moe."

"Catch a rebellion…"

"…Member."

"By his…"

"…Or."

"Her…"

"…Toe."

"If they laugh…."

"…If they cry."

"Gotta be sure…."

"To…"

"…Make 'em."

"Die."

More children crowded into the room, creating a large horde. Each child grabbed hold of their face, dug fingernails into flesh, clawed skin away to view glistening red fur, whiskers dripping blood, fangs lining open maws, affirming their hunger.

In the doorway stood the clown.

"You cannot win, Case," the entity said. "Give up. Allow us to show you our warmest welcome."

To her men, Case said: "All of you. Take Jonas and get in the bouncer. It's less than twenty feet away. I got this." She took aim with her rifle.

"We aren't leaving you," Bonner said.

"I agree," Harrens spat a glob of tobacco juice, reloaded his gun with more ammo.

"Not up for discussion. That is a direct order. Get out of here, you two!"

Bonner scowled. "Piss on your orders. Case. Grab the kid and get your ass in the bouncer. You know as well as I do this fight is hopeless. Harrens and I can hold them off while you get Jonas to safety." Without looking at Bonner he added "We got this, right, Harrens?"

"Yup." Harrens flipped his cap around, spat another glob. "They won't get through us. Get the hells out of here. Get the kid to safety."

Case knew she couldn't argue with the guys. Stubborn as they were. "Jonas, head to the bouncer."

Jonas started off.

"Gods be with you both," Case took aim, blasted into the crowd, picked off two kids, rocketed off behind Jonas.

Harrens and Bonner took aim, fired.

Small heads exploded.

Bullets burrowed holes into their bodies and chewed off their limbs as the rat children rocketed forward. Wet residue and streaks of crimson appeared as their feetless stumps smacked the floor. Claws out, a few launched themselves into Harrens and Bonner, piling atop the two.

Screams and shrieks of pain reverberated off the walls.

Jonas drifted into the passenger seat of the bouncer. Case slammed the door, hit the ignition. The Wankel-McMeyers spun.

Two of the demonic creatures landed on the hood, pounding on the windshield with fists, causing it to crack and spider web.

Case blasted the bouncer through the hole in the roof.

The creatures hung on. One ripped off a the driver's side door and swung into the cab, knocked Case into Jonas' lap. The other followed suit, grabbed Case by the hair, repeatedly slammed her head into the dash, knocking her unconscious. Her body slumped face-first into the passenger side floorboard.

The bouncer jarred to the side and one of the creatures slid behind the wheel, gained control of the craft. "Let's get you back home, Jonas. You'll love living with us and the master."

"It's a carnival ride!" the other guffawed.

Jonas couldn't go back. No way. He attacked the driver, wrapped an arm around its throat, squeezed.

The creature gasped, losing control of the craft.

The bouncer flipped on its side, careened the side of a building.

The other creature snatched a grab at Jonas, failing to do so because of Jonas' ghostly shape.

Squeezing the creature's neck until feeling a pop, Jonas let go. The head slumped forward. The dead body's claws dropped from the controls. Outside the ground rushed forward as the craft nose-dived.

Jonas attacked the other creature, shoved him toward the open door.

One claw wrapped around the steering wheel, the other dug into the headrest of the seat. The creature hissed. "You will not win, Jonas! We are strong! We are many! We will survive in this world where you freaks and mortals will not!"

"Not…if…I…can…help…it!" Jonas struggled, using as much strength as he could muster, using his legs, planting a foot on the creature's face and giving it a hard shove. The creature tried wrapping its claws around Jonas' ankle, failing to grasp his ectoplasmic shape.

The bouncer swerved into the side of a building, setting it into a tail-spin.

The creature let go and became ground rat inside one of the Wankel-McMeyers. Crimson splattered the windshield, flaked the interior, as the craft whipped around.

Jonas thumped against the passenger seat, his legs over Case. The outside world whirled around as if forced into a funnel cloud.

Jonas needed to get Case out of this bouncer ASAP. But how?

The bouncer plummeted.

*What did Walts' grandpa say about Ekto-Leaping? Nothing…he said he couldn't show him. It'd be too hard to do at the time… Wait. The BRD had the rules written out:*

A ghost Ekto-Leaps by concentrating on one spot. For example, if said ghost is standing outside a house he/she knows the floorplan, said ghost could easily Leap inside.

Jonas grabbed onto Case, squeezed his eyes shut, concentrated. And both vanished.
#
An explosion ricocheted through the air as Terrance drove the bouncer crossed the river, the other bouncers in tow.

DO NOT PASS BEYOND THIS LINE
FOR YOUR SAFETY AND OTHERS PLEASE TURN
AROUND AND RETURN TO         THE COLCNY
HAVE A NICE DAY

Warning signs inside the craft shrieked once it crossed over multiple dead eyes gazing up from their watery grave.
And plunged out of the sky.

# Prologue

Sprawled out in the floorboard, Benny twitched.

The unit's circuits and sensors failed to spark a response to its neurotransmitters in its brain, fighting to live. Benny's small lips trembled "M-m-m-m-mommy" before the robot shut down for good, mimicking the low hum of the bouncer's turbines dying down in the wake of skimming over a small copse of trees, blocking out Ozarium, though not the river. A larger copse of green hid away what lay beyond, stretched from where the craft landed in the field.

Sarah unclicked her seatbelt, scooped him up, held him to her breast and wept.

A strong breeze whipped Sarah's hair. Giving her only son a kiss on his forehead, she allowed the river to take him away.

She had no idea how long she stood there, watching the current kidnap her Benny, observing others who wore bloated flesh camouflaging their bones, before hearing a rumble, cresting over a nearby hill.

\*\*\*

Ray Manisquaski woke up in a Cryptronica. Pain crashed into the side of his skull. The injection the agent gave him right after his vid-cam was destroyed knocked him out cold. Through the glass others lined against the wall, a few familiar, such as Tyler Ray Jim Bob Elrod III, imprisoned just like himself. Eyes shut, their faces were very pale. A rock wall gave him a sense of an underground room.

"Ray Manisquaski," a recorded monotone voice spoke inside the chamber, "welcome to your new life as a TransmoG, an upgrade the Slader Corporation had been working on. Rest up, enjoy the ride. There will be much for you to download into your new positronic brain."

A tap on the glass.

A rat grinned at Ray.

***

Chains rattled.

"Well, buddy, ain't nothing left here for us to do. Let's see if someone else will pay our salary."

"Bleep."

"Sure, someone will want our services."

"Bleep?"

"How the hells should I know? Whoever wishes to pay our fee, I suppose."

"Bleep?"

"Yeah, get one of those Hula Hoop Orbitors out. Set the codes on for another colony."

"Bleep."

Moree's mechanical buddy reached a three-fingered hand inside its small door, withdrew an object the size of a pill, squeezed its gel surface, dropped it. An orange circle burst open, large enough for the mobile suicide unit to fit.

"Hop in, Chains," Moree slid behind the wheel.

Chains rolled inside the van, the rear doors closed. Moree steered the van into the orange glow. Within seconds they vanished.

\*\*\*

Grumbling, the four robot gnomes for hire who posed on their customer's lawn scurried down the street.

Unemployed, they needed to look for more work.

Logging into the Gridd via HeadKase, a job offer in the colony of Gorph looked pretty good...

# About the Author

Brick Marlin has been writing since he was a child. From an early age he was exposed to older, original horror movies. The great ones that have made a mark in history. He also tackled reading the likes of Stephen King, Clive Barker, Ray Bradbury, Kurt Vonnegut, Dean Koontz, Charles Dickens, Harper Lee, H.G. Wells, W. W. Jacobs, etc. Thus, he decided to engage himself and write horror and dark fantasy, scaring readers such as his parents, his friends, a handful of neighbors, and even leaving a few school teachers scratching their heads wondering if the boy should be committed or not with his gruesome tales of terror. Short story ideas continued to visit. A book idea or two sometimes stopped by for a sit. In 2007 he decided to take a more professional approach with his work. Hence, as a member of the Horror Writers Association, already having five books published by small presses with one more in the works coming soon, nearly twenty-five short stories published, adding to the few anthologies and collaborations with other authors, Brick Marlin trudges onward, hoping to achieve more creations, living in the minds of his characters making decisions such as whether to turn the knob and enter through the Red Door, or perhaps try and take a chance at the Blue Door, the one that is already ajar, a bony finger beckoning the next visitor.

Married to the best woman in the world, she allows him to tuck himself away inside his office, donning his Anti-Literary Gremlin helmet, and produce his bizarre tales.

Check out the following pages
to see more from

All Seventh Star Press titles available in
print and an array of specially priced eBook
formats.

Visit www.seventhstarpress.com for further
information

Connect with Seventh Star Press at
www.seventhstarpress.com
seventhstarpress.blogspot.com
www.facebook.com/seventhstarpress
www.twitter.com/7thstarpress

Transcend Reality!

Shadows Over Somerset from Bob Freeman!

Softcover: 978-1-941706-11-4
eBook: 978-1-941706-12-1

Michael Somers is brought to Cairnwood, an isolated manor in rural Indiana, to sit at the deathbed of a grandfather he never knew existed. He soon finds himself drawn into a strange and esoteric world filled with werewolves, vampires, witches... and a family curse that dates back to fourteenth century Scotland. In the sleepy little town of Somerset, an ancient evil awakens, hungering for blood and vengeance... and if Michael is to survive he must face his inner demons and embrace his family's dark past. Shadows Over Somerset is the first Cairnwood Manor Novel.

Now Available from Seventh Star Press,
the horror stylings of
# Michael West!

Trade Paperback ISBN: 9780983740209
eBook ISBN: 9780983740216

Trade Paperback ISBN: 9781937929718
eBook ISBN: 9781937929725

Trade Paperback ISBN: 9781937929954
eBook ISBN:9781937929831

Trade Paperback ISBN: 978-1-937929-18-3
eBook ISBN: 978-1-937929-19-0

16 Tales of the Paranormal and Ghostly from editors Alexander S. Brown and J.L. Mulvihill!

eBook ISBN: 978-1-937929-14-5

Softcover ISBN: 978-1-937929-12-1

From the shadowed realms of the paranormal comes 16 chilling tales that dwell in the South and South West. From 16 authors, learn of haunted homes, buildings, landmarks and roads where restless entities from beyond the grave desire acknowledgement amongst the living. Become acquainted with the aftermath of an eclipse that awakens the dead in a Memphis cemetery, see what horrors dwell in the woods at Hell's Gate, learn the dark secrets of Sidney's Cotton, and dare to travel down Ghost Road. These and many other tales are sure to keep you awake as you are introduced to what makes the South and South West so unique.... History and GHOSTS!!!!! So, sit back, dim the lights and prepare yourself to face the spirits that walk among us.

Now available!   A Seventh Star Press Anthology
from editor Michael West!

eBook ISBN: 978-1-937929-69-5
Softcover ISBN: 978-1-937929-60-2

Vampires Don't Sparkle! poses the question: What would
you do if you had unlimited power and eternal life?

Would you...go back to high school? Attend the same classes
year after year, going through the pomp and circumstance
of one graduation after another, until you found the perfect
date to take to prom? Would you...spend your days moping
and brooding, finding your only joy in a game of baseball
on a stormy day? Or would you...do something else?

The authors of this collection have a few ideas; some fanciful,
some humorous, and some as dark as an endless night.

Join us, and discover what it truly means to be "vampyre."

Post-apocalyptic, zombie-infested military thriller from Peter Welmerink!

Softcover ISBN: 978-1-941706-03-9
eBook ISBN: 978-1-941706-02-2

The HURON, a 72-ton heavy transport vehicle and an army of four; tracked, racked and ready to roll, to serve and protect the walled metropolis of Grand Rapids-both her living and her undead. Captain Jacob Billet and his crew patrol the byways, ready for trouble. William Lettner, the North Shore Coalition High Commissioner, has enemies from the mainland to the lakeshore and needs to be covertly transported home after his helicopter is shot down en route to Grand Rapids. He has no love for a city that give unliving civilians the right to survive. Lettner's venomous outbursts assaults Billet and his crew along every mile travelled as they are assigned to safely bring him through the treacherous landscape outside the city back to his hometown. To complete their mission, the HURON and her crew will have to face domesticated zombies and the feral undead; marauders holding strategic chokepoints hostage; barricaded villages fighting for survival, and a group of geneticists who've lost control of one of their monstrous experiments. The crew will need to stay strong and trust one another in order to finish the mission and bring their "precious" cargo home, even knowing, all the while, the terrible deeds Lettner has done. Travelling through West Michigan was never so dangerous. Transport is the first book in the Transport series!

Hellscapes, Volume 1
Venture through the infernal, where angels
fear to tread!

From Stephen Zimmer, a new horror
series set in realms where the inhabitants
experience the ultimate nightmare!
softcover ISBN: 978-1-937929-36-7
eBook ISBN: 978-1-937929-37-4

Paranormal-laced Horror from Crymsyn Hart!

Softcover: 978-1-941706-13-8
eBook: 978-1-941706-14-5

Being a psychic, you would think talking to the dead was a walk in the park. However, it's not always that simple. The hooded specter haunting me is one I've been dreaming about since I was a kid. One day, he appeared in my bedroom mirror. Good. Evil. I don't know what his true intentions are.

Enter Jackson, ghost hunting show host extraordinaire, and my ex, to save me from the big bad ghost.

From there…well…it's been a world wind of complications. My house burnt down. I'm being stalked by an ancient evil and gotten myself back into the world of being a ghost hunting psychic. Jackson dragged me, along with a few other psychics, to a ghost town wiped off the map called Death's Dance.

From there things went from bad to worse.

Death's Dance is Book One of the Deathly Encounters Series

# Urban Fantasy from John F. Allen!
## Meet Ivory Blaque!

## Softcover: 978-1-937929-16-9
## eBook: 978-1-937929-17-6

In The God Killers, the first book of The God Killers Legacy, former professional art thief Ivory Blaque is hired to procure a pair of antique pistols and gets much more than she bargained for when several attempts are made on her life.

Her client turns out to be a shadowy government agent who reveals that she is descended from a race of immortals, and that the pistols are linked to her unique heritage and the special psychic gifts she possesses. He uses the memory of her father to guilt her into working for him.

Ivory eventually gives in to his request, and in return, he presents her with her father's journal, which was written in an unbreakable code. Bishop believes that she is the only one capable of breaking the code and unlocking the plans of the vampire hierarchy. But when the city's top vampire is a sexy incubus with an attraction for her and she's assigned a hot new lycan enforcer to protect her, she finds herself caught between two sets of rock hard abs.

To regain her autonomy, clear her name, unlock the secrets of her past, and protect the lives of those closest to her, Ivory must play along with the forces trying to manipulate her. Ivory's life is rapidly spiraling out of control and headed for an explosive conclusion which she just might not survive.

Appalachian Gothic! Jason Sizemore's Irredeemable!
18 Tales of dark fantasy, science fiction, and horror

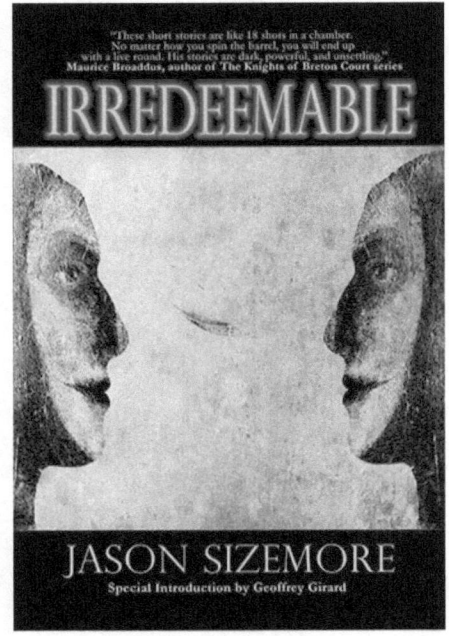

Softcover: 978-1-937929-59-6
eBook: 978-1-937929-68-8

Flowing like mists and shadows through the Appalachian Mountains come 18 tales from the mind of Jason Sizemore. Weaving together elements of southern gothic, science fiction, fantasy, horror, the supernatural, and much more, this diverse collection of short stories brings you an array of characters who must face accountability, responsibility, and, more ominously, retribution.

Whether it is Jack Taylor readying for a macabre, terrifying night in "The Sleeping Quartet," the Wayne brothers and mischief gone badly awry in "Pranks," the title character in "The Dead and Metty Crawford," or the church congregation and their welcoming of a special visitor in "Yellow Warblers," Irredeemable introduces you to a range of ordinary people who come face to face with extraordinary situations.

Whether the undead, aliens, ghosts, or killers of the yakuza, dangers of all kinds lurk within the darkness for those who dare tread upon its ground. Hop aboard and settle in, Irredeemable will take you on an unforgettable ride along a dark speculative fiction road.